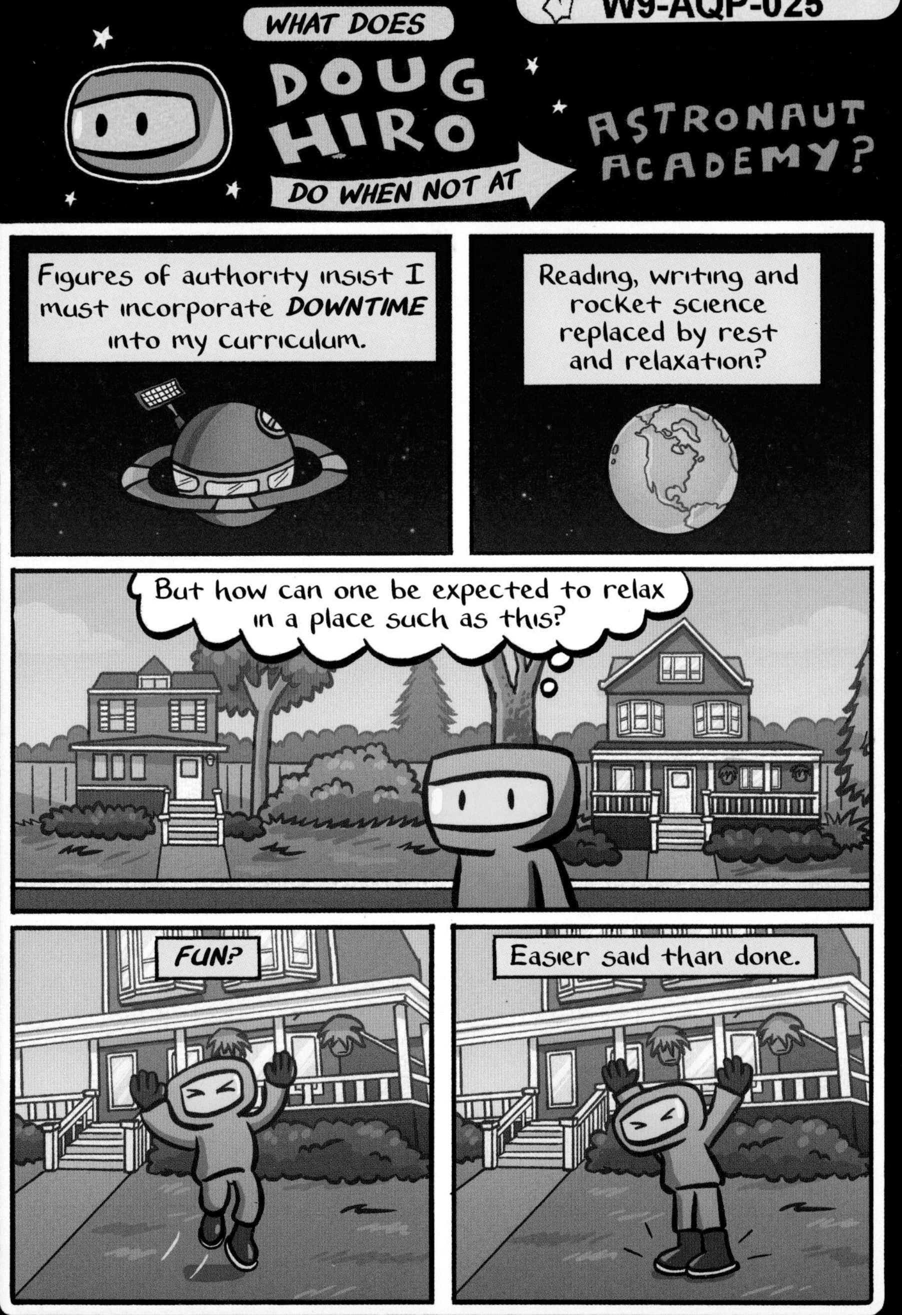
WHAT DOES
DOUG HIRO
DO WHEN NOT AT
ASTRONAUT ACADEMY?
Figures of authority insist I must incorporate DOWNTIME into my curriculum.
Reading, writing and rocket science replaced by rest and relaxation?
But how can one be expected to relax in a place such as this?
FUN?
Easier said than done.

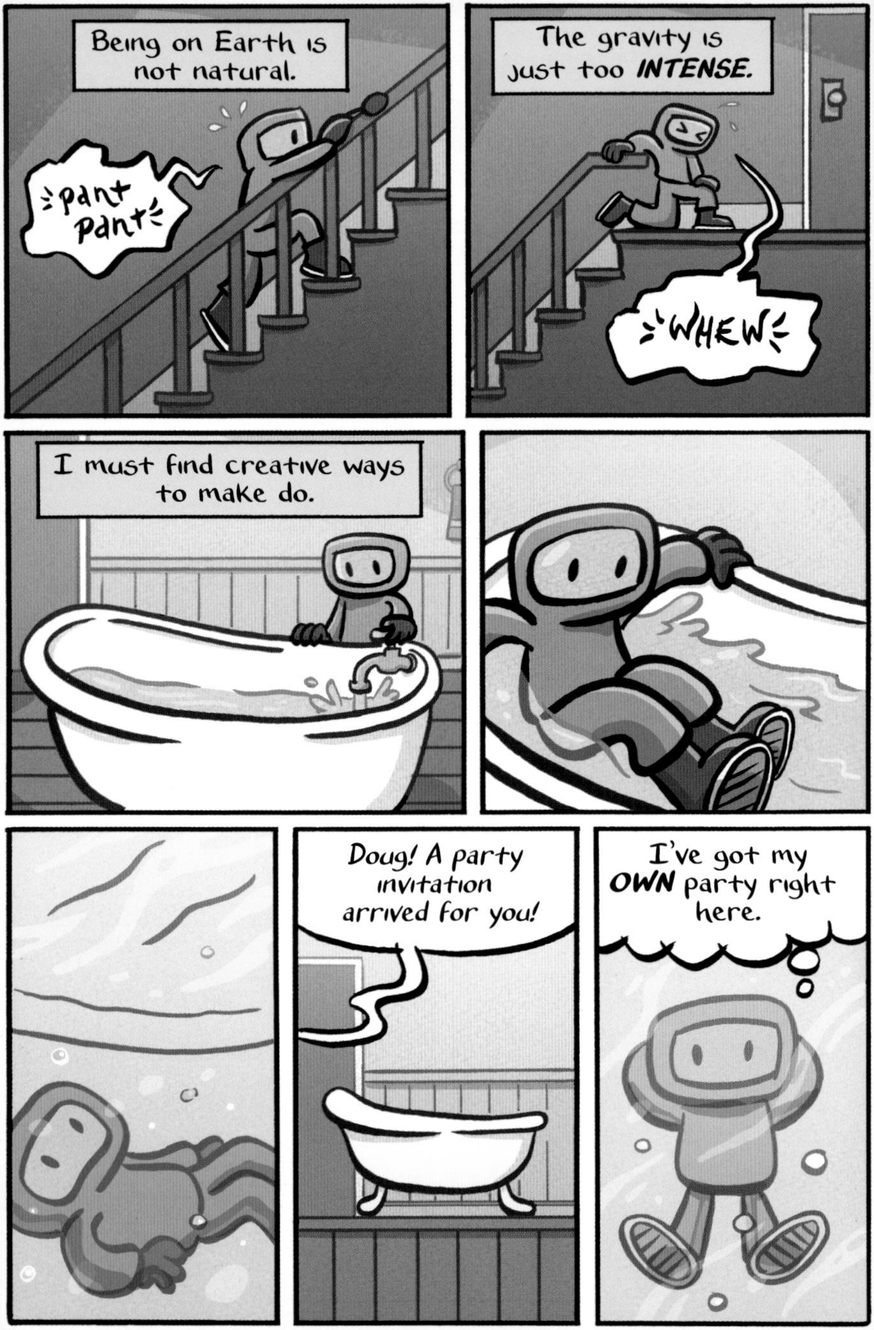
Being on Earth is not natural.
pant pant
The gravity is just too INTENSE.
WHEW
I must find creative ways to make do.
Doug! A party invitation arrived for you!
I've got my OWN party right here.

Thanks to all the awesome teachers, librarians, booksellers, and kids who inspire me to keep making comics. This book is for you.

First Second
New York

Text and illustrations copyright © 2021 by Dave Roman
Published by First Second
First Second is an imprint of Roaring Brook Press,
a division of Holtzbrinck Publishing Holdings Limited Partnership
120 Broadway, New York, NY 10271

Don't miss your next favorite book from First Second!
For the latest updates go to firstsecondnewsletter.com
and sign up for our enewsletter.

Library of Congress Control Number: 2020911254
Paperback ISBN: 978-1-250-21686-1
Hardcover ISBN: 978-1-250-21685-4

Our books may be purchased in bulk for promotional,
educational, or business use. Please contact your local bookseller or the
Macmillan Corporate and Premium Sales Department at (800) 221-7945
ext. 5442 or by email at MacmillanSpecialMarkets@macmillan.com.

Edited by Calista Brill and Rachel Stark
Color by JesnCin
Cover design by Kirk Benshoff
Interior design by Rob Steen

First edition, 2021

Printed in China by RR Donnelley Asia Printing Solutions Ltd.,
Dongguan City, Guangdong Province

Drawn with Paper Mate sharpwriter pencils on Strathmore 300 series Bristol
paper. Inked with Winsor & Newton Series 7 sable brushes, Speedball India ink, and
Pentel brush pens. Digital cleanup using Procreate and AstroPad on an iPad Pro.
Lettered (mostly) with Yaytime font. Colored in Photoshop.

Paperback: 10 9 8 7 6 5 4 3 2 1
Hardcover: 10 9 8 7 6 5 4 3 2 1

ASTRONAUT ACADEMY
SPLASHDOWN

WRITTEN AND ILLUSTRATED BY

DAVE ROMAN

WITH COLOR BY JESSICA AND JACINTA WIBOWO
JesnCin

:01

First Second
NEW YORK

summer break

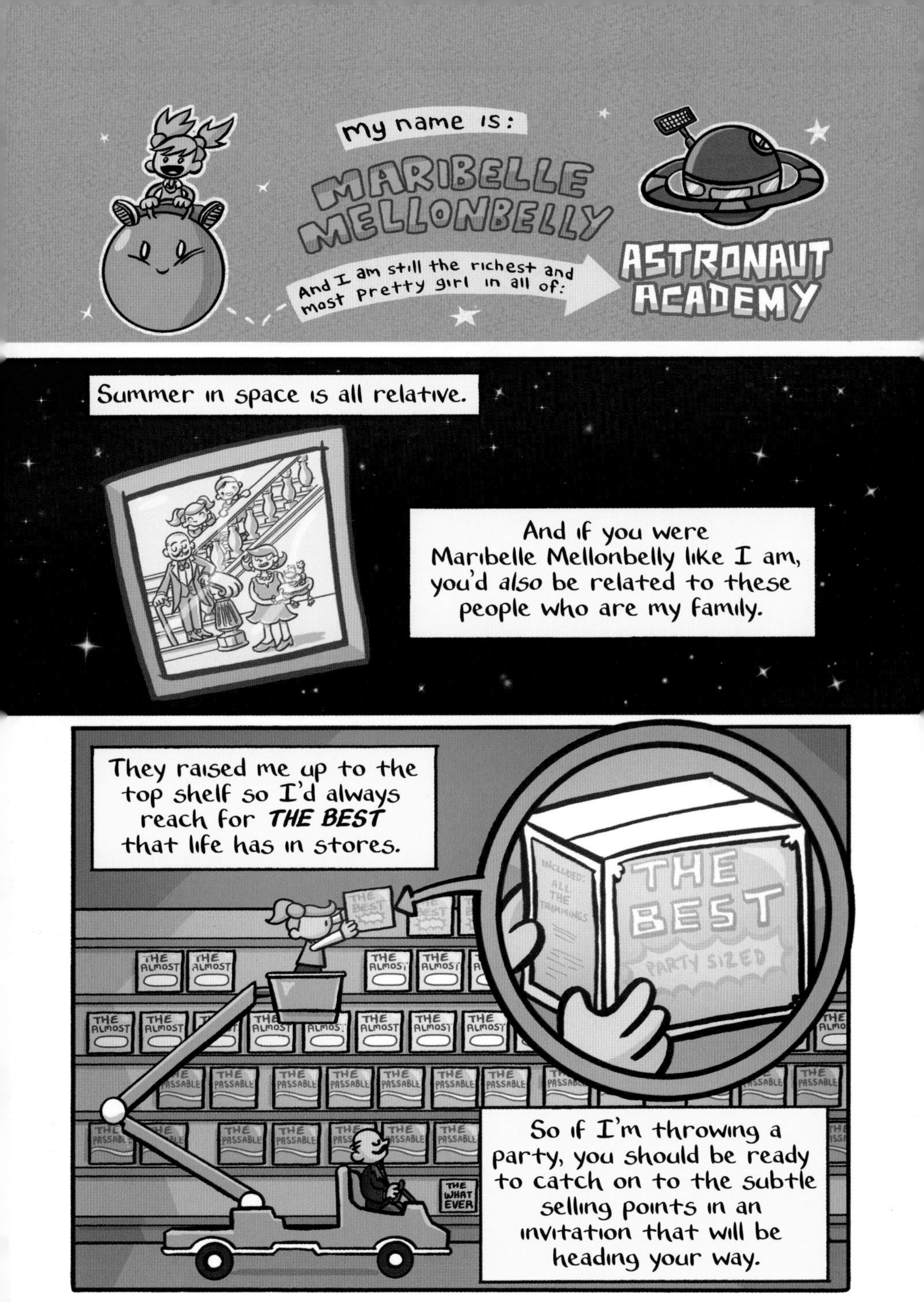

my name is:
MARIBELLE MELLONBELLY
And I am still the richest and most pretty girl in all of:
ASTRONAUT ACADEMY
Summer in space is all relative.
And if you were Maribelle Mellonbelly like I am, you'd *also* be related to these people who are my family.
They raised me up to the top shelf so I'd always reach for ***THE BEST*** that life has in stores.
THE BEST
INCLUDED: ALL THE TRIMMINGS
THE BEST
PARTY SIZED
THE ALMOST
THE PASSABLE
THE WHAT EVER
So if I'm throwing a party, you should be ready to catch on to the subtle selling points in an invitation that will be heading your way.

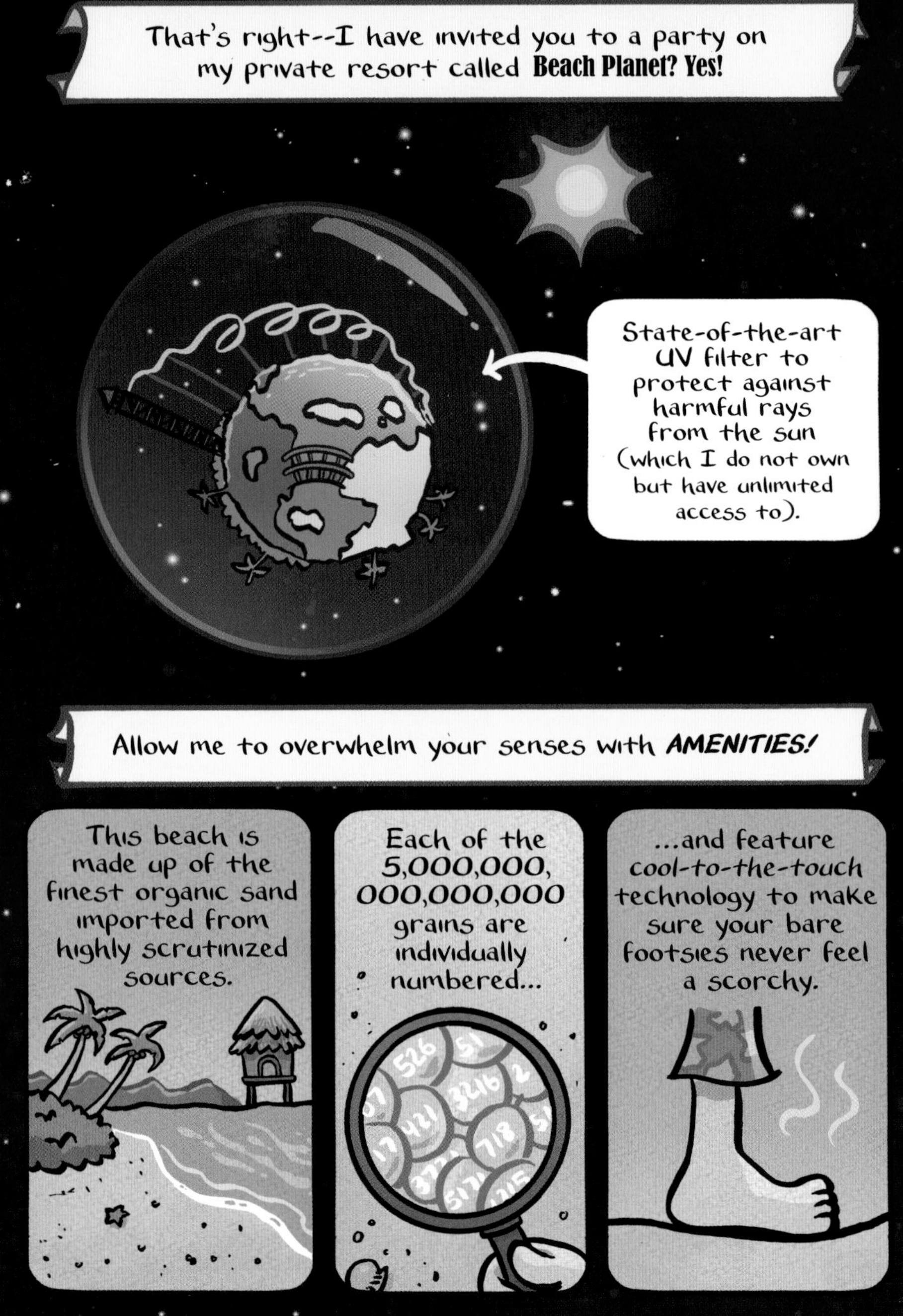
That's right--I have invited you to a party on my private resort called **Beach Planet? Yes!**
State-of-the-art UV filter to protect against harmful rays from the sun (which I do not own but have unlimited access to).
Allow me to overwhelm your senses with ***AMENITIES!***
This beach is made up of the finest organic sand imported from highly scrutinized sources.
Each of the 5,000,000,000,000,000 grains are individually numbered...
...and feature cool-to-the-touch technology to make sure your bare footsies never feel a scorchy.

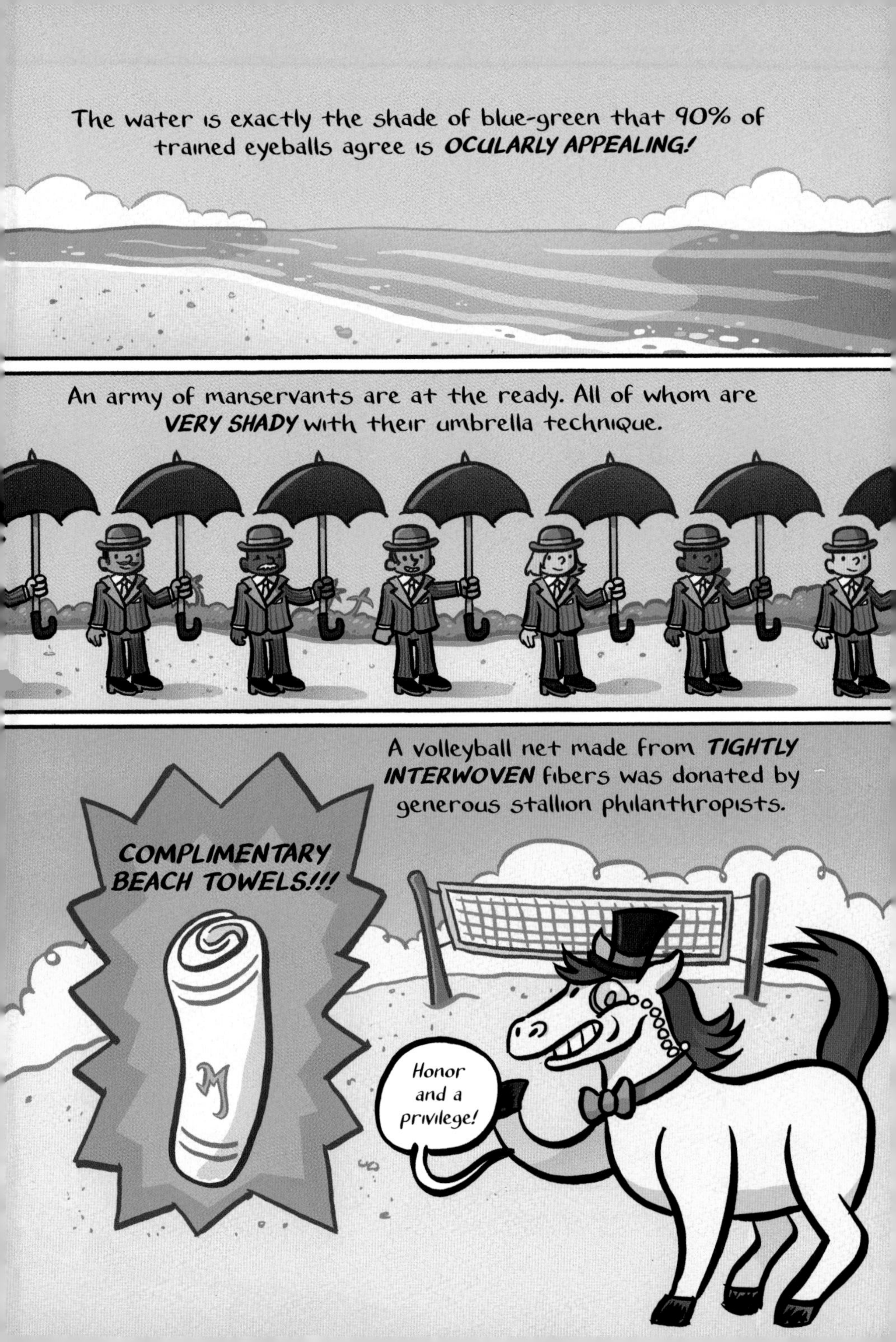
The water is exactly the shade of blue-green that 90% of trained eyeballs agree is OCULARLY APPEALING!
An army of manservants are at the ready. All of whom are VERY SHADY with their umbrella technique.
A volleyball net made from TIGHTLY INTERWOVEN fibers was donated by generous stallion philanthropists.
COMPLIMENTARY BEACH TOWELS!!!
Honor and a privilege!

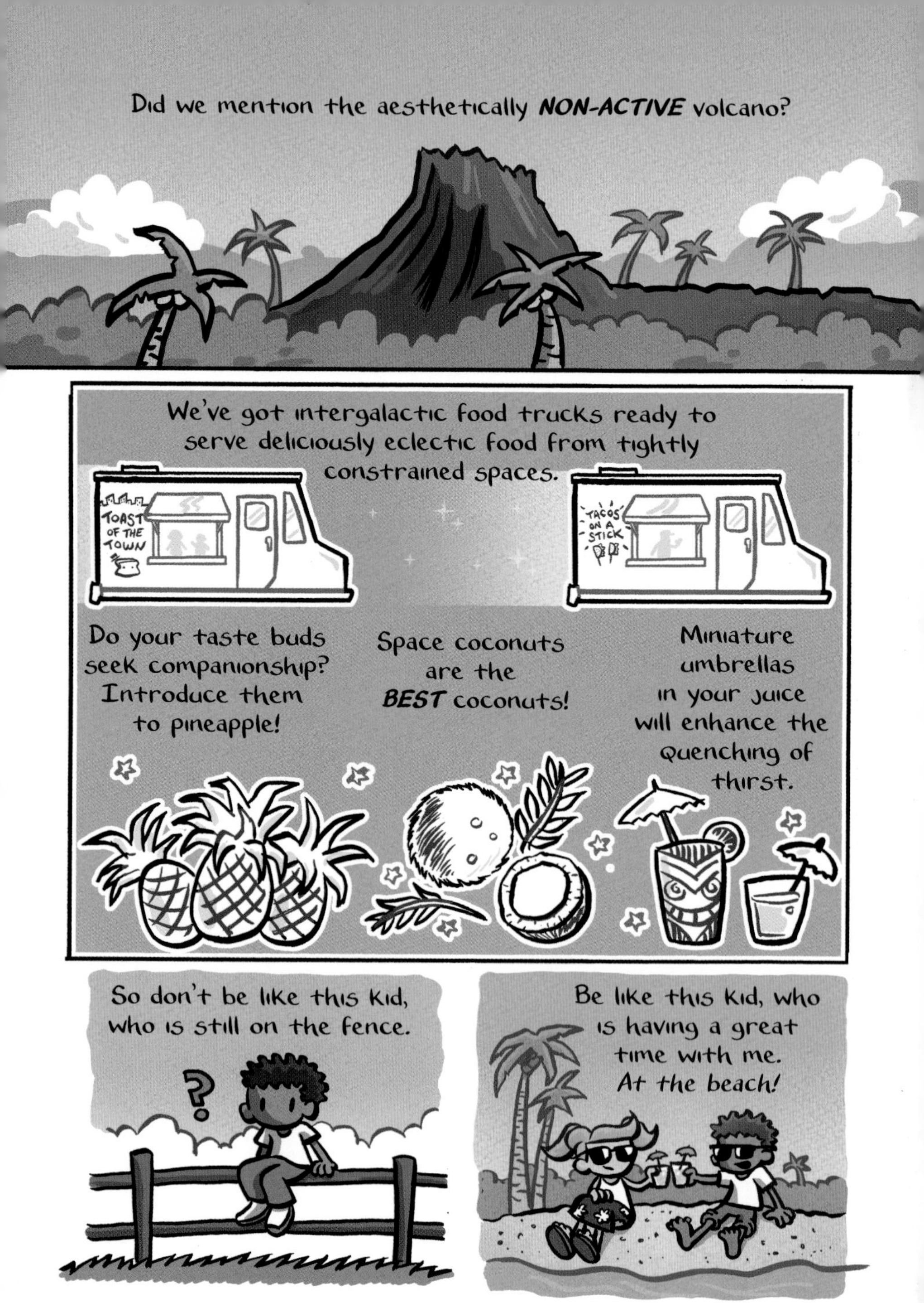
Did we mention the aesthetically ***NON-ACTIVE*** volcano?
We've got intergalactic food trucks ready to serve deliciously eclectic food from tightly constrained spaces.
TOAST OF THE TOWN
TACOS ON A STICK
Do your taste buds seek companionship? Introduce them to pineapple!
Space coconuts are the ***BEST*** coconuts!
Miniature umbrellas in your juice will enhance the quenching of thirst.
So don't be like this kid, who is still on the fence.
?
Be like this kid, who is having a great time with me. At the beach!

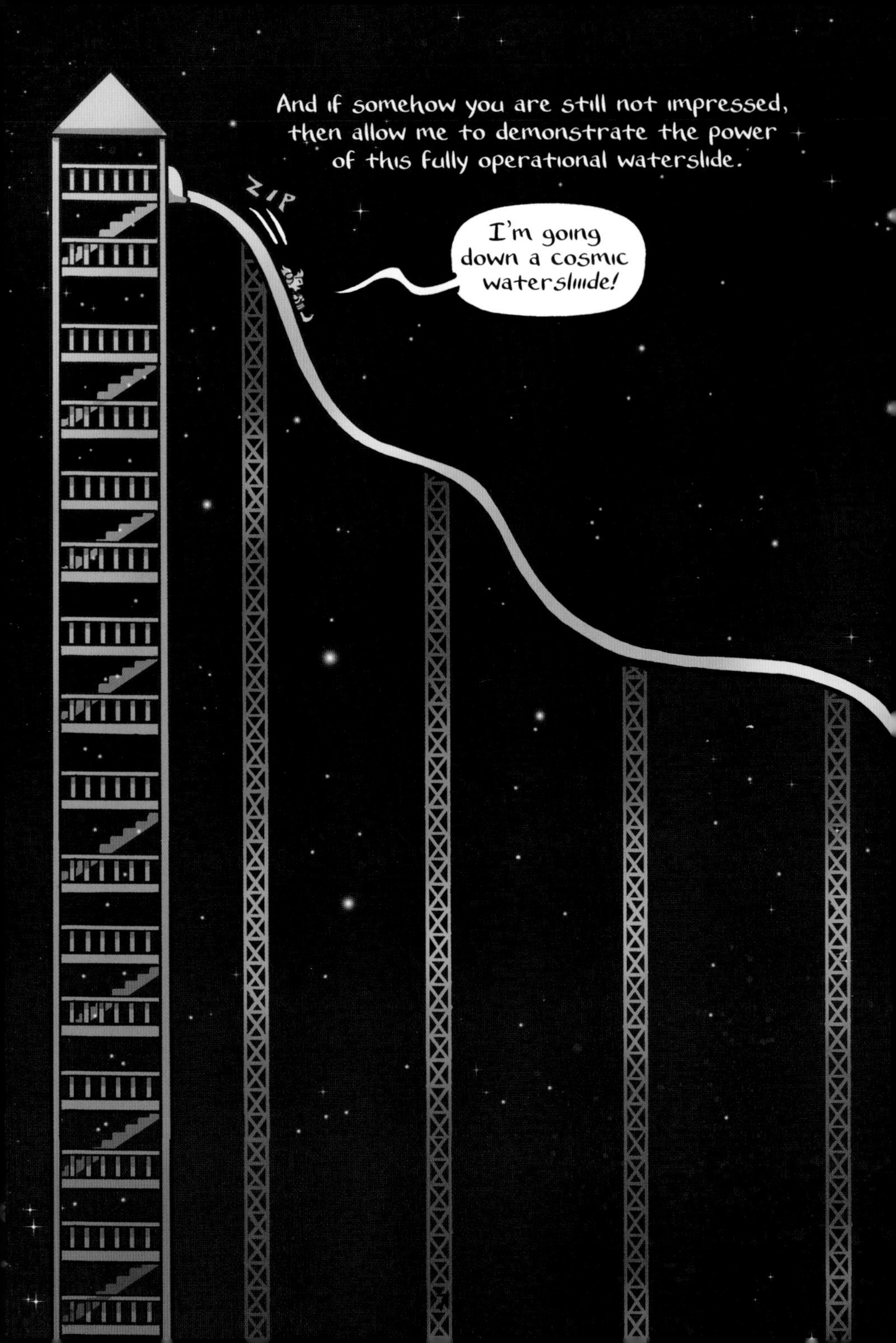
And if somehow you are still not impressed, then allow me to demonstrate the power of this fully operational waterslide.
ZIR
I'm going down a cosmic waterslide!

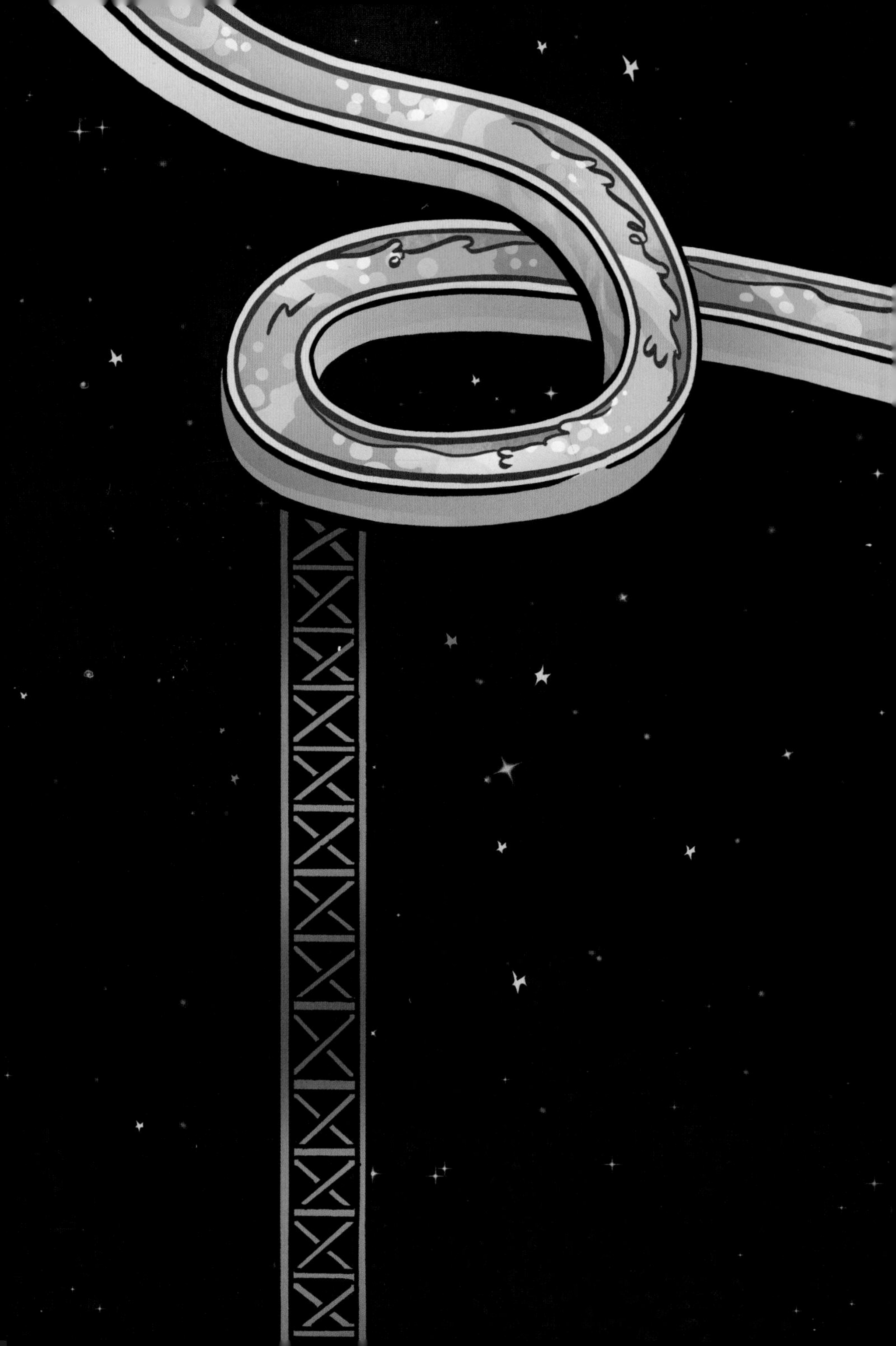

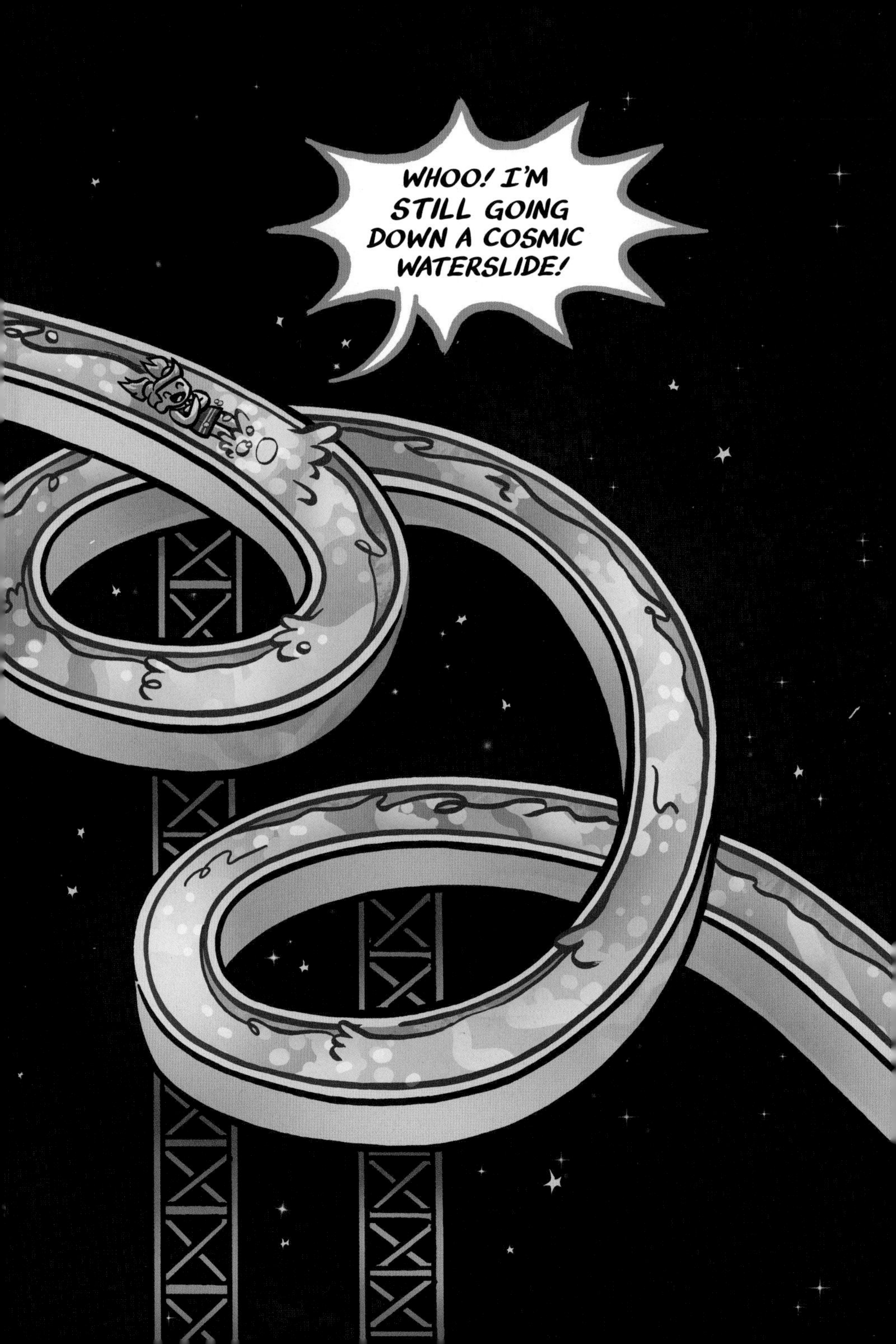
WHOO! I'M STILL GOING DOWN A COSMIC WATERSLIDE!

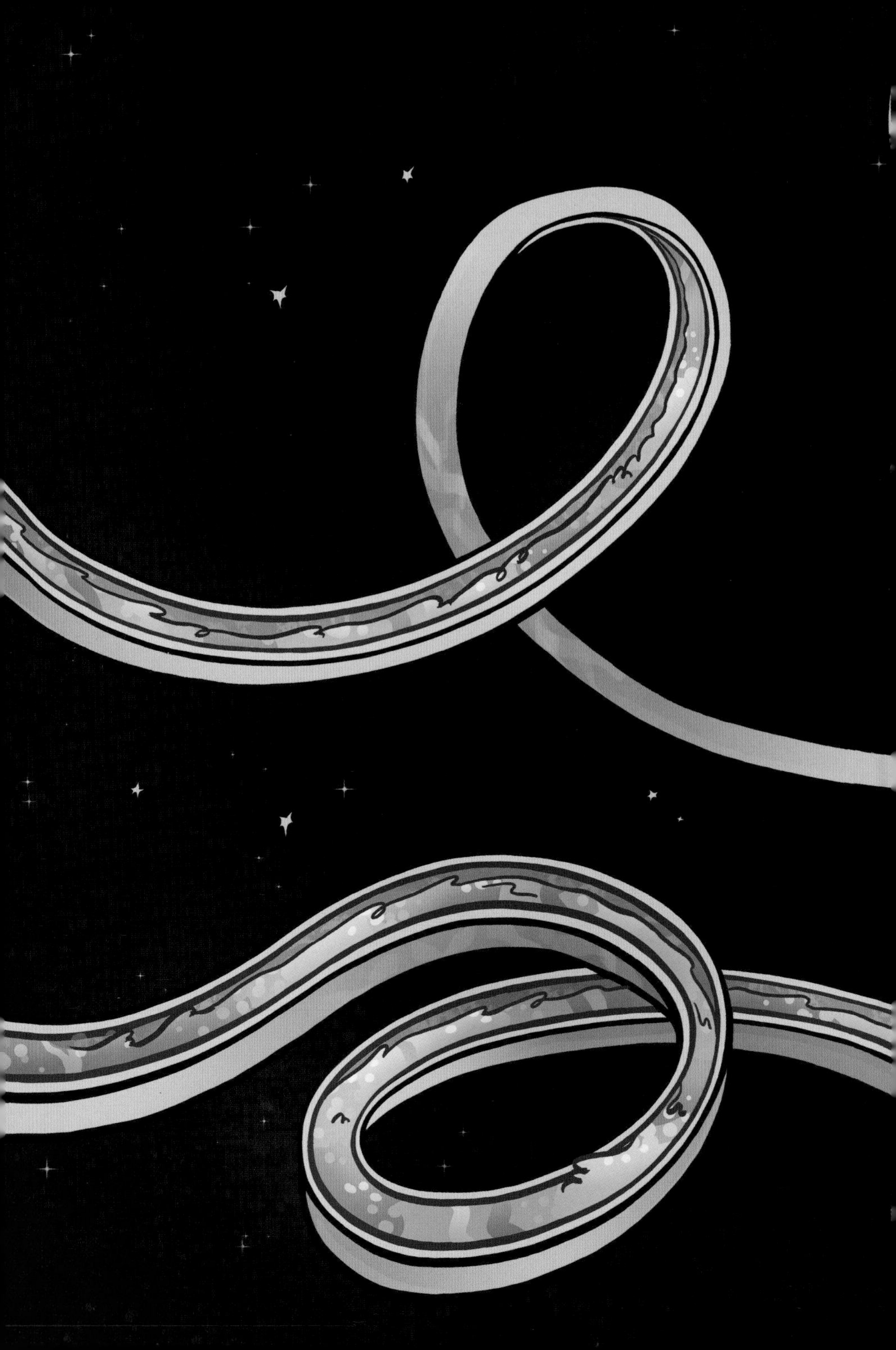

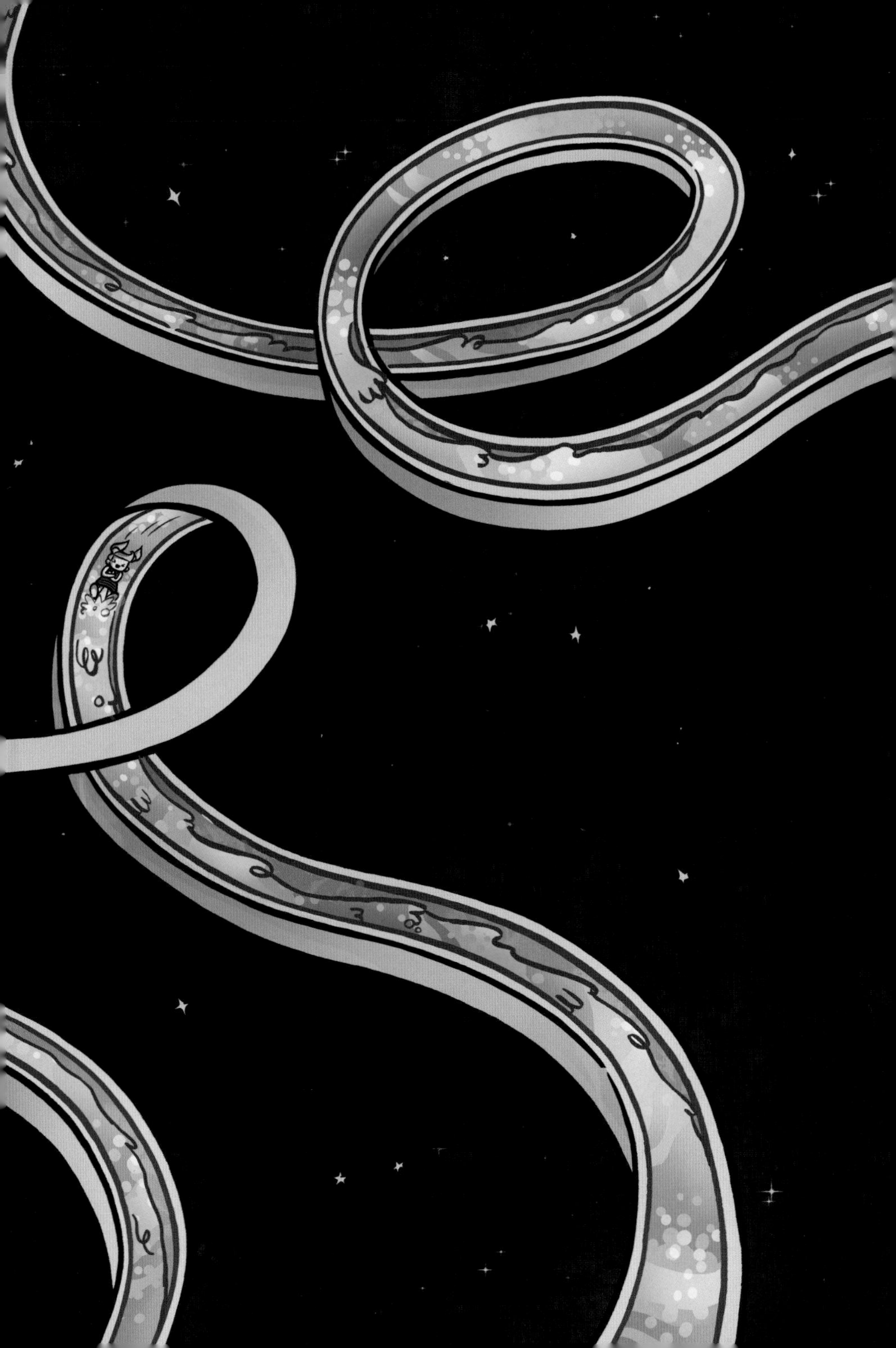

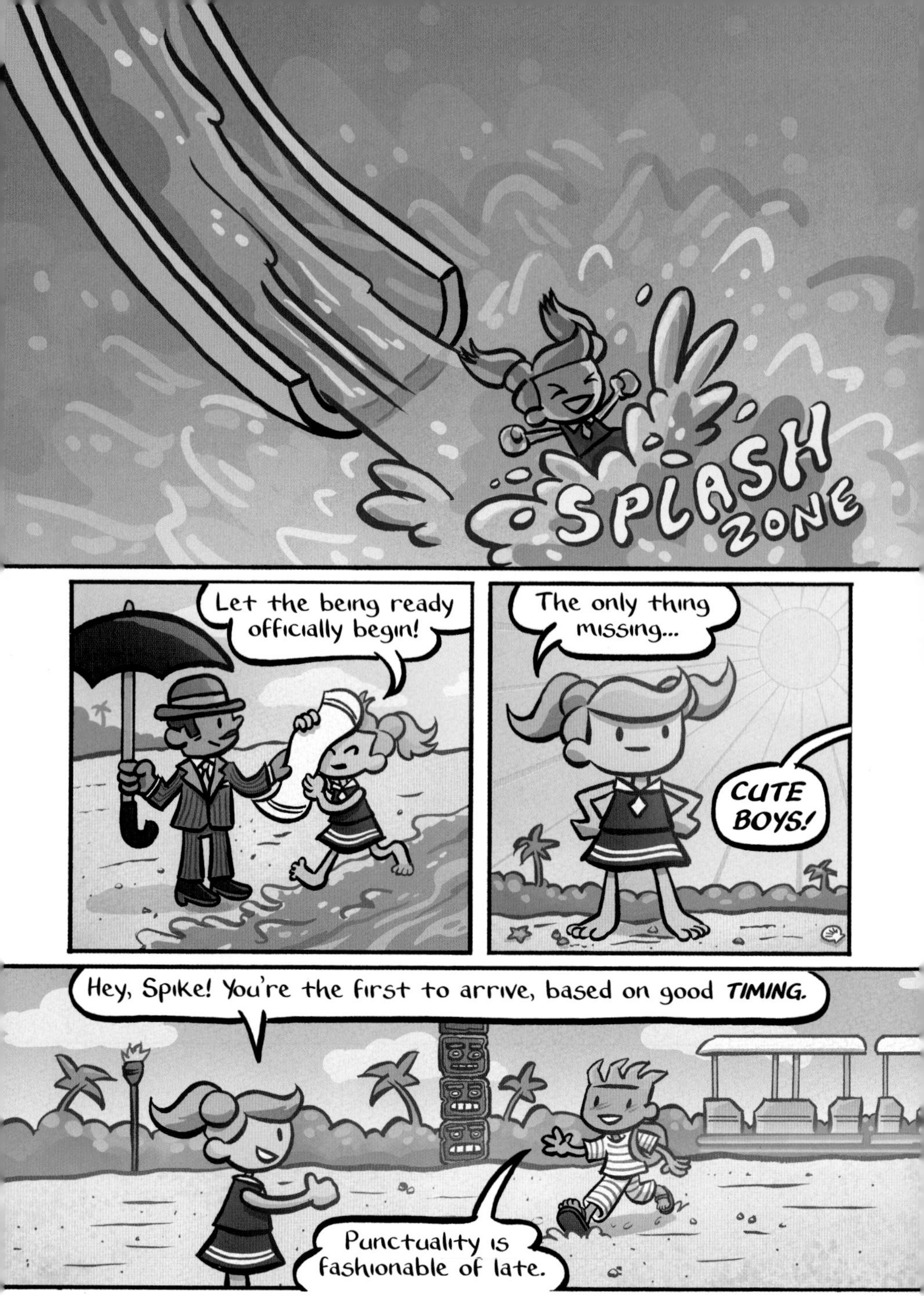

SPLASH ZONE
Let the being ready officially begin!
The only thing missing...
CUTE BOYS!
Hey, Spike! You're the first to arrive, based on good TIMING.
Punctuality is fashionable of late.

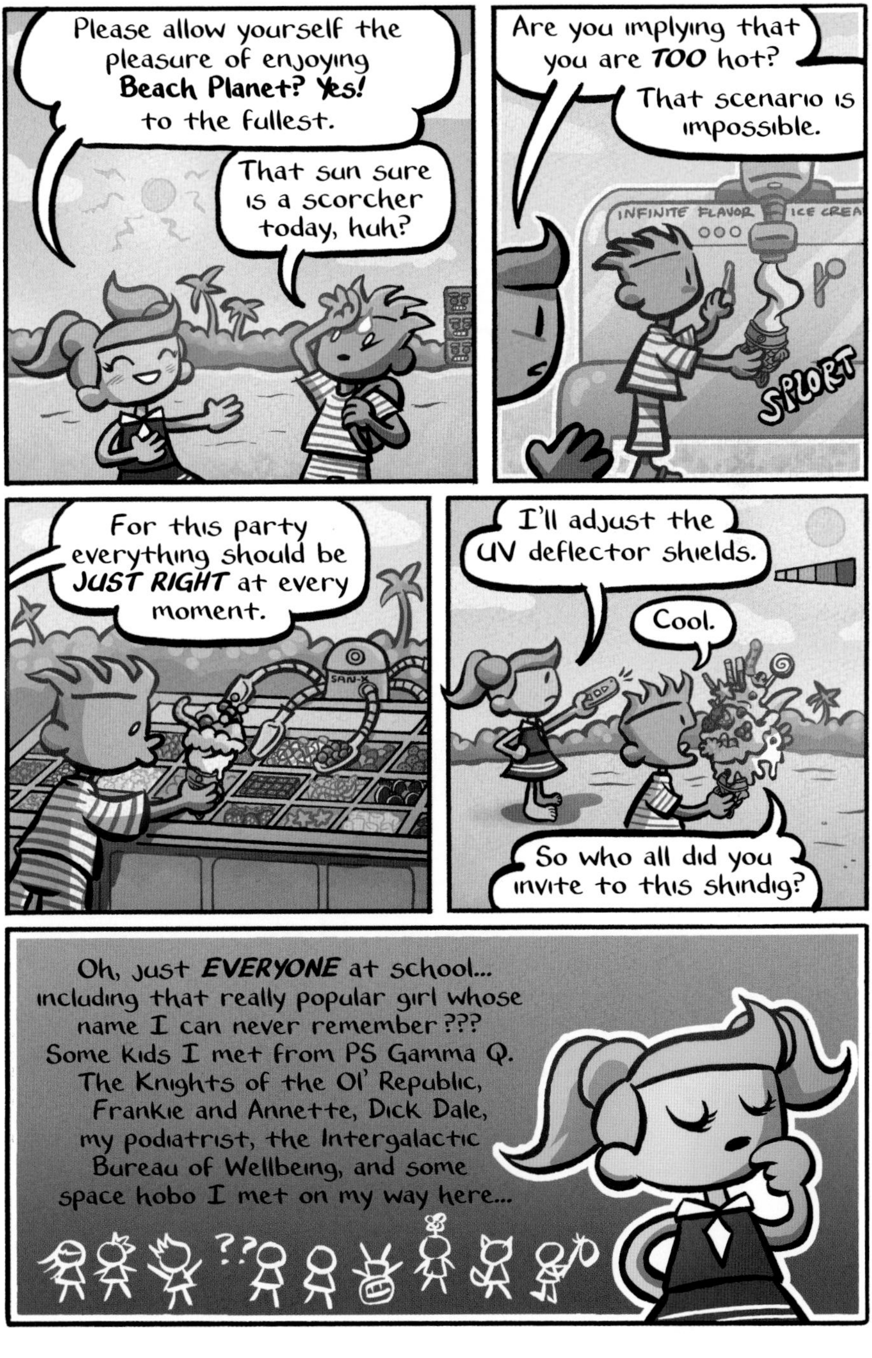
Please allow yourself the pleasure of enjoying Beach Planet? Yes! to the fullest.
That sun sure is a scorcher today, huh?
Are you implying that you are TOO hot?
That scenario is impossible.
INFINITE FLAVOR
ICE CREA
SPLORT
For this party everything should be JUST RIGHT at every moment.
SAN-X
I'll adjust the UV deflector shields.
Cool.
So who all did you invite to this shindig?
Oh, just EVERYONE at school... including that really popular girl whose name I can never remember??? Some kids I met from PS Gamma Q. The Knights of the Ol' Republic, Frankie and Annette, Dick Dale, my podiatrist, the Intergalactic Bureau of Wellbeing, and some space hobo I met on my way here...

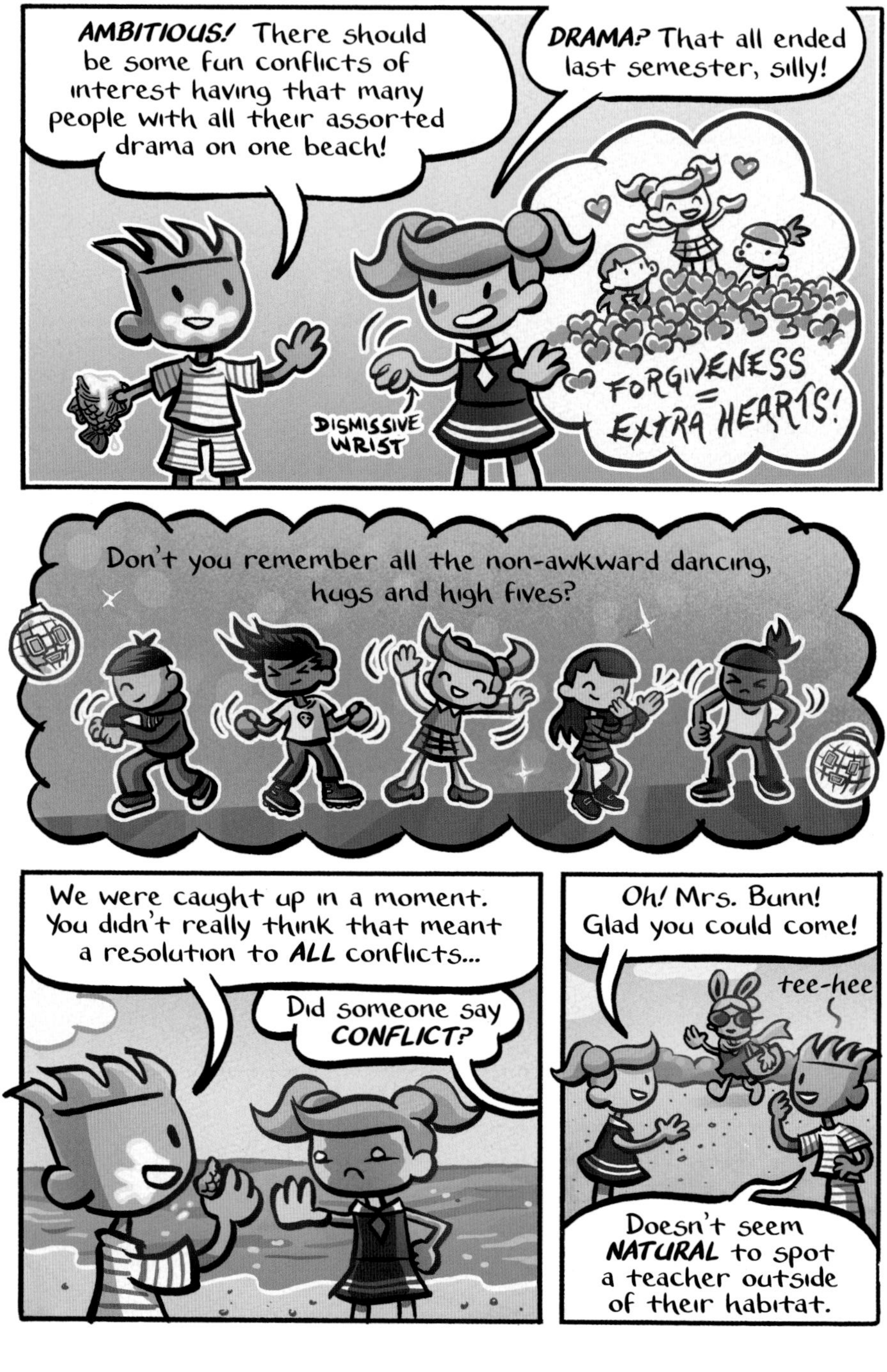
AMBITIOUS! There should be some fun conflicts of interest having that many people with all their assorted drama on one beach!
DRAMA? That all ended last semester, silly!
DISMISSIVE WRIST
FORGIVENESS = EXTRA HEARTS!
Don't you remember all the non-awkward dancing, hugs and high fives?
We were caught up in a moment. You didn't really think that meant a resolution to ALL conflicts...
Did someone say CONFLICT?
Oh! Mrs. Bunn! Glad you could come!
tee-hee
Doesn't seem NATURAL to spot a teacher outside of their habitat.

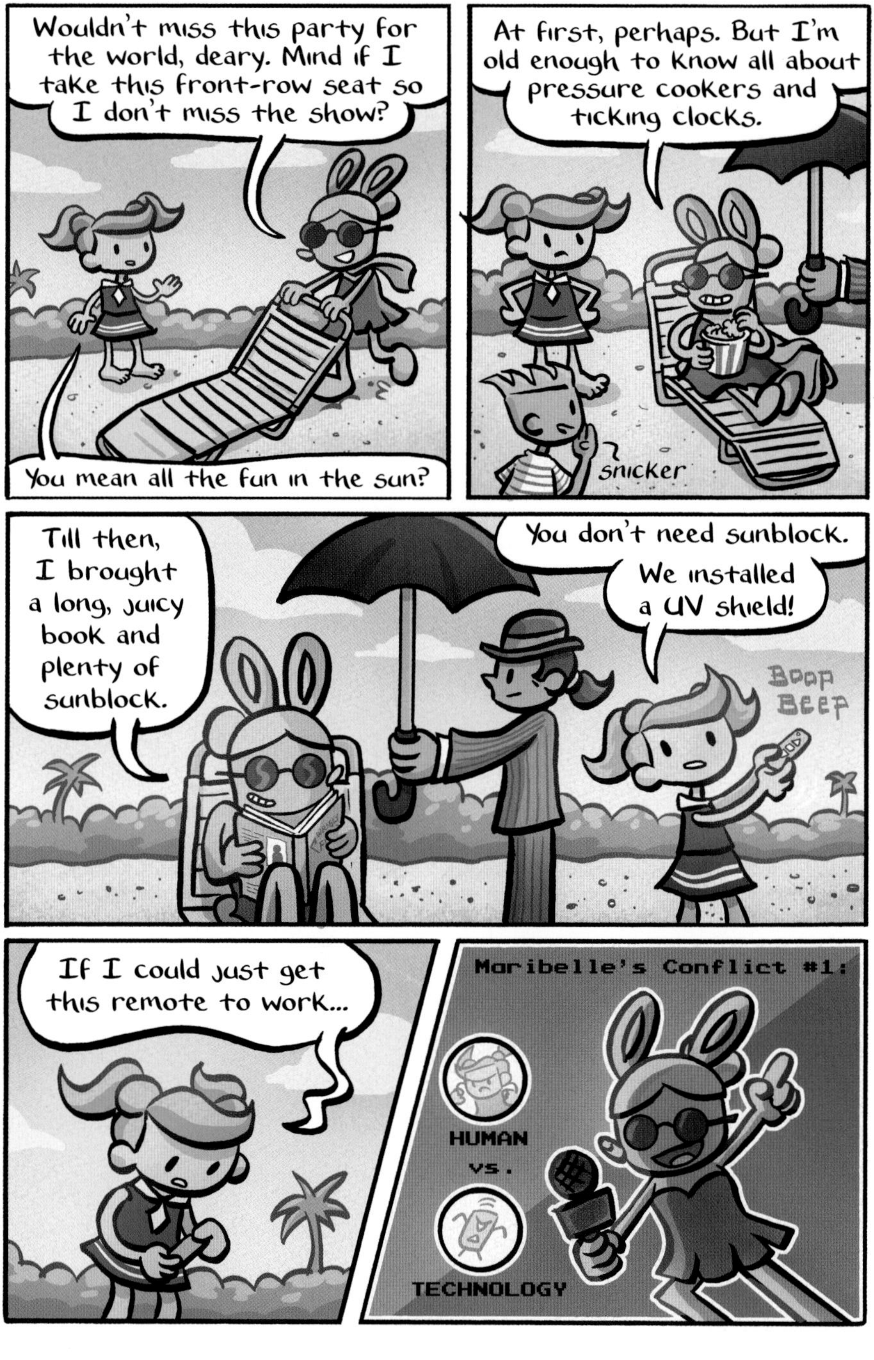

Wouldn't miss this party for the world, deary. Mind if I take this front-row seat so I don't miss the show?
You mean all the fun in the sun?
At first, perhaps. But I'm old enough to know all about pressure cookers and ticking clocks.
snicker
Till then, I brought a long, juicy book and plenty of sunblock.
You don't need sunblock.
We installed a UV shield!
BOOP BEEP
If I could just get this remote to work...
Maribelle's Conflict #1:
HUMAN
vs.
TECHNOLOGY

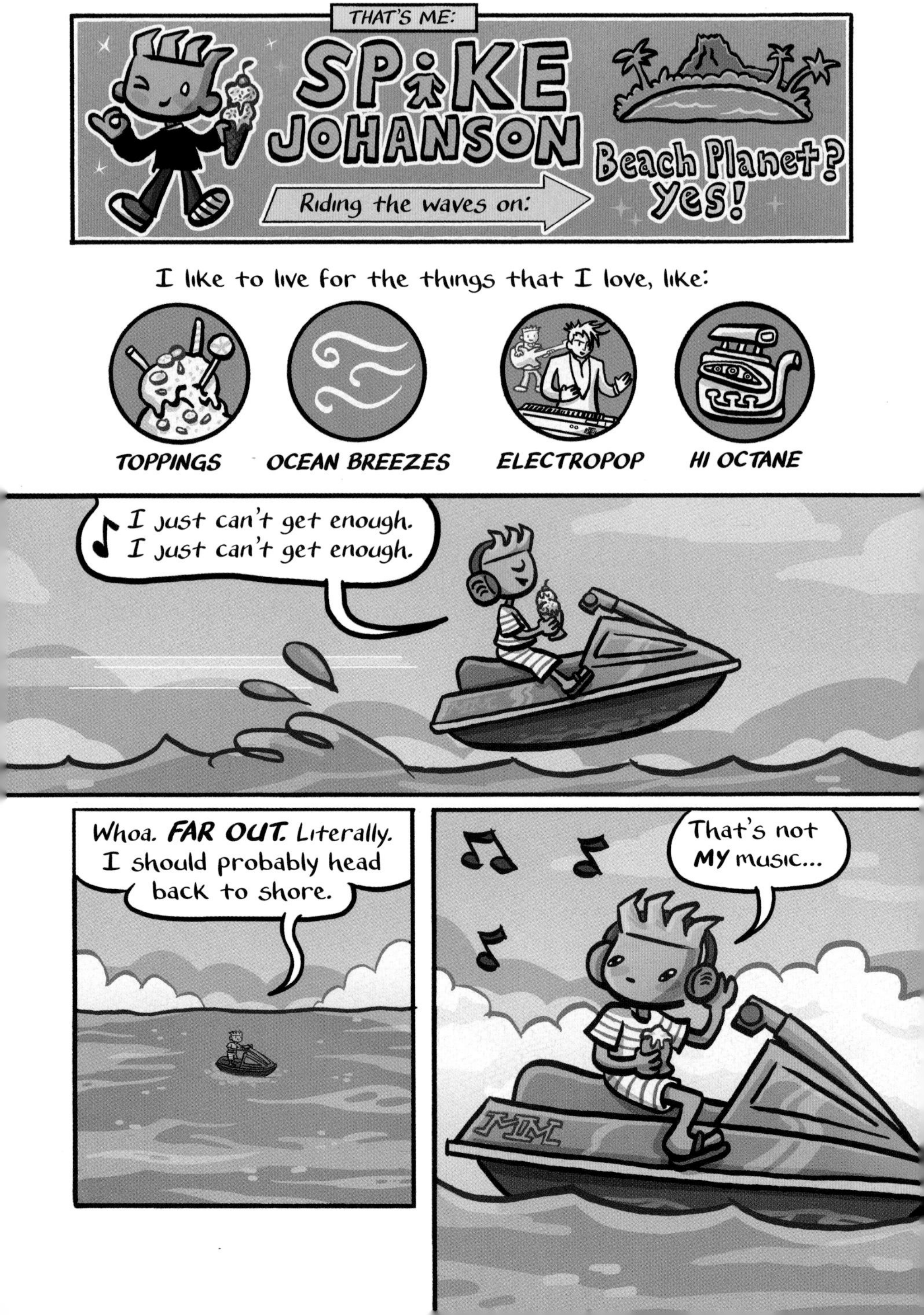

THAT'S ME:
SPIKE JOHANSON
Riding the waves on:
Beach Planet? yes!
I like to live for the things that I love, like:
TOPPINGS
OCEAN BREEZES
ELECTROPOP
HI OCTANE
I just can't get enough.
I just can't get enough.
Whoa. FAR OUT. Literally. I should probably head back to shore.
That's not MY music...

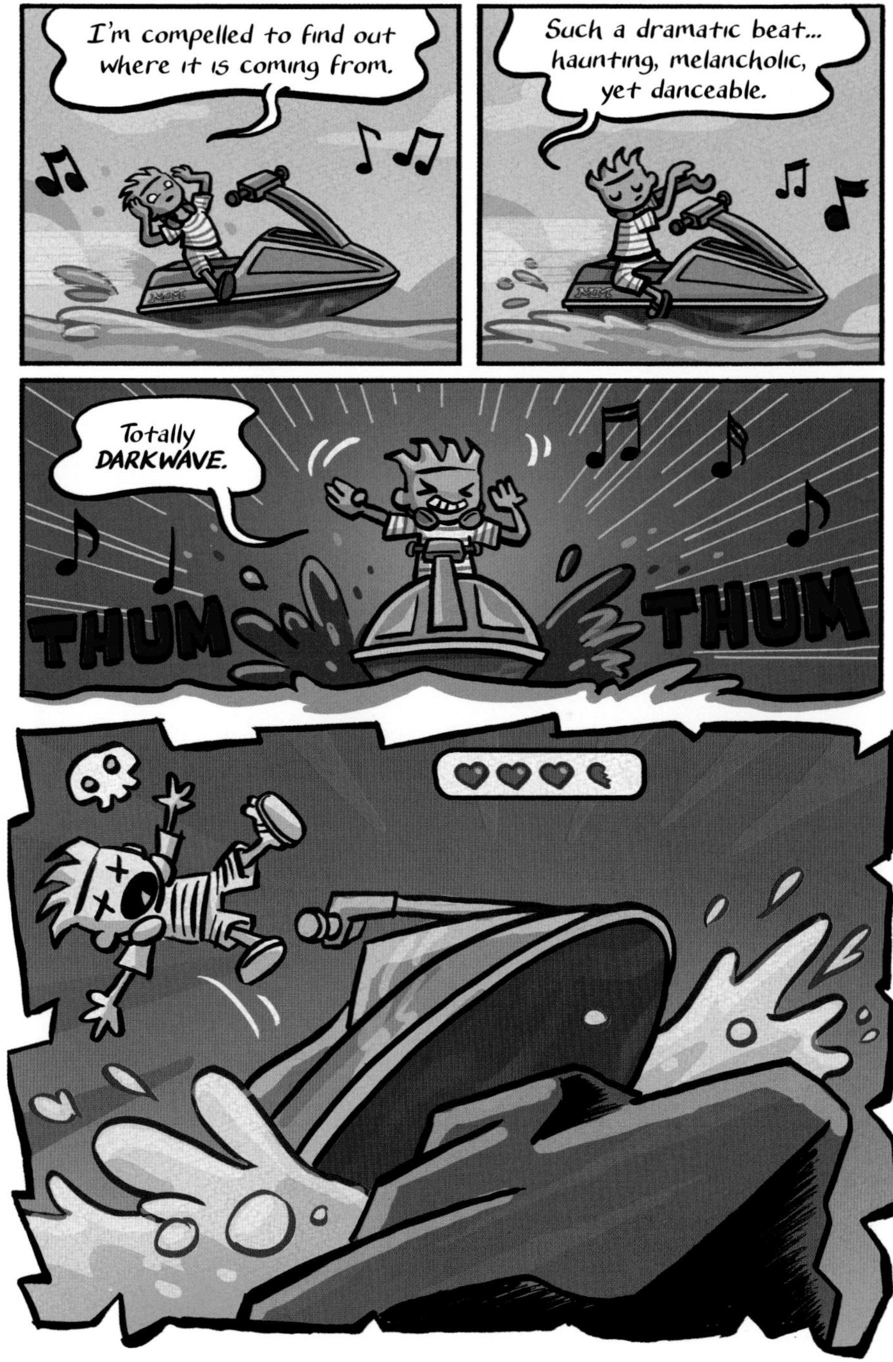
I'm compelled to find out where it is coming from.
Such a dramatic beat... haunting, melancholic, yet danceable.
Totally DARKWAVE.
THUM
THUM

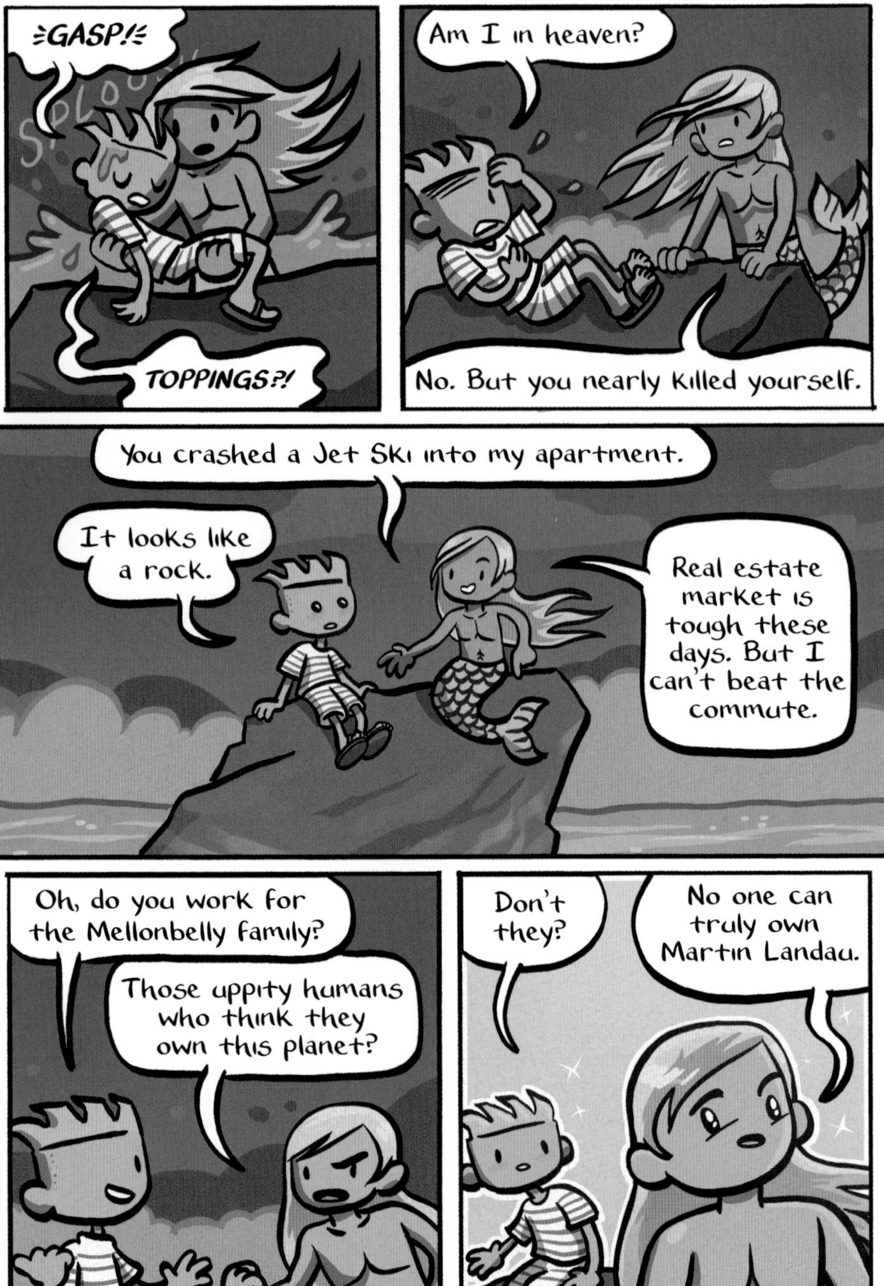
GASP!
TOPPINGS?!
Am I in heaven?
No. But you nearly killed yourself.
You crashed a Jet Ski into my apartment.
It looks like a rock.
Real estate market is tough these days. But I can't beat the commute.
Oh, do you work for the Mellonbelly family?
Those uppity humans who think they own this planet?
Don't they?
No one can truly own Martin Landau.

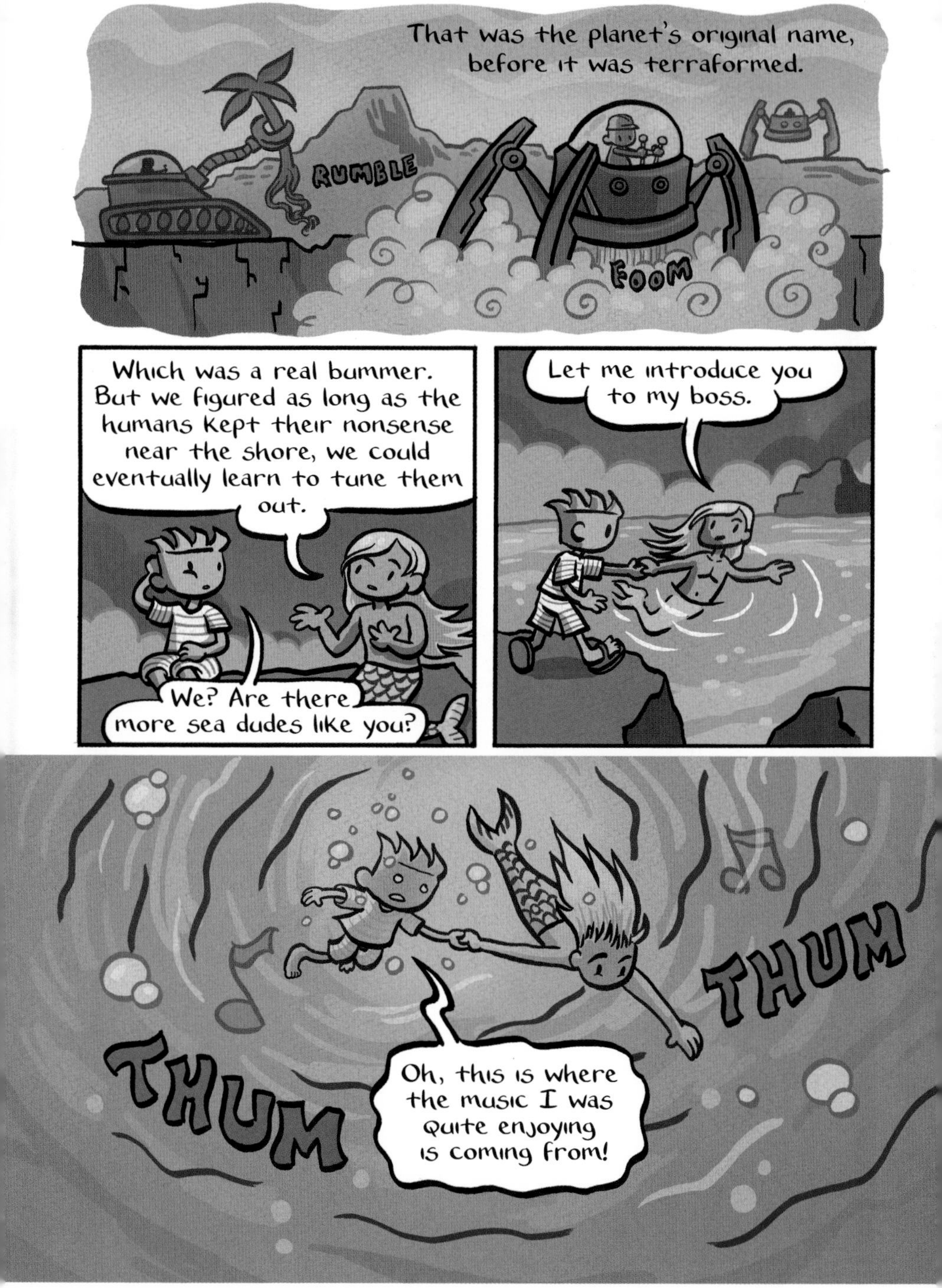
That was the planet's original name, before it was terraformed.
RUMBLE
FOOM
Which was a real bummer. But we figured as long as the humans kept their nonsense near the shore, we could eventually learn to tune them out.
We? Are there more sea dudes like you?
Let me introduce you to my boss.
THUM
THUM
Oh, this is where the music I was quite enjoying is coming from!

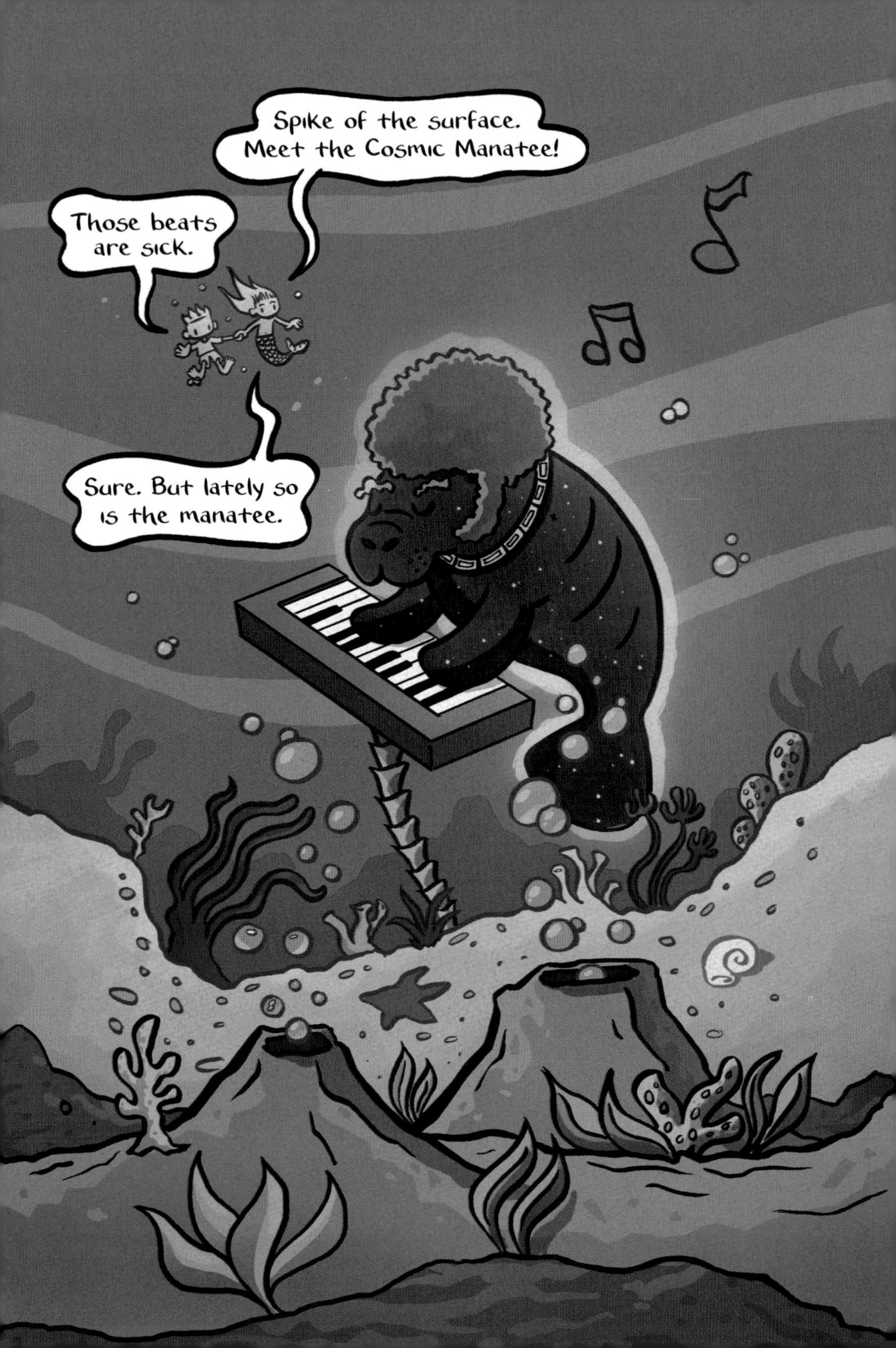
Spike of the surface. Meet the Cosmic Manatee!
Those beats are sick.
Sure. But lately so is the manatee.

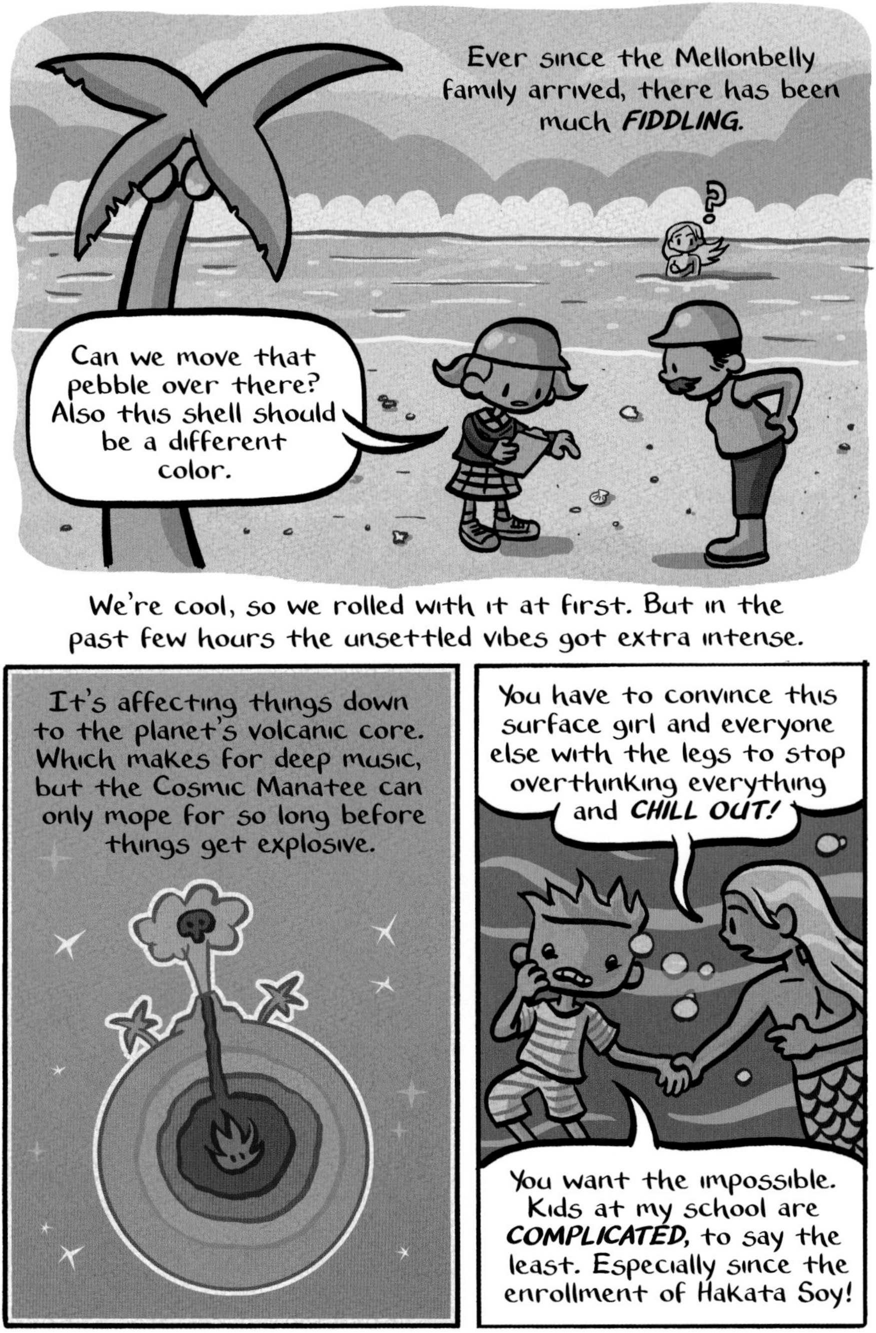
Ever since the Mellonbelly family arrived, there has been much *FIDDLING.*
?
Can we move that pebble over there? Also this shell should be a different color.
We're cool, so we rolled with it at first. But in the past few hours the unsettled vibes got extra intense.
It's affecting things down to the planet's volcanic core. Which makes for deep music, but the Cosmic Manatee can only mope for so long before things get explosive.
You have to convince this surface girl and everyone else with the legs to stop overthinking everything and *CHILL OUT!*
You want the impossible. Kids at my school are *COMPLICATED,* to say the least. Especially since the enrollment of Hakata Soy!

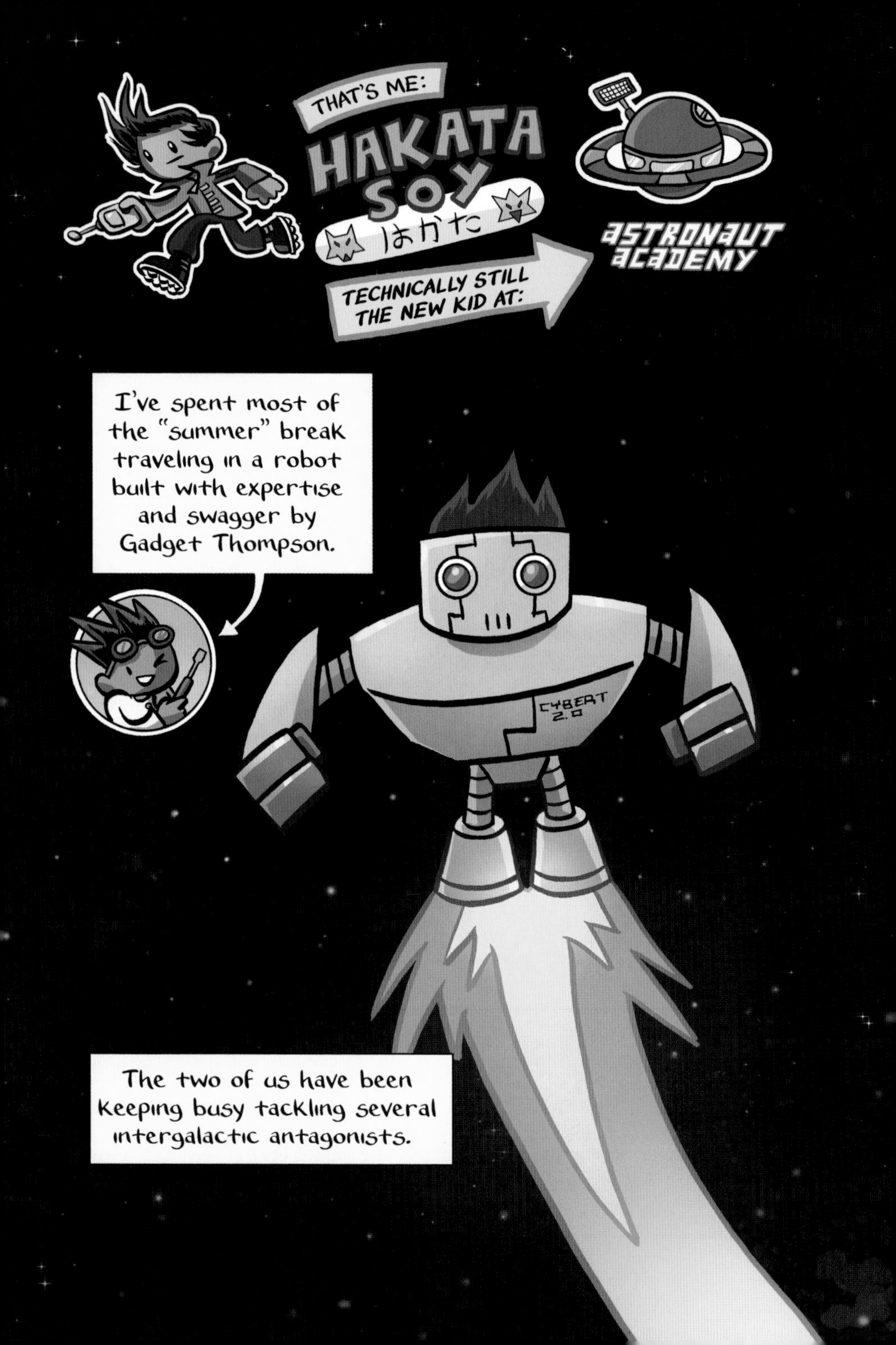

THAT'S ME:
HAKATA SOY
はかた
TECHNICALLY STILL THE NEW KID AT:
ASTRONAUT ACADEMY
I've spent most of the "summer" break traveling in a robot built with expertise and swagger by Gadget Thompson.
CYBERT 2.0
The two of us have been keeping busy tackling several intergalactic antagonists.

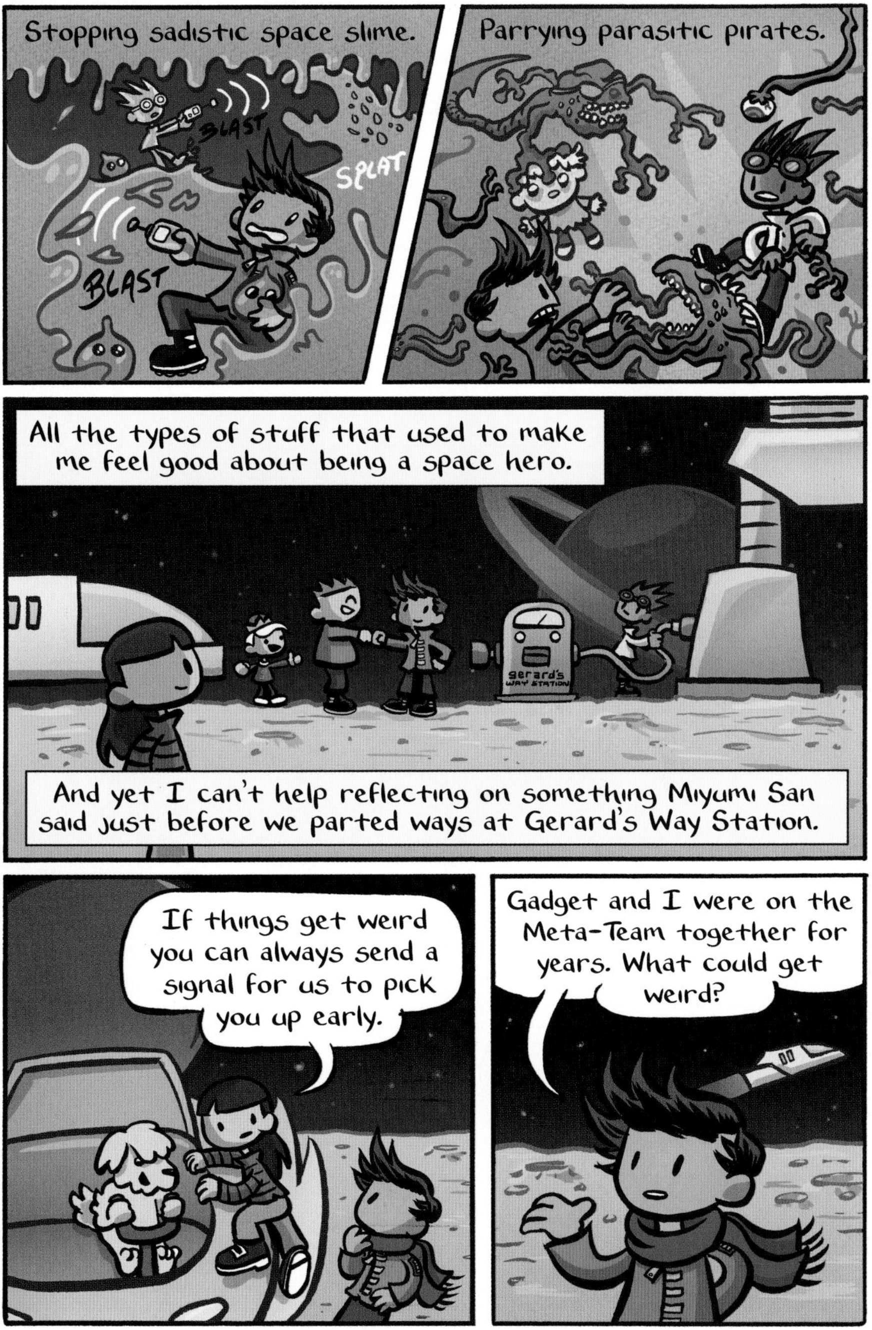
Stopping sadistic space slime.
BLAST
SPLAT
BLAST
Parrying parasitic pirates.
All the types of stuff that used to make me feel good about being a space hero.
Gerard's WAY STATION
And yet I can't help reflecting on something Miyumi San said just before we parted ways at Gerard's Way Station.
If things get weird you can always send a signal for us to pick you up early.
Gadget and I were on the Meta-Team together for years. What could get weird?

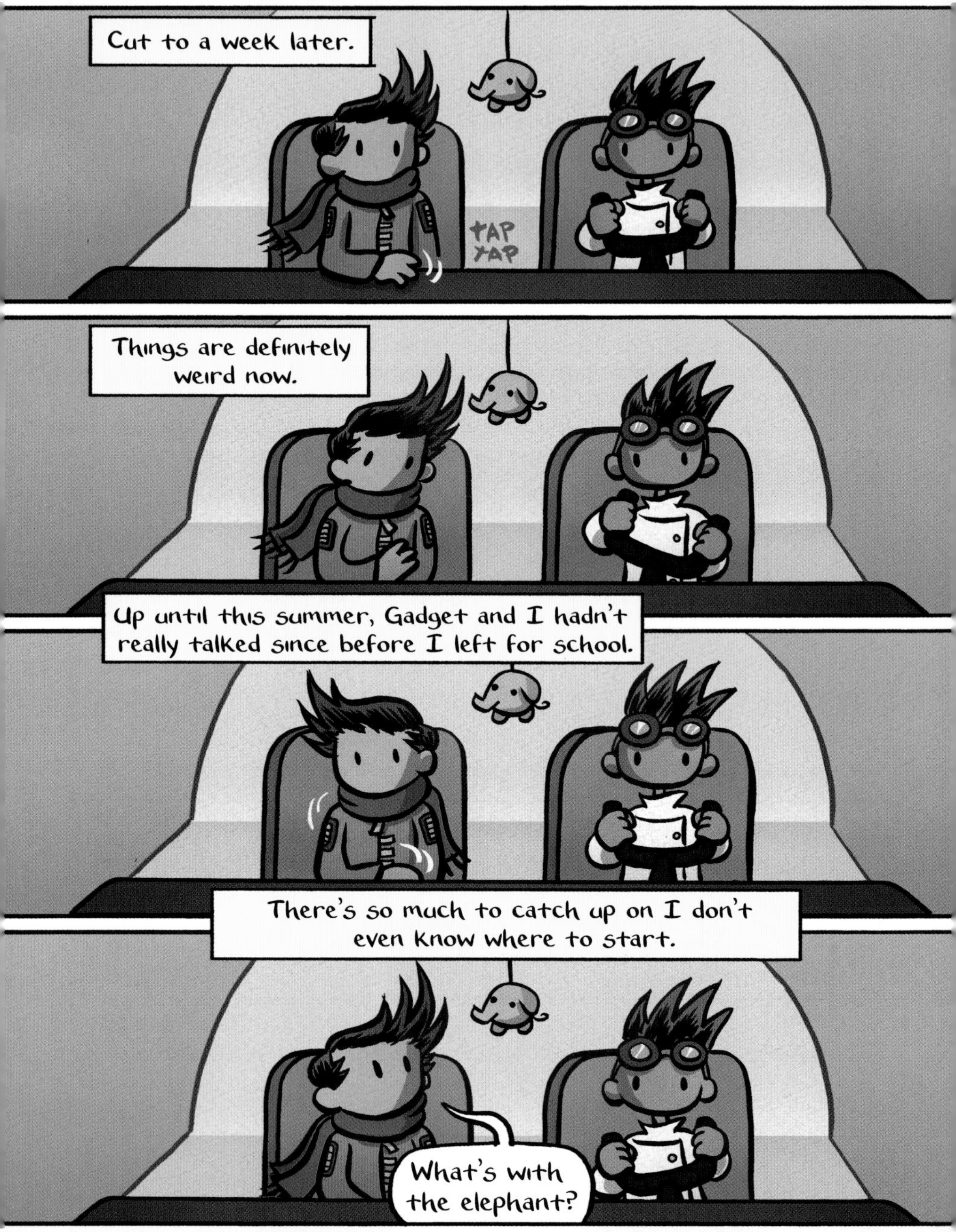
Cut to a week later.
TAP TAP
Things are definitely weird now.
Up until this summer, Gadget and I hadn't really talked since before I left for school.
There's so much to catch up on I don't even know where to start.
What's with the elephant?

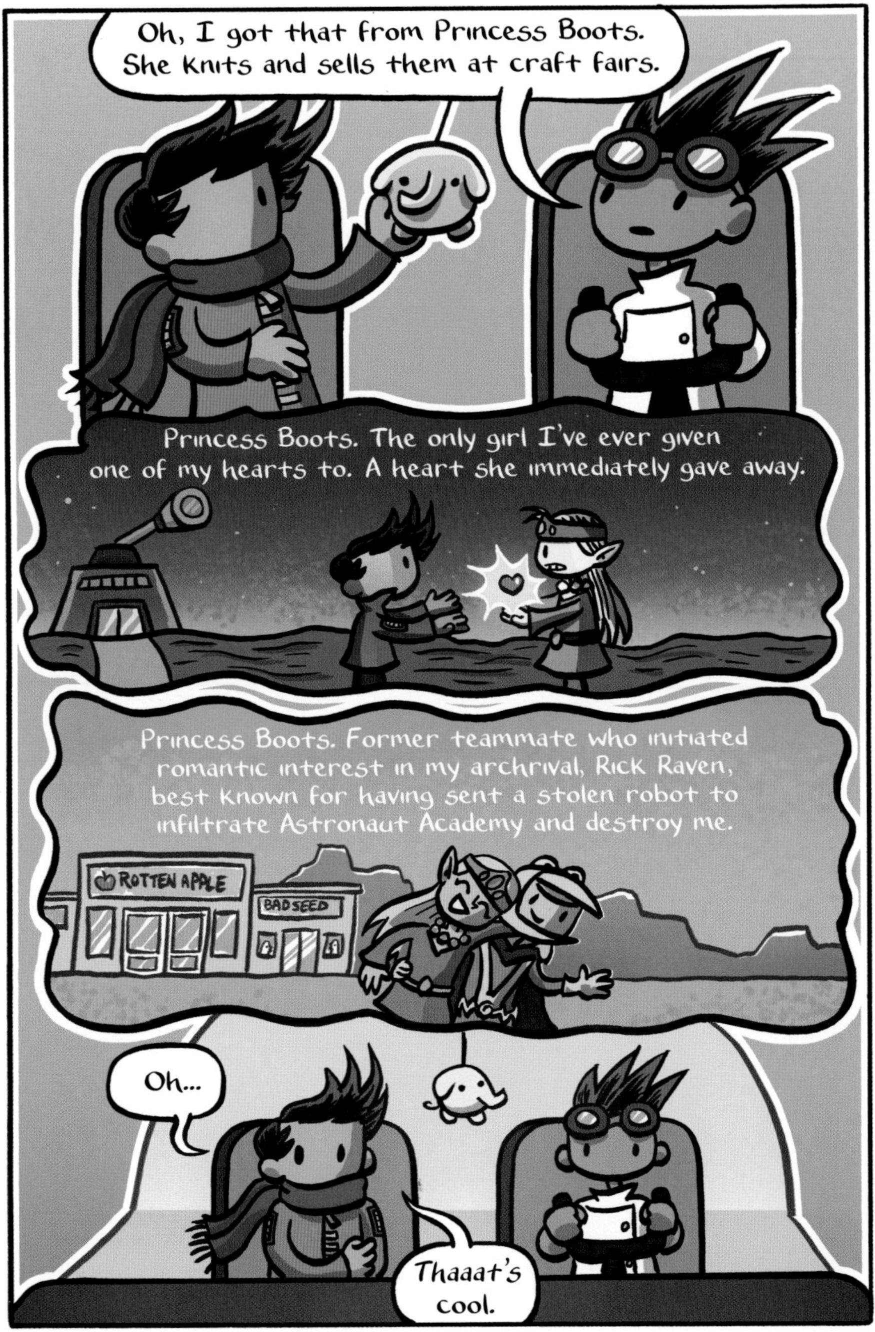
Oh, I got that from Princess Boots. She knits and sells them at craft fairs.
Princess Boots. The only girl I've ever given one of my hearts to. A heart she immediately gave away.
Princess Boots. Former teammate who initiated romantic interest in my archrival, Rick Raven, best known for having sent a stolen robot to infiltrate Astronaut Academy and destroy me.
ROTTEN APPLE
BAD SEED
Oh...
Thaaat's cool.

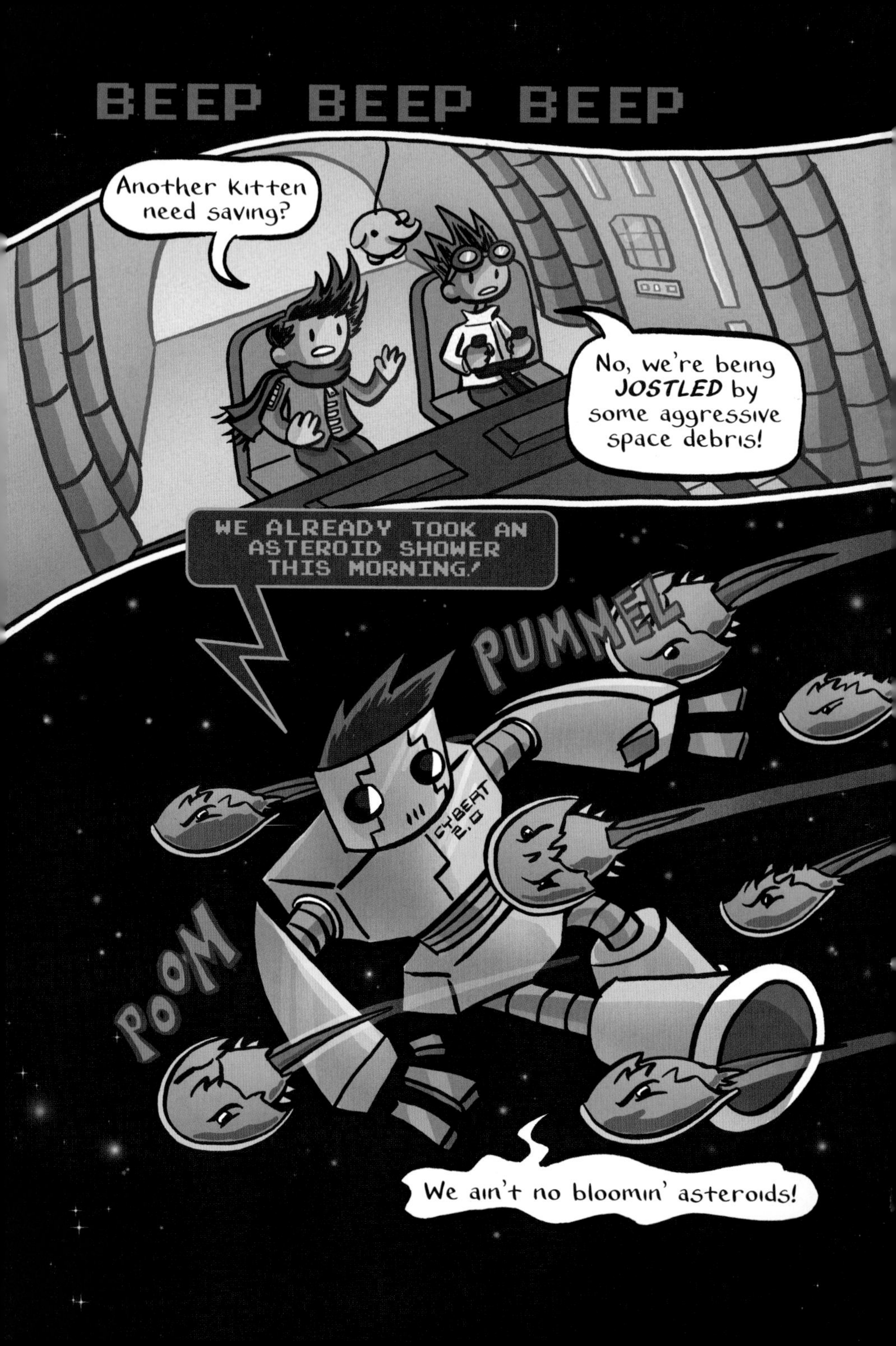
BEEP BEEP BEEP
Another kitten need saving?
No, we're being JOSTLED by some aggressive space debris!
WE ALREADY TOOK AN ASTEROID SHOWER THIS MORNING!
PUMMEL
CYBEAT 2.0
POOM
We ain't no bloomin' asteroids!

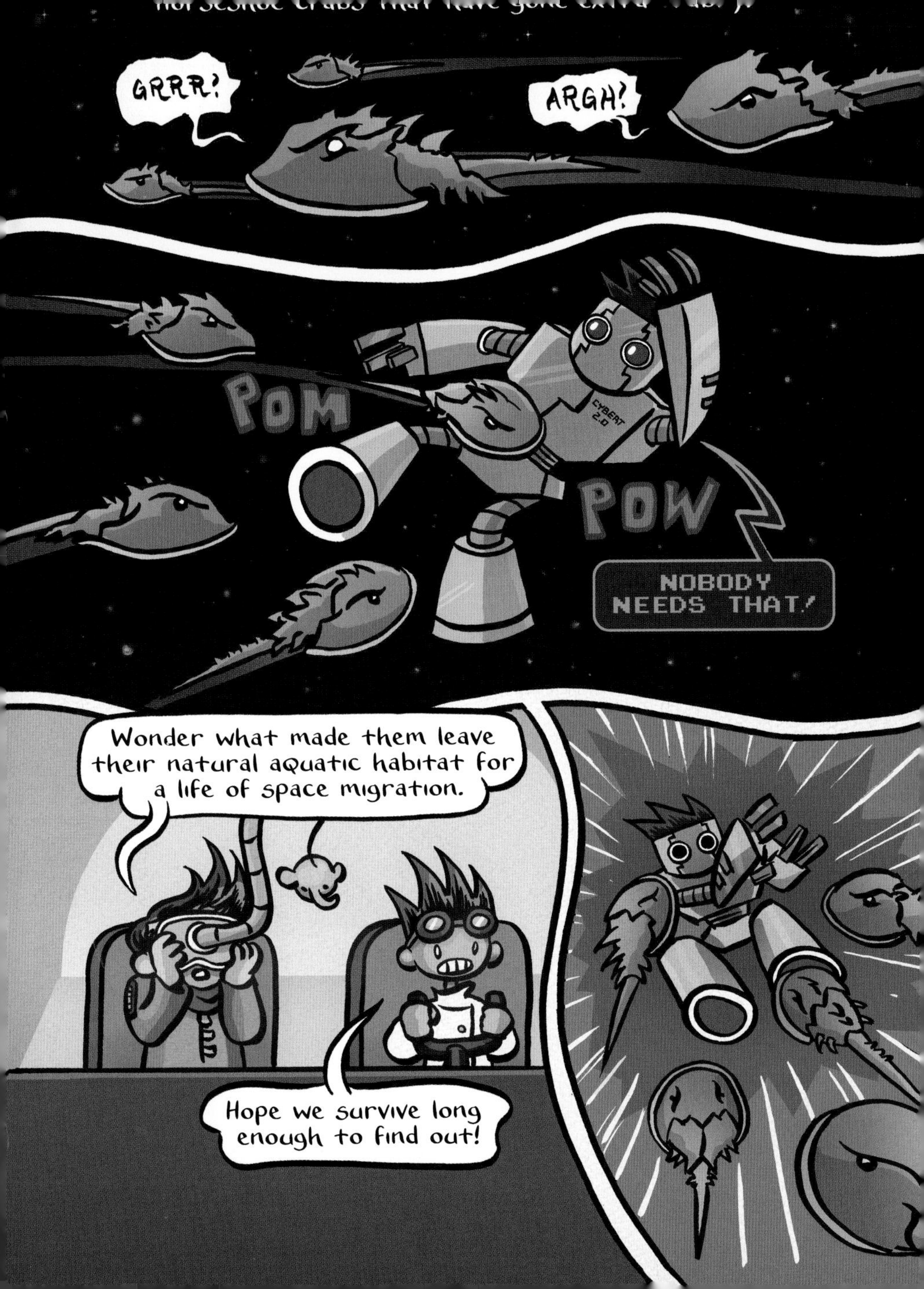
GRRR?
ARGH?
POM
POW
NOBODY NEEDS THAT!
Wonder what made them leave their natural aquatic habitat for a life of space migration.
Hope we survive long enough to find out!

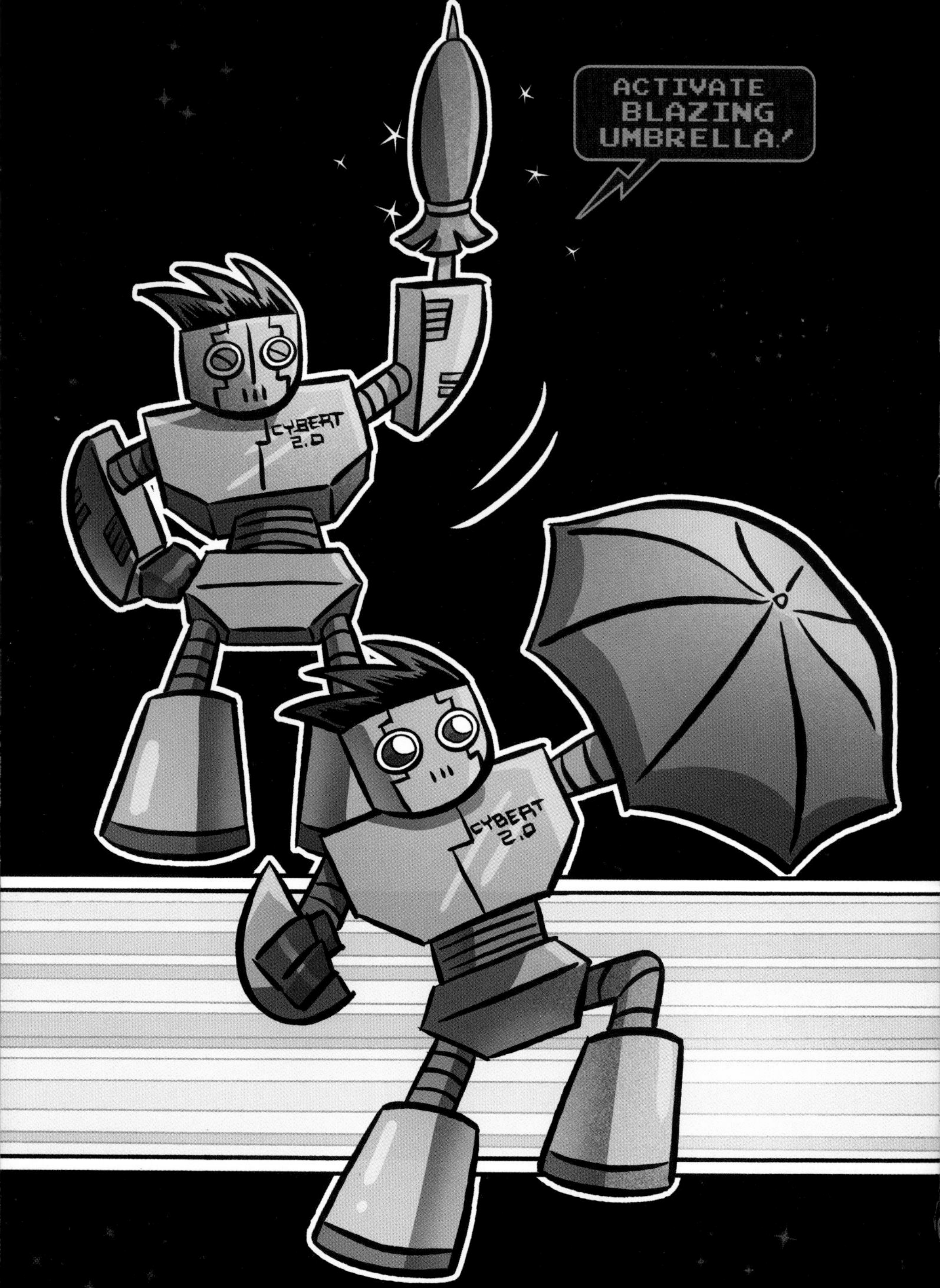
ACTIVATE BLAZING UMBRELLA!
CYBERT 2.0
CYBERT 2.0

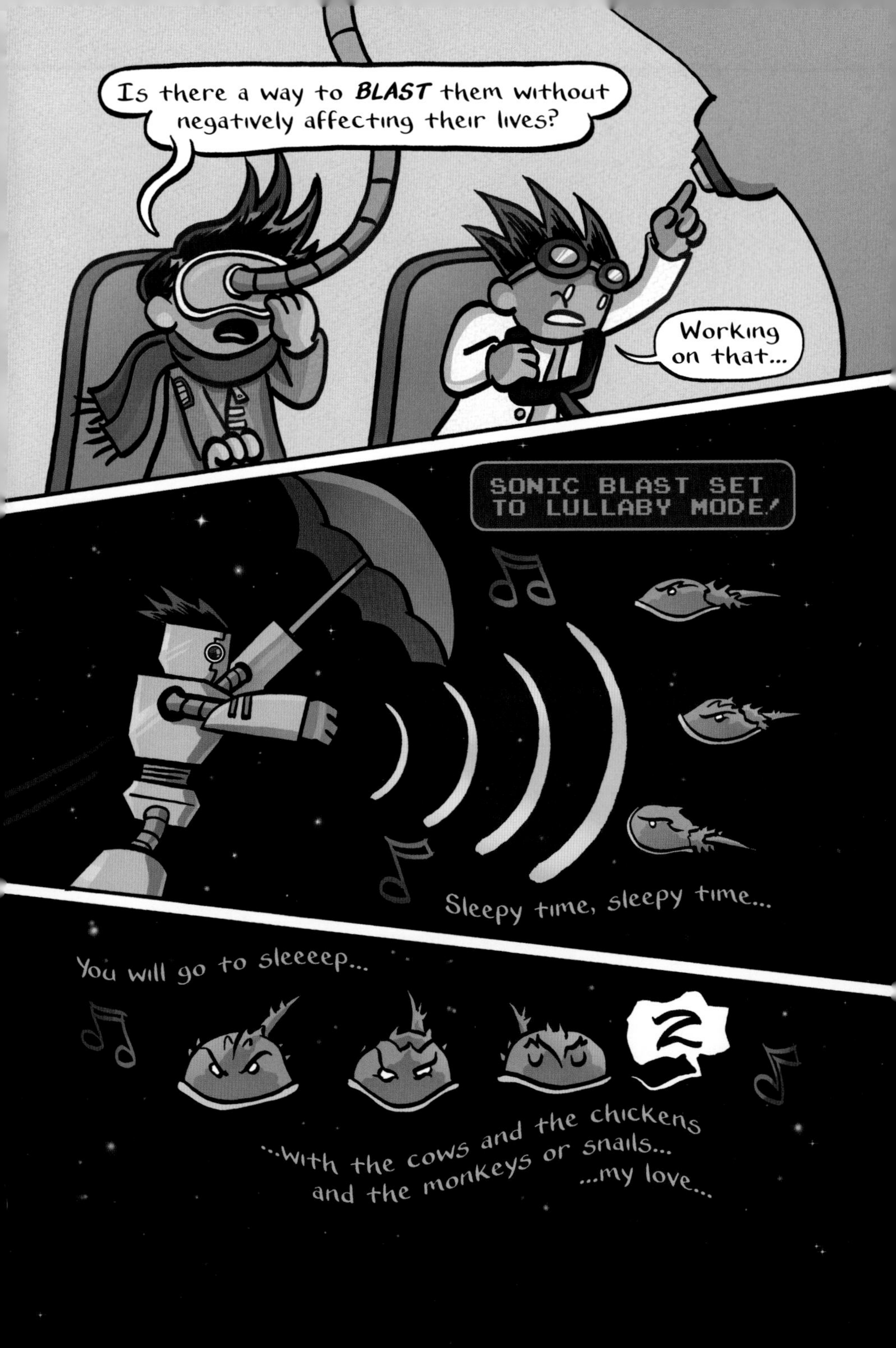
Is there a way to BLAST them without negatively affecting their lives?
Working on that...
SONIC BLAST SET TO LULLABY MODE!
Sleepy time, sleepy time...
You will go to sleeeep...
Z
...with the cows and the chickens and the monkeys or snails...
...my love...

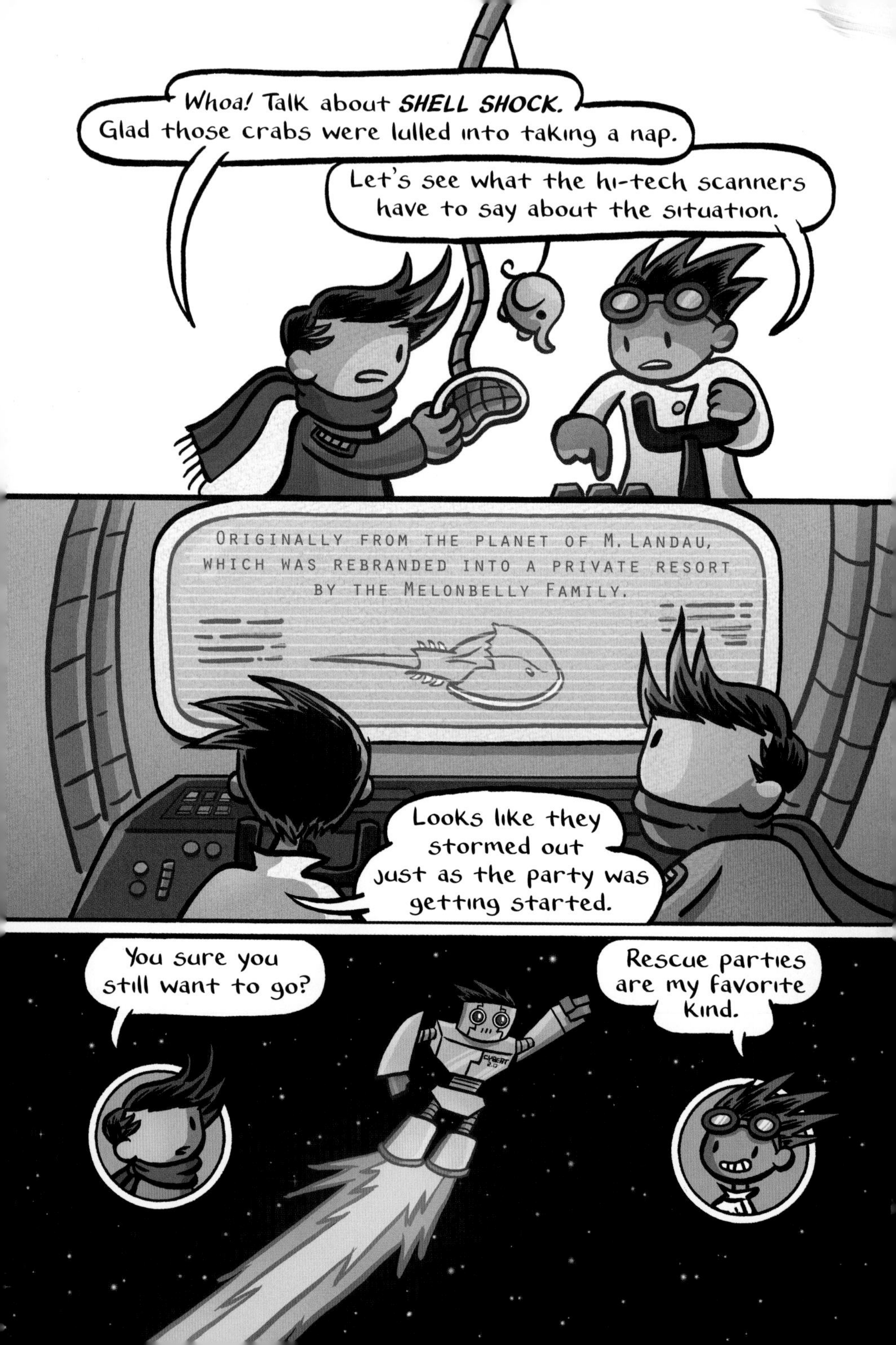
Whoa! Talk about **SHELL SHOCK.** Glad those crabs were lulled into taking a nap.
Let's see what the hi-tech scanners have to say about the situation.
ORIGINALLY FROM THE PLANET OF M. LANDAU, WHICH WAS REBRANDED INTO A PRIVATE RESORT BY THE MELONBELLY FAMILY.
Looks like they stormed out just as the party was getting started.
You sure you still want to go?
Rescue parties are my favorite kind.

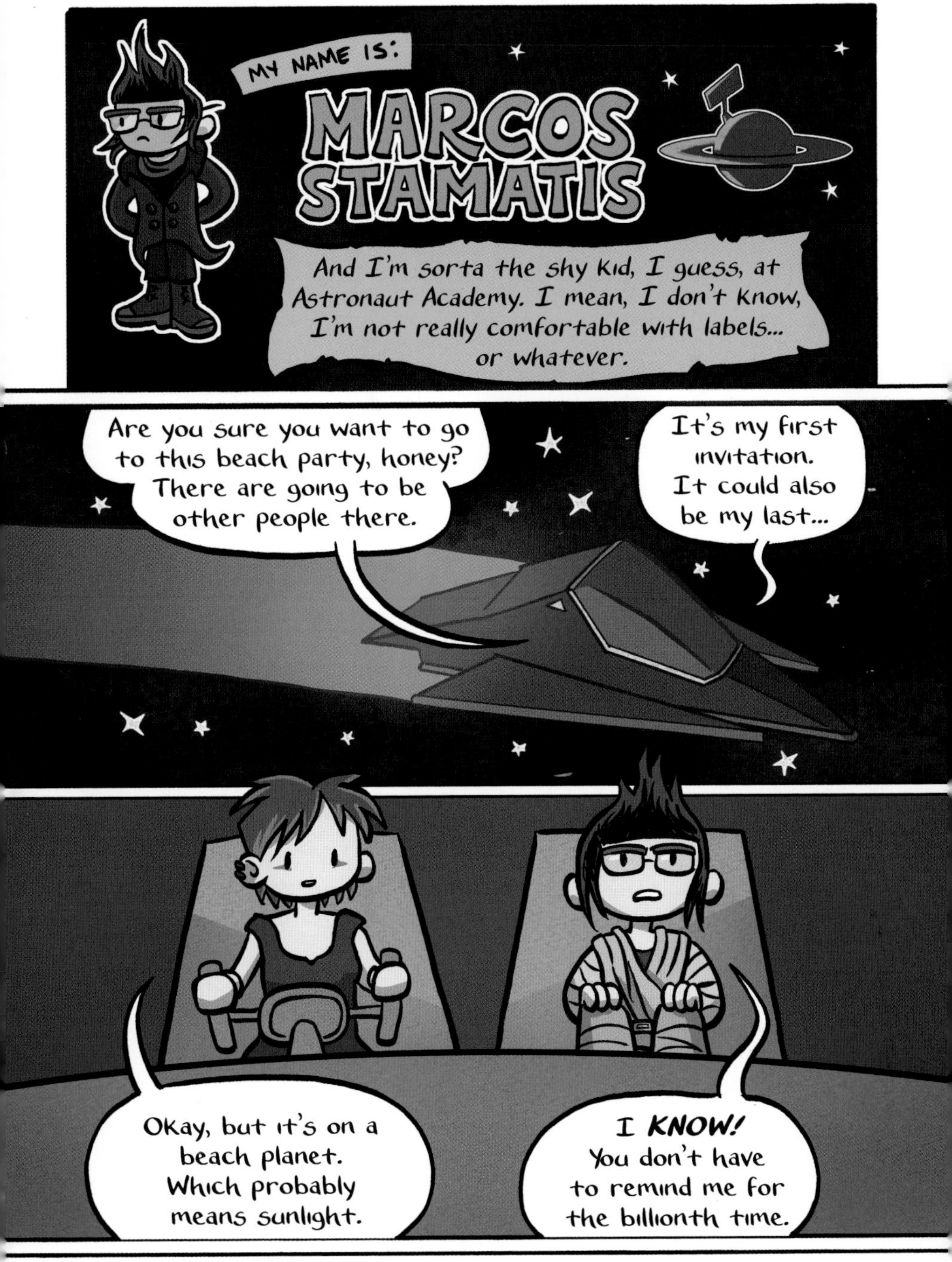
MY NAME IS:
MARCOS STAMATIS
And I'm sorta the shy kid, I guess, at Astronaut Academy. I mean, I don't know, I'm not really comfortable with labels... or whatever.
Are you sure you want to go to this beach party, honey? There are going to be other people there.
It's my first invitation. It could also be my last...
Okay, but it's on a beach planet. Which probably means sunlight.
I KNOW! You don't have to remind me for the billionth time.

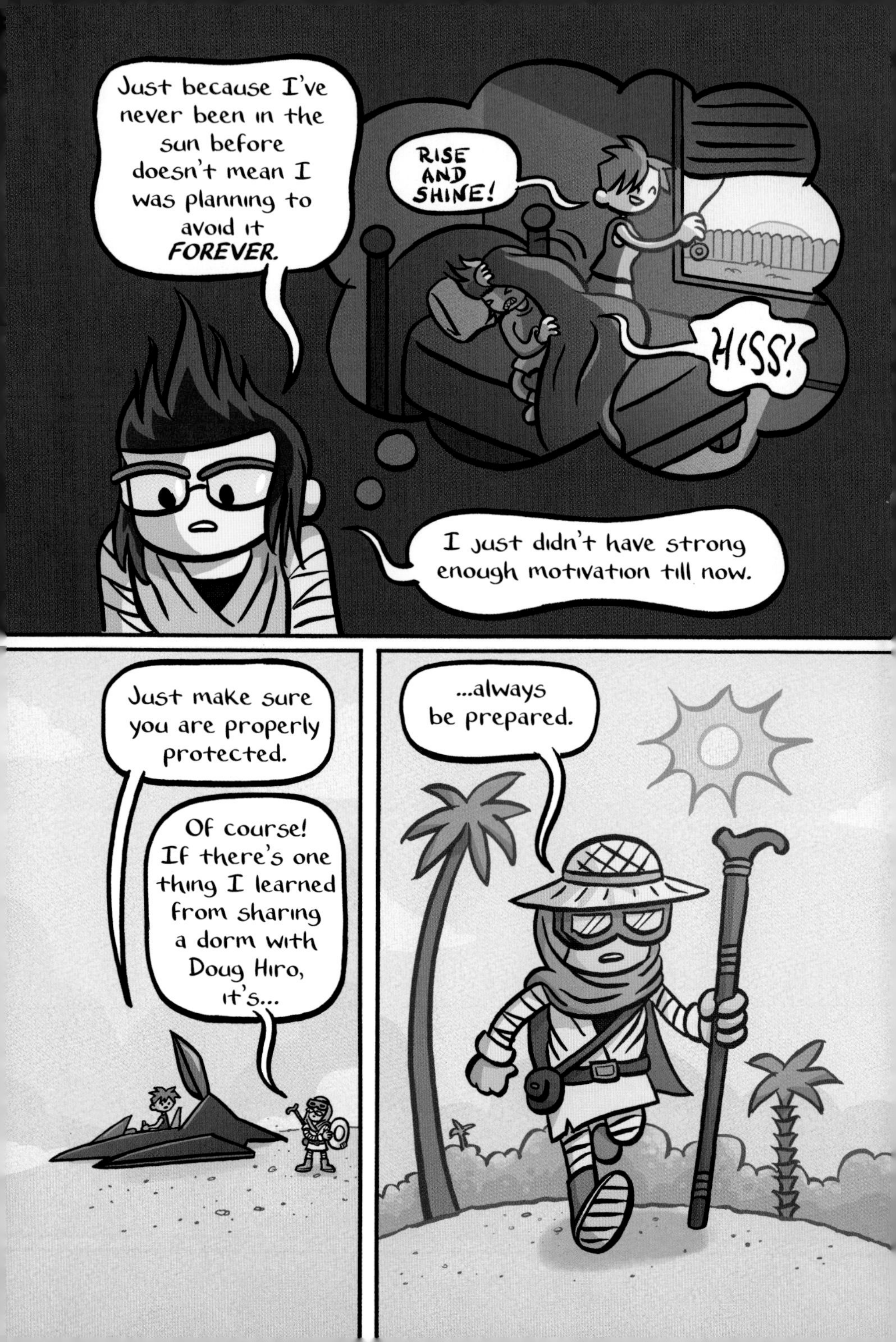
Just because I've never been in the sun before doesn't mean I was planning to avoid it FOREVER.
RISE AND SHINE!
HISS!
I just didn't have strong enough motivation till now.
Just make sure you are properly protected.
Of course! If there's one thing I learned from sharing a dorm with Doug Hiro, it's...
...always be prepared.

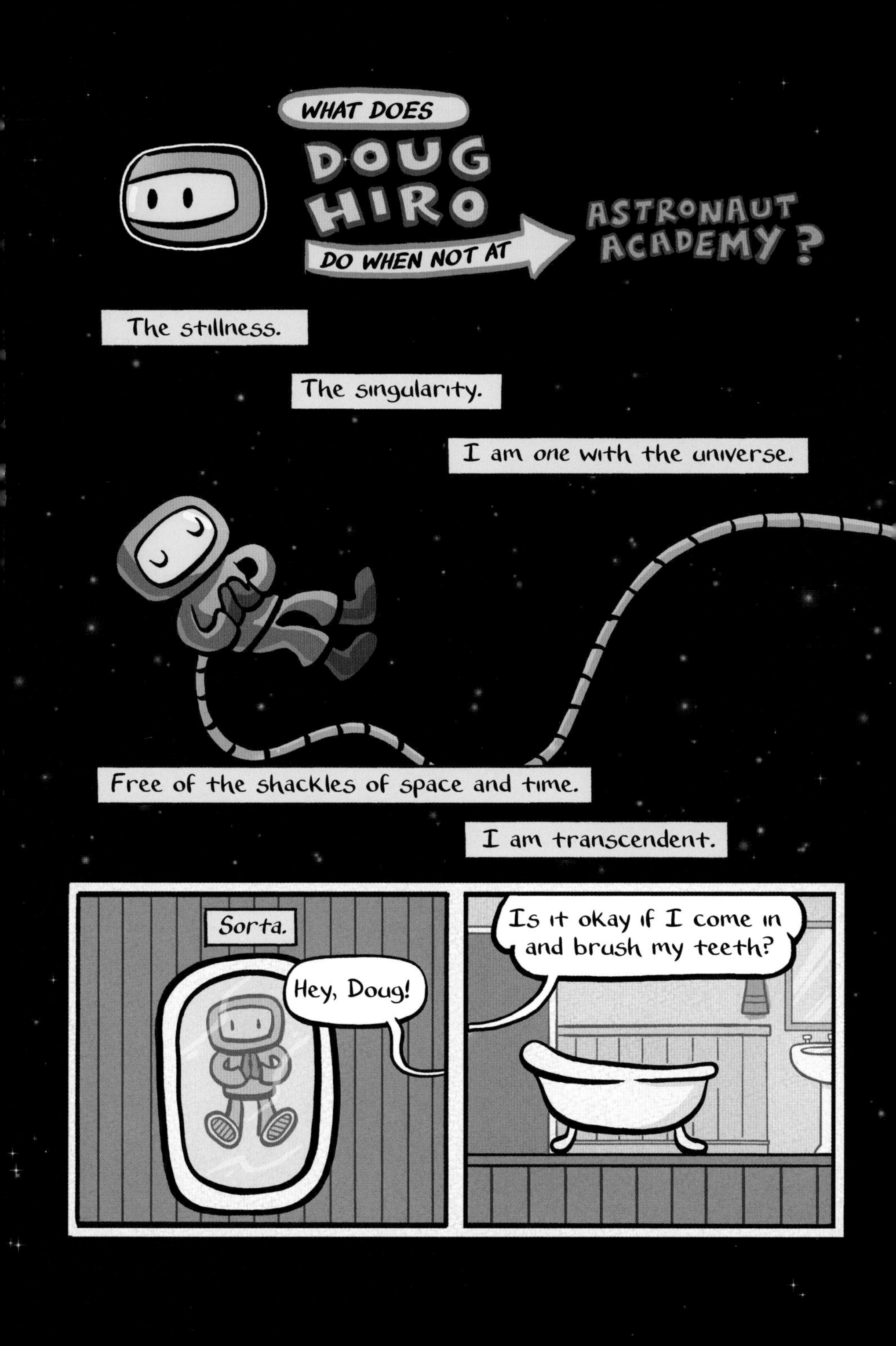
WHAT DOES
DOUG HIRO
DO WHEN NOT AT
ASTRONAUT ACADEMY?
The stillness.
The singularity.
I am one with the universe.
Free of the shackles of space and time.
I am transcendent.
Sorta.
Hey, Doug!
Is it okay if I come in and brush my teeth?

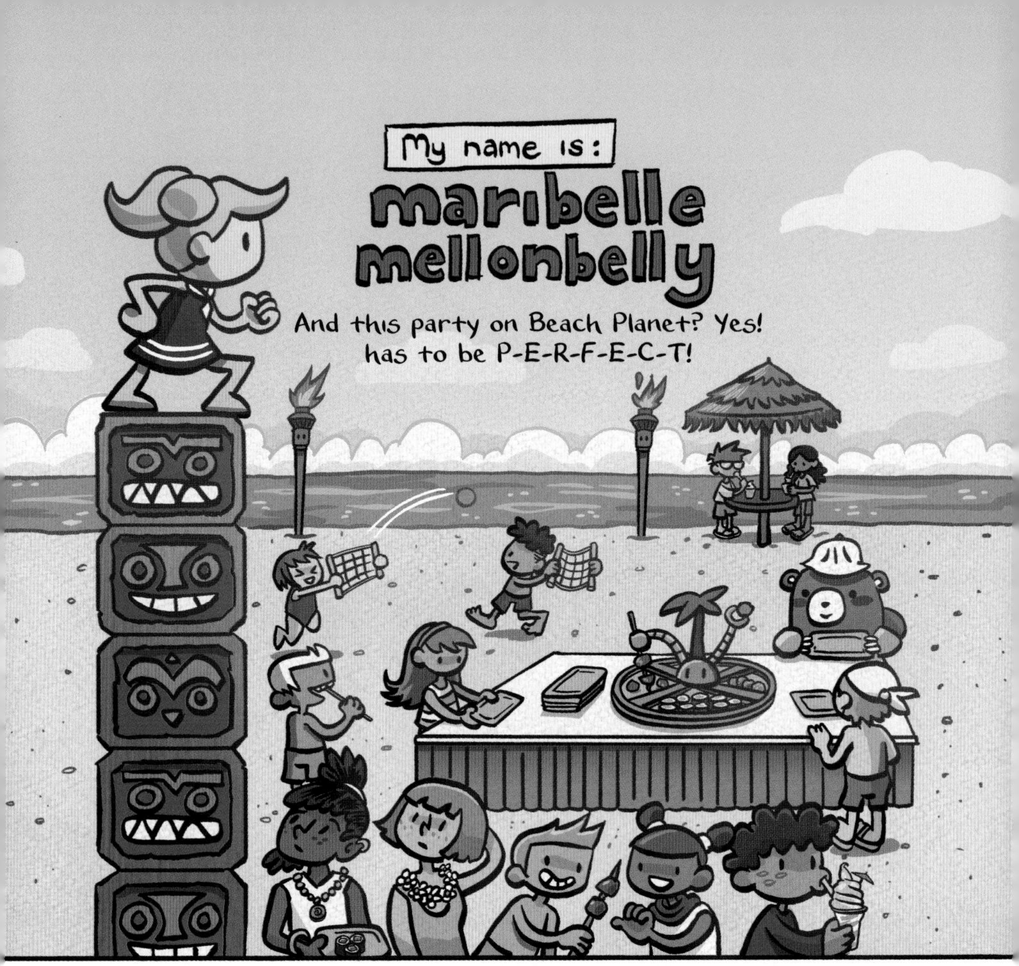
My name is:
maribelle mellonbelly
And this party on Beach Planet? Yes! has to be P-E-R-F-E-C-T!

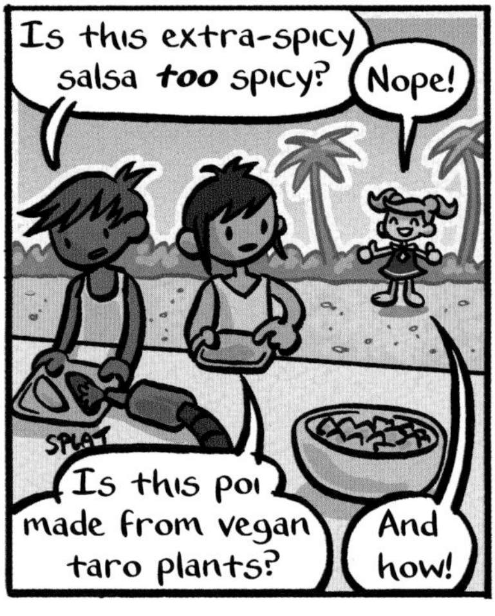
Is this extra-spicy salsa *too* spicy?
Nope!
SPLAT
Is this poi made from vegan taro plants?
And how!

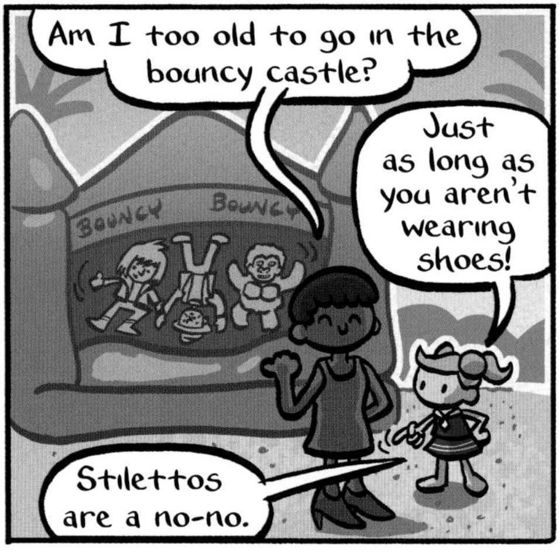
Am I too old to go in the bouncy castle?
Just as long as you aren't wearing shoes!
Stilettos are a no-no.

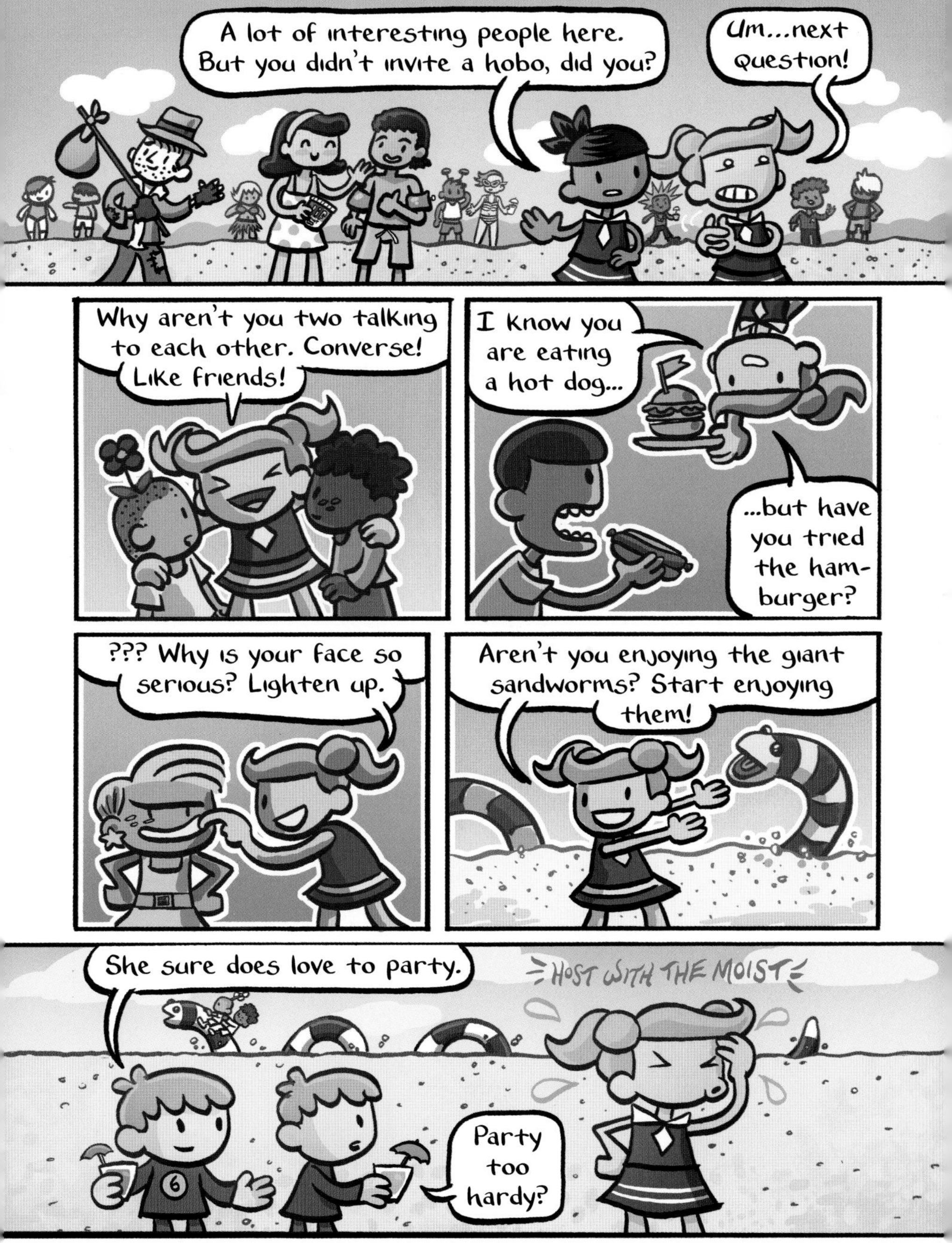
A lot of interesting people here. But you didn't invite a hobo, did you?
Um...next question!
Why aren't you two talking to each other. Converse! Like friends!
I know you are eating a hot dog...
...but have you tried the ham-burger?
??? Why is your face so serious? Lighten up.
Aren't you enjoying the giant sandworms? Start enjoying them!
She sure does love to party.
HOST WITH THE MOIST
6
Party too hardy?

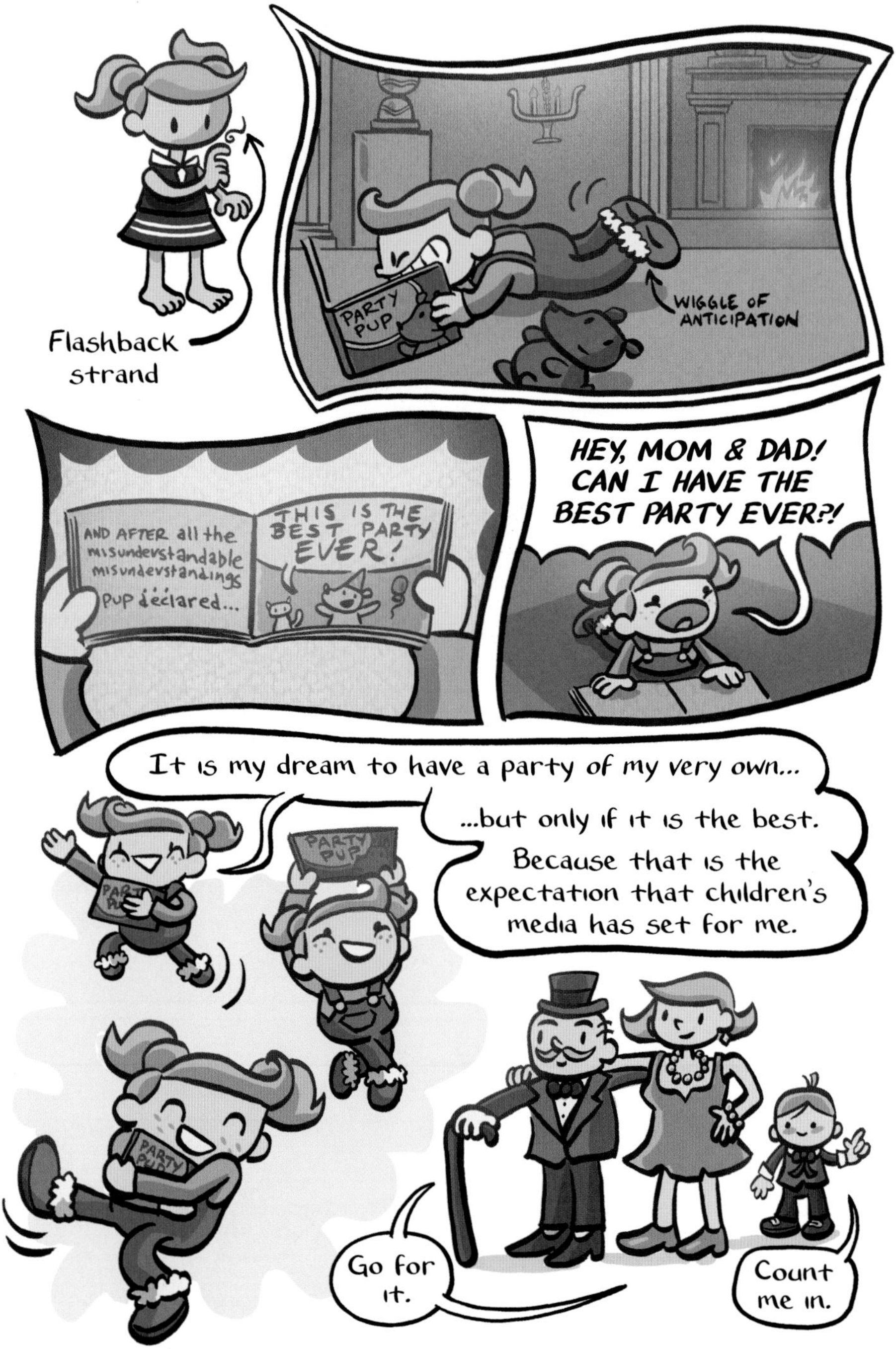
Flashback strand
PARTY PUP
WIGGLE OF ANTICIPATION
AND AFTER all the misunderstandable misunderstandings pup declared...
THIS IS THE BEST PARTY EVER!
HEY, MOM & DAD! CAN I HAVE THE BEST PARTY EVER?!
It is my dream to have a party of my very own...
...but only if it is the best.
Because that is the expectation that children's media has set for me.
PARTY PUP
PARTY PUP
PARTY PUP
Go for it.
Count me in.

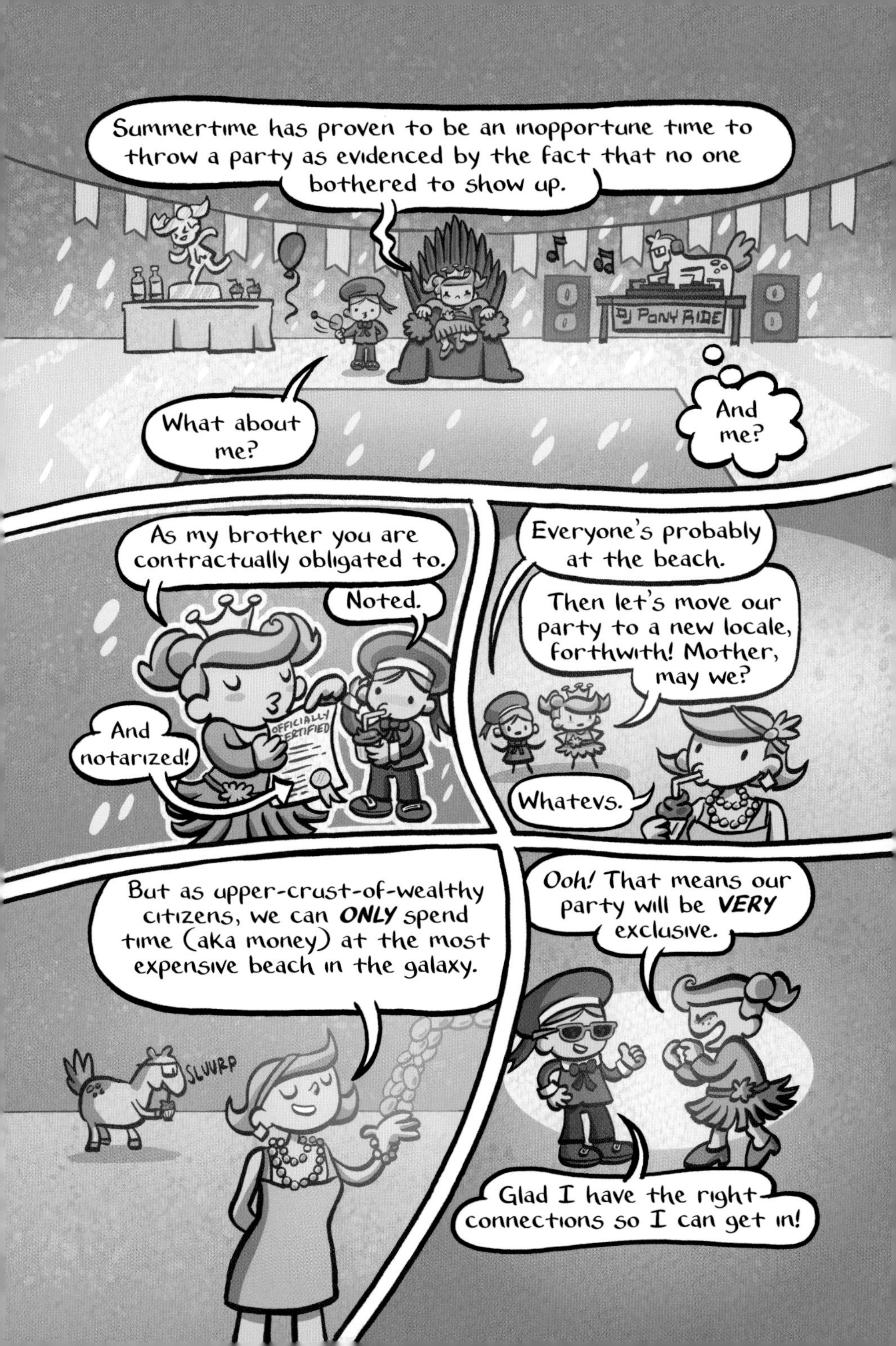
Summertime has proven to be an inopportune time to throw a party as evidenced by the fact that no one bothered to show up.
DJ PONY RIDE
What about me?
And me?
As my brother you are contractually obligated to.
Noted.
OFFICIALLY CERTIFIED
And notarized!
Everyone's probably at the beach.
Then let's move our party to a new locale, forthwith! Mother, may we?
Whatevs.
But as upper-crust-of-wealthy citizens, we can ONLY spend time (aka money) at the most expensive beach in the galaxy.
SLUURP
Ooh! That means our party will be VERY exclusive.
Glad I have the right connections so I can get in!

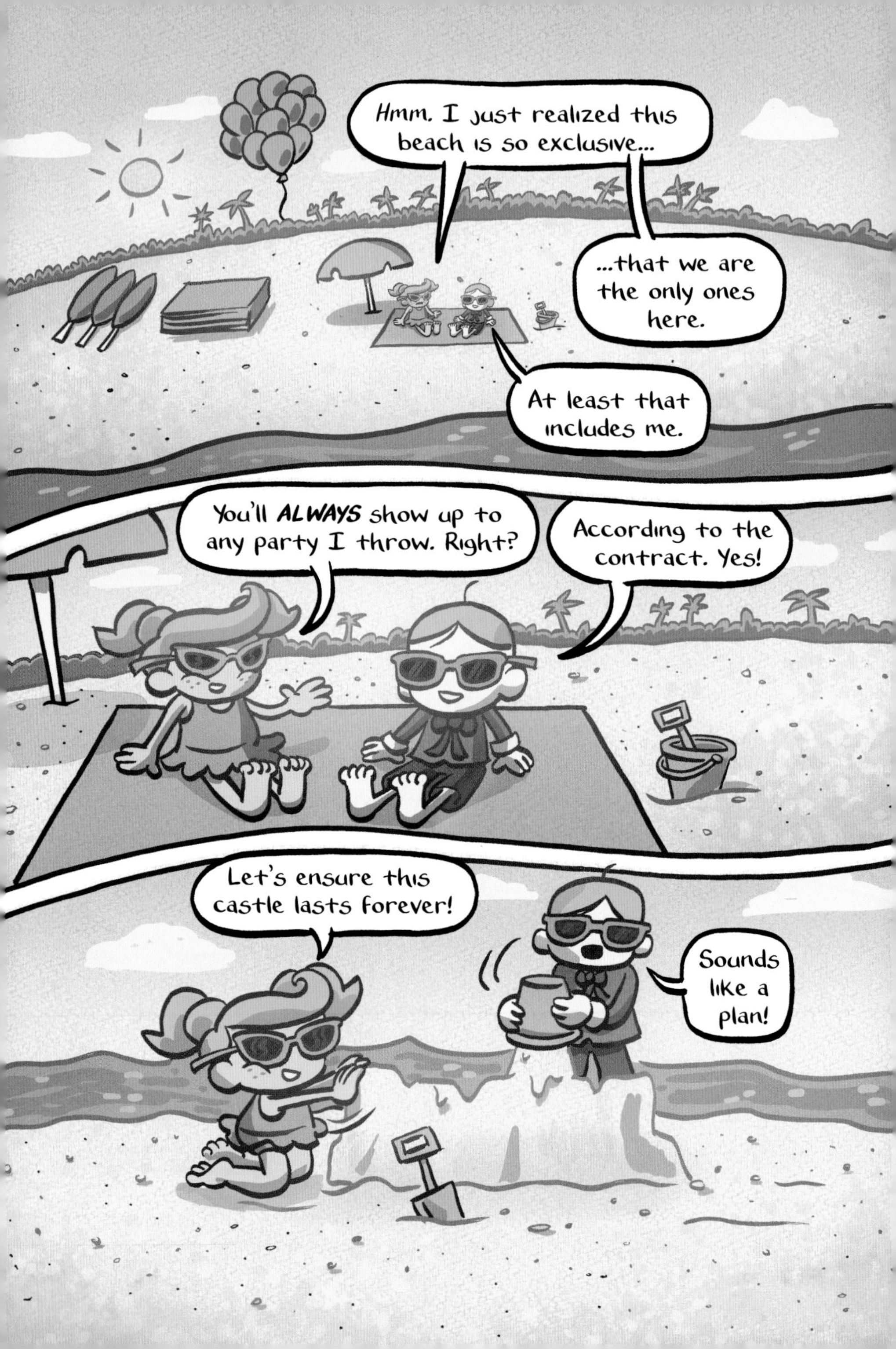
Hmm. I just realized this beach is so exclusive...
...that we are the only ones here.
At least that includes me.
You'll **ALWAYS** show up to any party I throw. Right?
According to the contract. Yes!
Let's ensure this castle lasts forever!
Sounds like a plan!

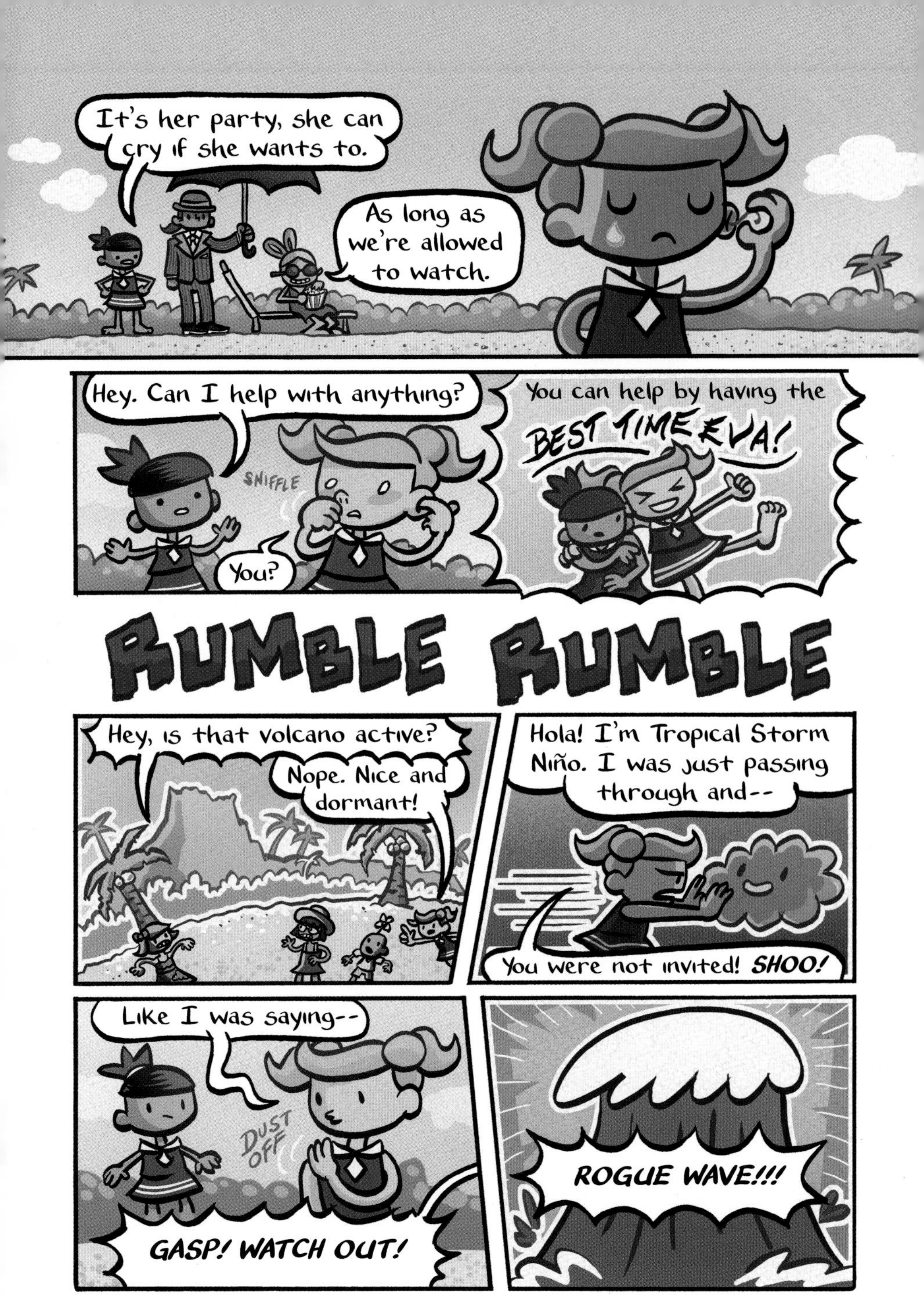
It's her party, she can cry if she wants to.
As long as we're allowed to watch.
Hey. Can I help with anything?
SNIFFLE
You?
You can help by having the
BEST TIME EVA!
RUMBLE RUMBLE
Hey, is that volcano active?
Nope. Nice and dormant!
Hola! I'm Tropical Storm Niño. I was just passing through and--
You were not invited! SHOO!
Like I was saying--
DUST OFF
GASP! WATCH OUT!
ROGUE WAVE!!!

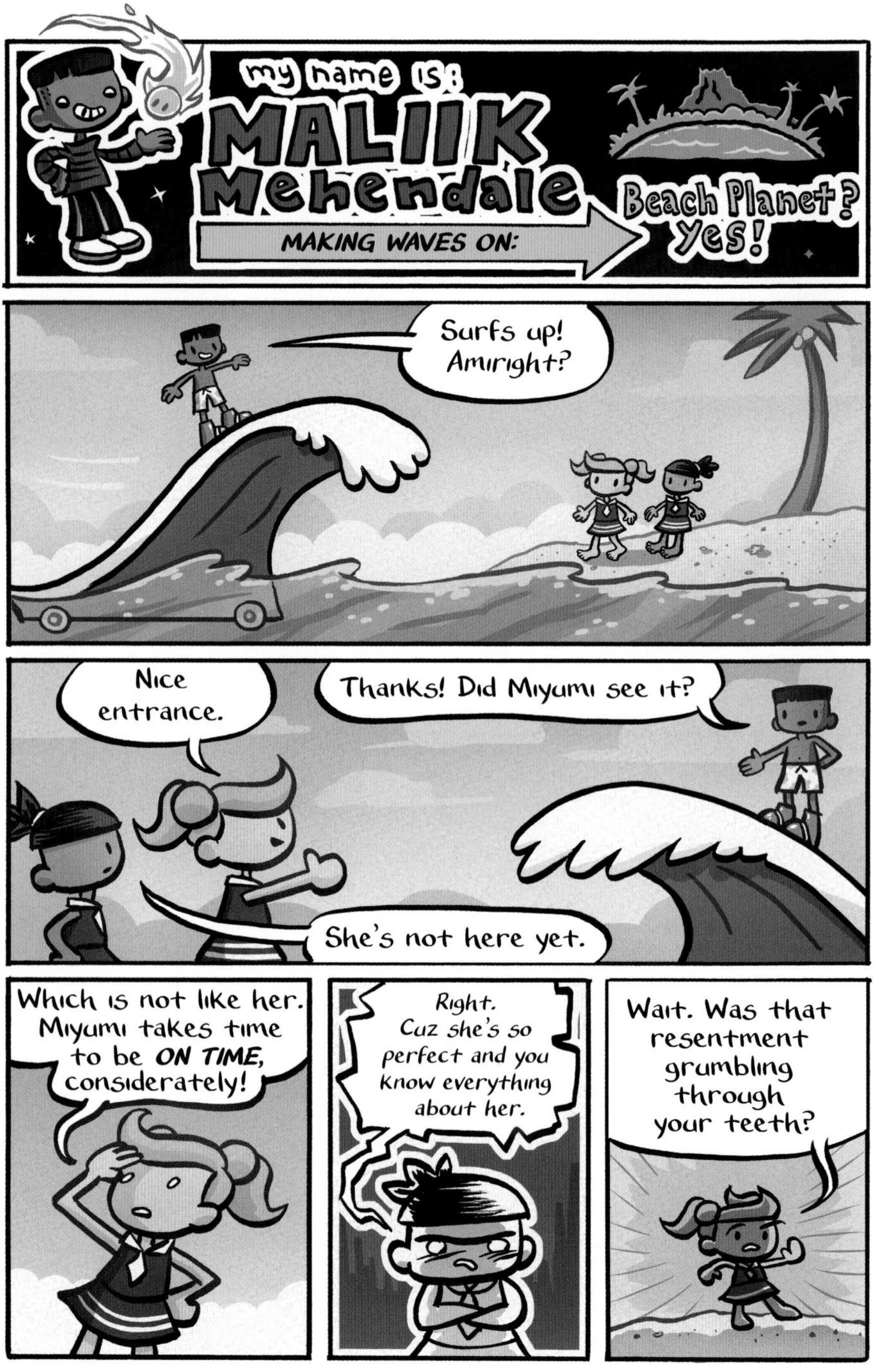
my name is:
MALIIK Mehendale
MAKING WAVES ON:
Beach Planet? yes!
Surfs up! Amiright?
Nice entrance.
Thanks! Did Miyumi see it?
She's not here yet.
Which is not like her. Miyumi takes time to be ON TIME, considerately!
Right. Cuz she's so perfect and you know everything about her.
Wait. Was that resentment grumbling through your teeth?

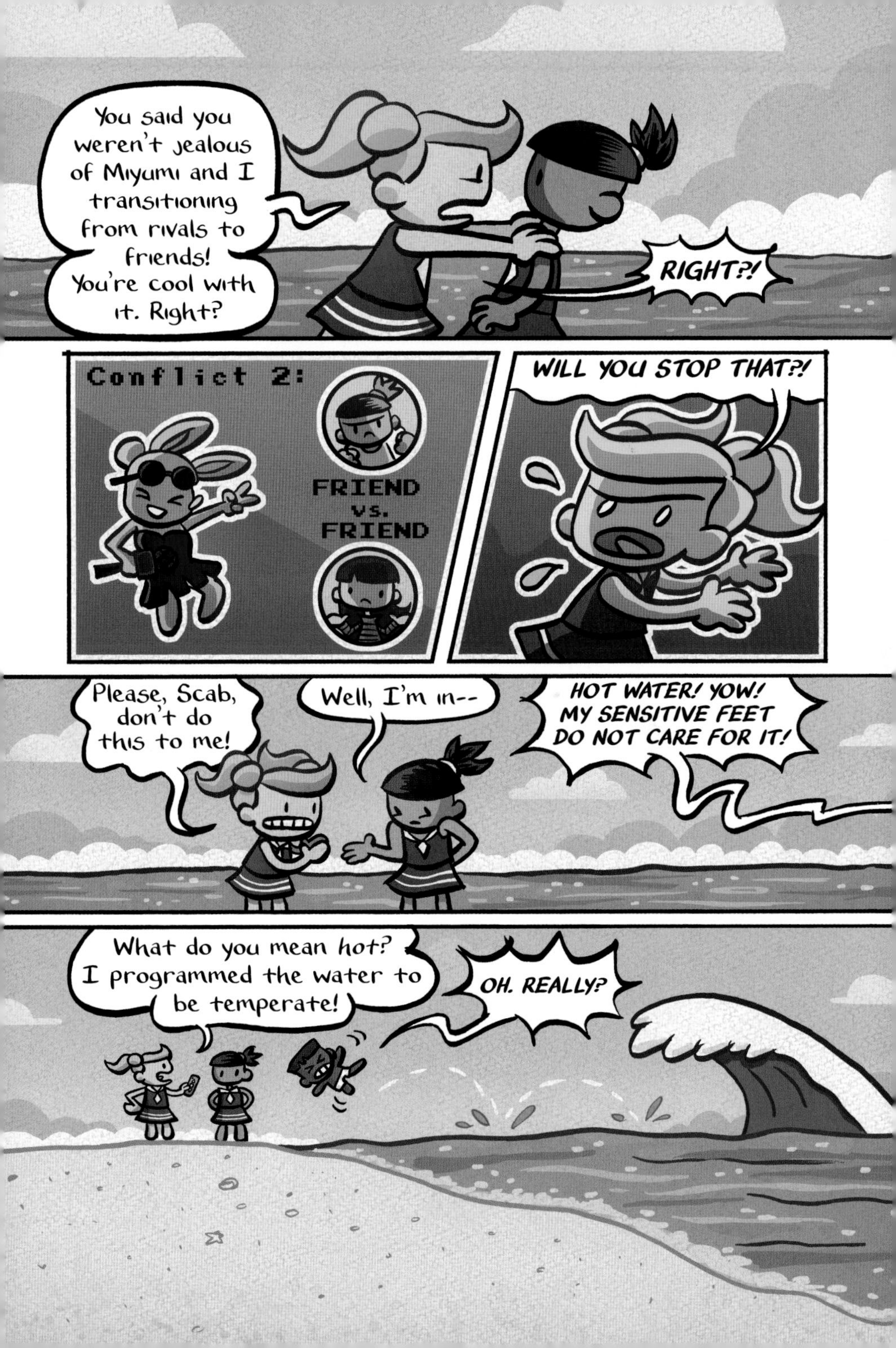

You said you weren't jealous of Miyumi and I transitioning from rivals to friends! You're cool with it. Right?
RIGHT?!
Conflict 2:
FRIEND vs. FRIEND
WILL YOU STOP THAT?!
Please, Scab, don't do this to me!
Well, I'm in--
HOT WATER! YOW! MY SENSITIVE FEET DO NOT CARE FOR IT!
What do you mean hot? I programmed the water to be temperate!
OH. REALLY?

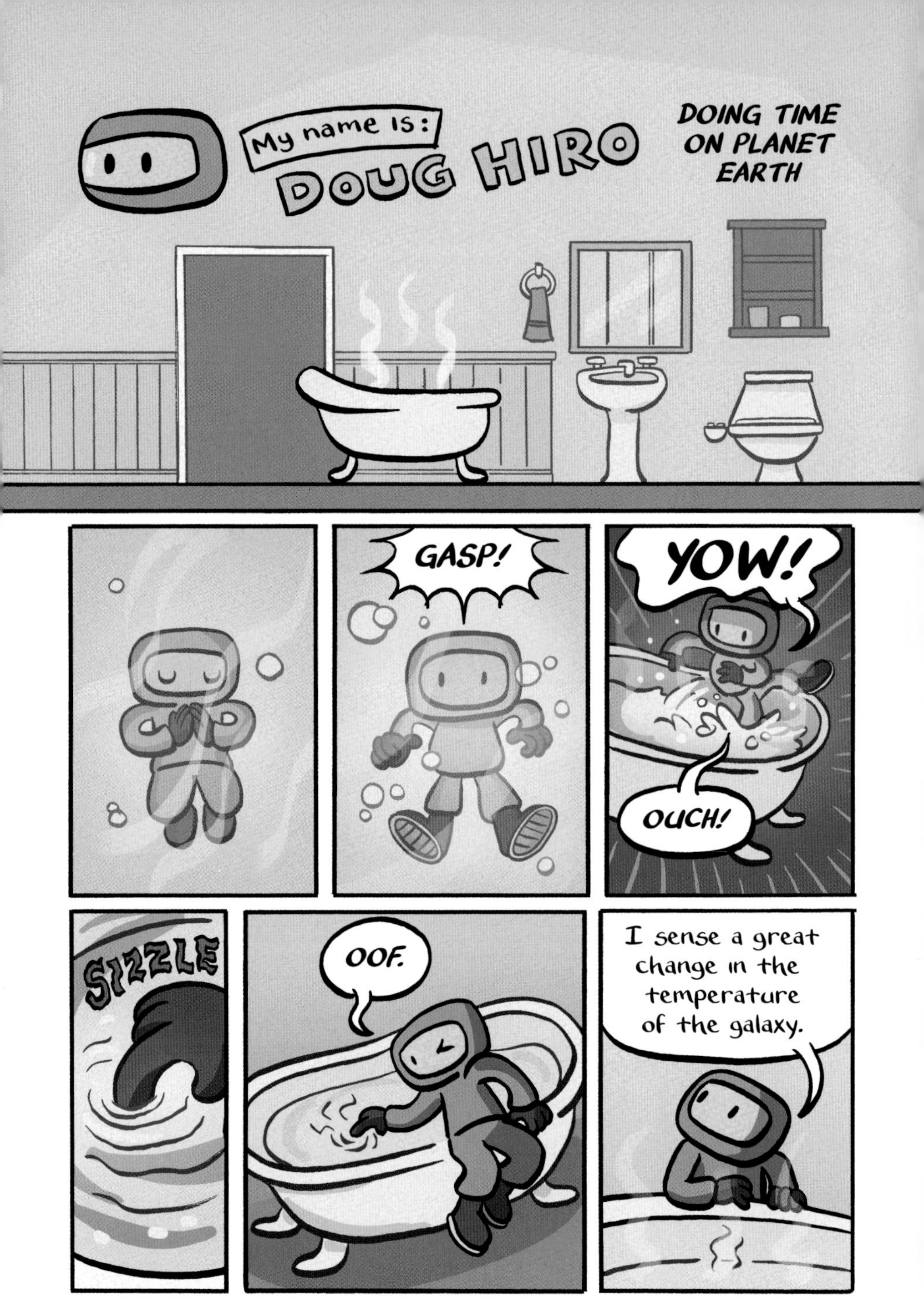
My name is:
DOUG HIRO
DOING TIME ON PLANET EARTH
GASP!
YOW!
OUCH!
SIZZLE
OOF.
I sense a great change in the temperature of the galaxy.

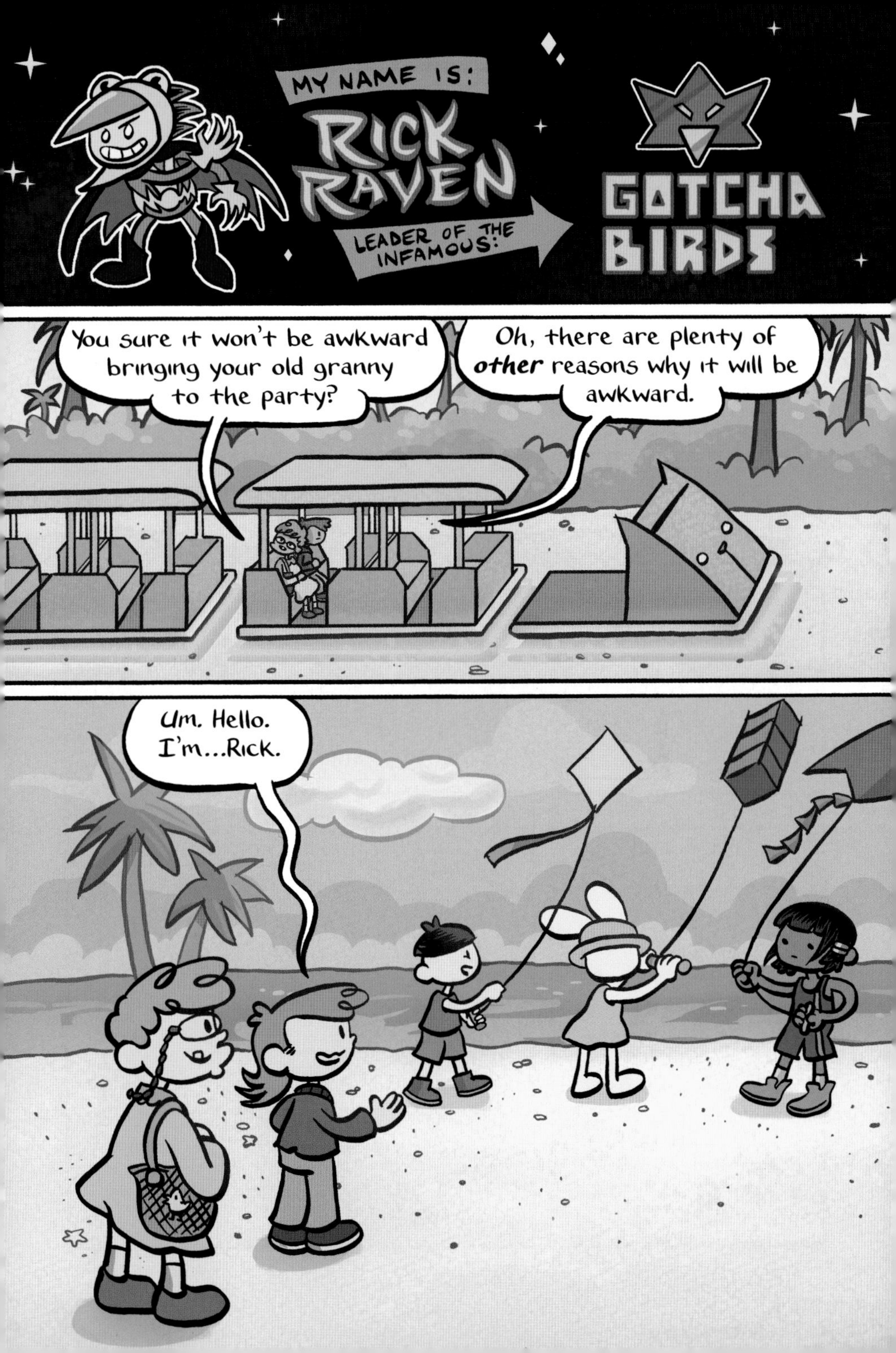
MY NAME IS:
RICK RAVEN
LEADER OF THE INFAMOUS:
GOTCHA BIRDS
You sure it won't be awkward bringing your old granny to the party?
Oh, there are plenty of *other* reasons why it will be awkward.
Um. Hello. I'm...Rick.

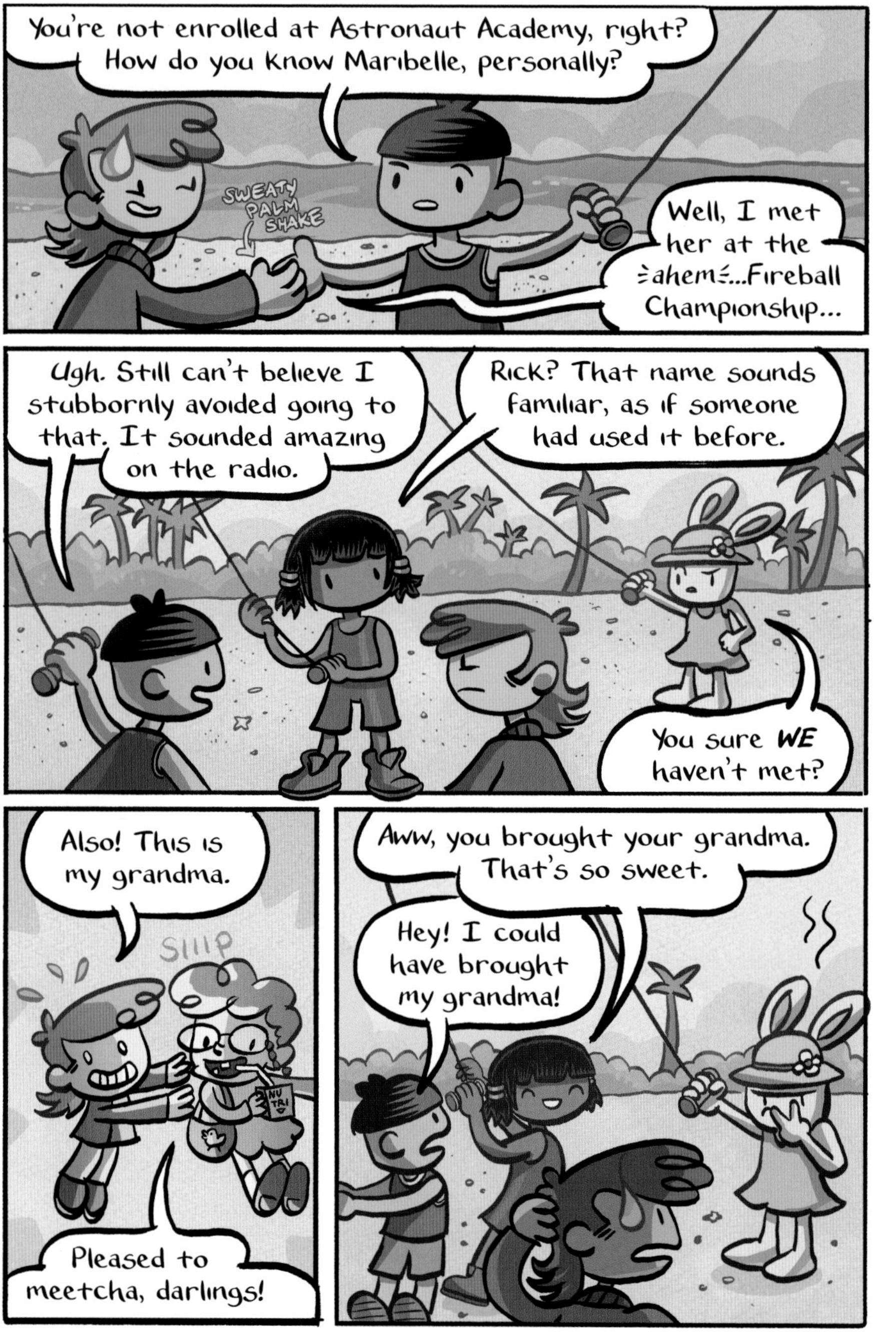
You're not enrolled at Astronaut Academy, right? How do you know Maribelle, personally?
SWEATY PALM SHAKE
Well, I met her at the ahem...Fireball Championship...
Ugh. Still can't believe I stubbornly avoided going to that. It sounded amazing on the radio.
Rick? That name sounds familiar, as if someone had used it before.
You sure WE haven't met?
Also! This is my grandma.
SIIIP
NU TRI
Pleased to meetcha, darlings!
Aww, you brought your grandma. That's so sweet.
Hey! I could have brought my grandma!

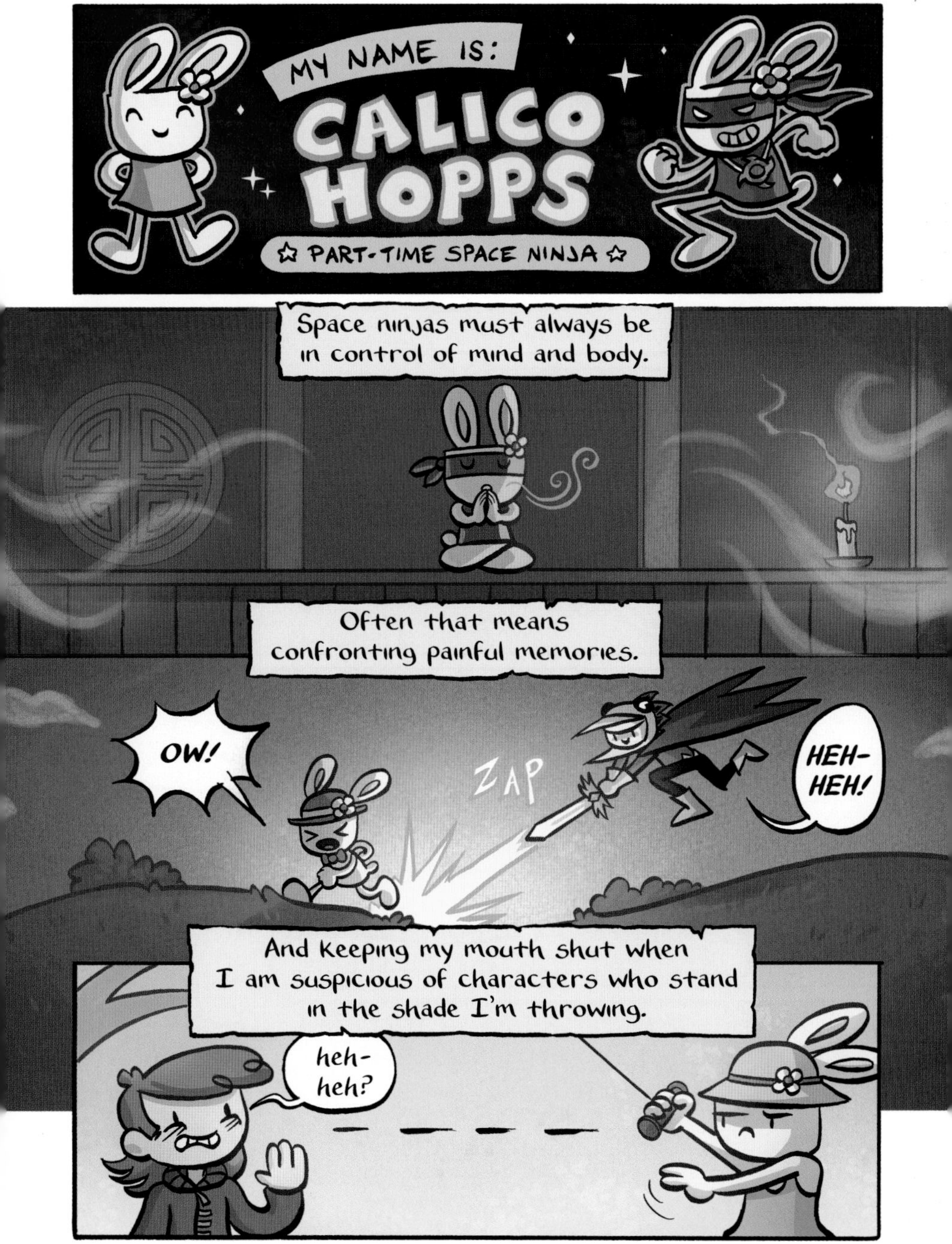
MY NAME IS:
CALICO HOPPS
☆ PART-TIME SPACE NINJA ☆
Space ninjas must always be in control of mind and body.
Often that means confronting painful memories.
OW!
ZAP
HEH-HEH!
And keeping my mouth shut when I am suspicious of characters who stand in the shade I'm throwing.
heh-heh?

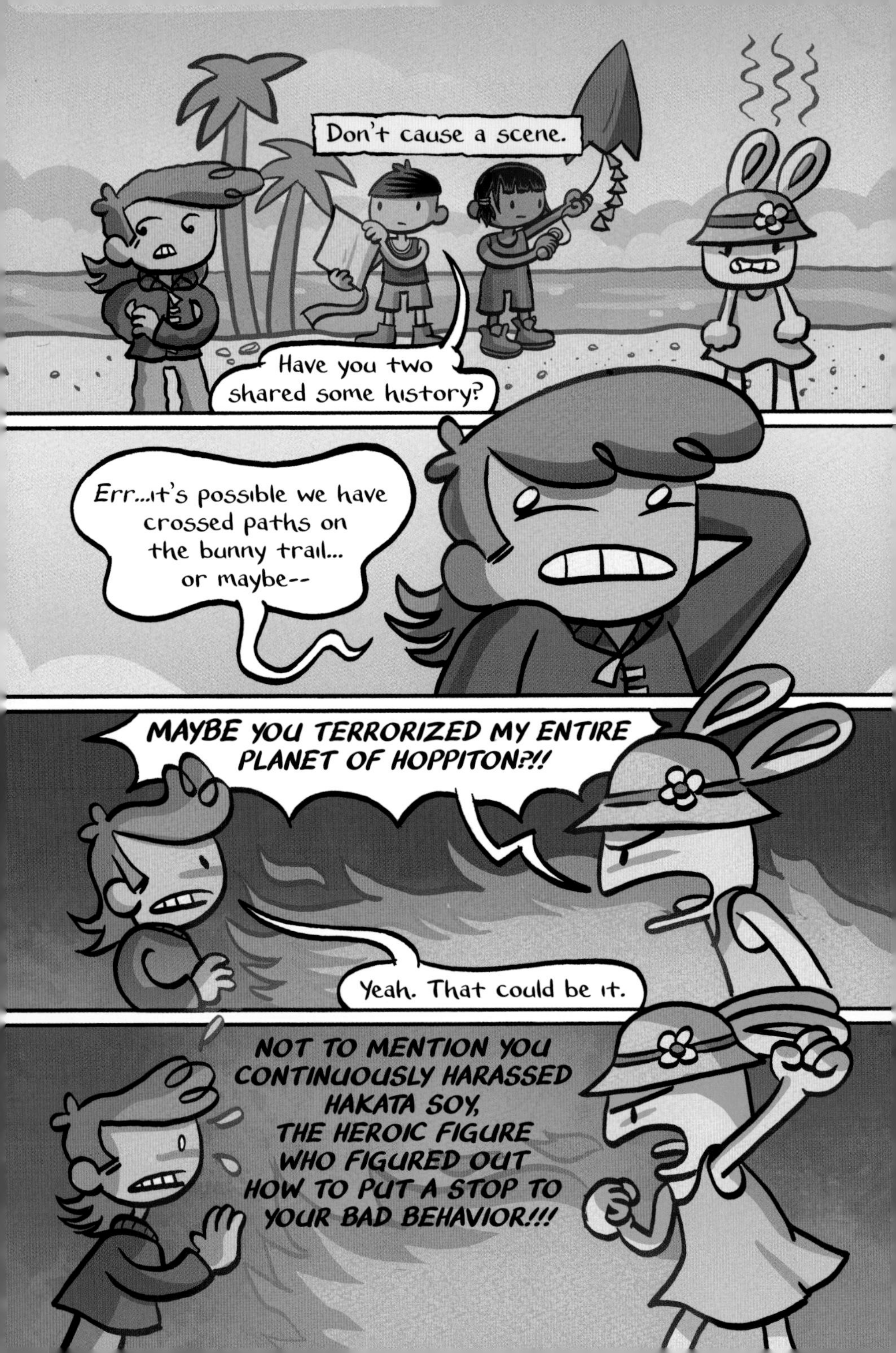
Don't cause a scene.
Have you two shared some history?
Err...it's possible we have crossed paths on the bunny trail... or maybe--
MAYBE YOU TERRORIZED MY ENTIRE PLANET OF HOPPITON?!!
Yeah. That could be it.
NOT TO MENTION YOU CONTINUOUSLY HARASSED HAKATA SOY, THE HEROIC FIGURE WHO FIGURED OUT HOW TO PUT A STOP TO YOUR BAD BEHAVIOR!!!

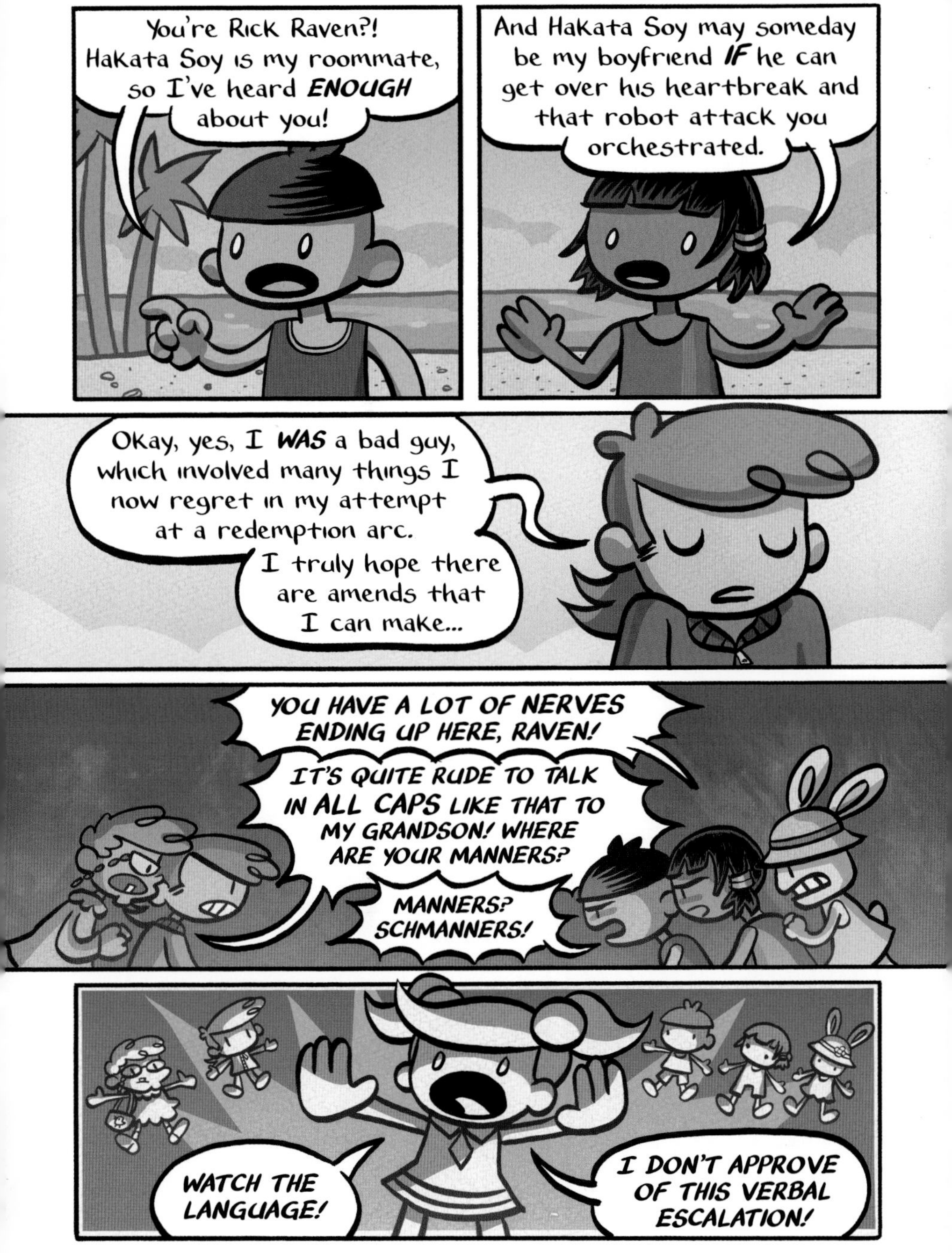
You're Rick Raven?! Hakata Soy is my roommate, so I've heard ENOUGH about you!
And Hakata Soy may someday be my boyfriend IF he can get over his heartbreak and that robot attack you orchestrated.
Okay, yes, I WAS a bad guy, which involved many things I now regret in my attempt at a redemption arc.
I truly hope there are amends that I can make...
YOU HAVE A LOT OF NERVES ENDING UP HERE, RAVEN!
IT'S QUITE RUDE TO TALK IN ALL CAPS LIKE THAT TO MY GRANDSON! WHERE ARE YOUR MANNERS?
MANNERS? SCHMANNERS!
WATCH THE LANGUAGE!
I DON'T APPROVE OF THIS VERBAL ESCALATION!

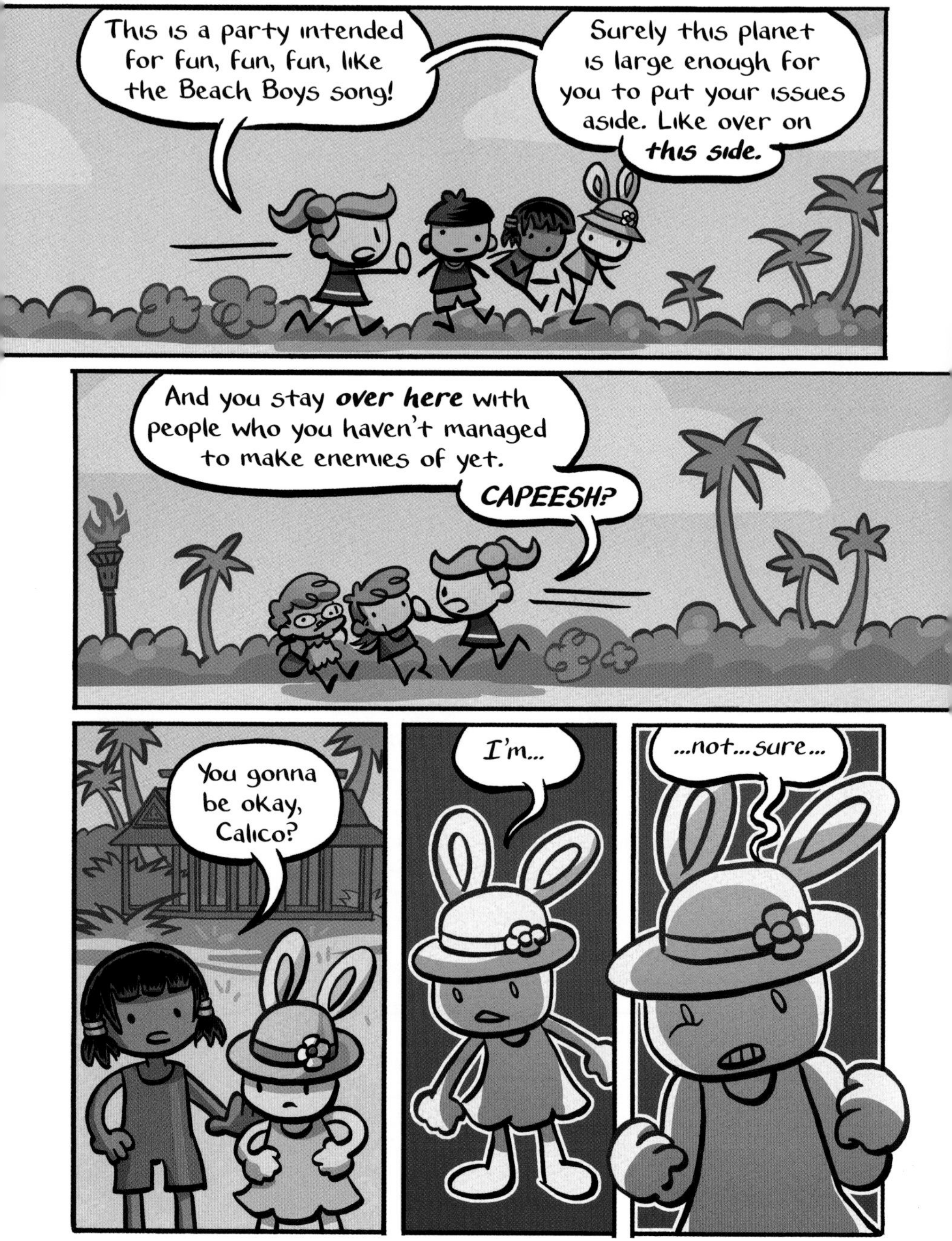
This is a party intended for fun, fun, fun, like the Beach Boys song!
Surely this planet is large enough for you to put your issues aside. Like over on **this side.**
And you stay **over here** with people who you haven't managed to make enemies of yet.
CAPEESH?
You gonna be okay, Calico?
I'm...
...not...sure...

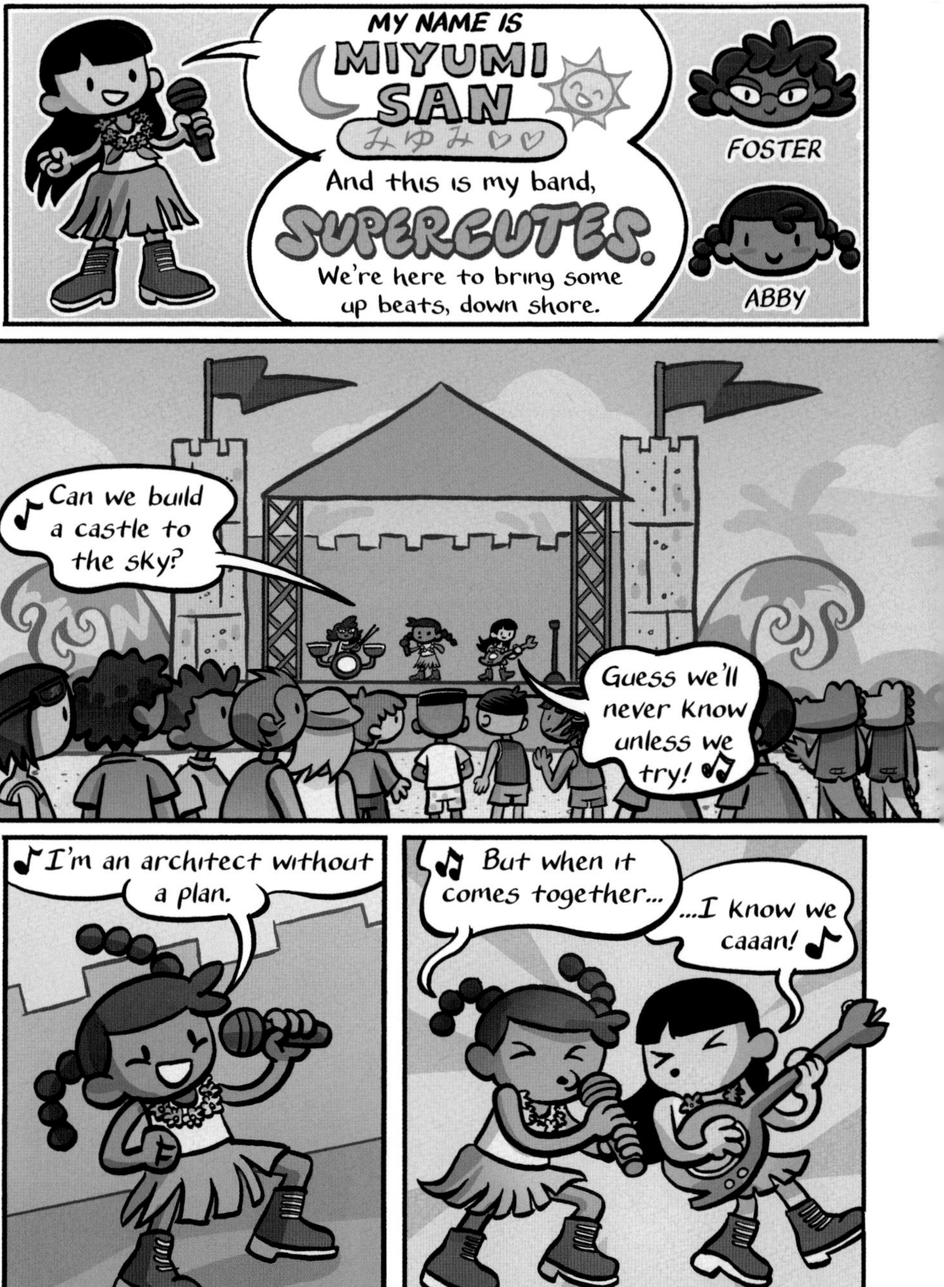
MY NAME IS
MIYUMI SAN
みゆみ
And this is my band,
SUPERCUTES.
We're here to bring some up beats, down shore.
FOSTER
ABBY
Can we build a castle to the sky?
Guess we'll never know unless we try!
I'm an architect without a plan.
But when it comes together...
...I know we caaan!

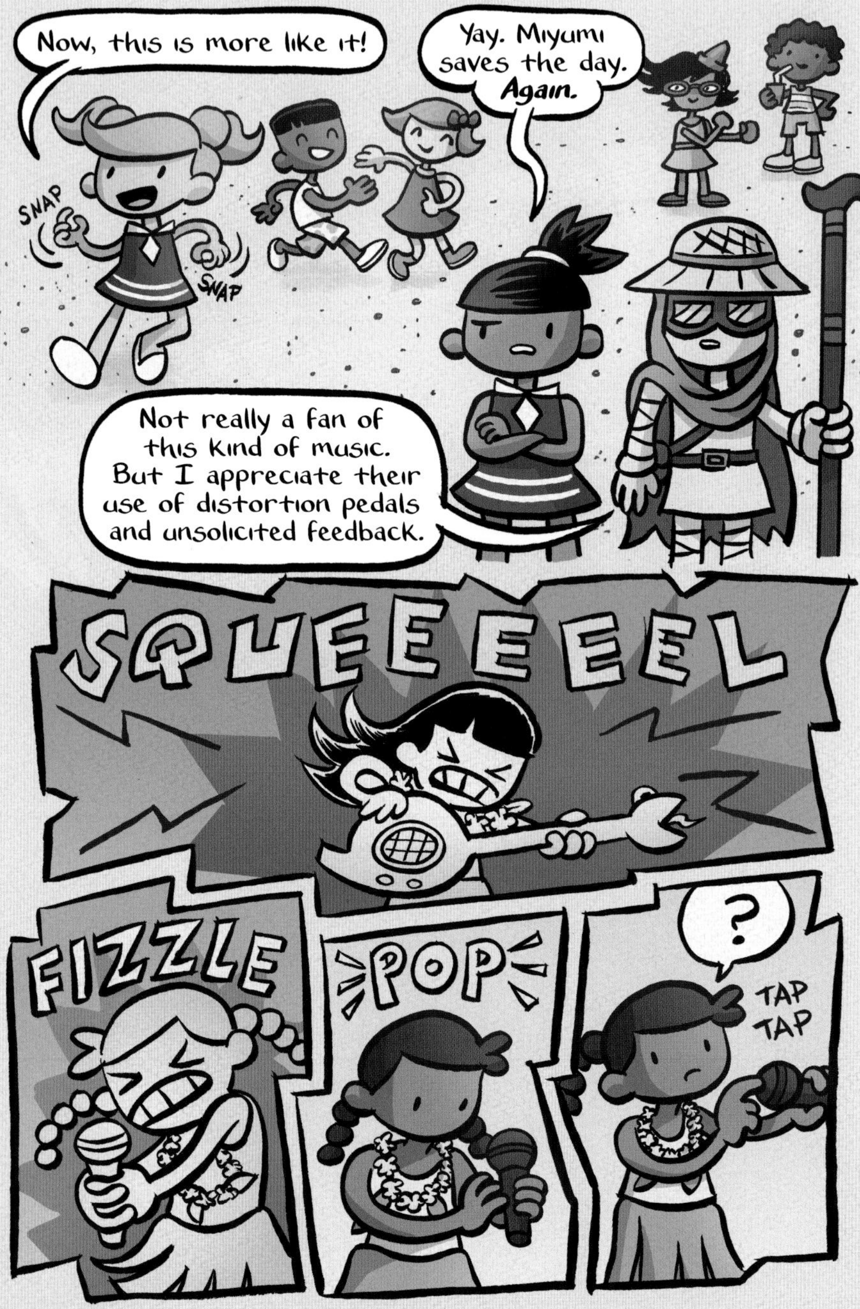

Now, this is more like it!
SNAP
SNAP
Yay. Miyumi saves the day. **Again.**
Not really a fan of this kind of music. But I appreciate their use of distortion pedals and unsolicited feedback.
SQUEEEEEL
FIZZLE
POP
?
TAP TAP

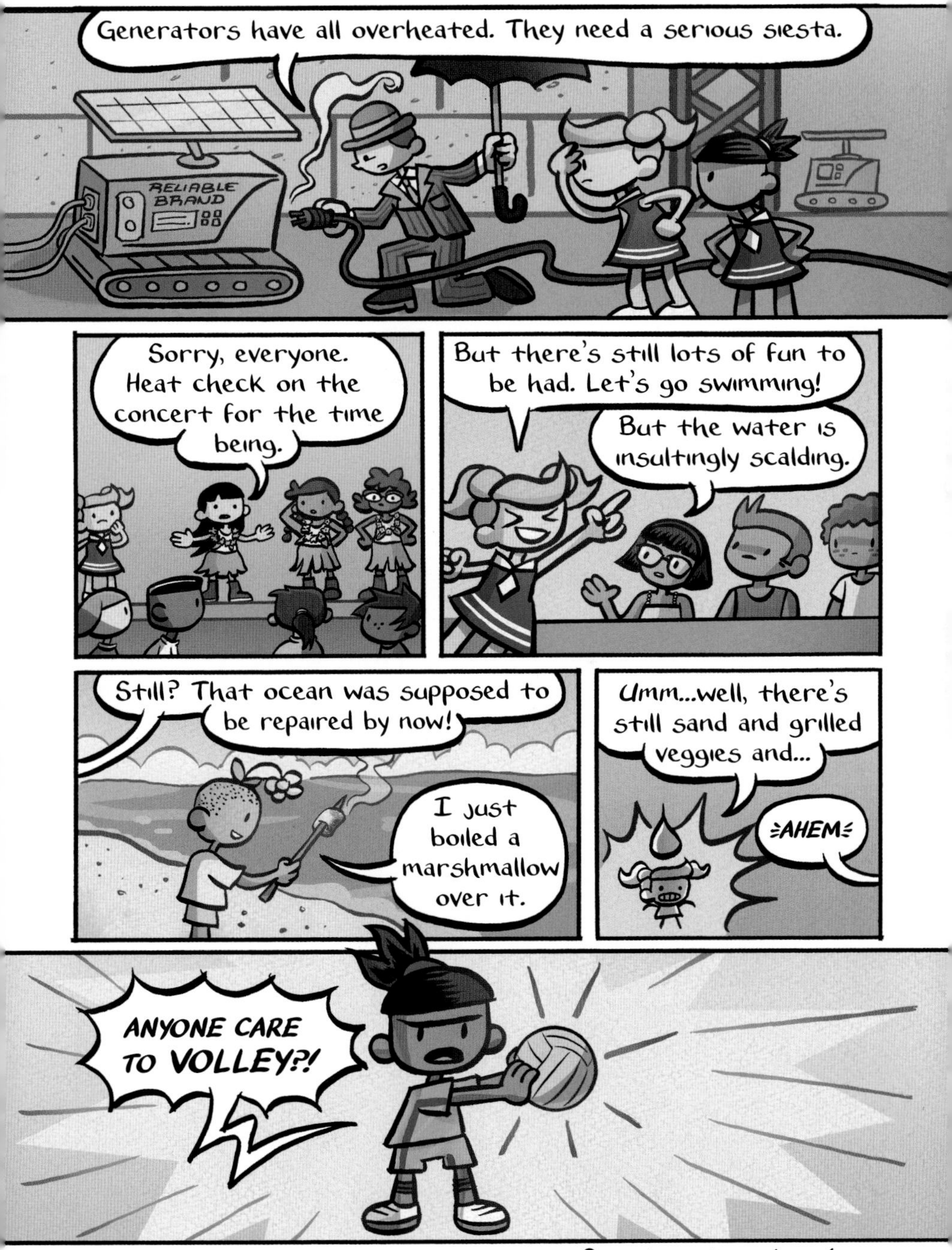
Generators have all overheated. They need a serious siesta.
RELIABLE BRAND
Sorry, everyone. Heat check on the concert for the time being.
But there's still lots of fun to be had. Let's go swimming!
But the water is insultingly scalding.
Still? That ocean was supposed to be repaired by now!
I just boiled a marshmallow over it.
Umm...well, there's still sand and grilled veggies and...
AHEM
ANYONE CARE TO VOLLEY?!

Dramatic costume change!

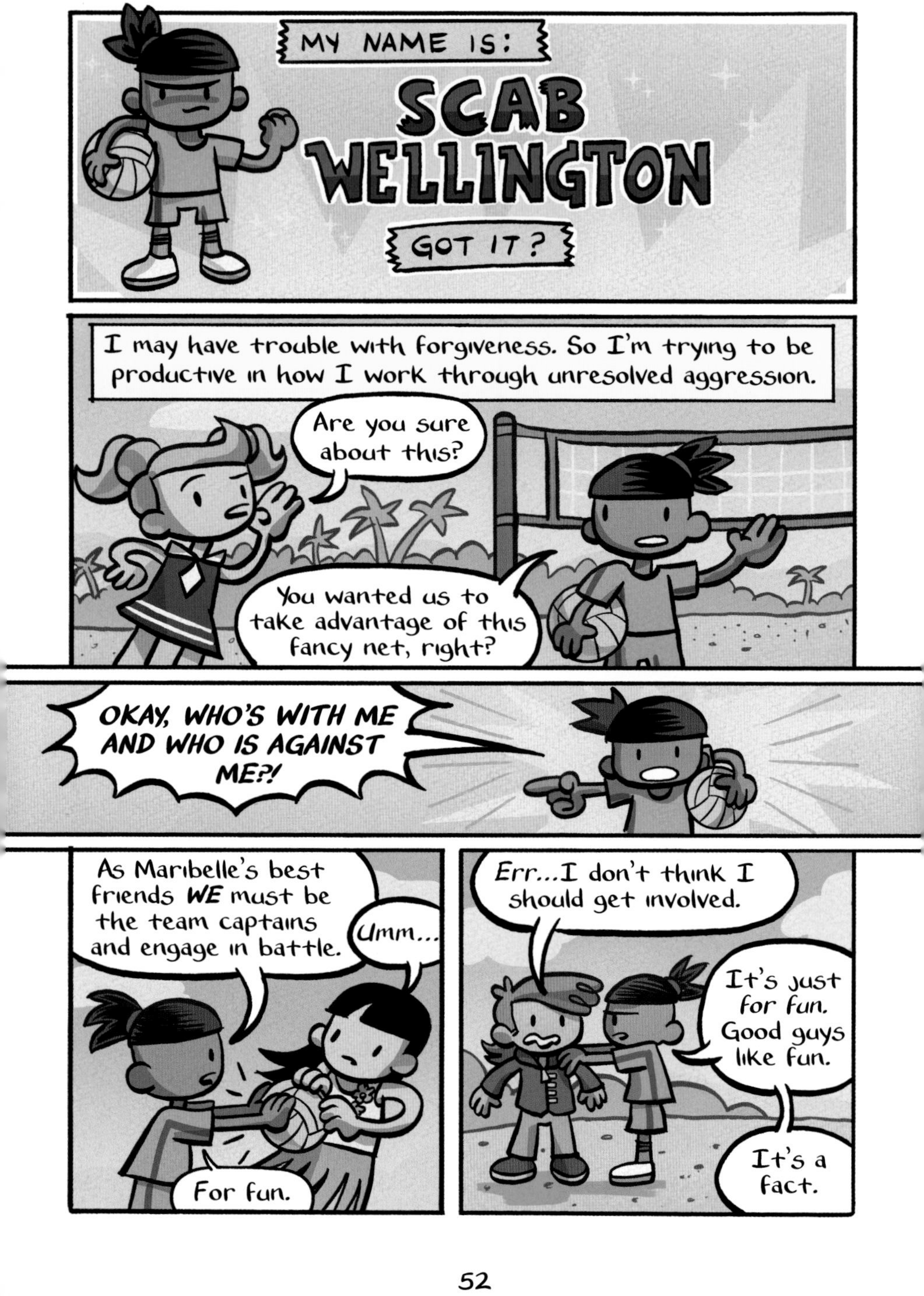
MY NAME IS:
SCAB WELLINGTON
GOT IT?
I may have trouble with forgiveness. So I'm trying to be productive in how I work through unresolved aggression.
Are you sure about this?
You wanted us to take advantage of this fancy net, right?
OKAY, WHO'S WITH ME AND WHO IS AGAINST ME?!
As Maribelle's best friends WE must be the team captains and engage in battle.
Umm...
For fun.
Err...I don't think I should get involved.
It's just for fun. Good guys like fun.
It's a fact.

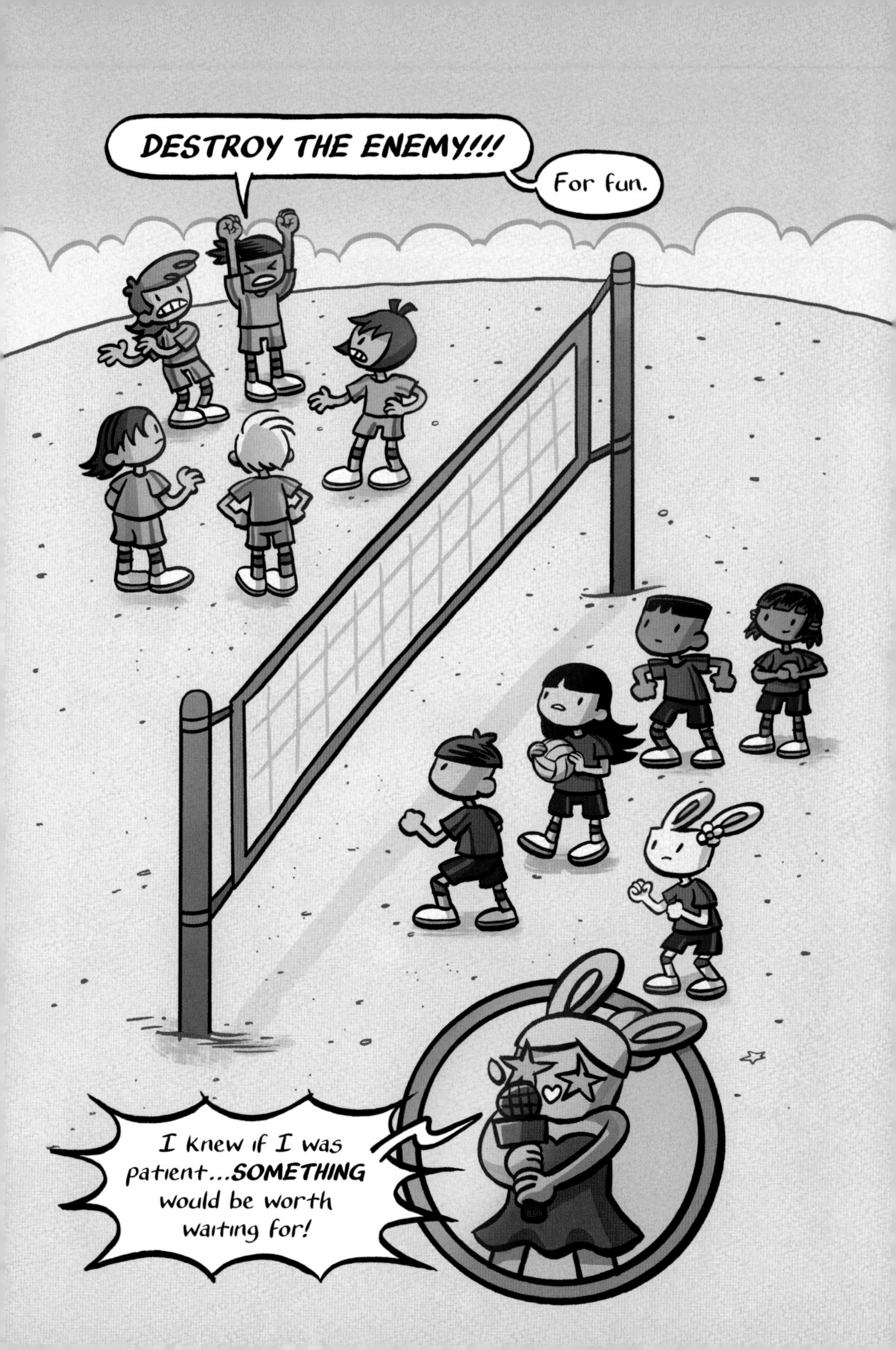
DESTROY THE ENEMY!!!
For fun.
I knew if I was patient...SOMETHING would be worth waiting for!

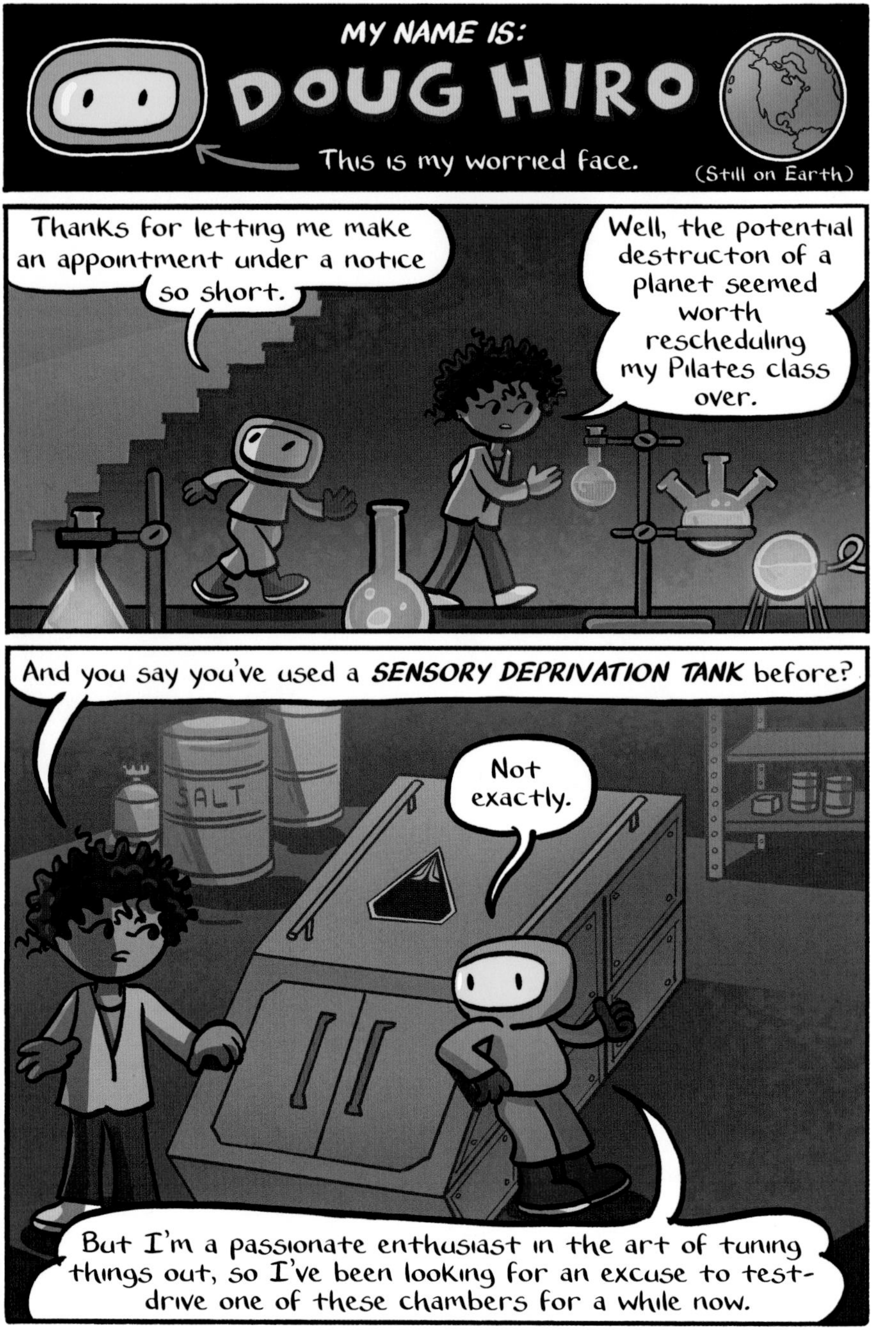
MY NAME IS:
DOUG HIRO
This is my worried face.
(Still on Earth)
Thanks for letting me make an appointment under a notice so short.
Well, the potential destructon of a planet seemed worth rescheduling my Pilates class over.
And you say you've used a SENSORY DEPRIVATION TANK before?
SALT
Not exactly.
But I'm a passionate enthusiast in the art of tuning things out, so I've been looking for an excuse to test-drive one of these chambers for a while now.

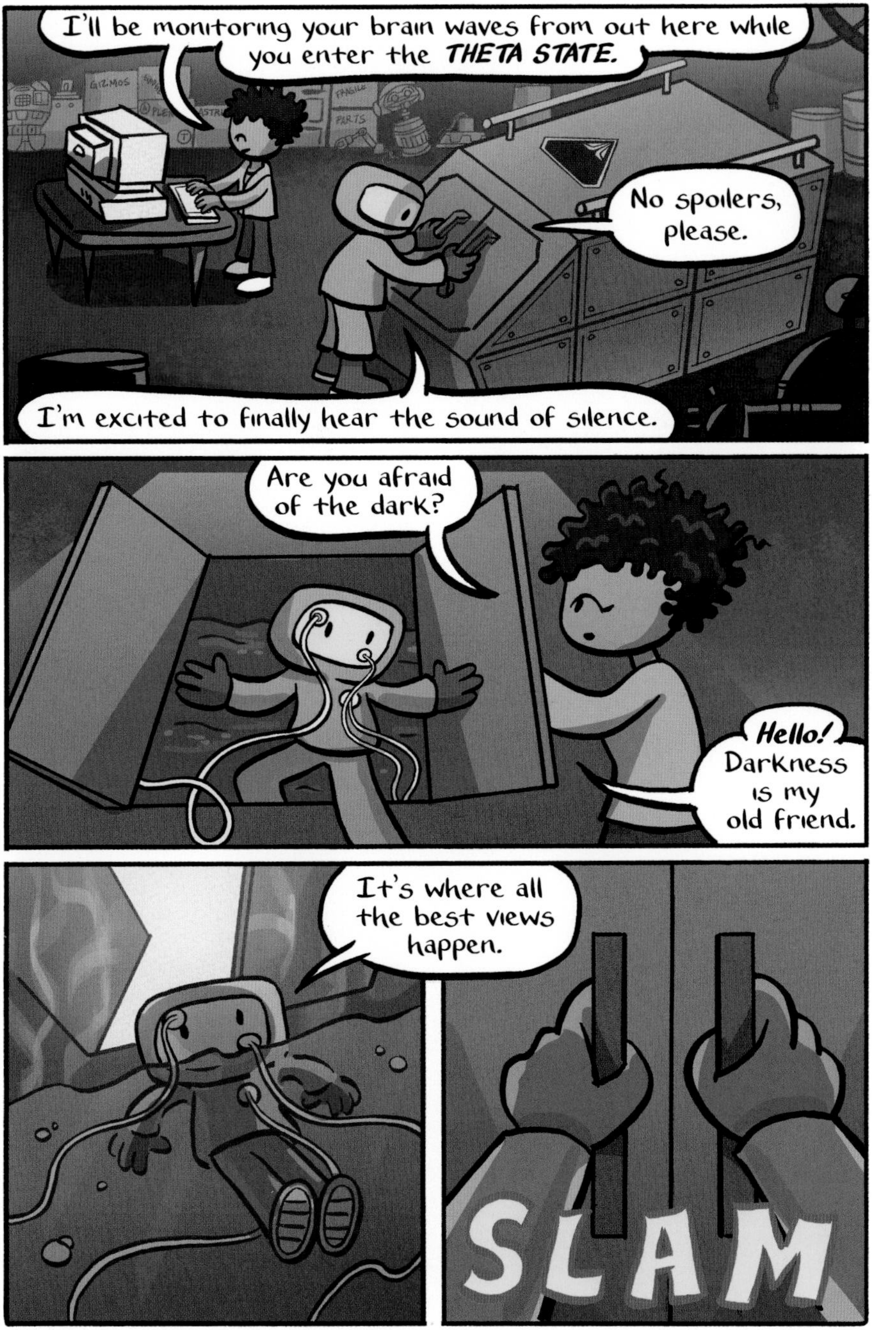
I'll be monitoring your brain waves from out here while you enter the *THETA STATE.*
No spoilers, please.
I'm excited to finally hear the sound of silence.
Are you afraid of the dark?
Hello! Darkness is my old friend.
It's where all the best views happen.
SLAM

Okay.

This is some *legit* vacuum.

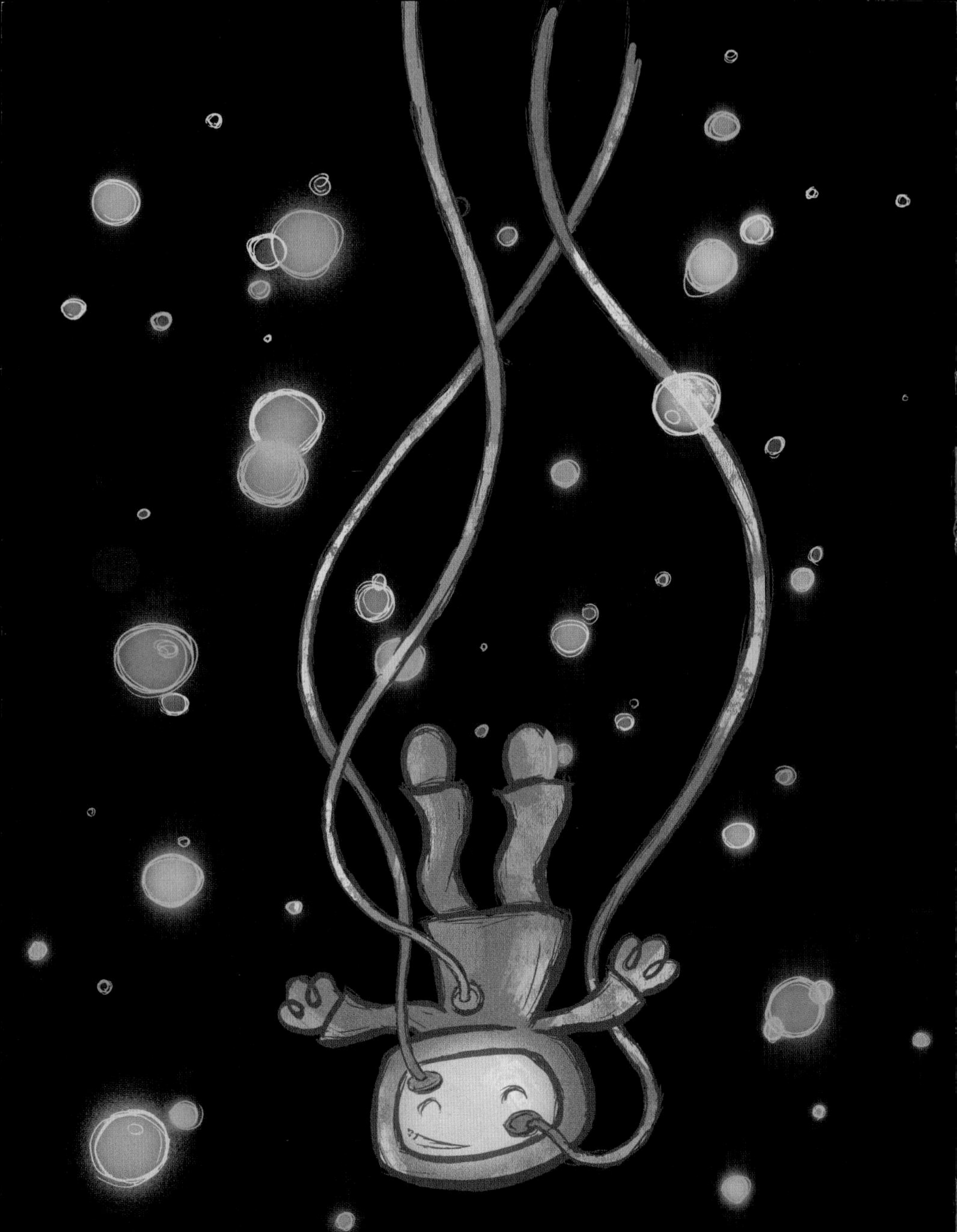

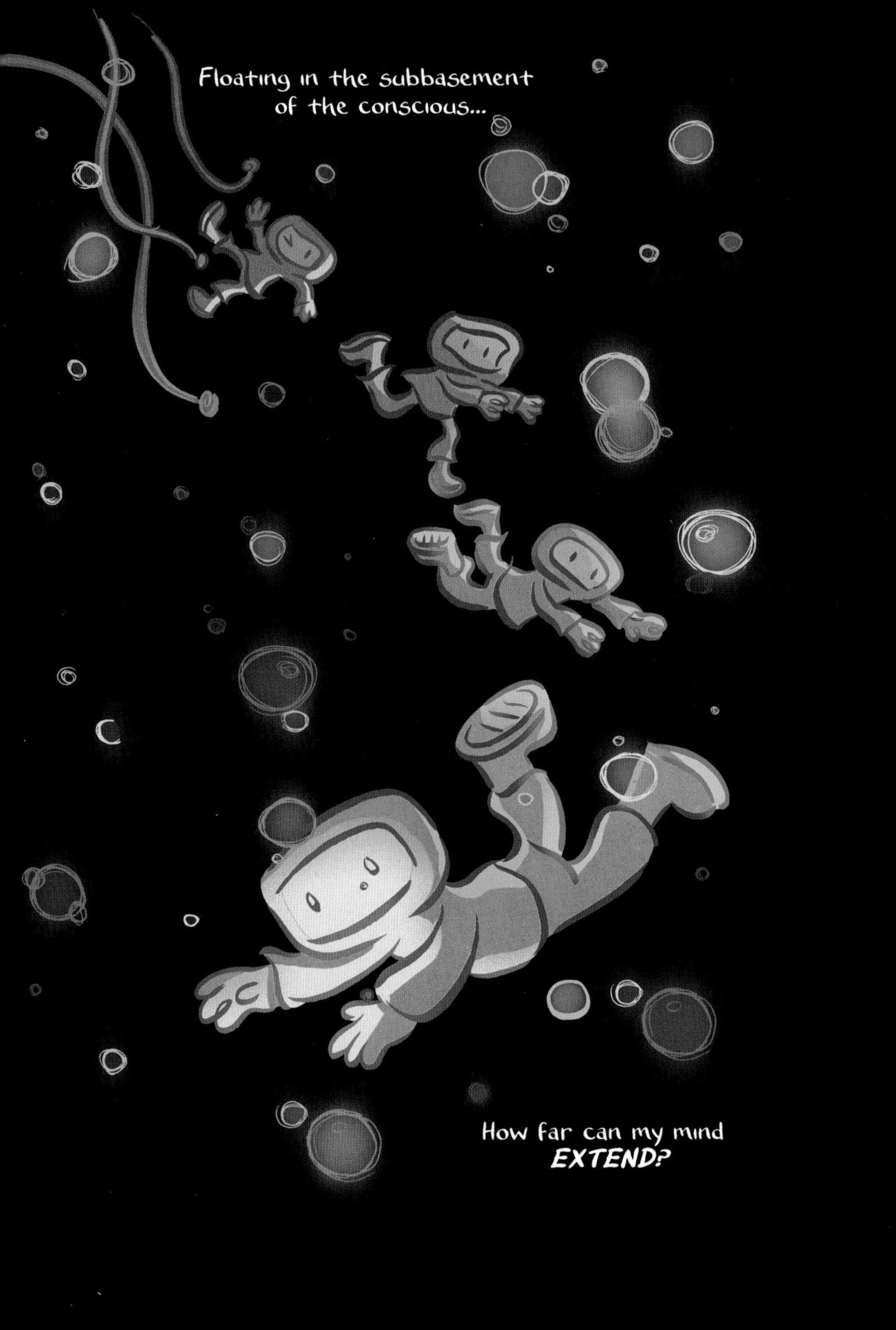
Floating in the subbasement of the conscious...
How far can my mind EXTEND?

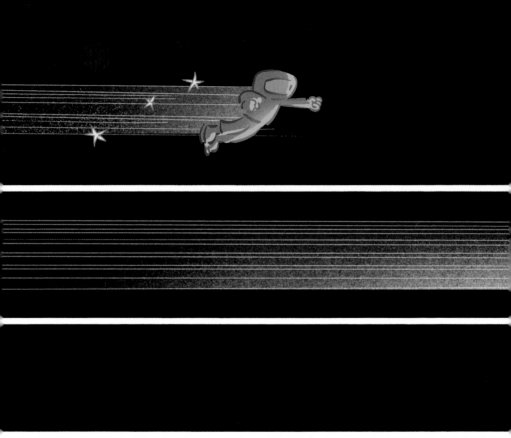

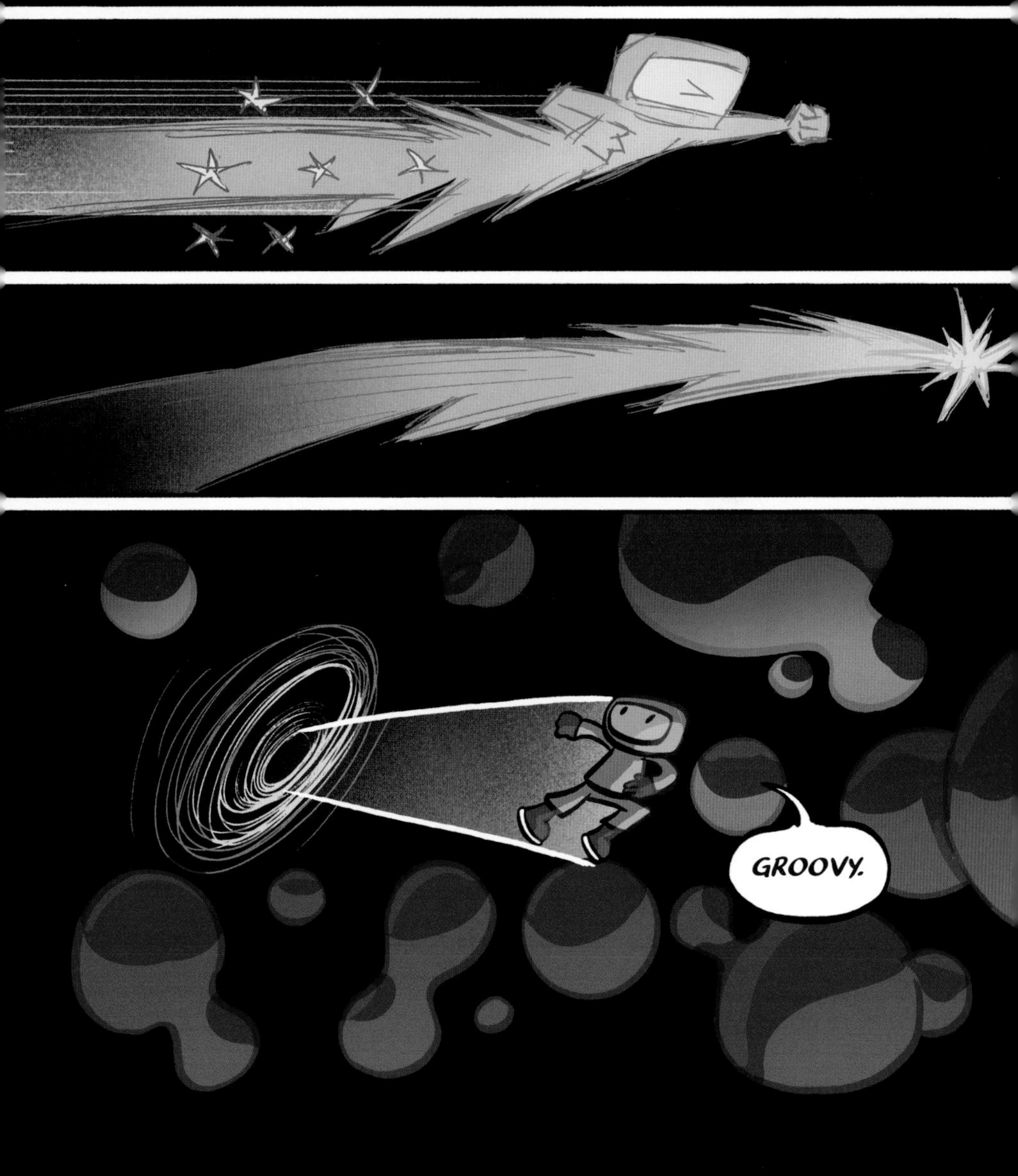
GROOVY.

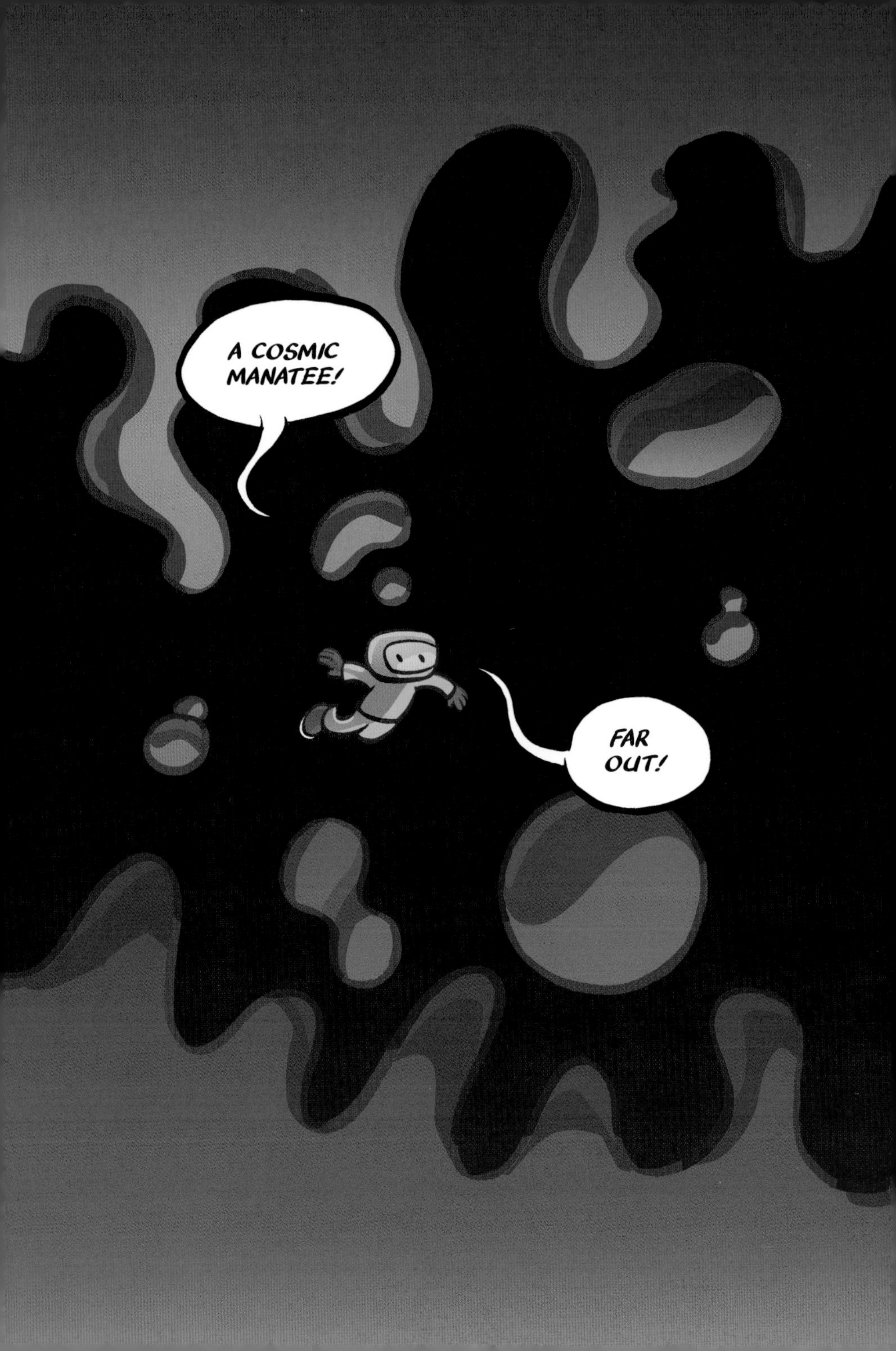
A COSMIC MANATEE!
FAR OUT!

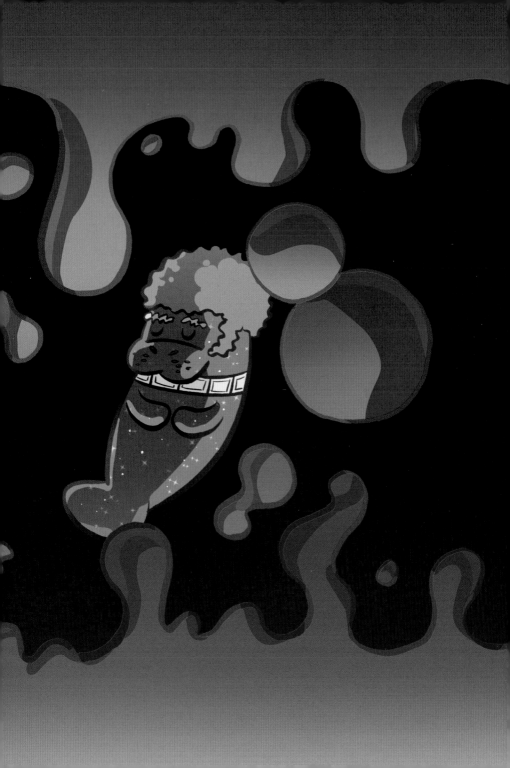

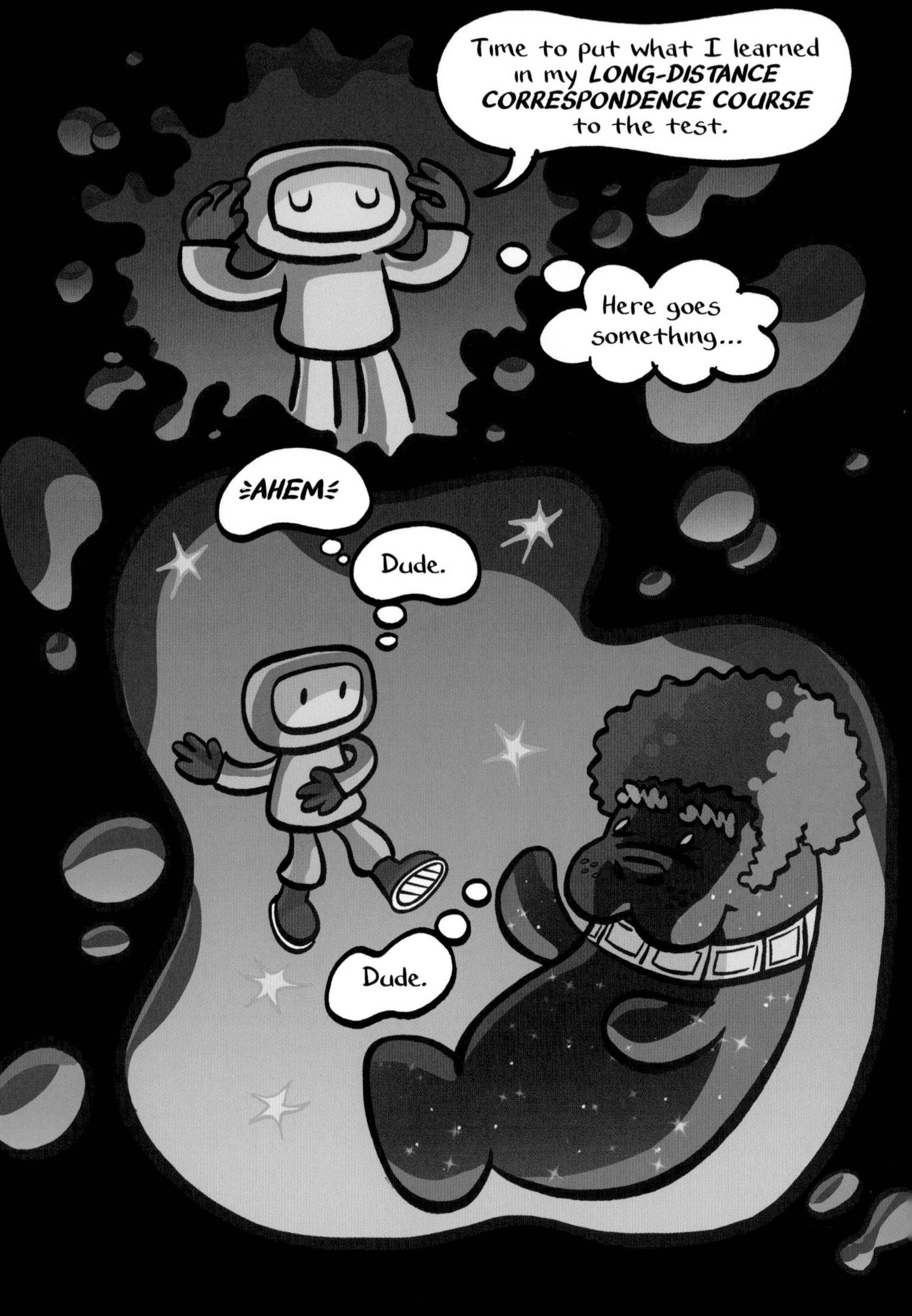

Time to put what I learned in my **LONG-DISTANCE CORRESPONDENCE COURSE** to the test.
Here goes something...
AHEM
Dude.
Dude.

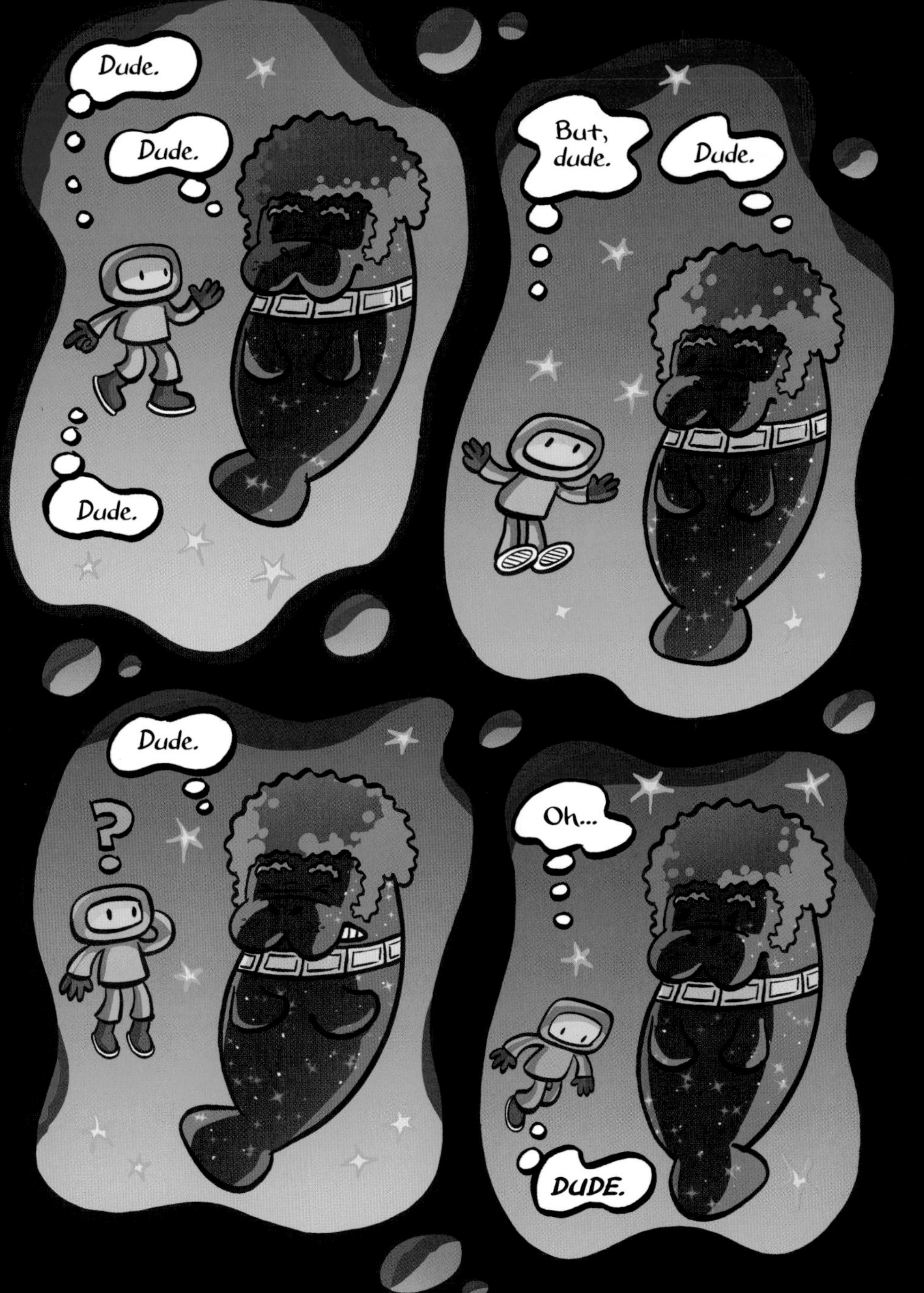
Dude.
Dude.
Dude.
But, dude.
Dude.
Dude.
Oh...
DUDE.

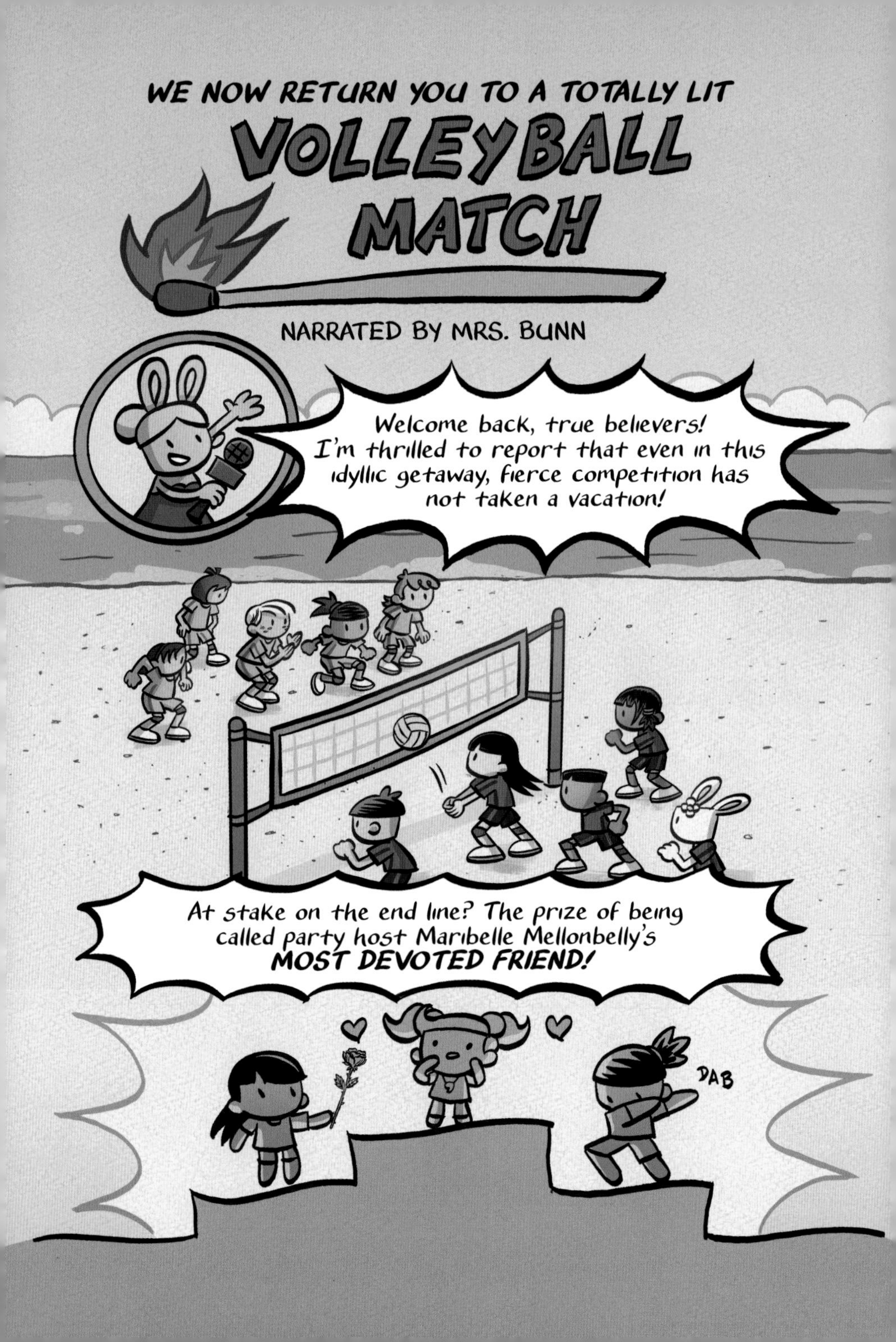
WE NOW RETURN YOU TO A TOTALLY LIT
VOLLEYBALL MATCH
NARRATED BY MRS. BUNN
Welcome back, true believers! I'm thrilled to report that even in this idyllic getaway, fierce competition has not taken a vacation!
At stake on the end line? The prize of being called party host Maribelle Mellonbelly's MOST DEVOTED FRIEND!
DAB

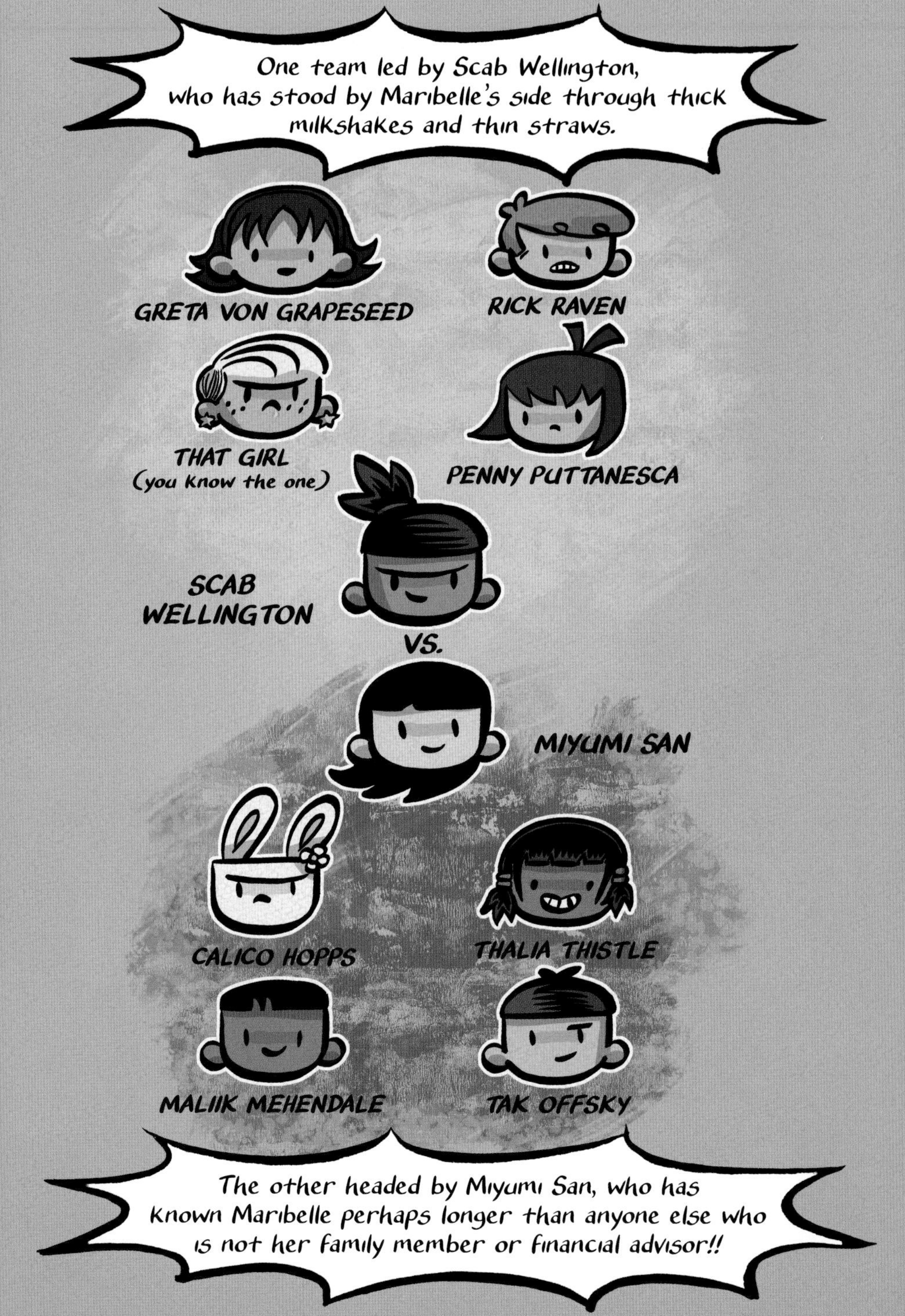
One team led by Scab Wellington, who has stood by Maribelle's side through thick milkshakes and thin straws.
GRETA VON GRAPESEED
RICK RAVEN
THAT GIRL (you know the one)
PENNY PUTTANESCA
SCAB WELLINGTON
VS.
MIYUMI SAN
CALICO HOPPS
THALIA THISTLE
MALIIK MEHENDALE
TAK OFFSKY
The other headed by Miyumi San, who has known Maribelle perhaps longer than anyone else who is not her family member or financial advisor!!

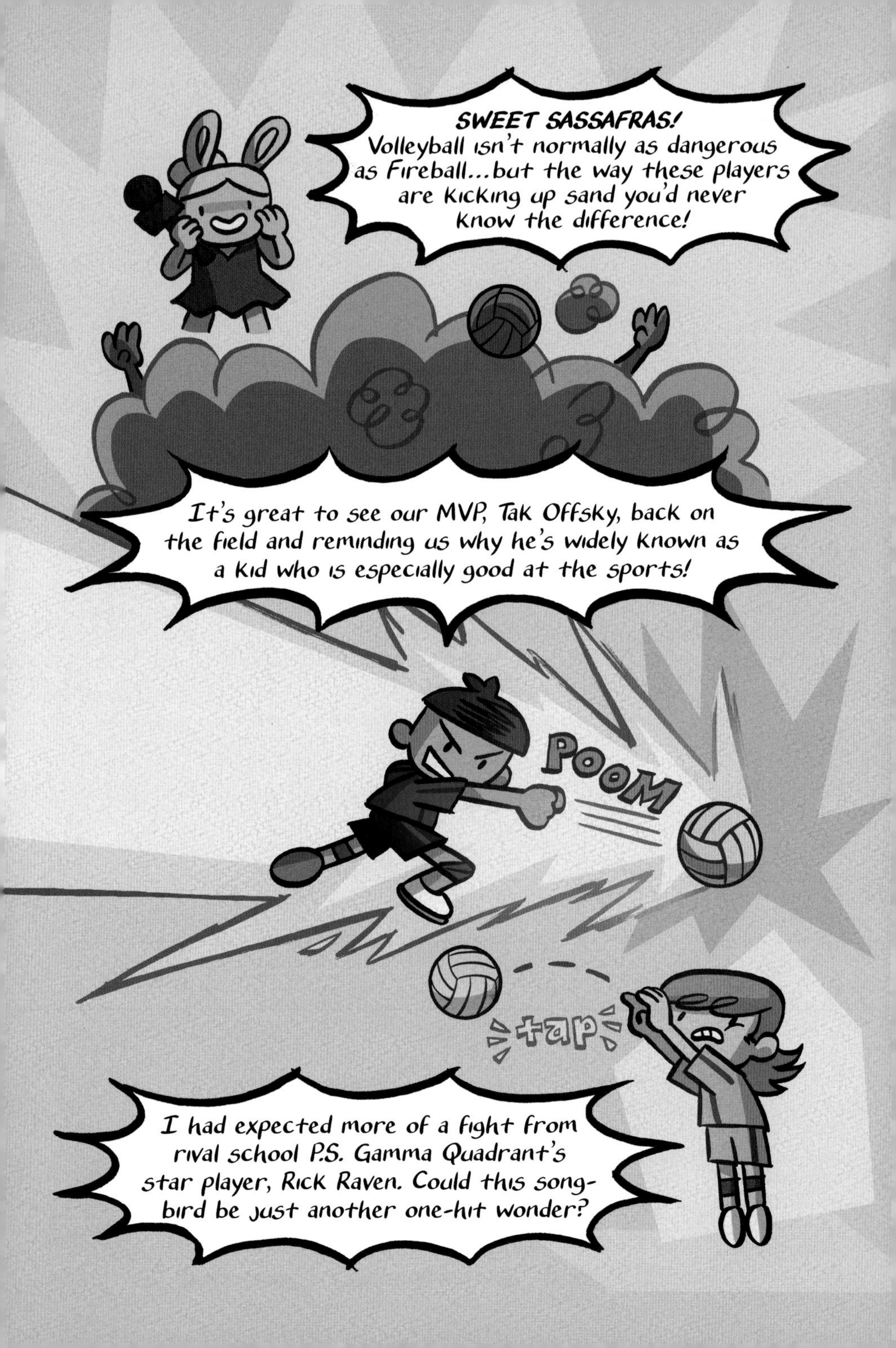
SWEET SASSAFRAS! Volleyball isn't normally as dangerous as Fireball...but the way these players are kicking up sand you'd never know the difference!
It's great to see our MVP, Tak Offsky, back on the field and reminding us why he's widely known as a kid who is especially good at the sports!
POOM
tap
I had expected more of a fight from rival school P.S. Gamma Quadrant's star player, Rick Raven. Could this song-bird be just another one-hit wonder?

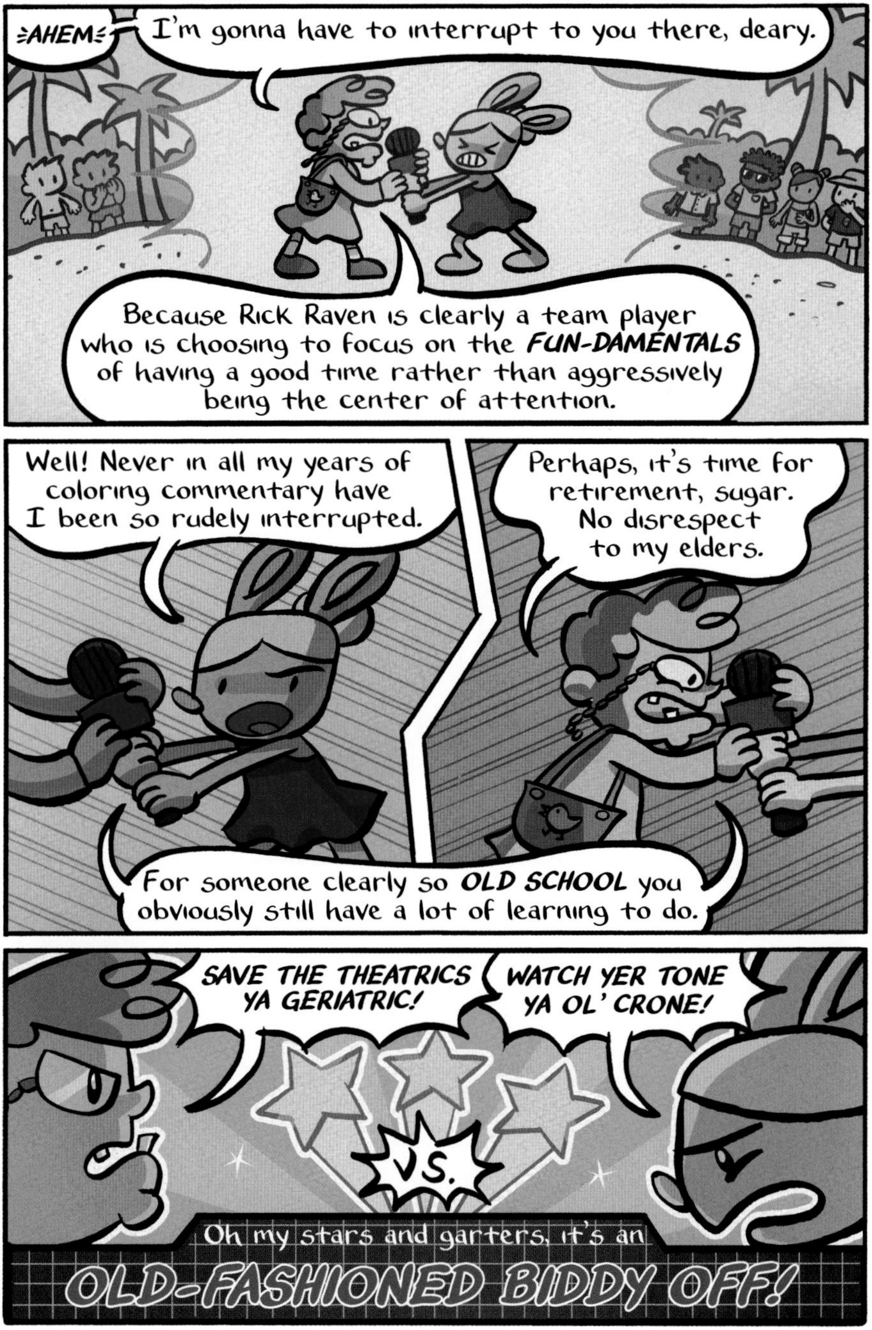

AHEM
I'm gonna have to interrupt to you there, deary.
Because Rick Raven is clearly a team player who is choosing to focus on the FUN-DAMENTALS of having a good time rather than aggressively being the center of attention.
Well! Never in all my years of coloring commentary have I been so rudely interrupted.
Perhaps, it's time for retirement, sugar. No disrespect to my elders.
For someone clearly so OLD SCHOOL you obviously still have a lot of learning to do.
SAVE THE THEATRICS YA GERIATRIC!
WATCH YER TONE YA OL' CRONE!
VS.
Oh my stars and garters, it's an
OLD-FASHIONED BIDDY OFF!

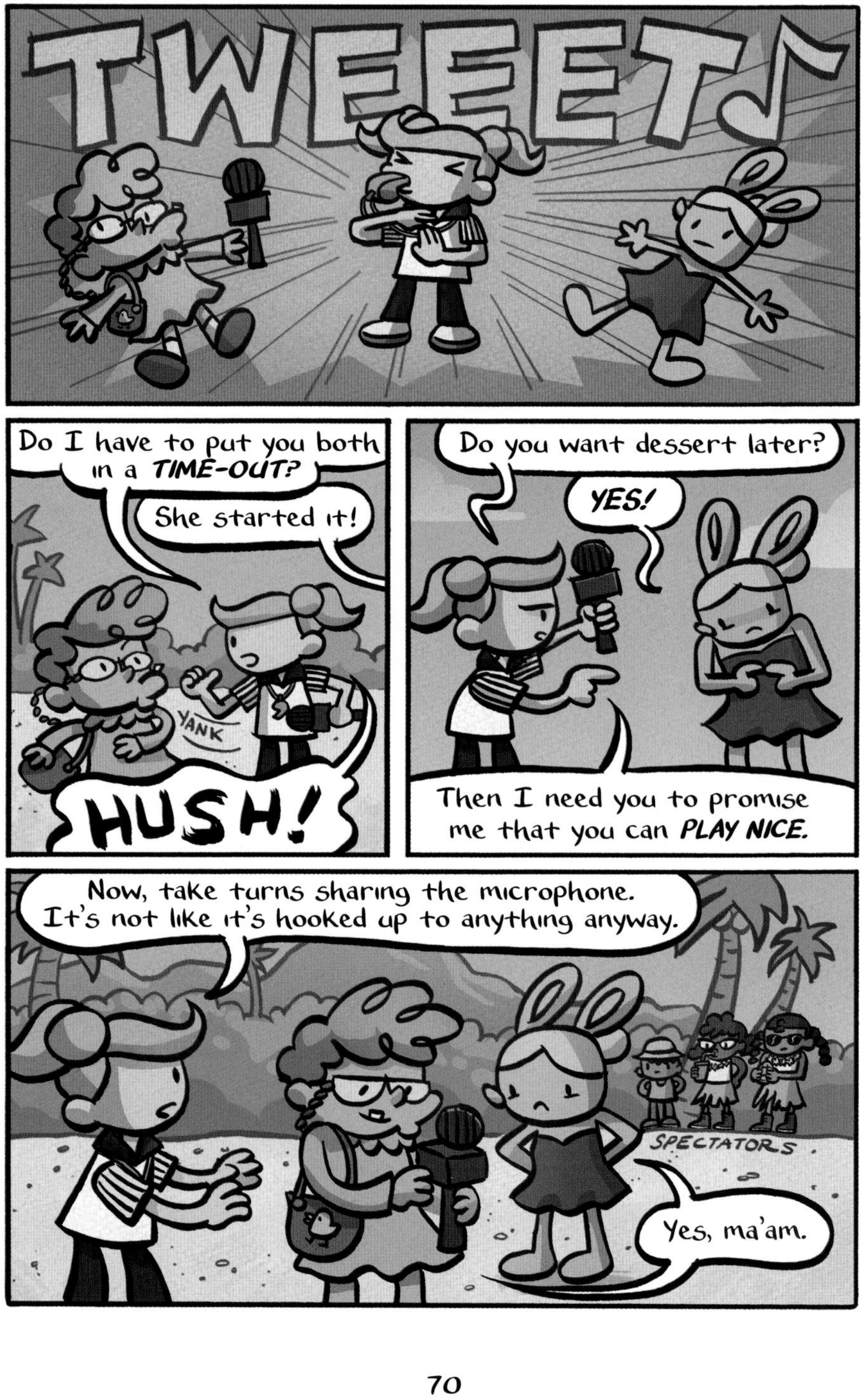
TWEEET♪
Do I have to put you both in a TIME-OUT?
She started it!
YANK
HUSH!
Do you want dessert later?
YES!
Then I need you to promise me that you can PLAY NICE.
Now, take turns sharing the microphone. It's not like it's hooked up to anything anyway.
SPECTATORS
Yes, ma'am.

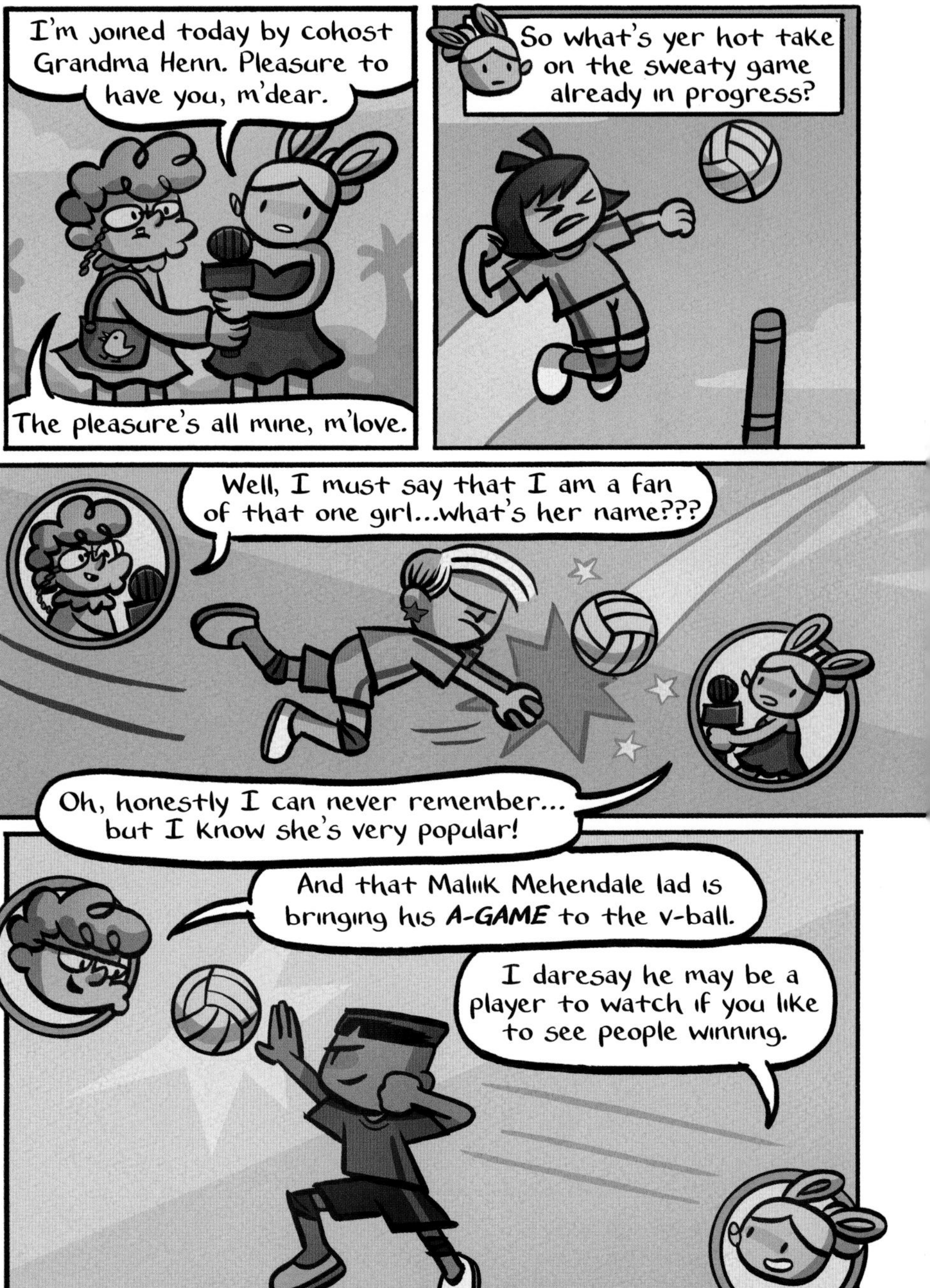

I'm joined today by cohost Grandma Henn. Pleasure to have you, m'dear.
The pleasure's all mine, m'love.
So what's yer hot take on the sweaty game already in progress?
Well, I must say that I am a fan of that one girl...what's her name???
Oh, honestly I can never remember... but I know she's very popular!
And that Malik Mehendale lad is bringing his ***A-GAME*** to the v-ball.
I daresay he may be a player to watch if you like to see people winning.

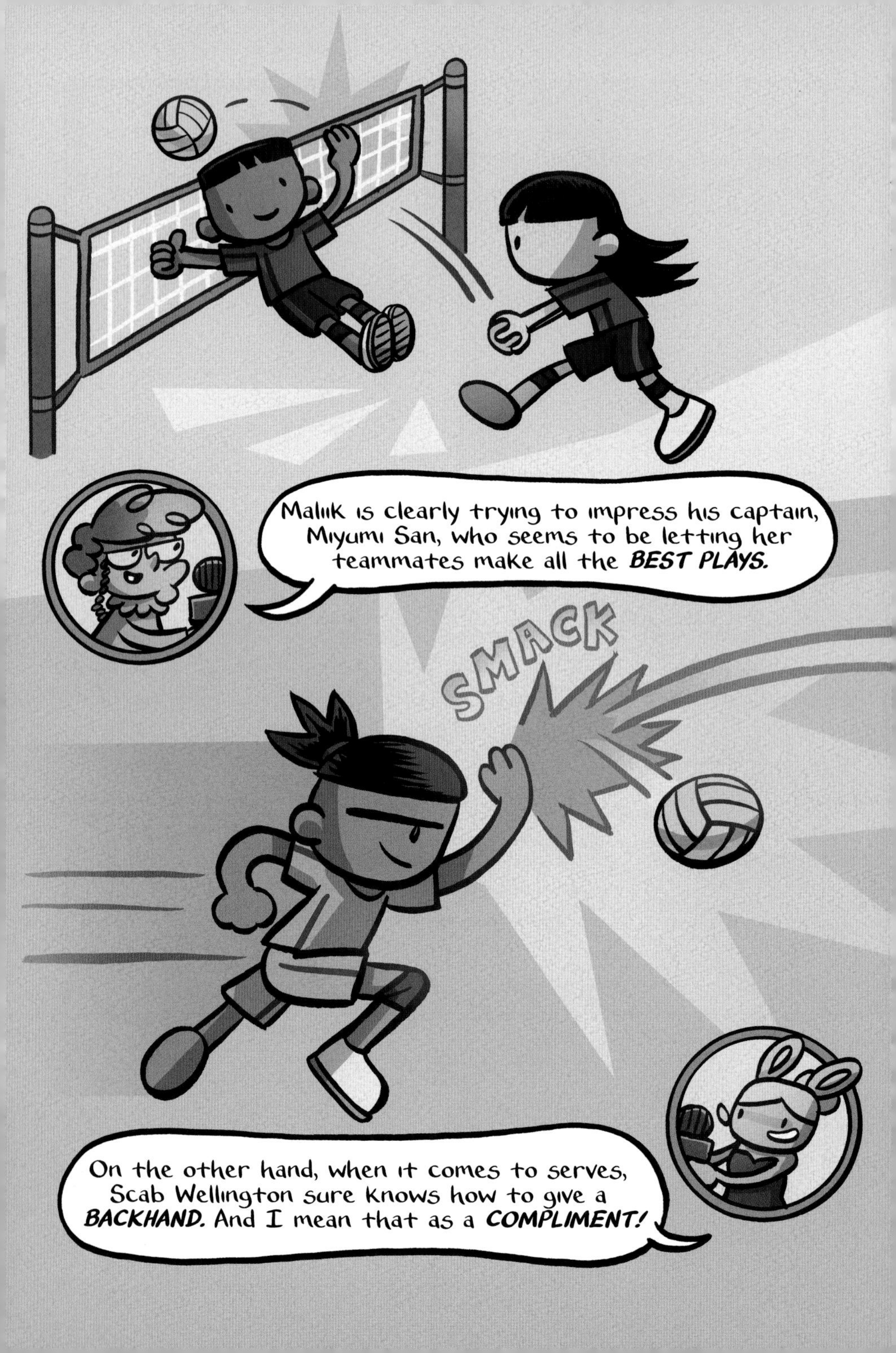
Maliik is clearly trying to impress his captain, Miyumi San, who seems to be letting her teammates make all the BEST PLAYS.
SMACK
On the other hand, when it comes to serves, Scab Wellington sure knows how to give a BACKHAND. And I mean that as a COMPLIMENT!

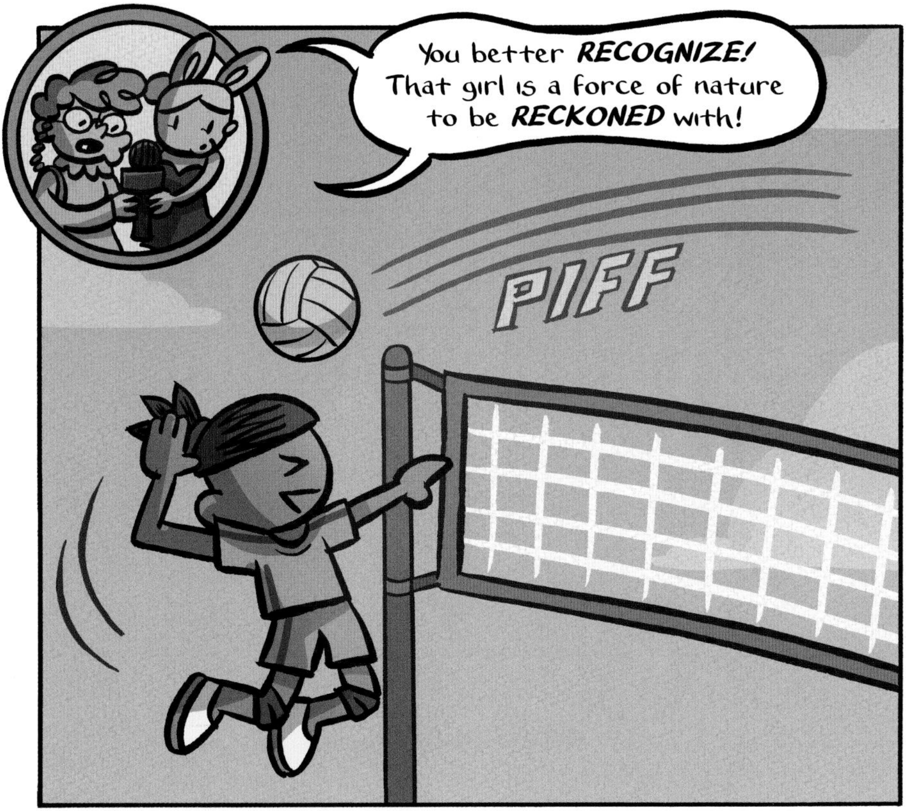
You better **RECOGNIZE!** That girl is a force of nature to be **RECKONED** with!
PIFF

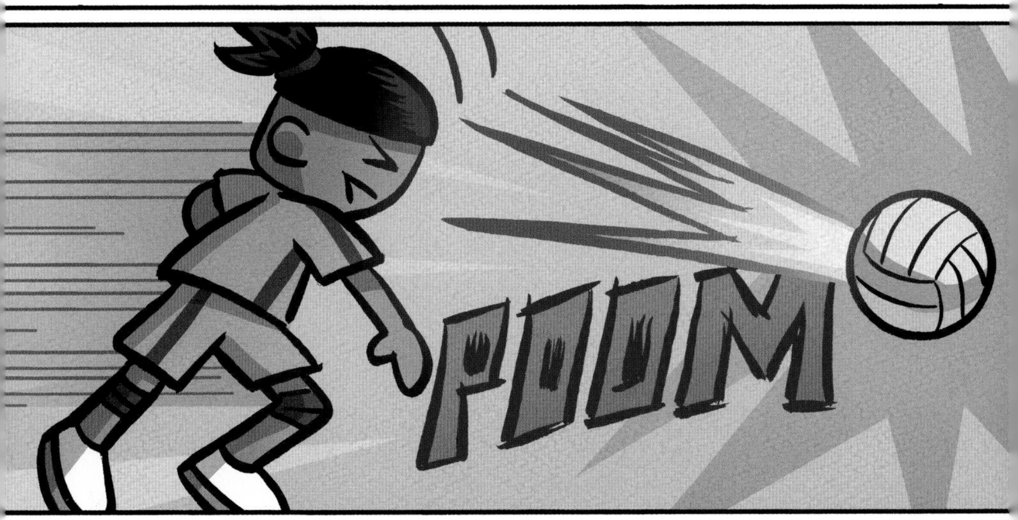
POOM

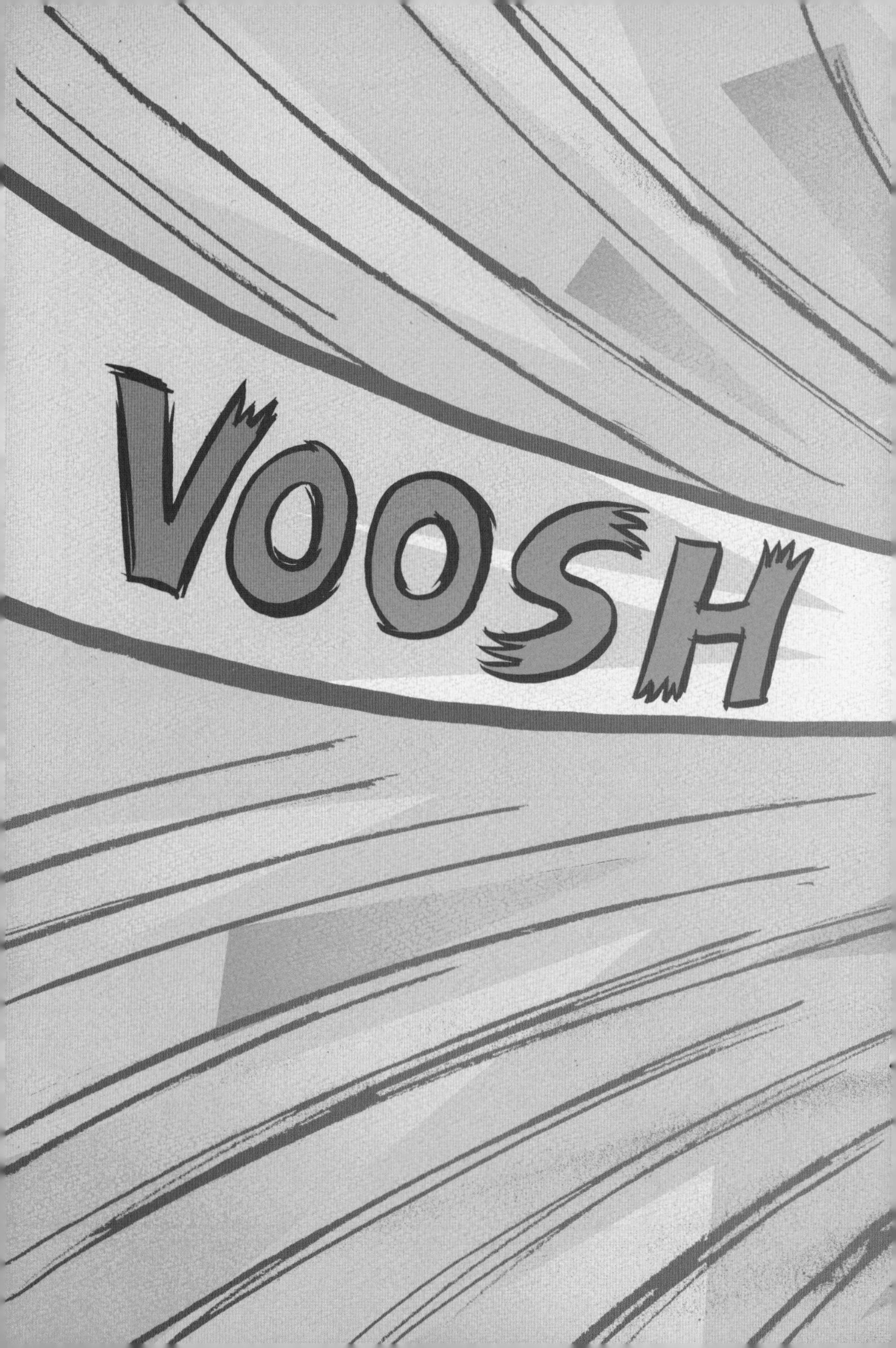
VOOSH

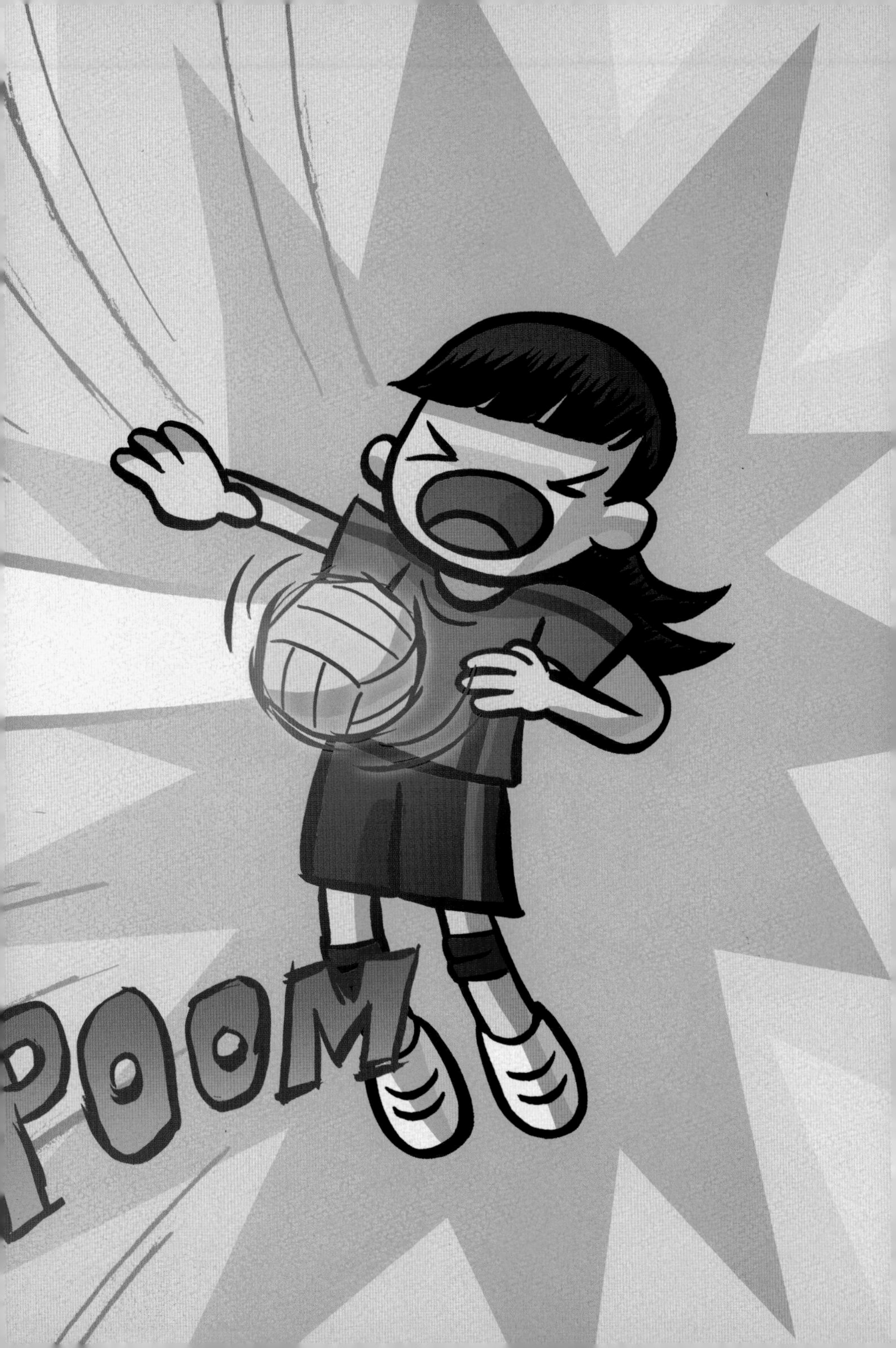
POOM

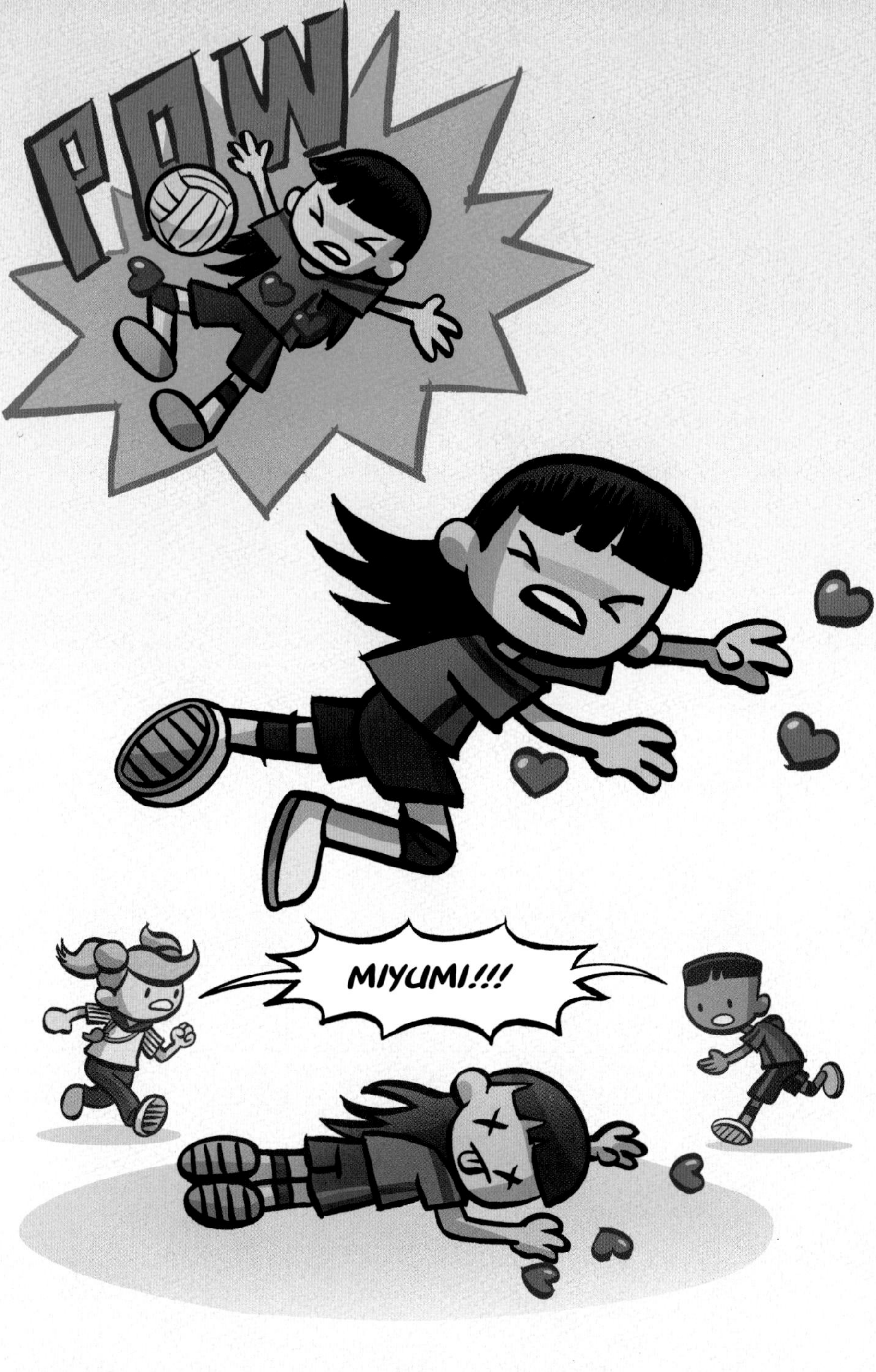
POW
MIYUMI!!!

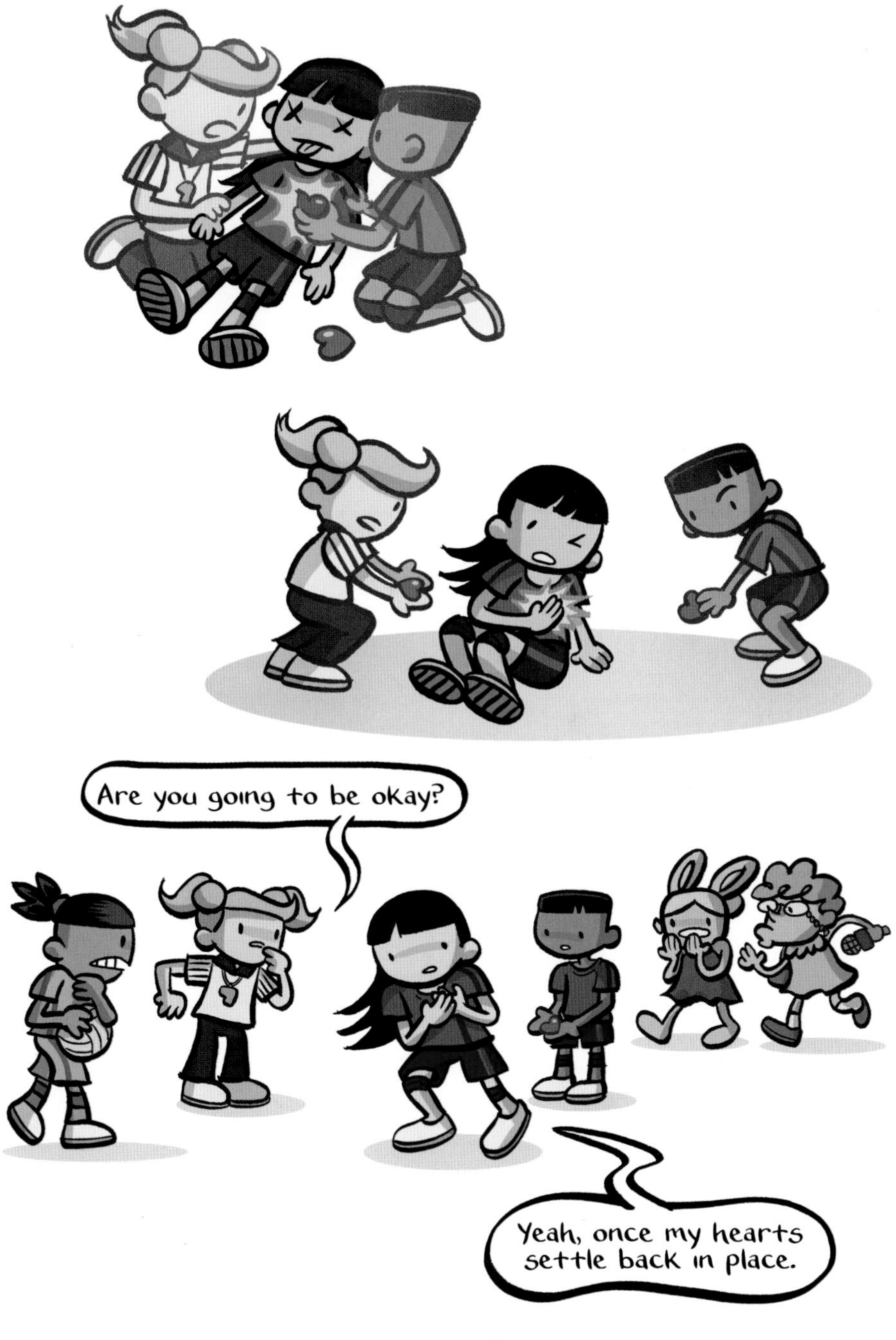
Are you going to be okay?
Yeah, once my hearts settle back in place.

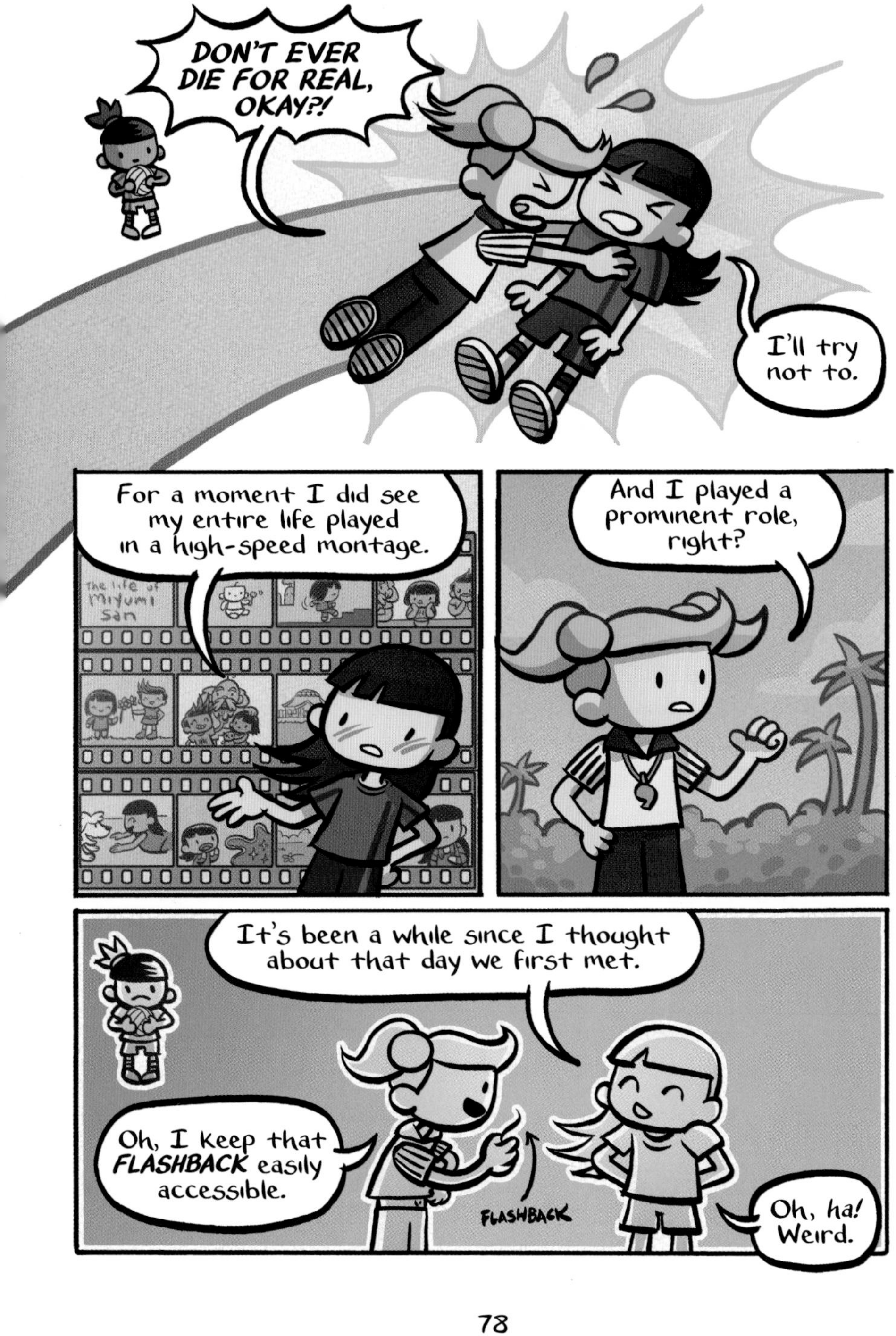
DON'T EVER DIE FOR REAL, OKAY?!
I'll try not to.
For a moment I did see my entire life played in a high-speed montage.
The life of Miyumi San
And I played a prominent role, right?
It's been a while since I thought about that day we first met.
Oh, I keep that *FLASHBACK* easily accessible.
FLASHBACK
Oh, ha! Weird.

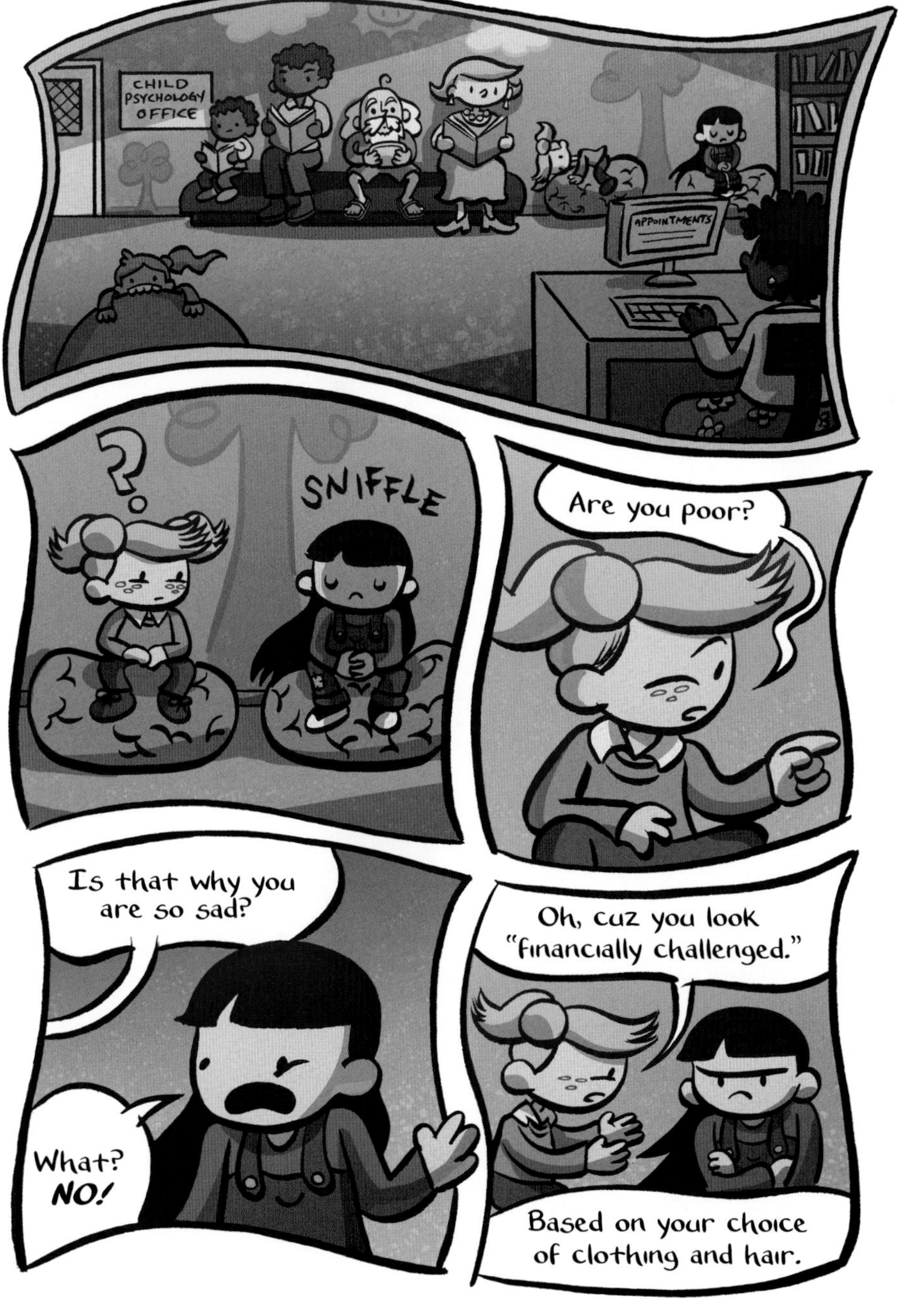
CHILD PSYCHOLOGY OFFICE
APPOINTMENTS
SNIFFLE
Are you poor?
Is that why you are so sad?
What? NO!
Oh, cuz you look "financially challenged."
Based on your choice of clothing and hair.

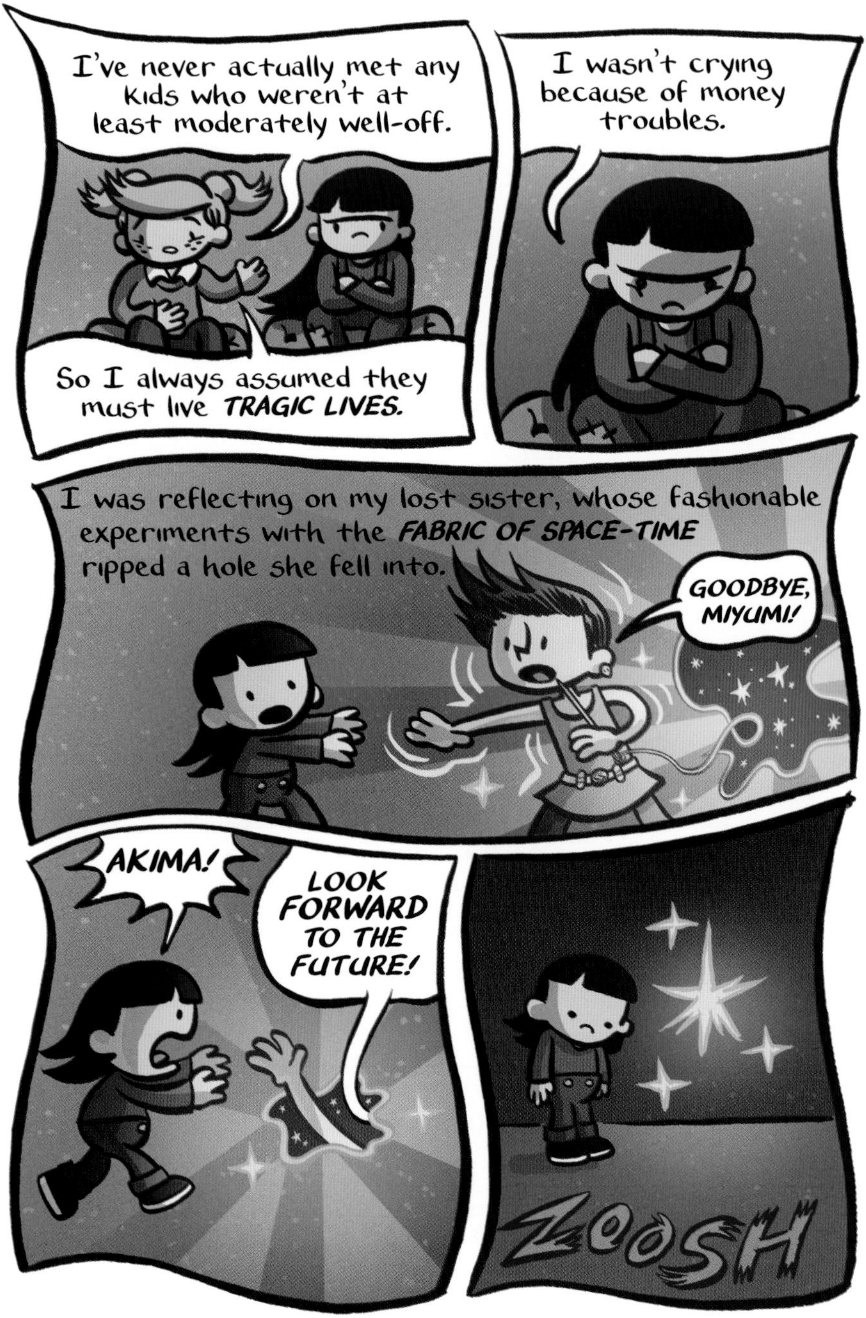
I've never actually met any kids who weren't at least moderately well-off.
So I always assumed they must live TRAGIC LIVES.
I wasn't crying because of money troubles.
I was reflecting on my lost sister, whose fashionable experiments with the FABRIC OF SPACE-TIME ripped a hole she fell into.
GOODBYE, MIYUMI!
AKIMA!
LOOK FORWARD TO THE FUTURE!
ZOOSH

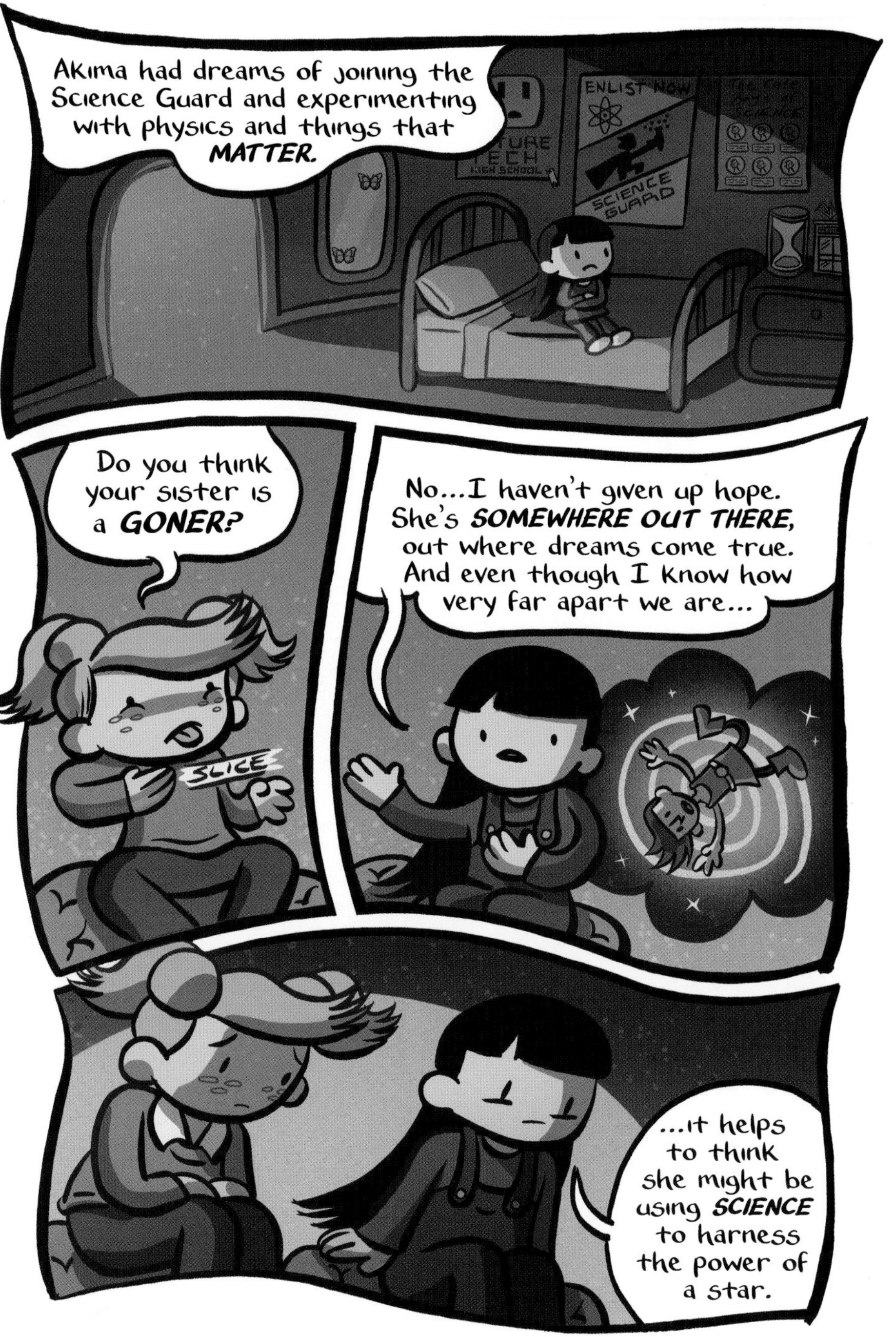
Akima had dreams of joining the Science Guard and experimenting with physics and things that MATTER.
ENLIST NOW
SCIENCE GUARD
HIGH SCHOOL
Do you think your sister is a GONER?
SLICE
No...I haven't given up hope. She's SOMEWHERE OUT THERE, out where dreams come true. And even though I know how very far apart we are...
...it helps to think she might be using SCIENCE to harness the power of a star.

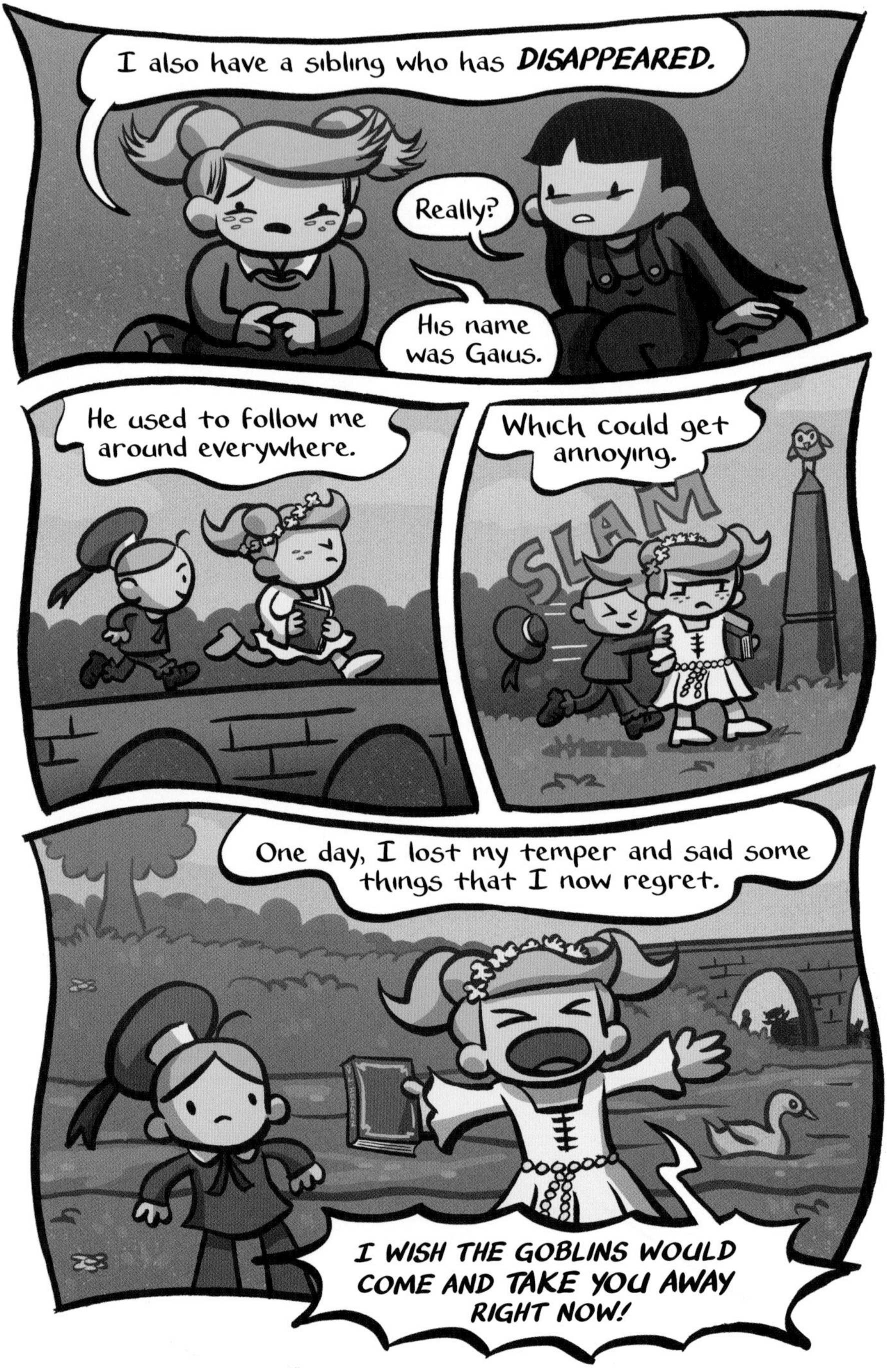
I also have a sibling who has DISAPPEARED.
Really?
His name was Gaius.
He used to follow me around everywhere.
Which could get annoying.
SLAM
One day, I lost my temper and said some things that I now regret.
I WISH THE GOBLINS WOULD COME AND TAKE YOU AWAY RIGHT NOW!

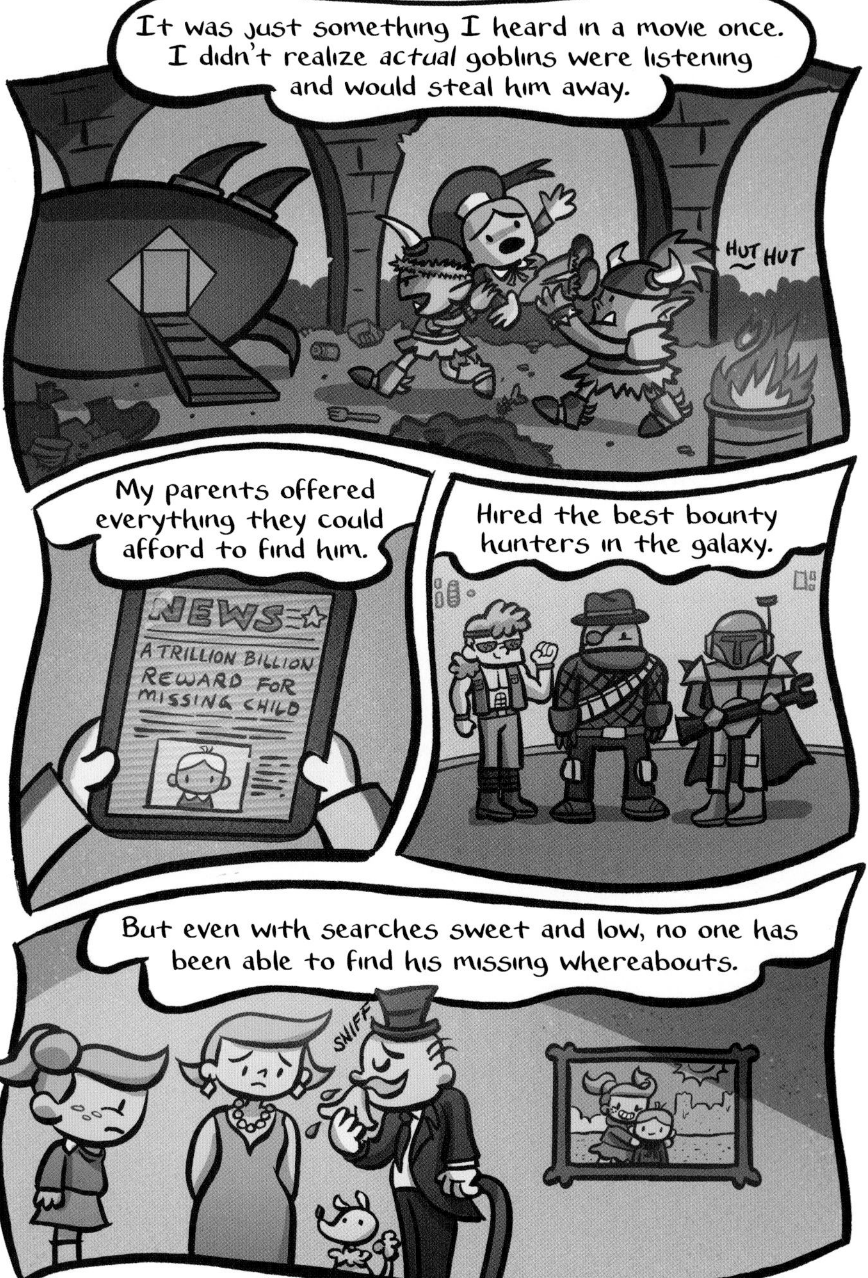

It was just something I heard in a movie once. I didn't realize actual goblins were listening and would steal him away.
HUT HUT
My parents offered everything they could afford to find him.
NEWS
A TRILLION BILLION REWARD FOR MISSING CHILD
Hired the best bounty hunters in the galaxy.
But even with searches sweet and low, no one has been able to find his missing whereabouts.
SNIFF

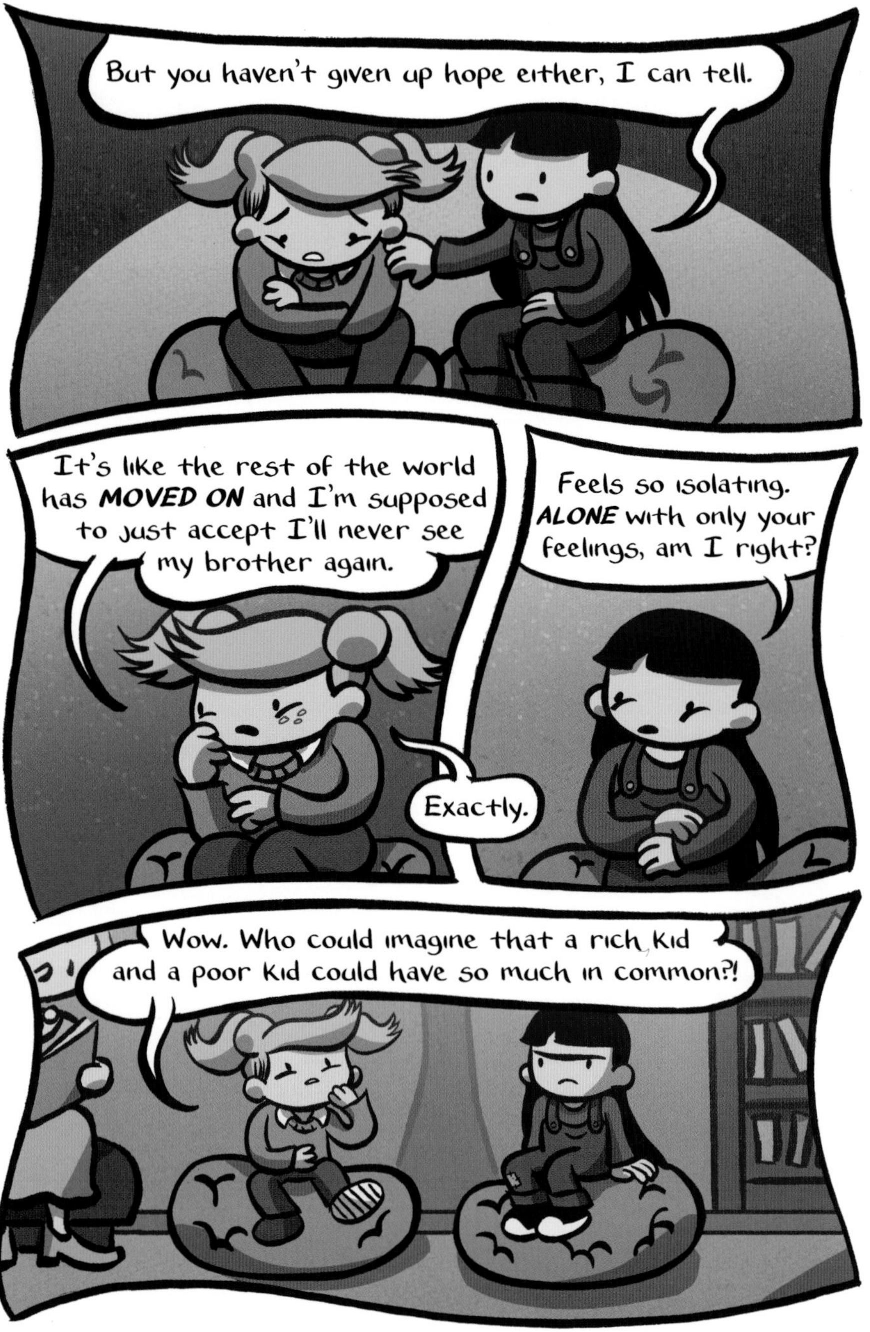
But you haven't given up hope either, I can tell.
It's like the rest of the world has MOVED ON and I'm supposed to just accept I'll never see my brother again.
Feels so isolating. ALONE with only your feelings, am I right?
Exactly.
Wow. Who could imagine that a rich kid and a poor kid could have so much in common?!

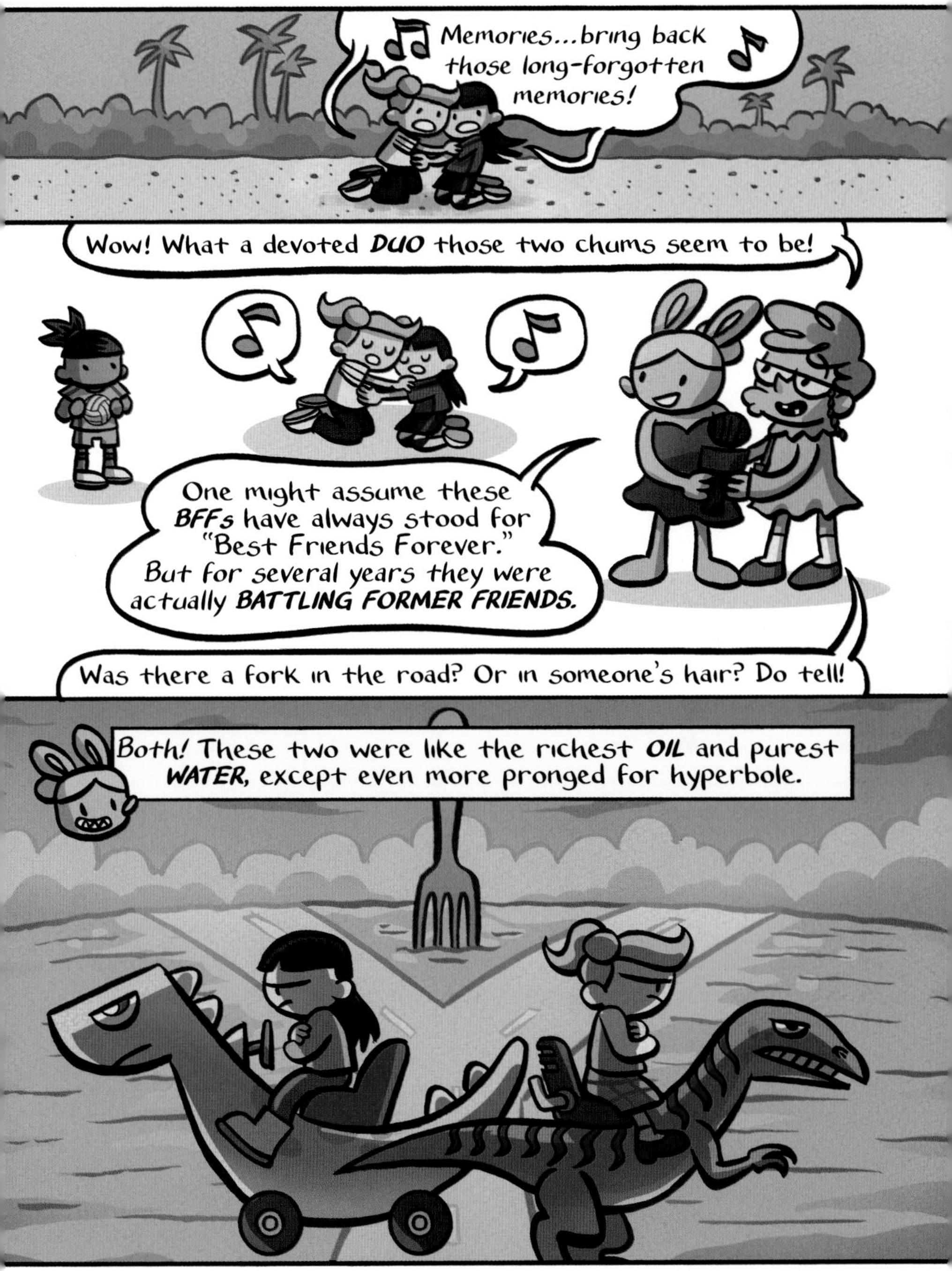

Memories...bring back those long-forgotten memories!
Wow! What a devoted DUO those two chums seem to be!
One might assume these BFFs have always stood for "Best Friends Forever." But for several years they were actually BATTLING FORMER FRIENDS.
Was there a fork in the road? Or in someone's hair? Do tell!
Both! These two were like the richest OIL and purest WATER, except even more pronged for hyperbole.

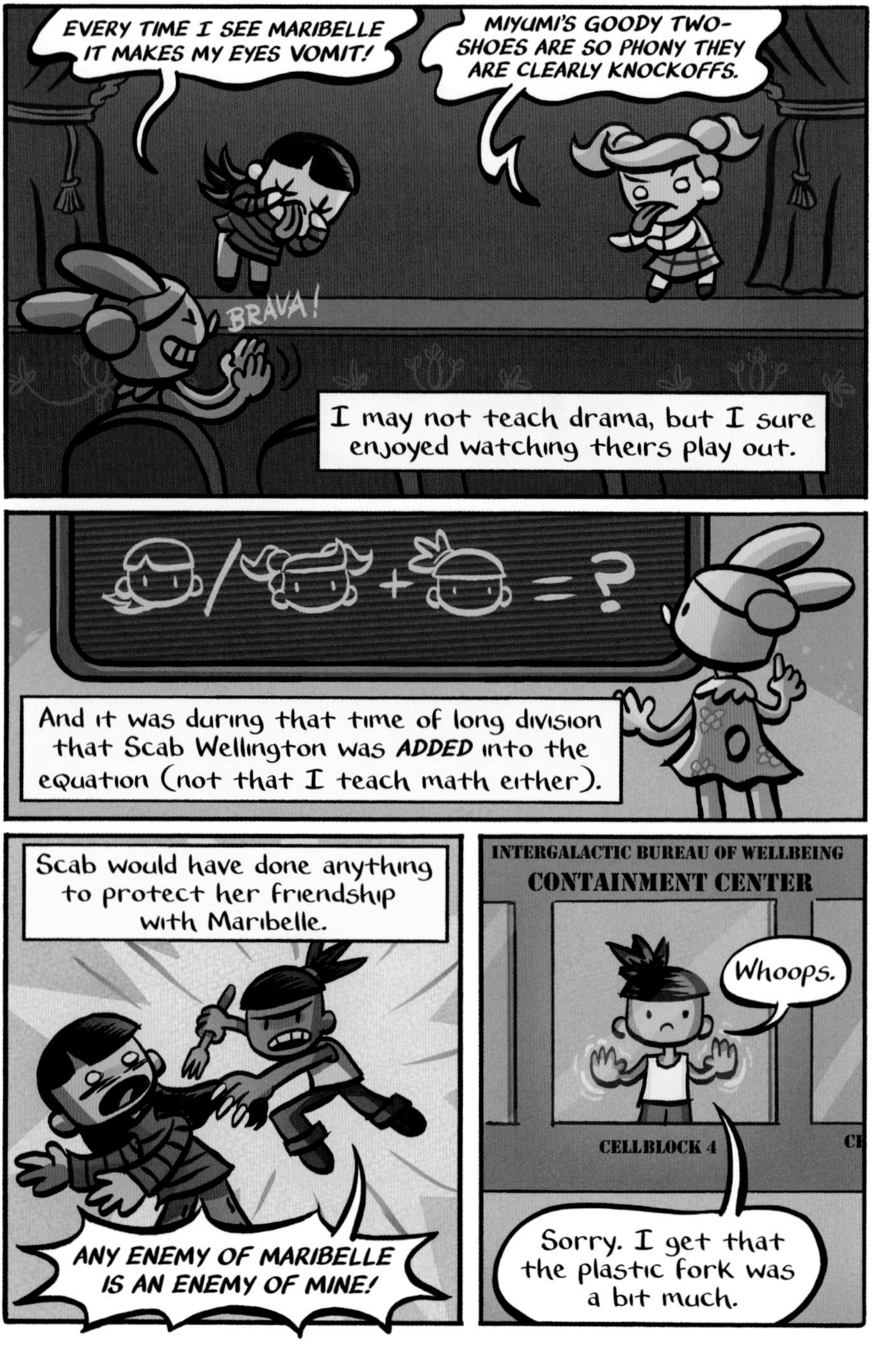
EVERY TIME I SEE MARIBELLE IT MAKES MY EYES VOMIT!
MIYUMI'S GOODY TWO-SHOES ARE SO PHONY THEY ARE CLEARLY KNOCKOFFS.
BRAVA!
I may not teach drama, but I sure enjoyed watching theirs play out.
And it was during that time of long division that Scab Wellington was ADDED into the equation (not that I teach math either).
Scab would have done anything to protect her friendship with Maribelle.
ANY ENEMY OF MARIBELLE IS AN ENEMY OF MINE!
INTERGALACTIC BUREAU OF WELLBEING
CONTAINMENT CENTER
Whoops.
CELLBLOCK 4
Sorry. I get that the plastic fork was a bit much.

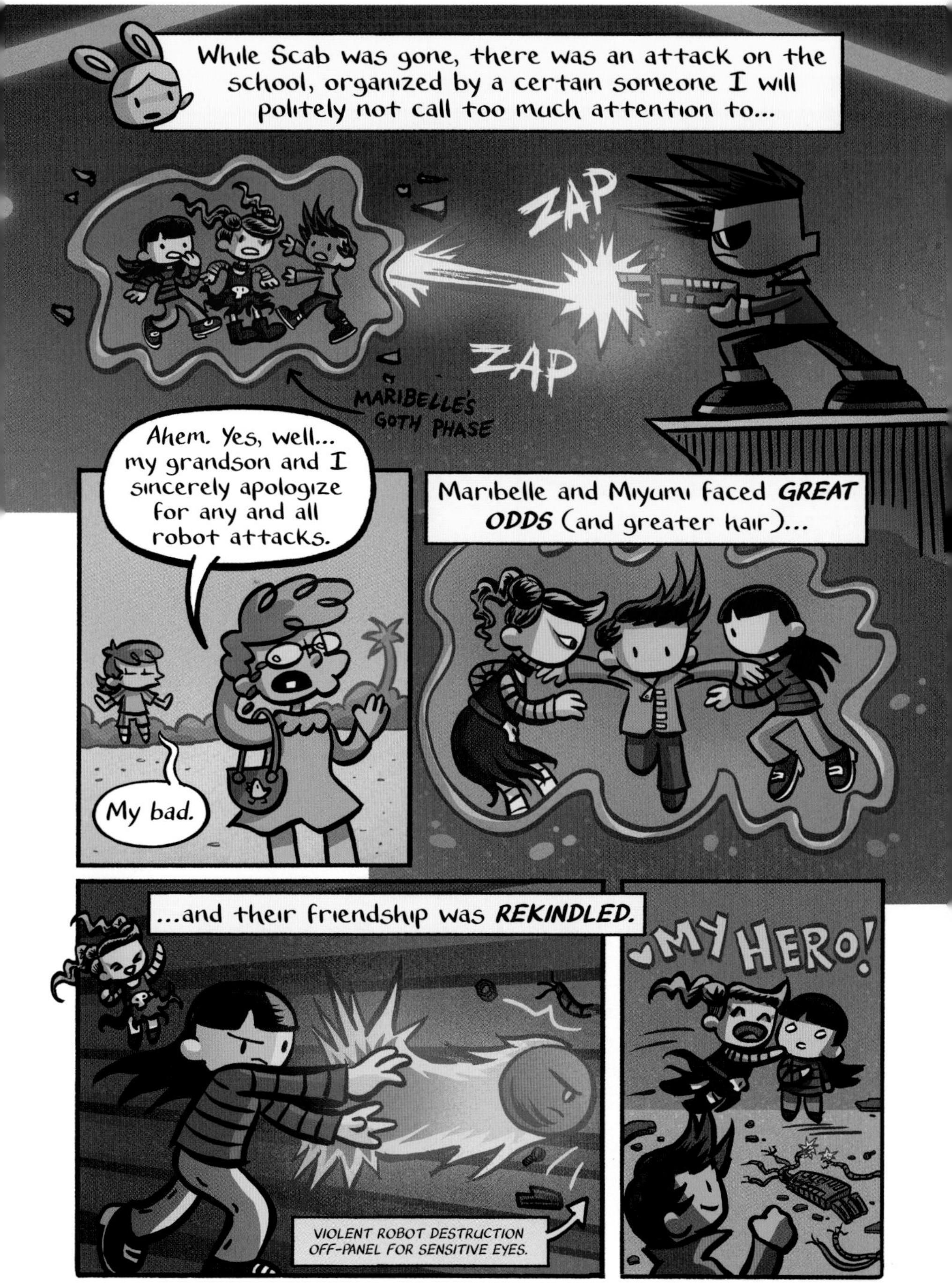
While Scab was gone, there was an attack on the school, organized by a certain someone I will politely not call too much attention to...
ZAP
ZAP
MARIBELLE'S GOTH PHASE
Ahem. Yes, well... my grandson and I sincerely apologize for any and all robot attacks.
My bad.
Maribelle and Miyumi faced GREAT ODDS (and greater hair)...
...and their friendship was REKINDLED.
VIOLENT ROBOT DESTRUCTION OFF-PANEL FOR SENSITIVE EYES.
MY HERO!

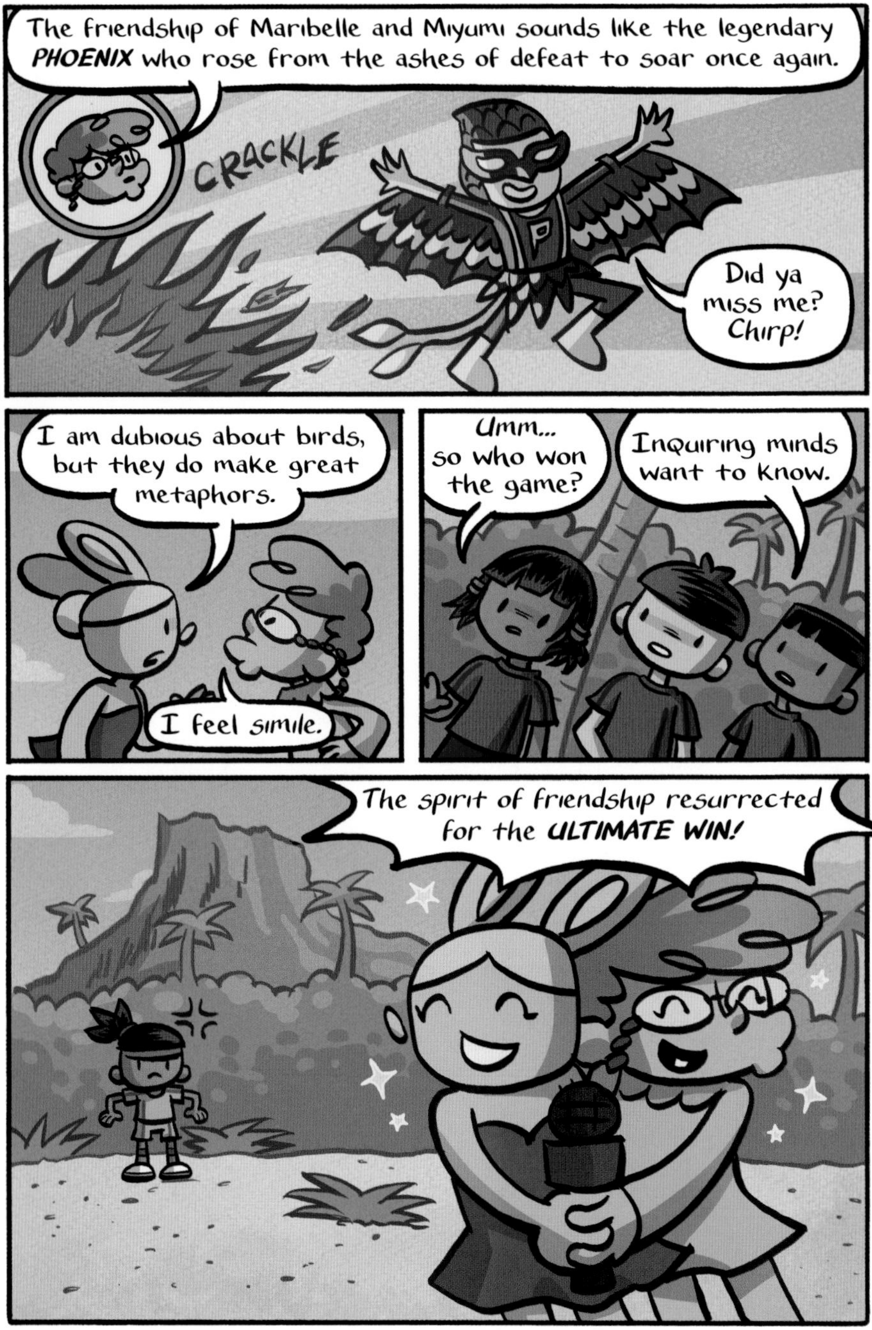
The friendship of Maribelle and Miyumi sounds like the legendary **PHOENIX** who rose from the ashes of defeat to soar once again.
CRACKLE
Did ya miss me? Chirp!
I am dubious about birds, but they do make great metaphors.
I feel simile.
Umm... so who won the game?
Inquiring minds want to know.
The spirit of friendship resurrected for the **ULTIMATE WIN!**

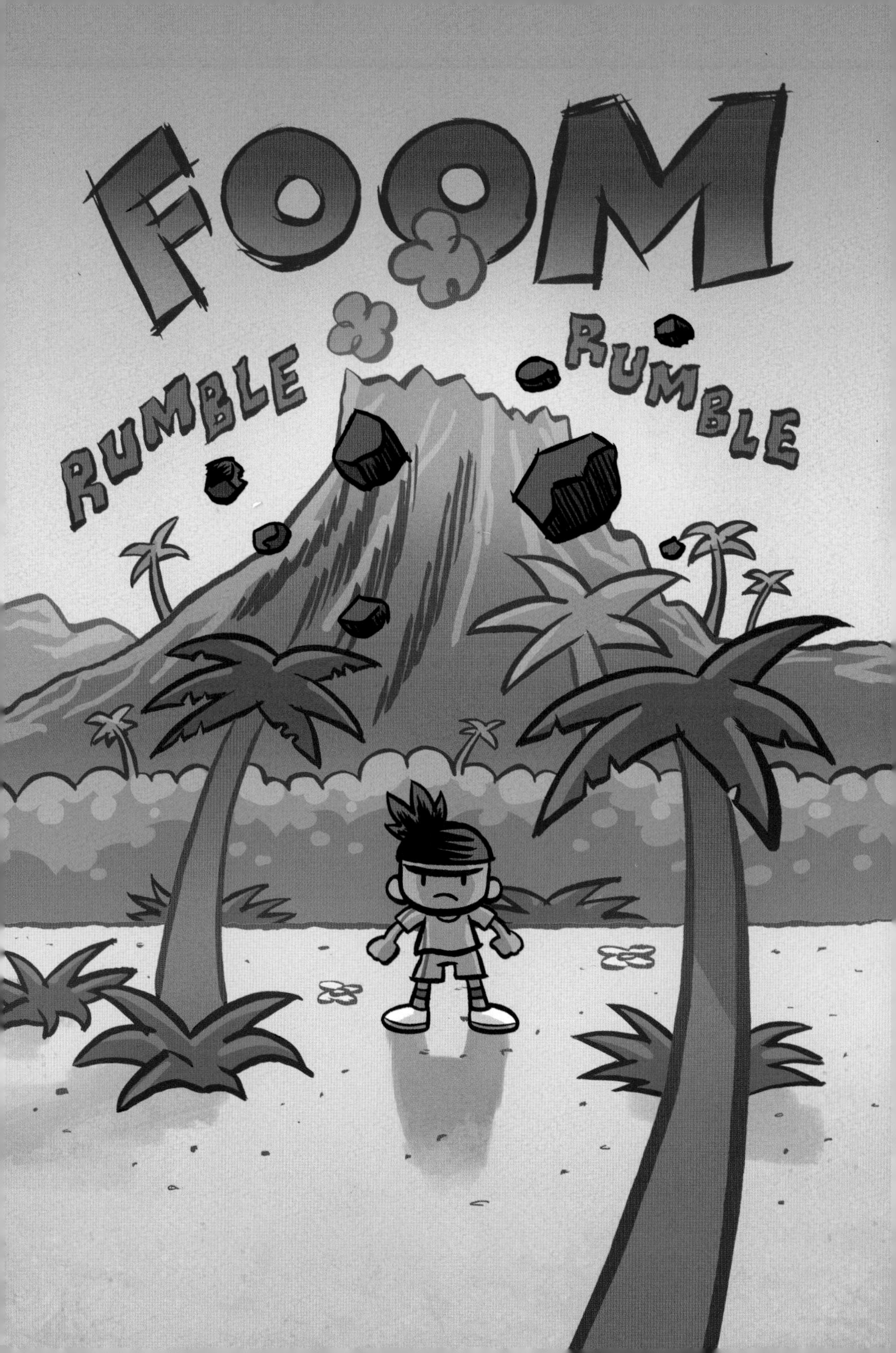
FOOM
RUMBLE
RUMBLE

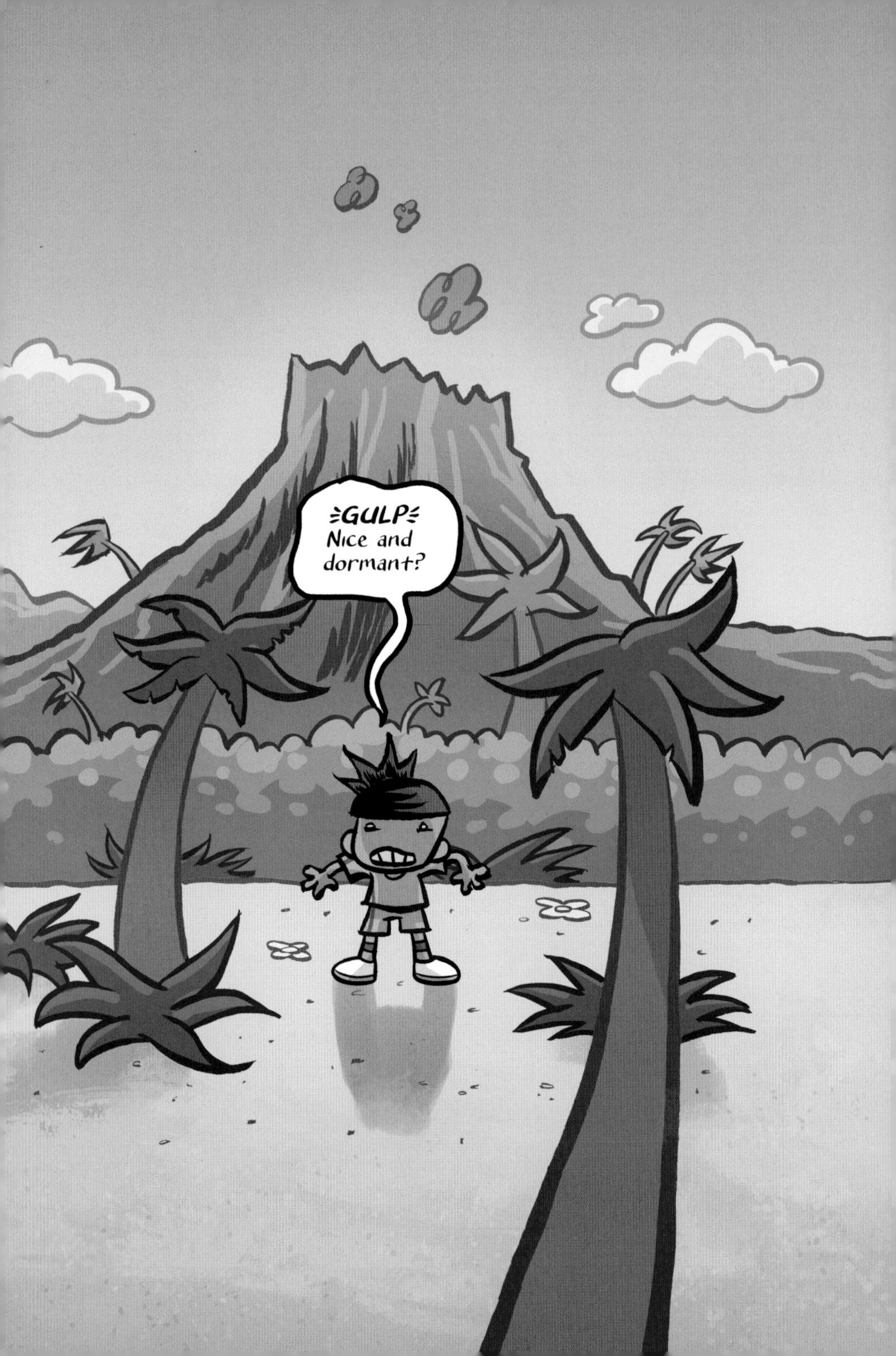
GULP
Nice and dormant?

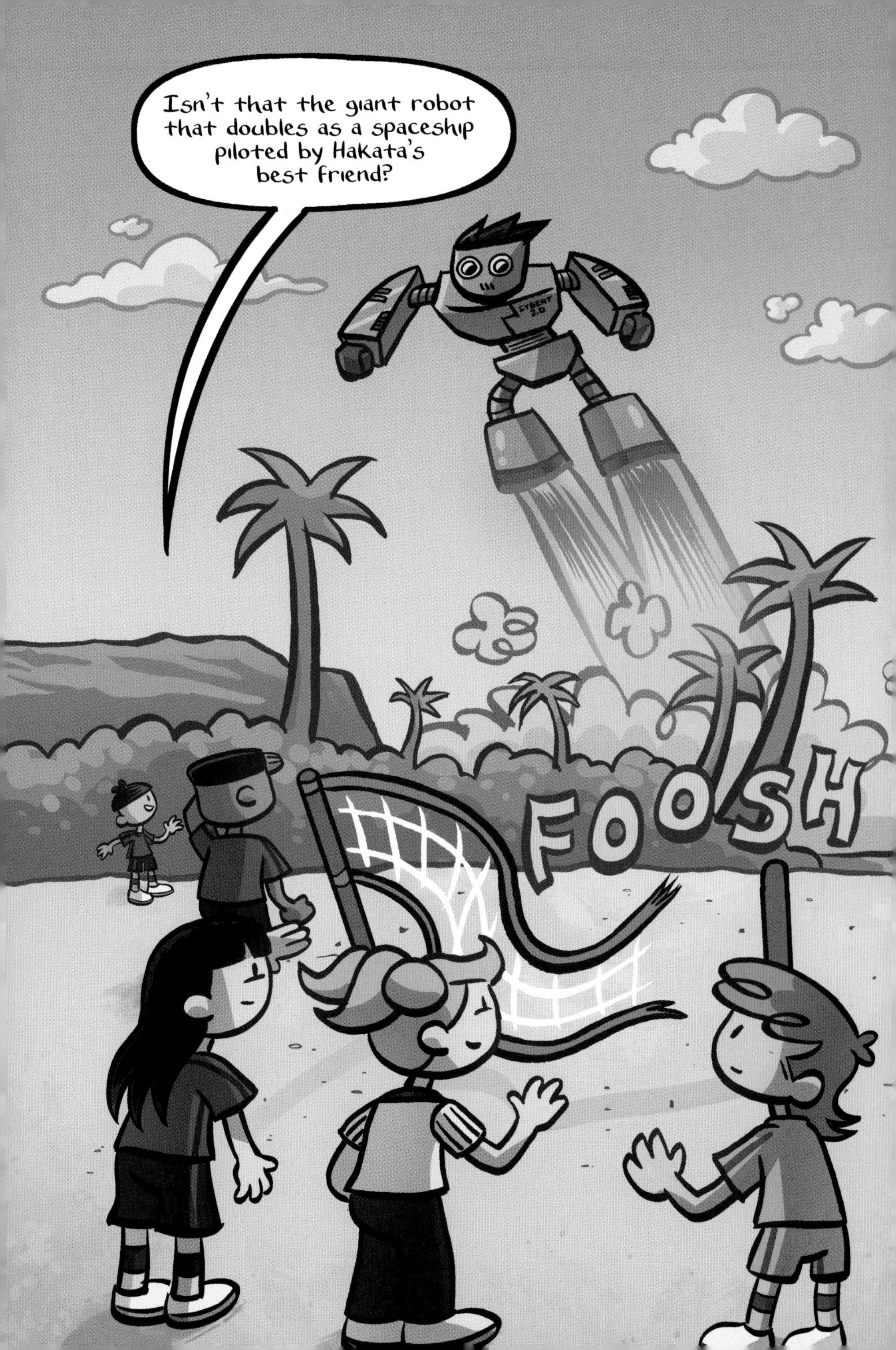
Isn't that the giant robot that doubles as a spaceship piloted by Hakata's best friend?
FOOSH

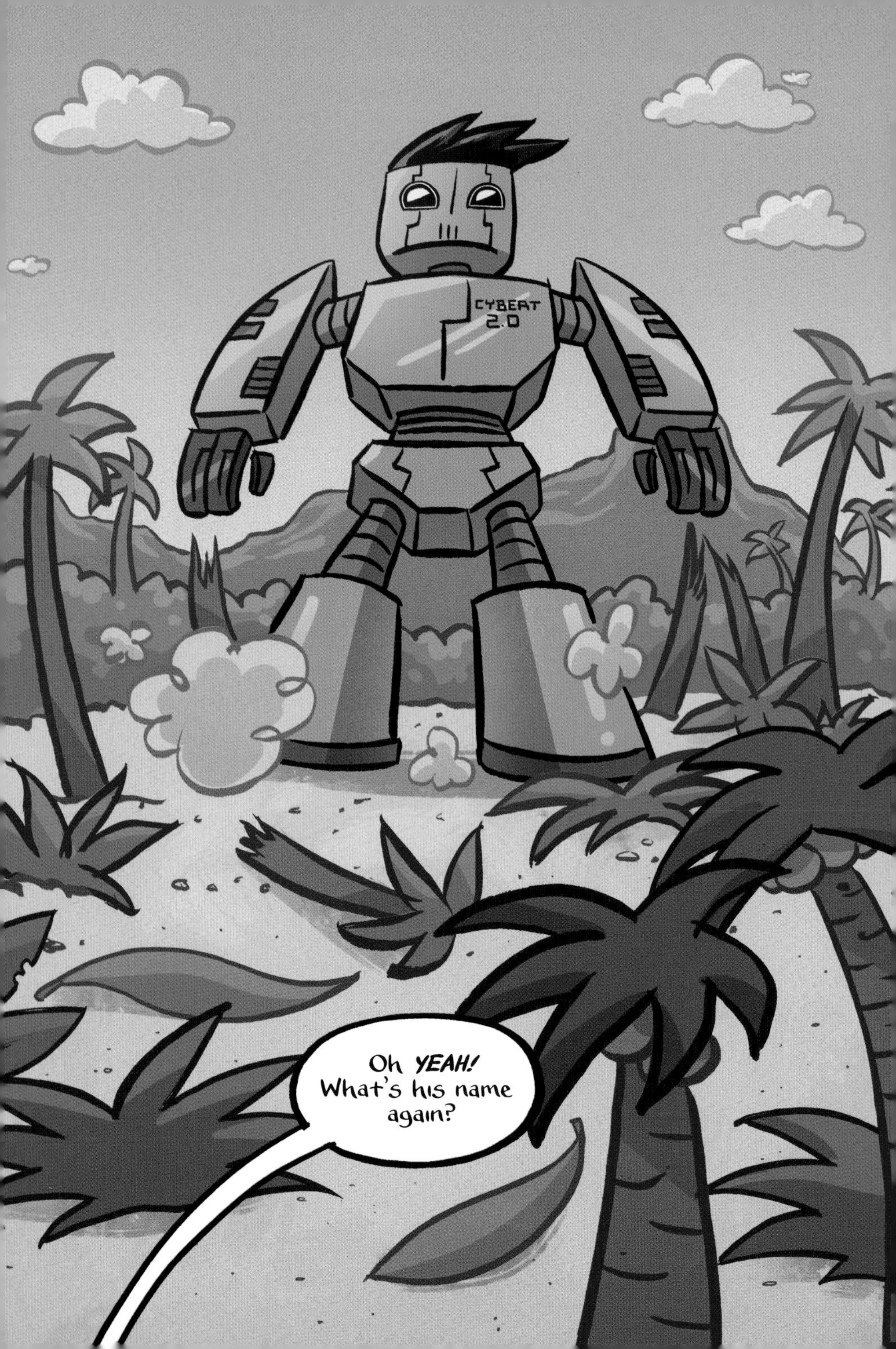
CYBEAT 2.0
Oh YEAH! What's his name again?

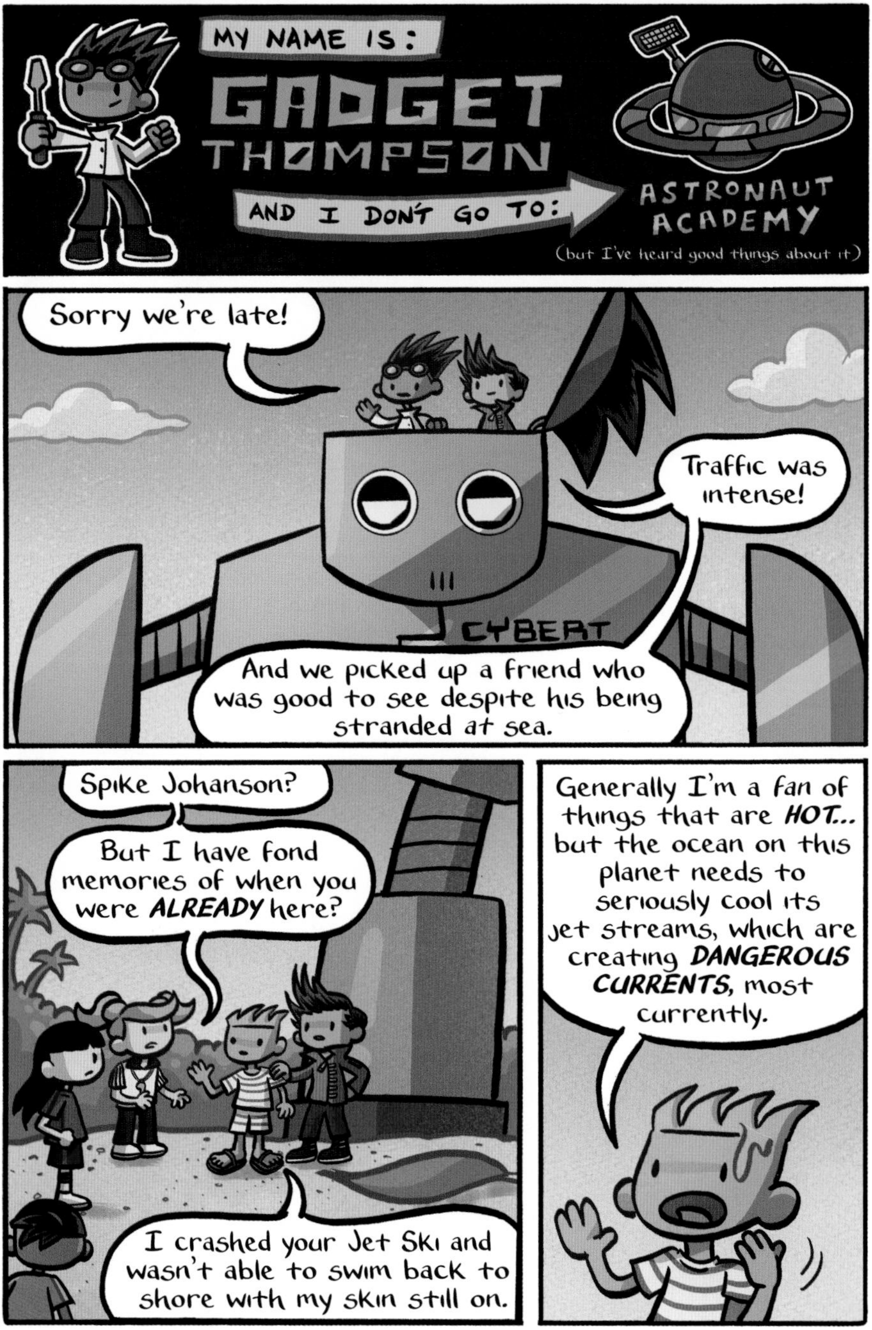
MY NAME IS:
GADGET THOMPSON
AND I DON'T GO TO:
ASTRONAUT ACADEMY
(but I've heard good things about it)
Sorry we're late!
Traffic was intense!
CYBERT
And we picked up a friend who was good to see despite his being stranded at sea.
Spike Johanson?
But I have fond memories of when you were ALREADY here?
I crashed your Jet Ski and wasn't able to swim back to shore with my skin still on.
Generally I'm a fan of things that are HOT... but the ocean on this planet needs to seriously cool its jet streams, which are creating DANGEROUS CURRENTS, most currently.

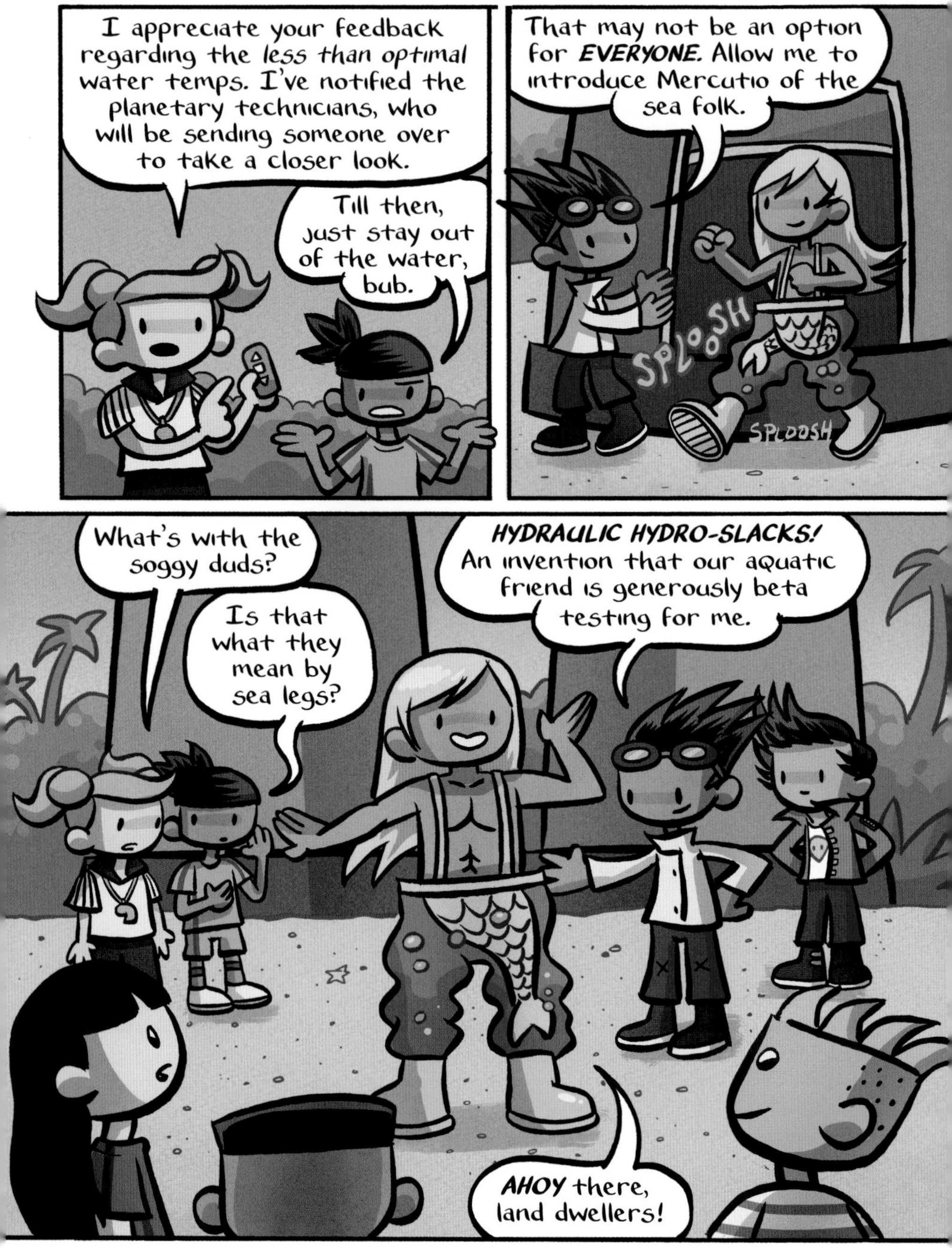

I appreciate your feedback regarding the *less than optimal* water temps. I've notified the planetary technicians, who will be sending someone over to take a closer look.
Till then, just stay out of the water, bub.
That may not be an option for ***EVERYONE.*** Allow me to introduce Mercutio of the sea folk.
SPLOOSH
SPLOOSH
What's with the soggy duds?
Is that what they mean by sea legs?
HYDRAULIC HYDRO-SLACKS! An invention that our aquatic friend is generously beta testing for me.
AHOY there, land dwellers!

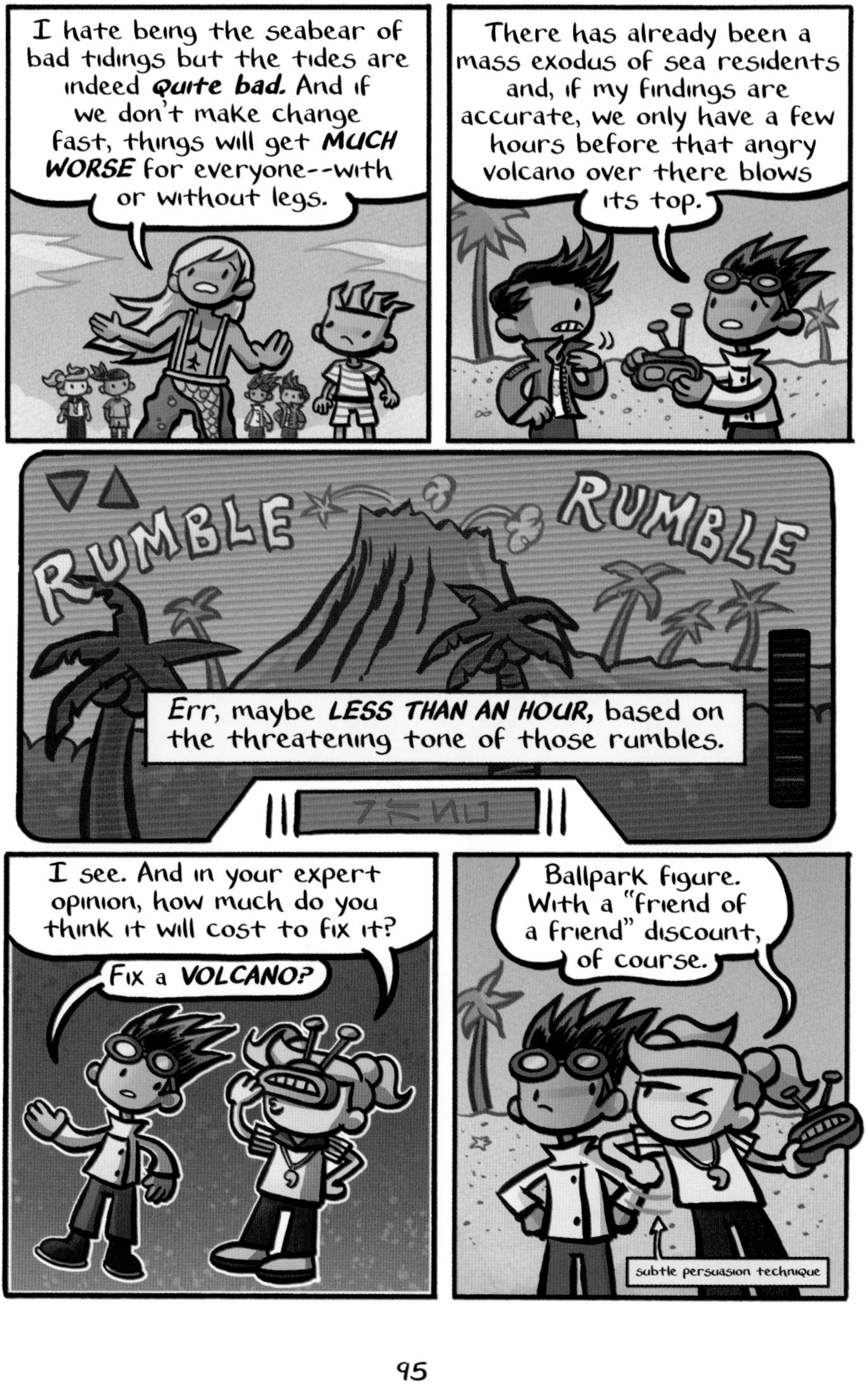
I hate being the seabear of bad tidings but the tides are indeed **Quite bad.** And if we don't make change fast, things will get **MUCH WORSE** for everyone--with or without legs.
There has already been a mass exodus of sea residents and, if my findings are accurate, we only have a few hours before that angry volcano over there blows its top.
RUMBLE
RUMBLE
Err, maybe **LESS THAN AN HOUR,** based on the threatening tone of those rumbles.
I see. And in your expert opinion, how much do you think it will cost to fix it?
Fix a **VOLCANO?**
Ballpark figure. With a "friend of a friend" discount, of course.
subtle persuasion technique

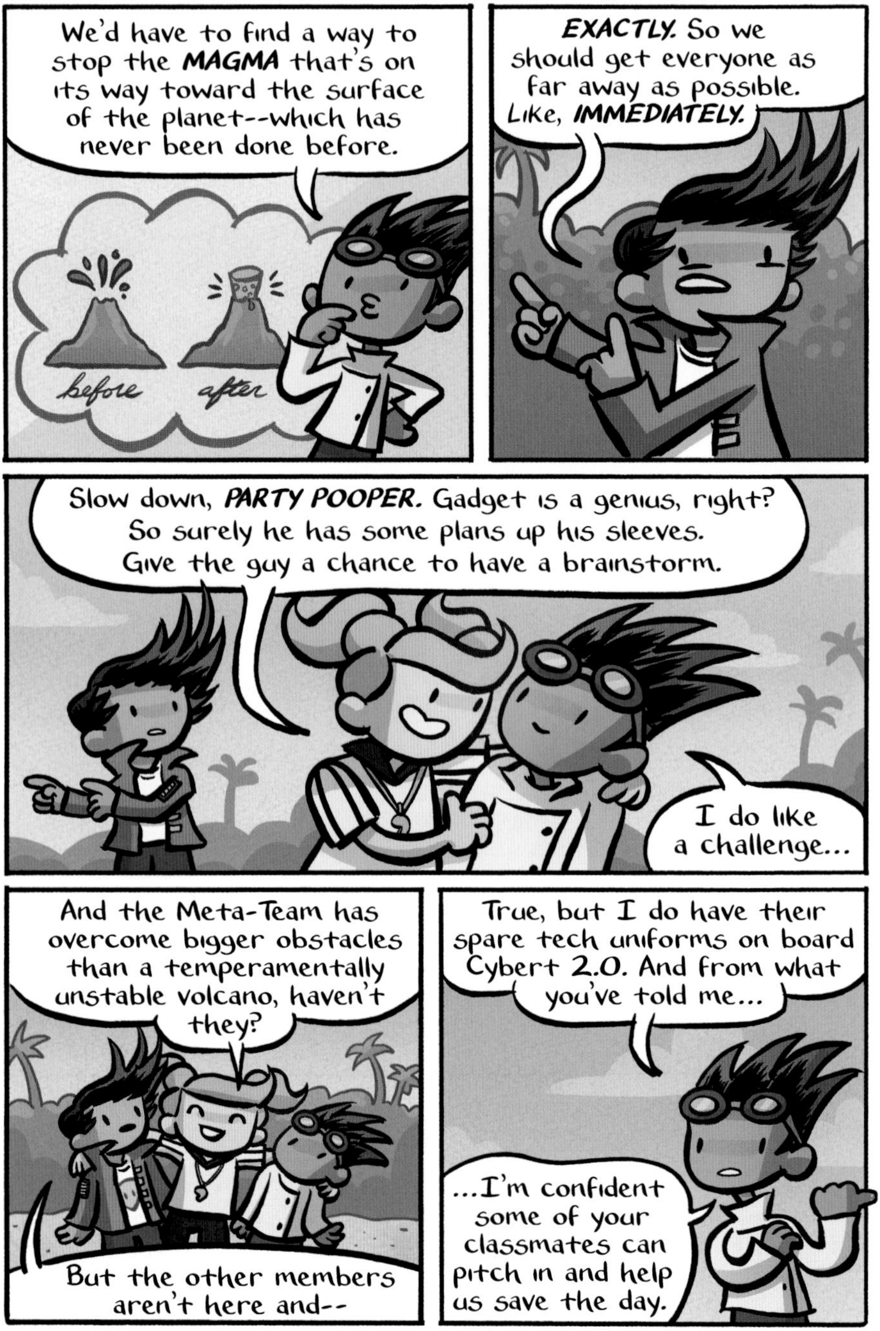
We'd have to find a way to stop the MAGMA that's on its way toward the surface of the planet--which has never been done before.
before
after
EXACTLY. So we should get everyone as far away as possible. Like, IMMEDIATELY.
Slow down, PARTY POOPER. Gadget is a genius, right? So surely he has some plans up his sleeves. Give the guy a chance to have a brainstorm.
I do like a challenge...
And the Meta-Team has overcome bigger obstacles than a temperamentally unstable volcano, haven't they?
But the other members aren't here and--
True, but I do have their spare tech uniforms on board Cybert 2.0. And from what you've told me...
...I'm confident some of your classmates can pitch in and help us save the day.

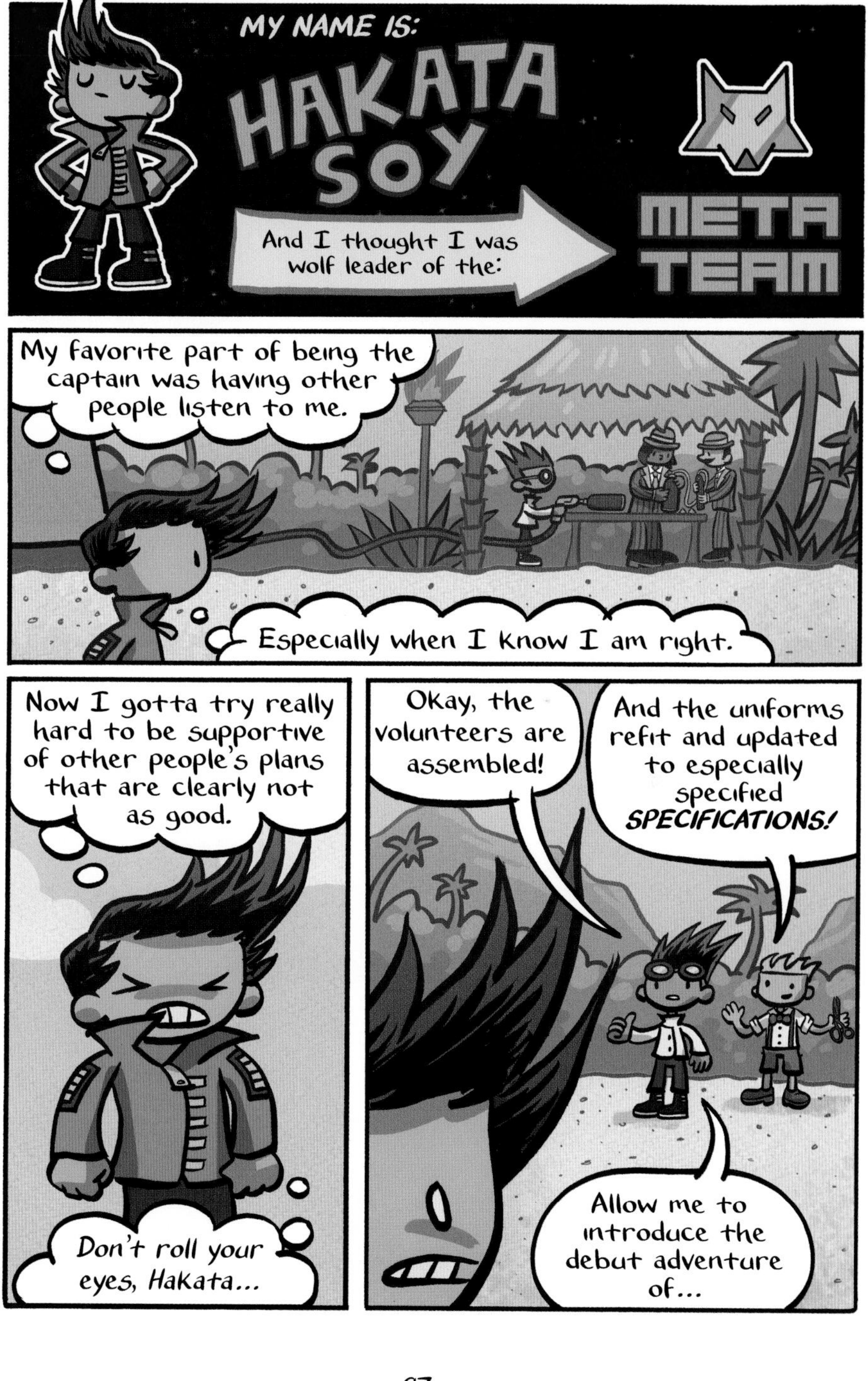
MY NAME IS:
HAKATA SOY
And I thought I was wolf leader of the:
META TEAM
My favorite part of being the captain was having other people listen to me.
Especially when I know I am right.
Now I gotta try really hard to be supportive of other people's plans that are clearly not as good.
Don't roll your eyes, Hakata...
Okay, the volunteers are assembled!
And the uniforms refit and updated to especially specified SPECIFICATIONS!
Allow me to introduce the debut adventure of...

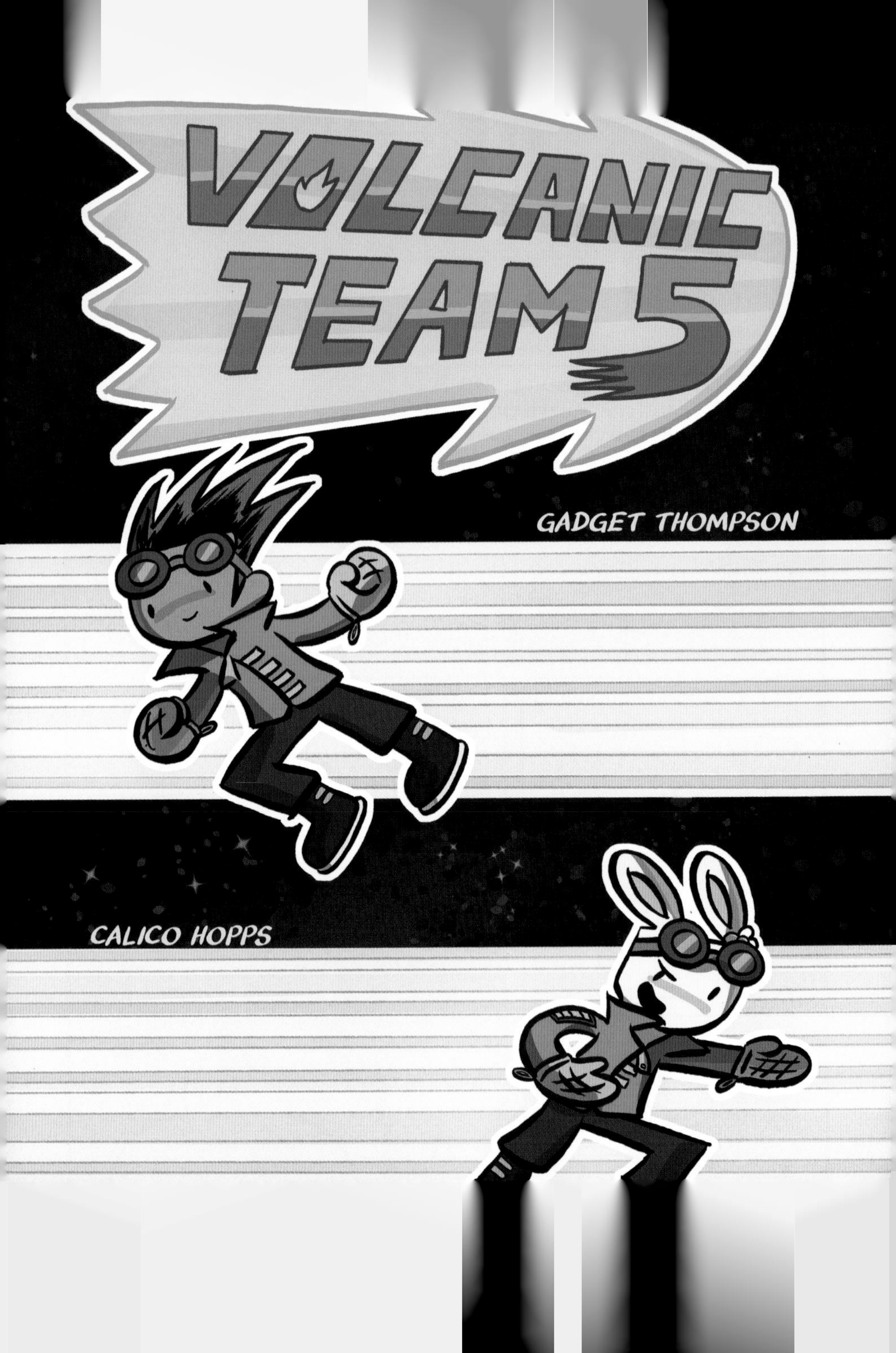
VOLCANIC TEAM 5
GADGET THOMPSON
CALICO HOPPS

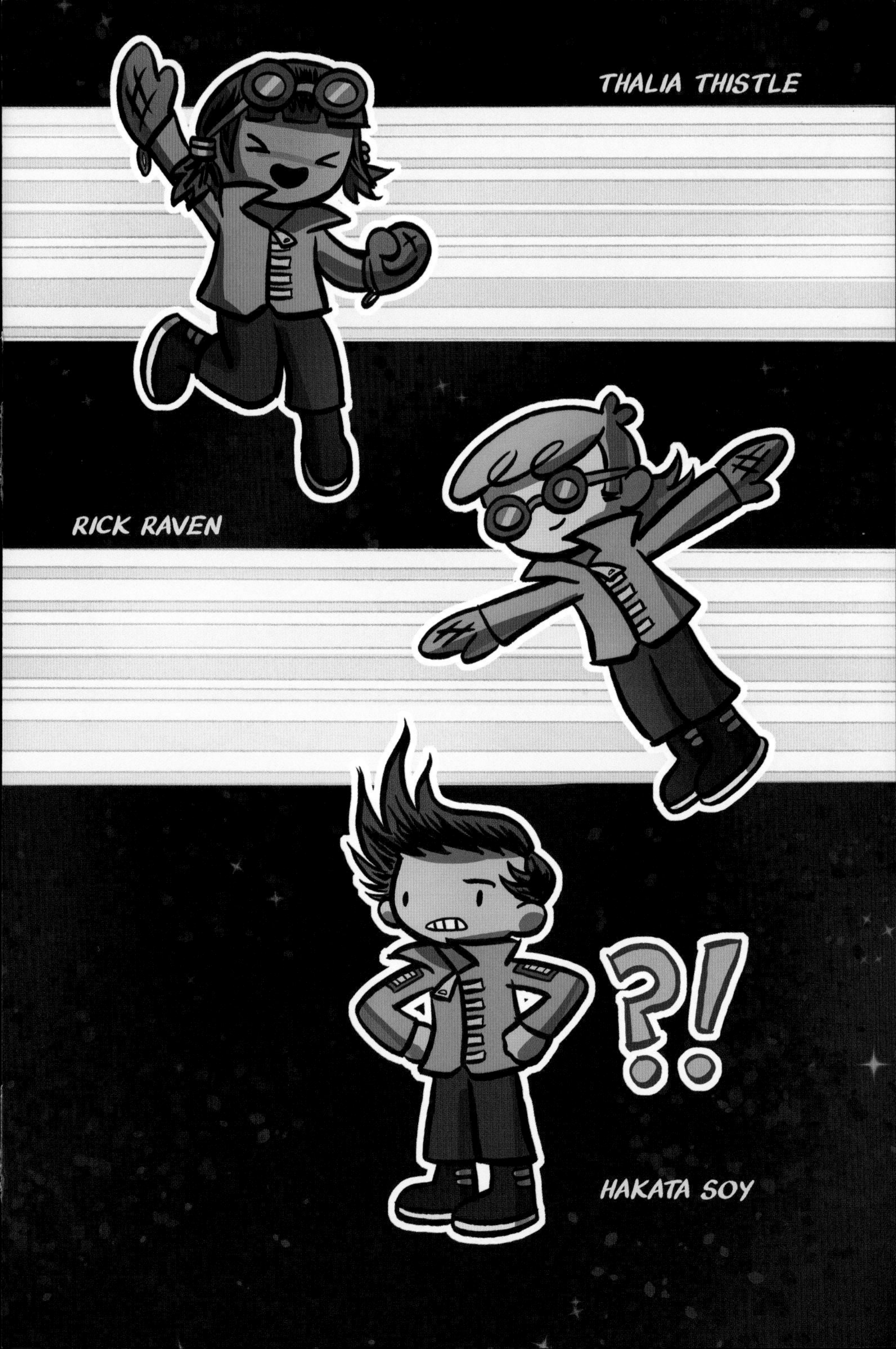
THALIA THISTLE
RICK RAVEN
?!
HAKATA SOY

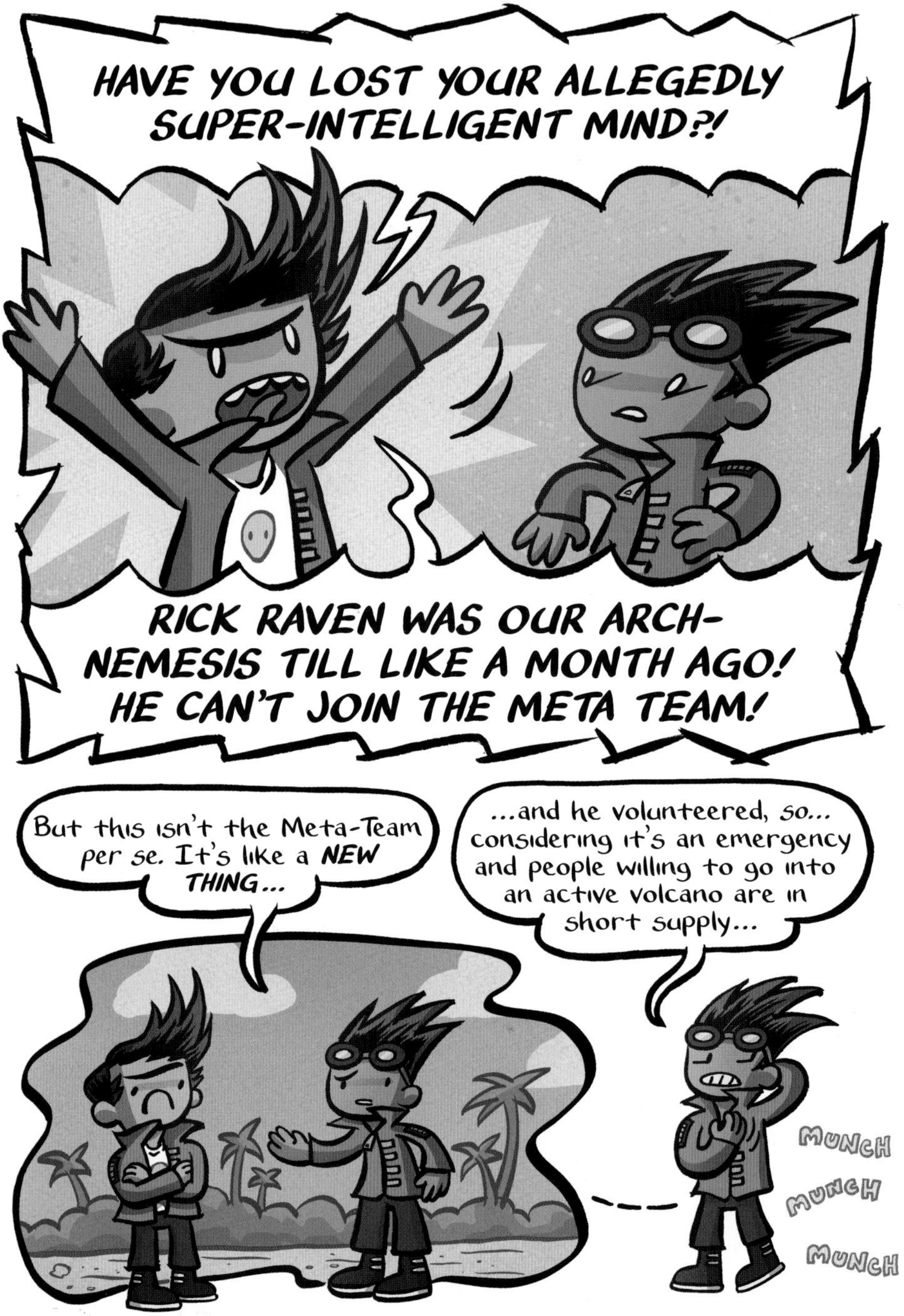
HAVE YOU LOST YOUR ALLEGEDLY SUPER-INTELLIGENT MIND?!
RICK RAVEN WAS OUR ARCH-NEMESIS TILL LIKE A MONTH AGO! HE CAN'T JOIN THE META TEAM!
But this isn't the Meta-Team per se. It's like a NEW THING...
...and he volunteered, so... considering it's an emergency and people willing to go into an active volcano are in short supply...
MUNCH
MUNCH
MUNCH

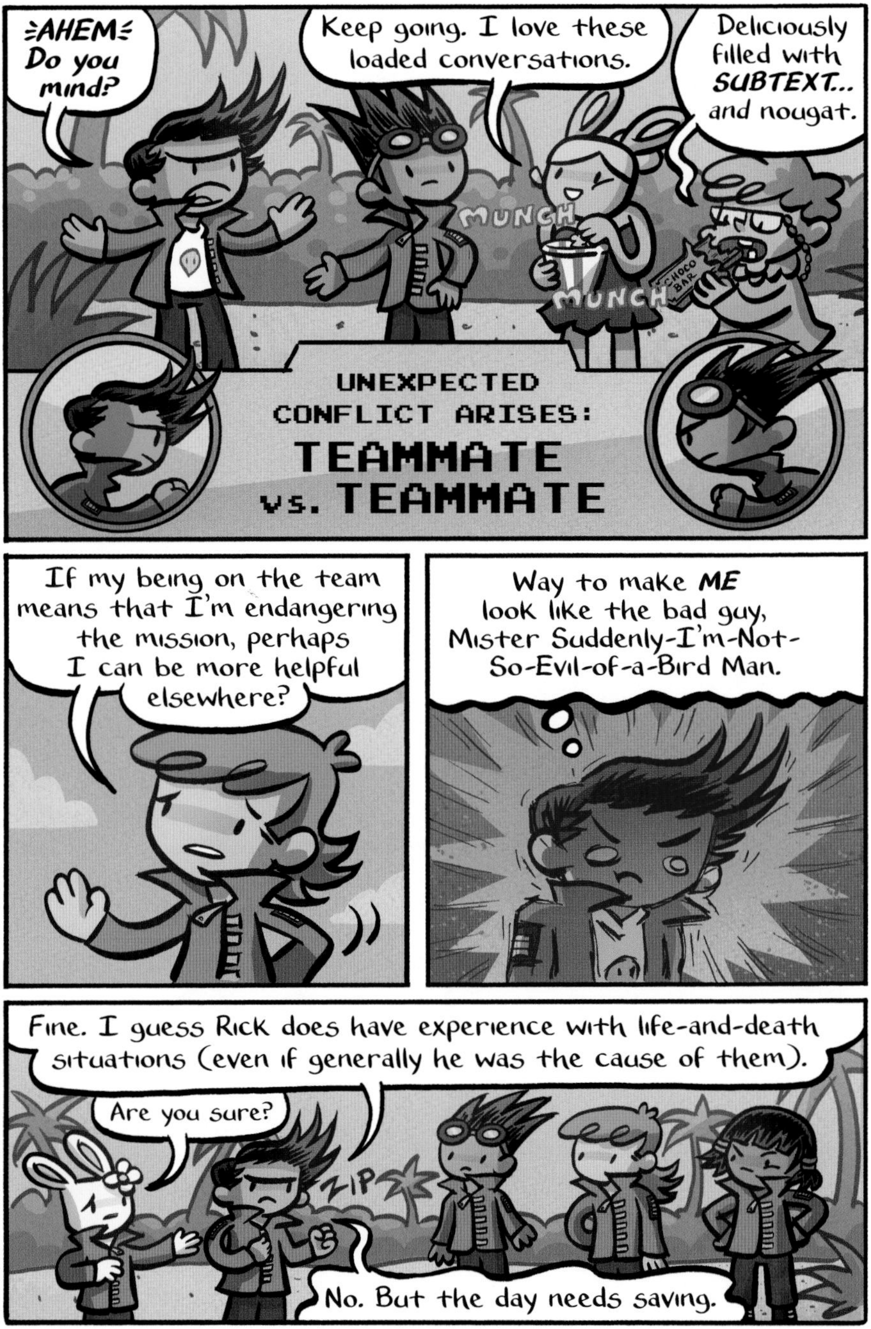
AHEM Do you mind?
Keep going. I love these loaded conversations.
Deliciously filled with SUBTEXT... and nougat.
MUNCH
MUNCH
CHOCO BAR
UNEXPECTED CONFLICT ARISES:
TEAMMATE vs. TEAMMATE
If my being on the team means that I'm endangering the mission, perhaps I can be more helpful elsewhere?
Way to make ME look like the bad guy, Mister Suddenly-I'm-Not-So-Evil-of-a-Bird Man.
Fine. I guess Rick does have experience with life-and-death situations (even if generally he was the cause of them).
Are you sure?
ZIP
No. But the day needs saving.

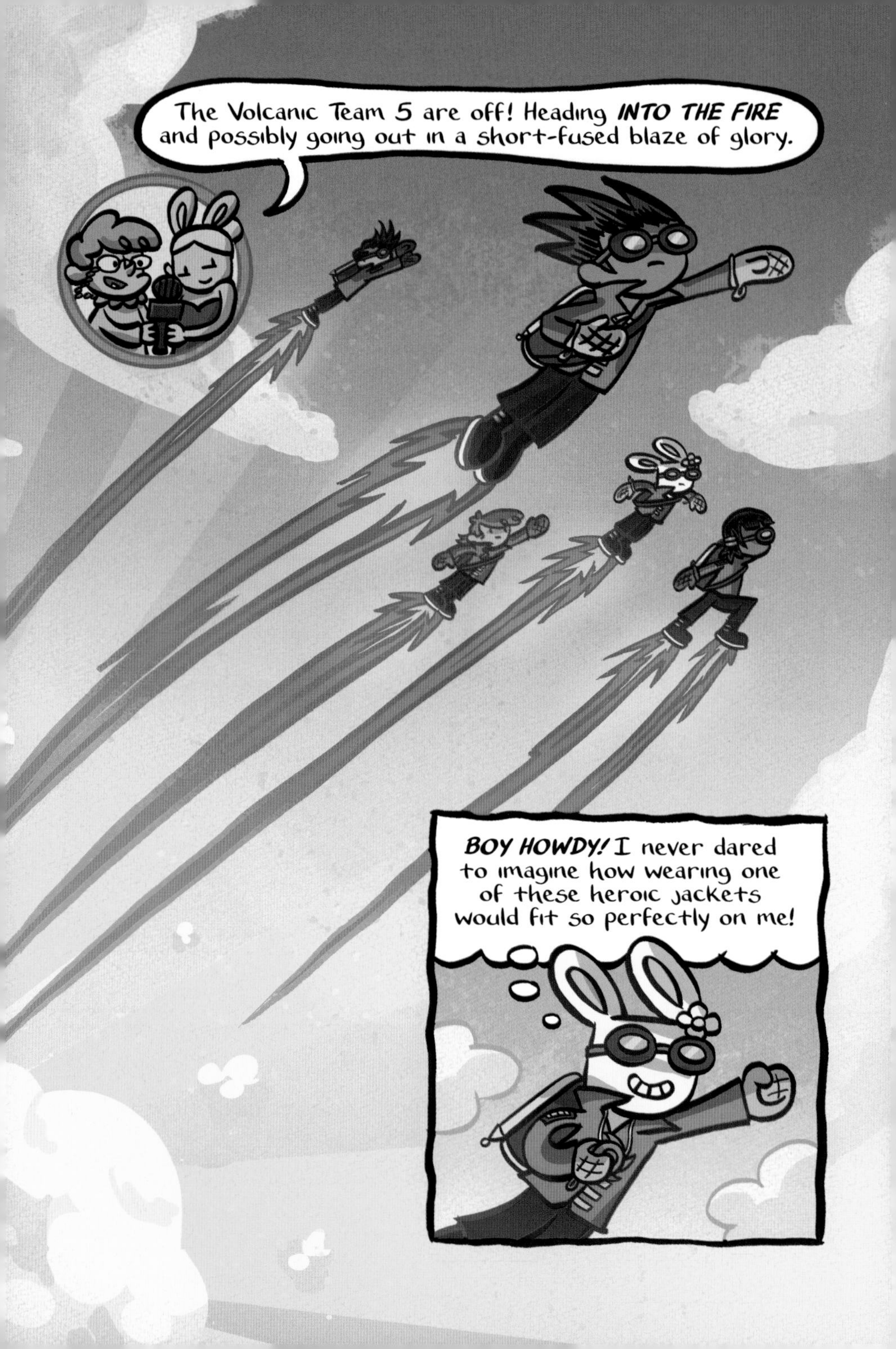
The Volcanic Team 5 are off! Heading ***INTO THE FIRE*** and possibly going out in a short-fused blaze of glory.
BOY HOWDY! I never dared to imagine how wearing one of these heroic jackets would fit so perfectly on me!

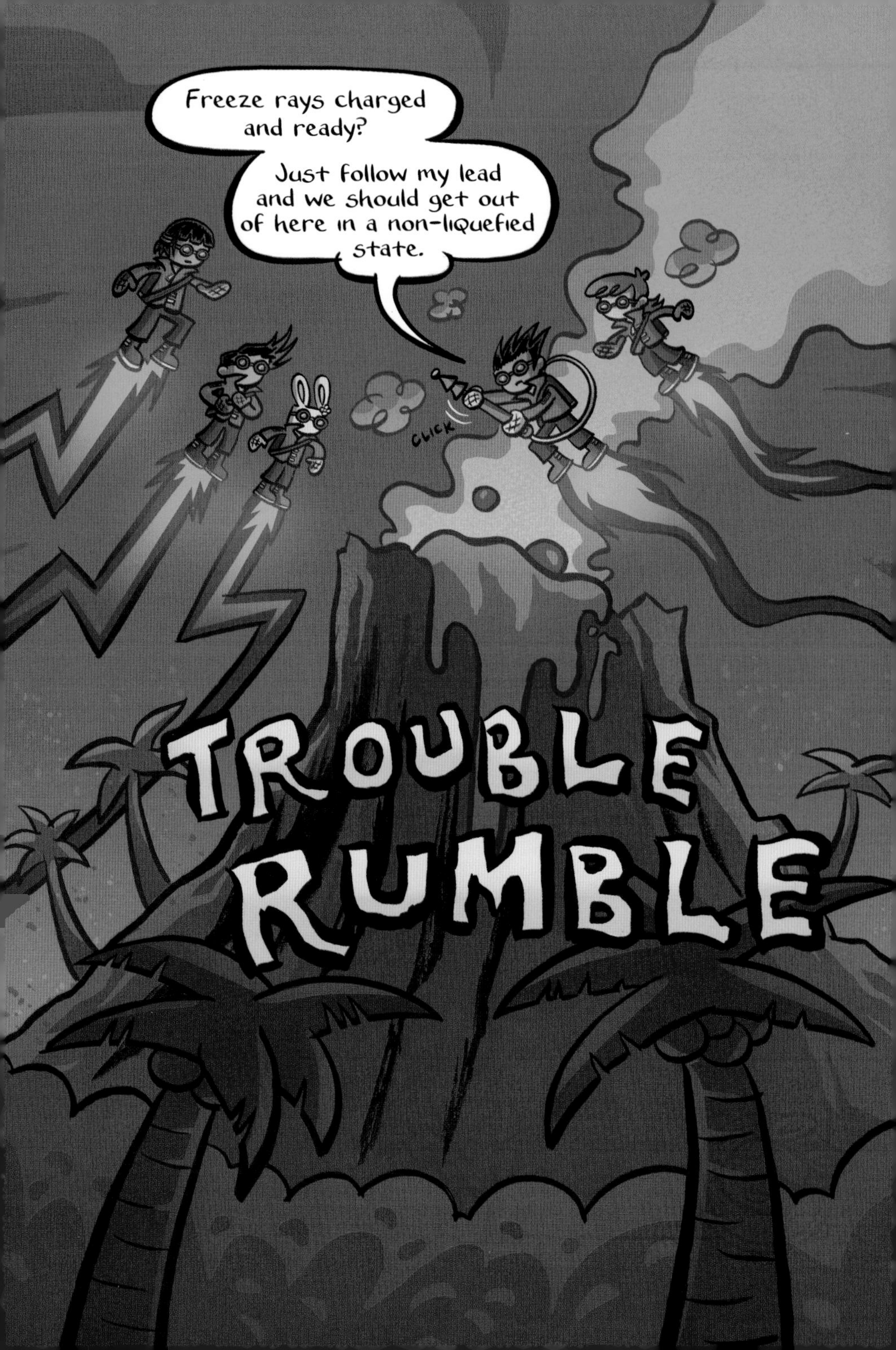
Freeze rays charged and ready?
Just follow my lead and we should get out of here in a non-liquefied state.
CLICK
TROUBLE RUMBLE

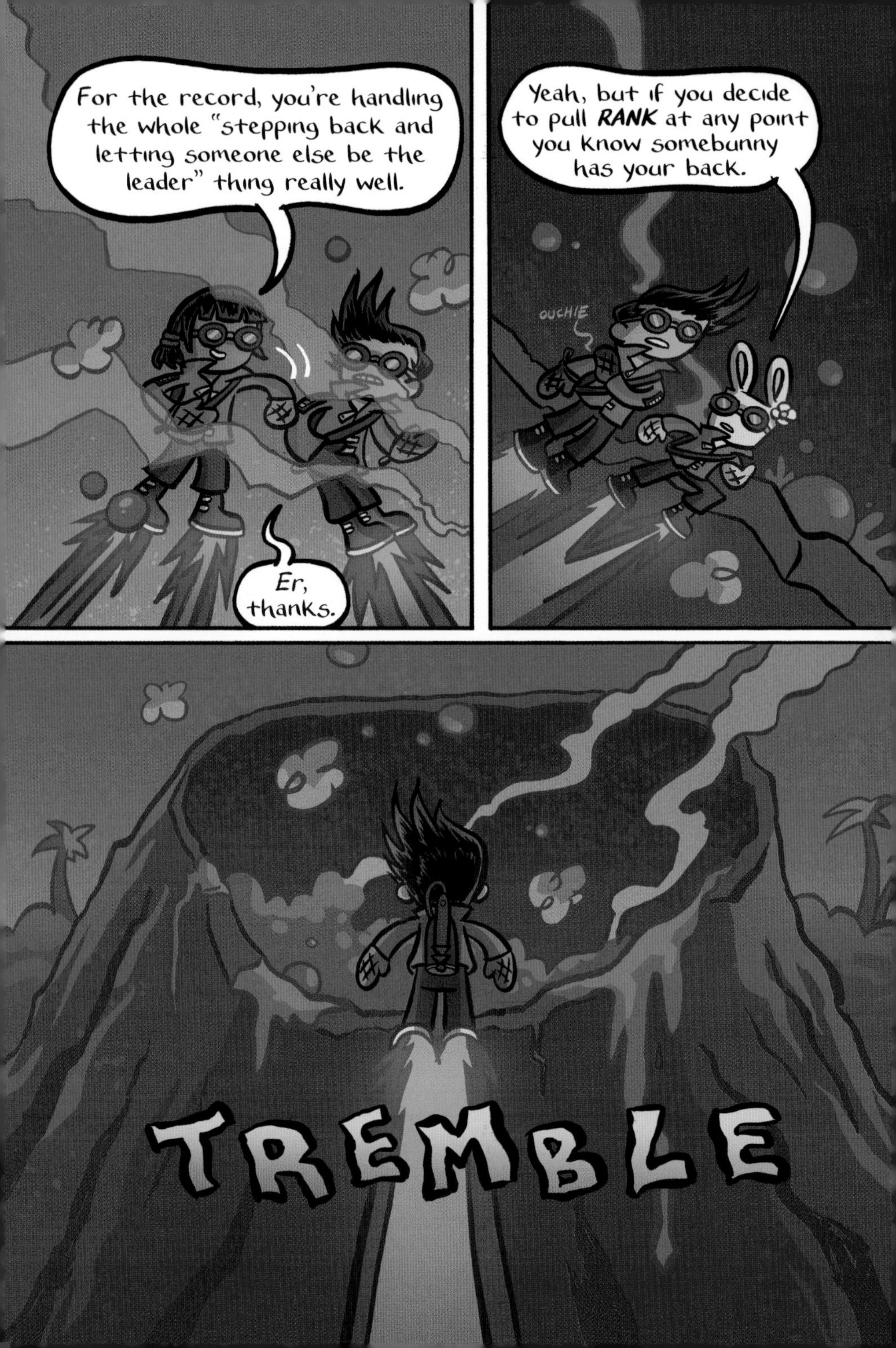
For the record, you're handling the whole "stepping back and letting someone else be the leader" thing really well.
Er, thanks.
OUCHIE
Yeah, but if you decide to pull ***RANK*** at any point you know somebunny has your back.
TREMBLE

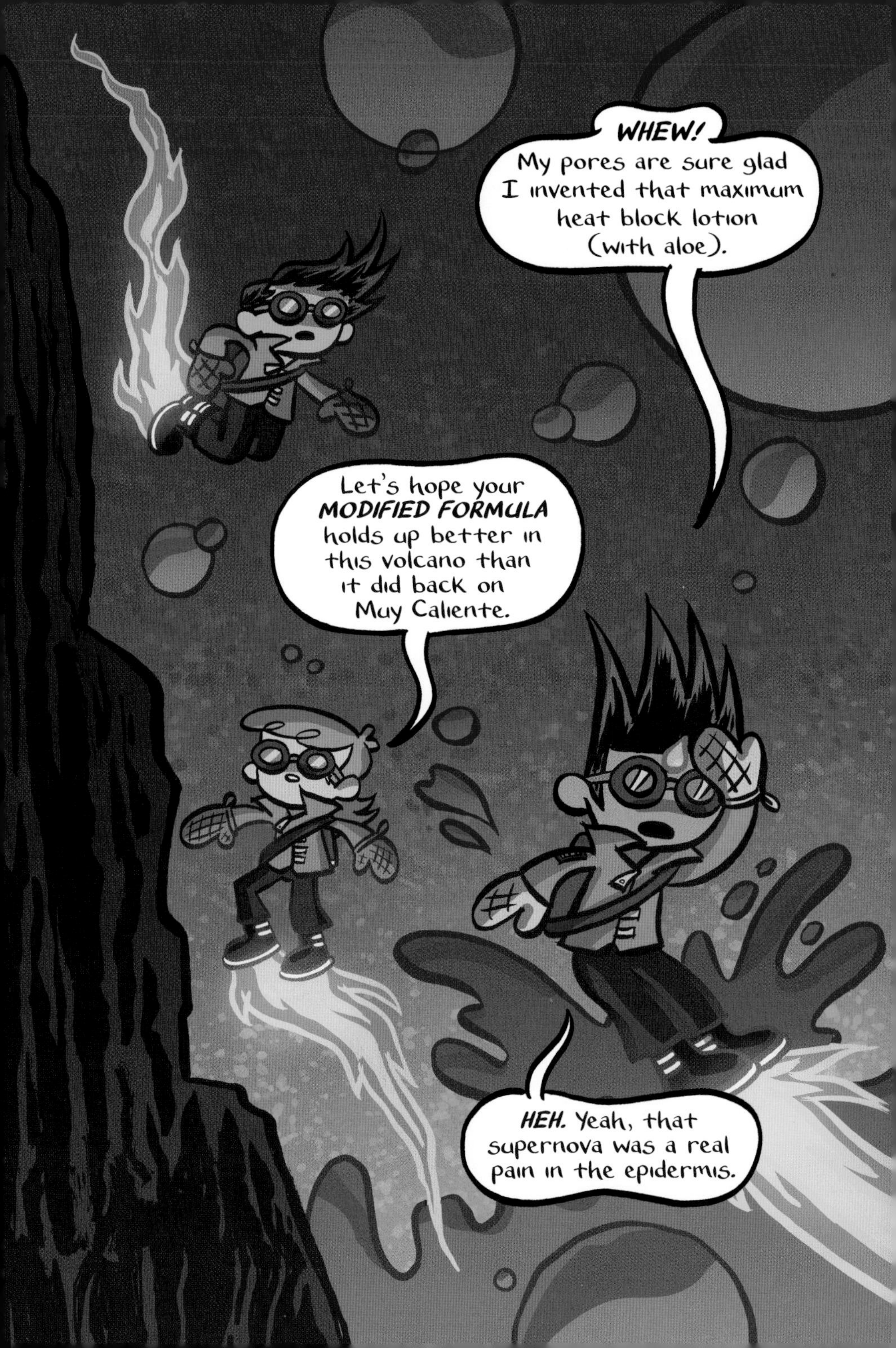
WHEW! My pores are sure glad I invented that maximum heat block lotion (with aloe).
Let's hope your MODIFIED FORMULA holds up better in this volcano than it did back on Muy Caliente.
HEH. Yeah, that supernova was a real pain in the epidermis.

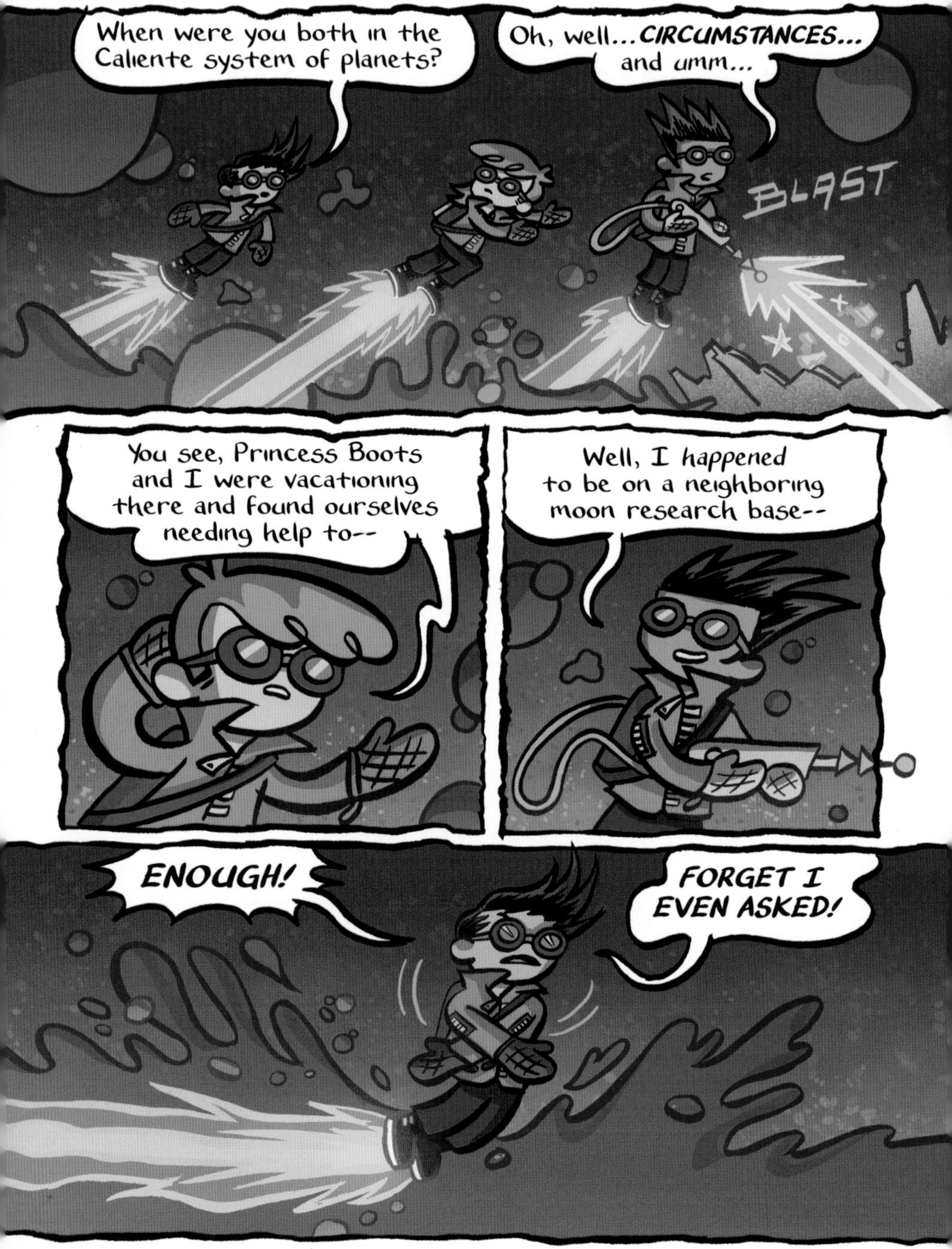
When were you both in the Caliente system of planets?
Oh, well... CIRCUMSTANCES... and umm...
BLAST
You see, Princess Boots and I were vacationing there and found ourselves needing help to--
Well, I happened to be on a neighboring moon research base--
ENOUGH!
FORGET I EVEN ASKED!

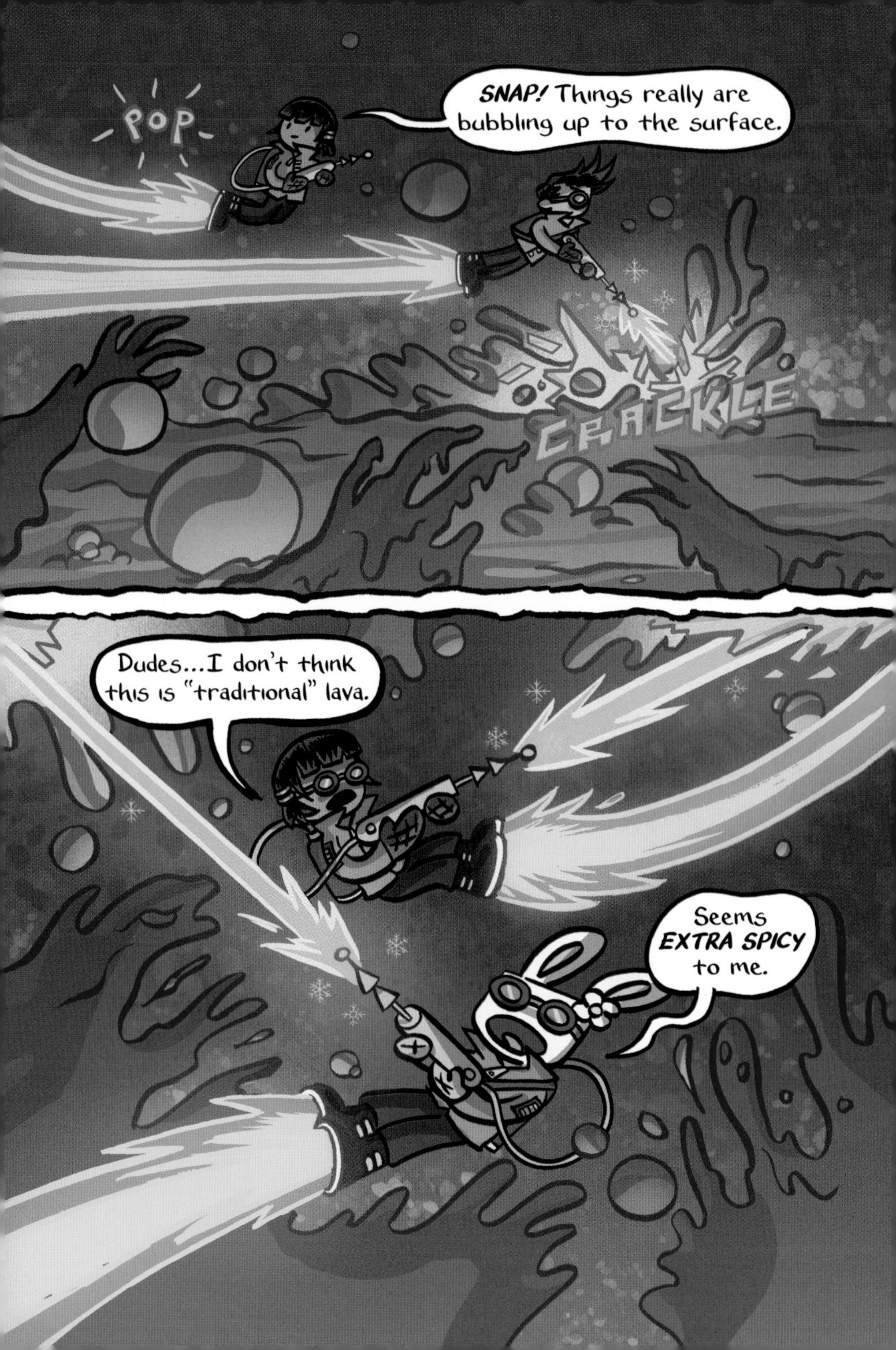
POP
SNAP! Things really are bubbling up to the surface.
CRACKLE
Dudes...I don't think this is "traditional" lava.
Seems EXTRA SPICY to me.

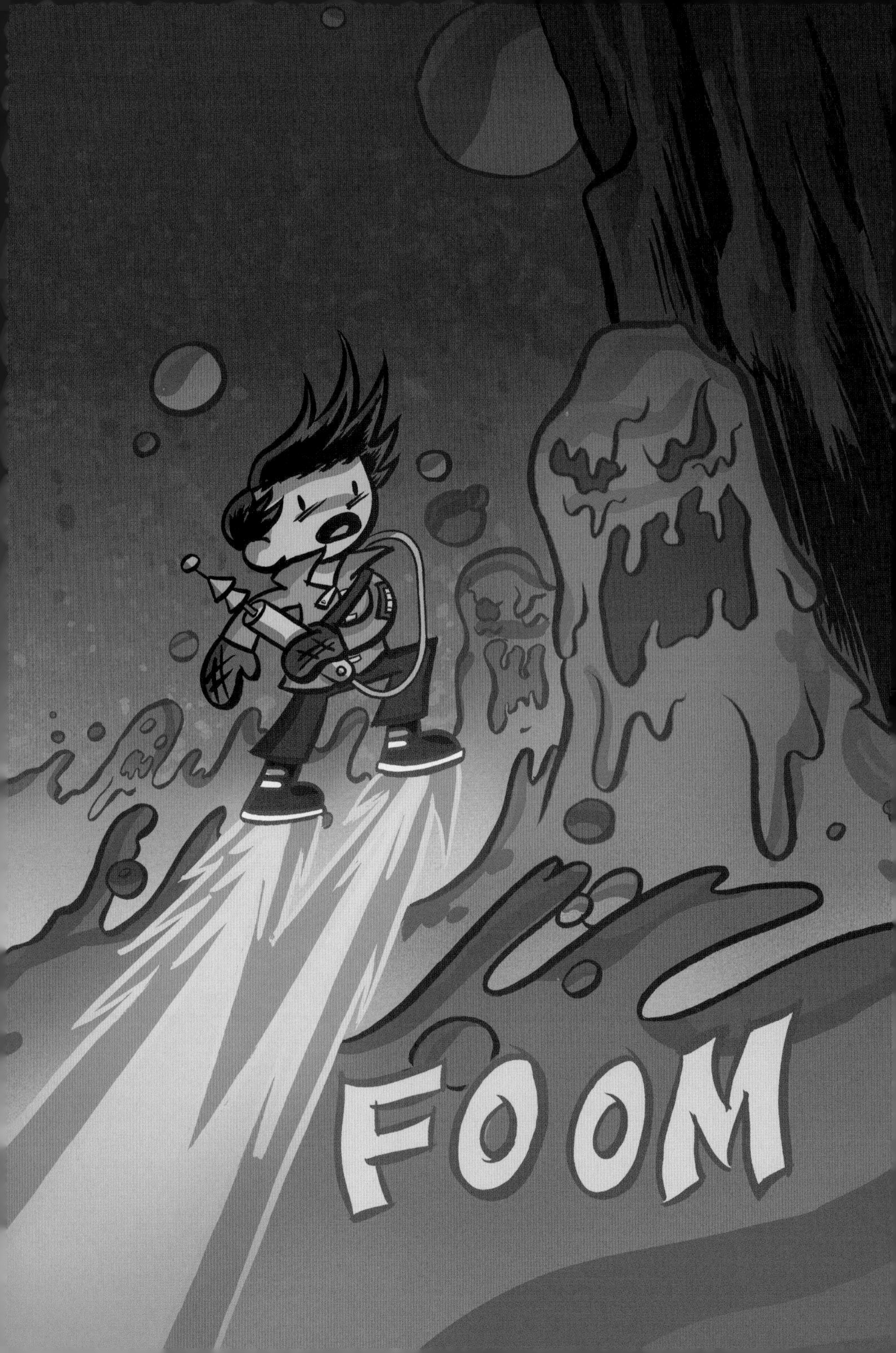
FOOM

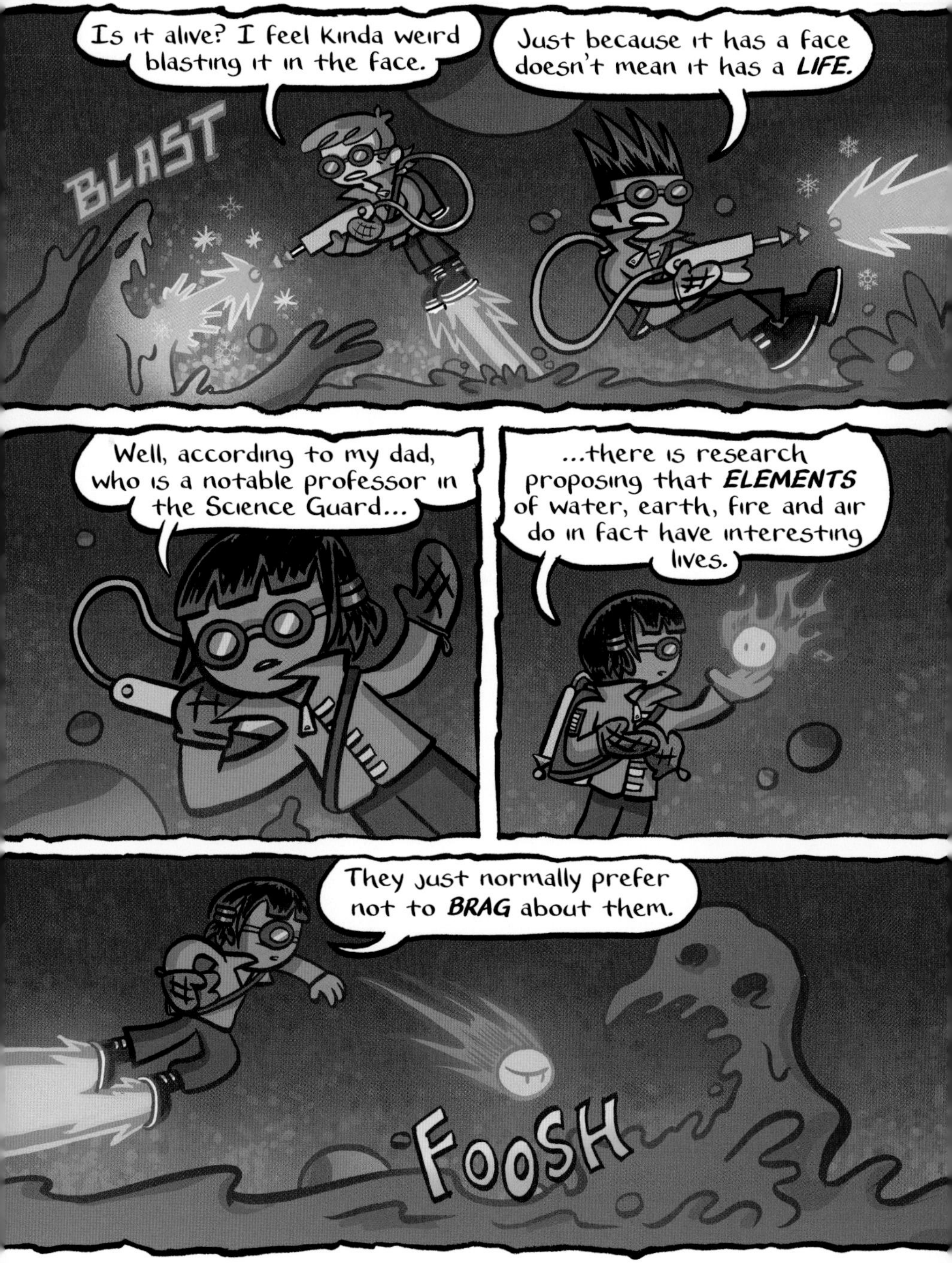
Is it alive? I feel kinda weird blasting it in the face.
Just because it has a face doesn't mean it has a LIFE.
BLAST
Well, according to my dad, who is a notable professor in the Science Guard...
...there is research proposing that ELEMENTS of water, earth, fire and air do in fact have interesting lives.
They just normally prefer not to BRAG about them.
FOOSH

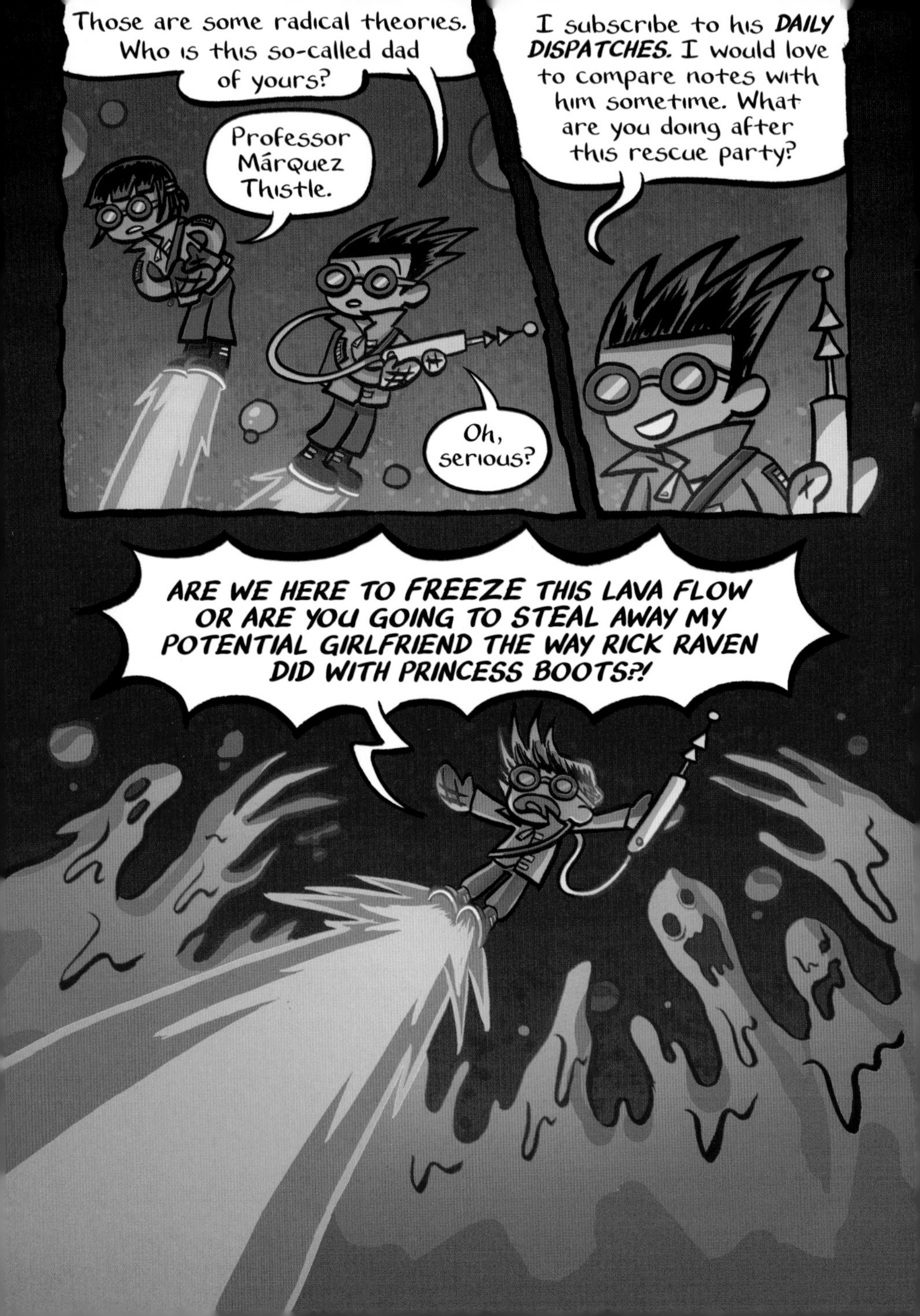
Those are some radical theories. Who is this so-called dad of yours?
Professor Márquez Thistle.
Oh, serious?
I subscribe to his DAILY DISPATCHES. I would love to compare notes with him sometime. What are you doing after this rescue party?
ARE WE HERE TO FREEZE THIS LAVA FLOW OR ARE YOU GOING TO STEAL AWAY MY POTENTIAL GIRLFRIEND THE WAY RICK RAVEN DID WITH PRINCESS BOOTS?!

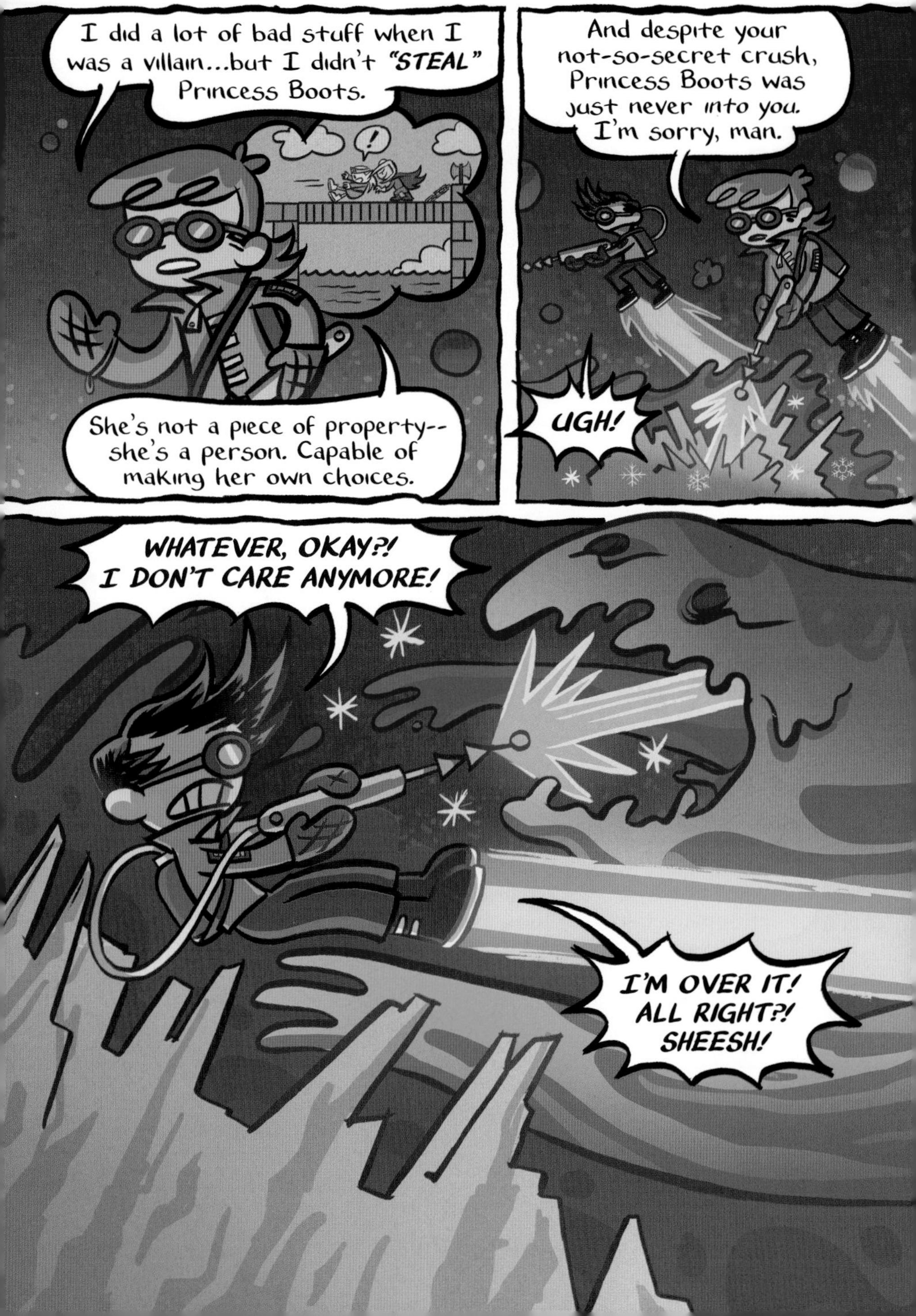
I did a lot of bad stuff when I was a villain...but I didn't "STEAL" Princess Boots.
!
She's not a piece of property--she's a person. Capable of making her own choices.
And despite your not-so-secret crush, Princess Boots was just never into you. I'm sorry, man.
UGH!
WHATEVER, OKAY?! I DON'T CARE ANYMORE!
I'M OVER IT! ALL RIGHT?! SHEESH!

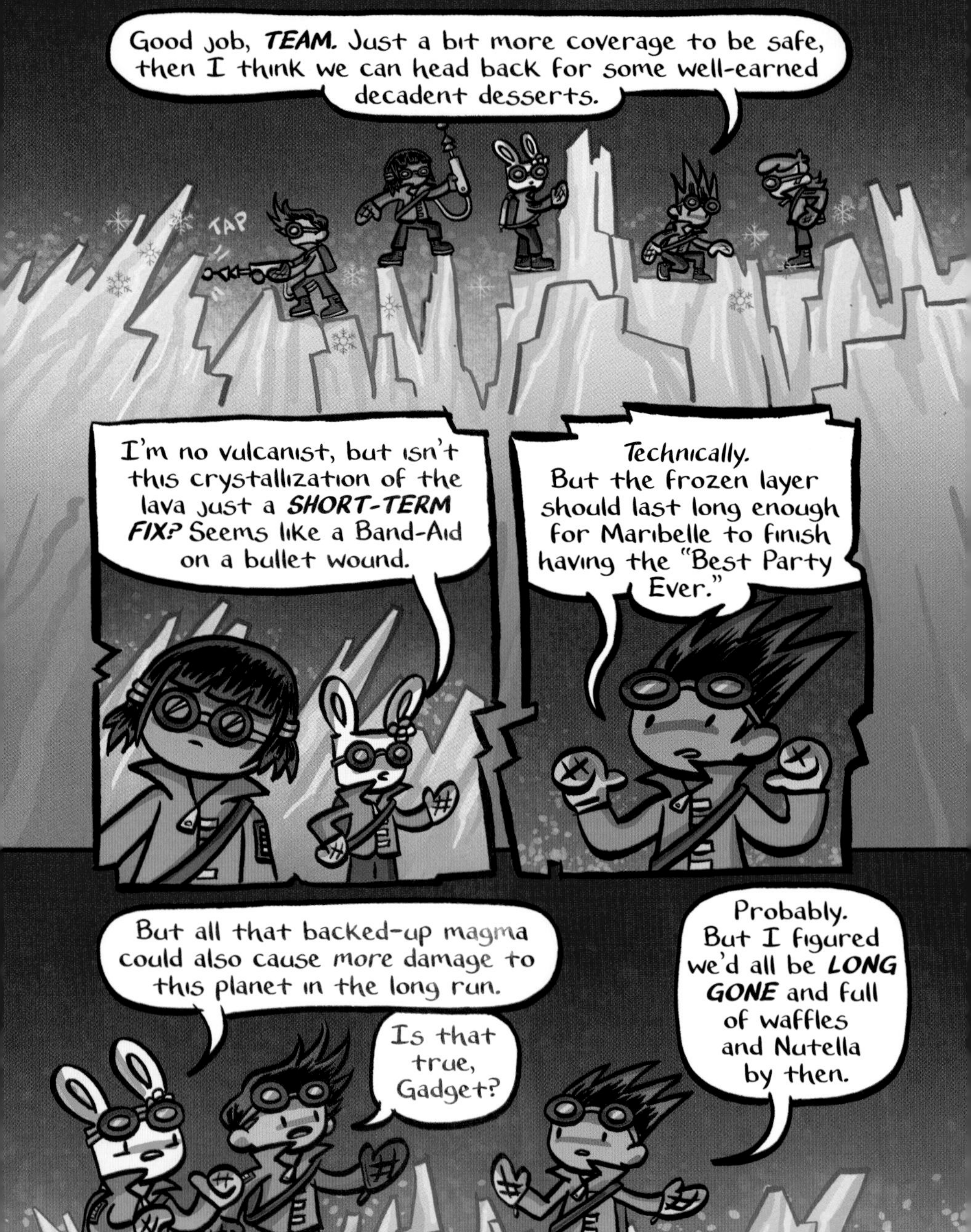

Good job, TEAM. Just a bit more coverage to be safe, then I think we can head back for some well-earned decadent desserts.
TAP
I'm no vulcanist, but isn't this crystallization of the lava just a SHORT-TERM FIX? Seems like a Band-Aid on a bullet wound.
Technically. But the frozen layer should last long enough for Maribelle to finish having the "Best Party Ever."
But all that backed-up magma could also cause more damage to this planet in the long run.
Is that true, Gadget?
Probably. But I figured we'd all be LONG GONE and full of waffles and Nutella by then.

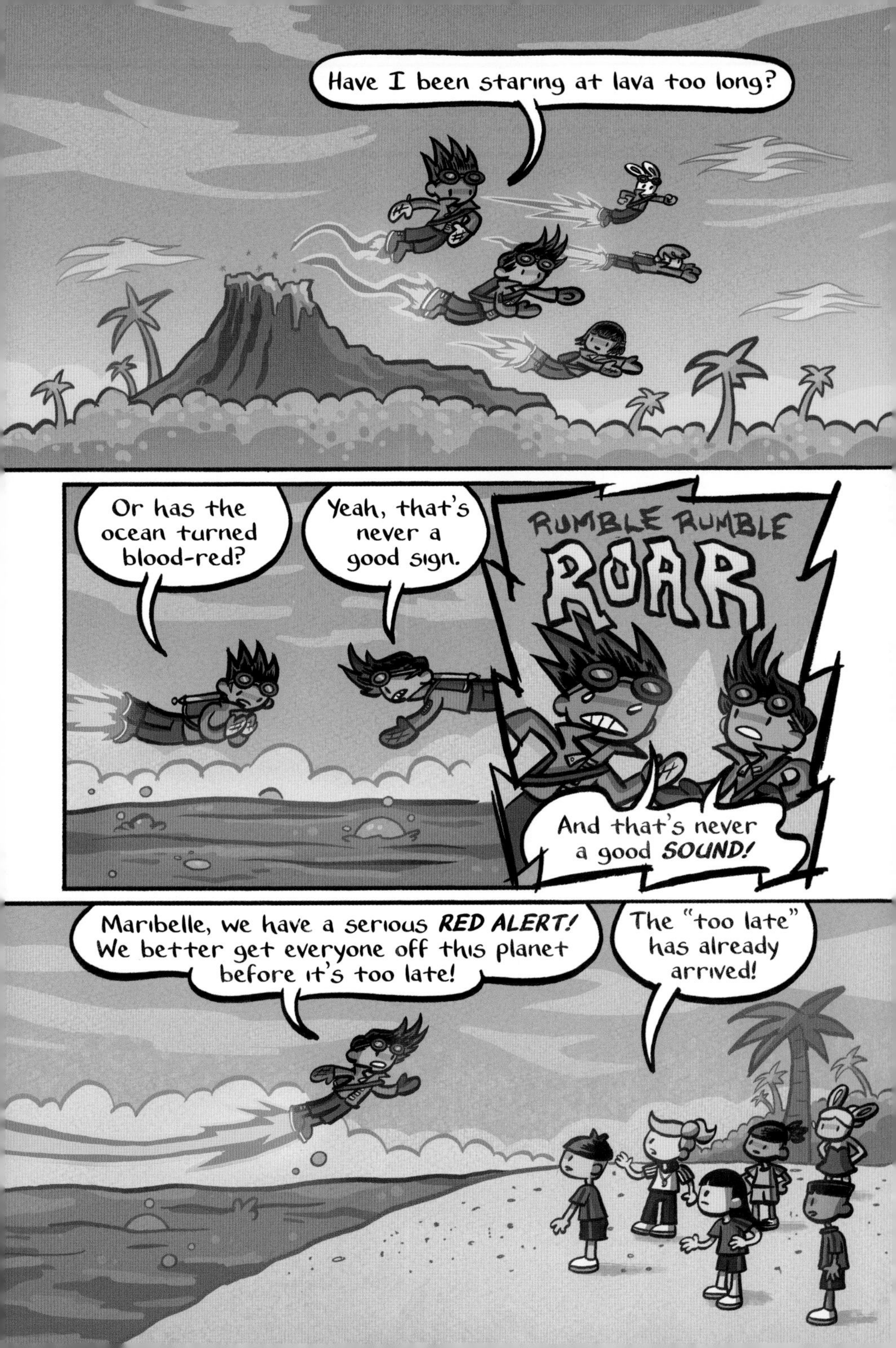
Have I been staring at lava too long?
Or has the ocean turned blood-red?
Yeah, that's never a good sign.
RUMBLE RUMBLE
ROAR
And that's never a good SOUND!
Maribelle, we have a serious RED ALERT! We better get everyone off this planet before it's too late!
The "too late" has already arrived!

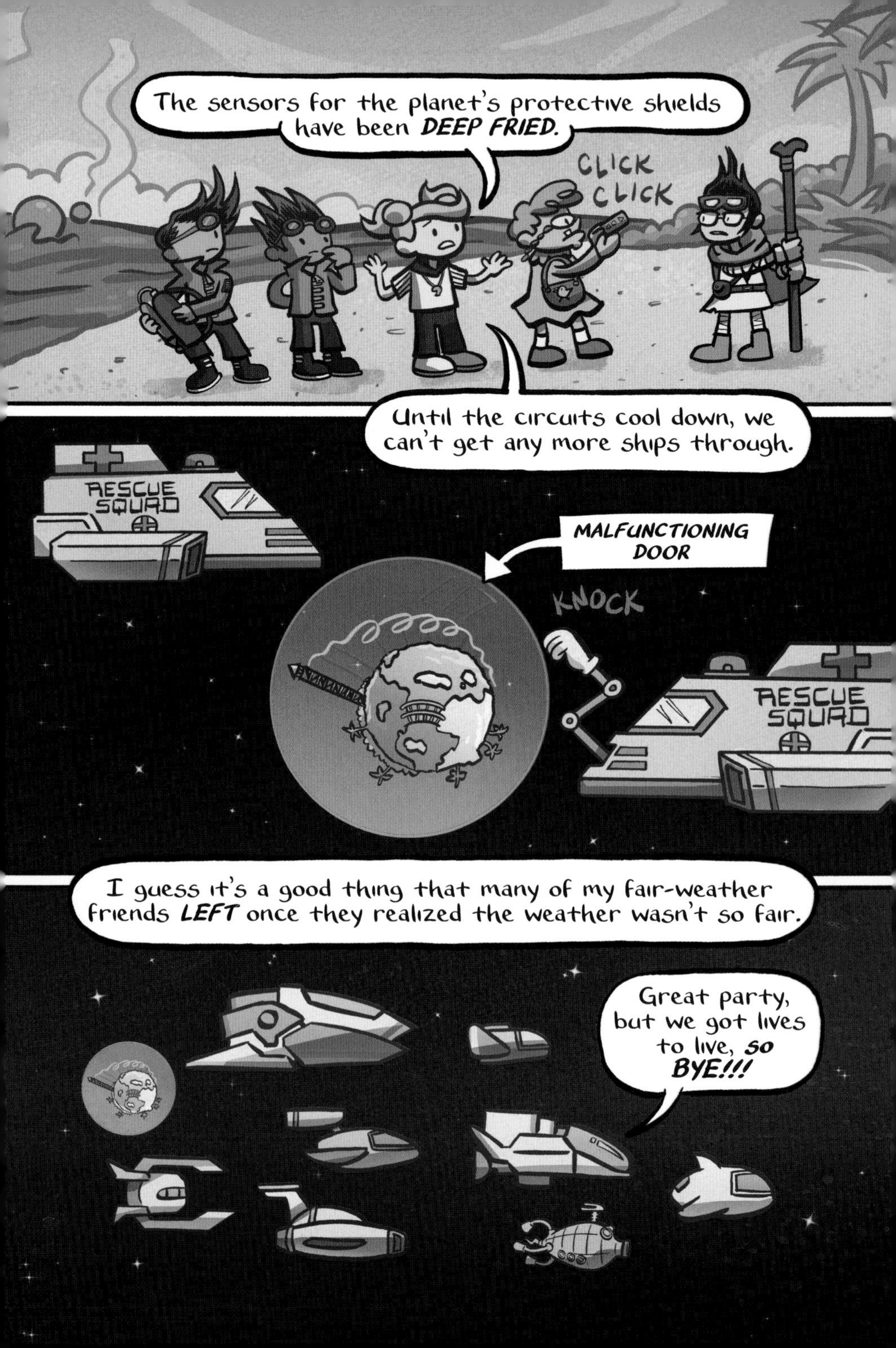
The sensors for the planet's protective shields have been DEEP FRIED.
CLICK CLICK
Until the circuits cool down, we can't get any more ships through.
RESCUE SQUAD
MALFUNCTIONING DOOR
KNOCK
RESCUE SQUAD
I guess it's a good thing that many of my fair-weather friends LEFT once they realized the weather wasn't so fair.
Great party, but we got lives to live, SO BYE!!!

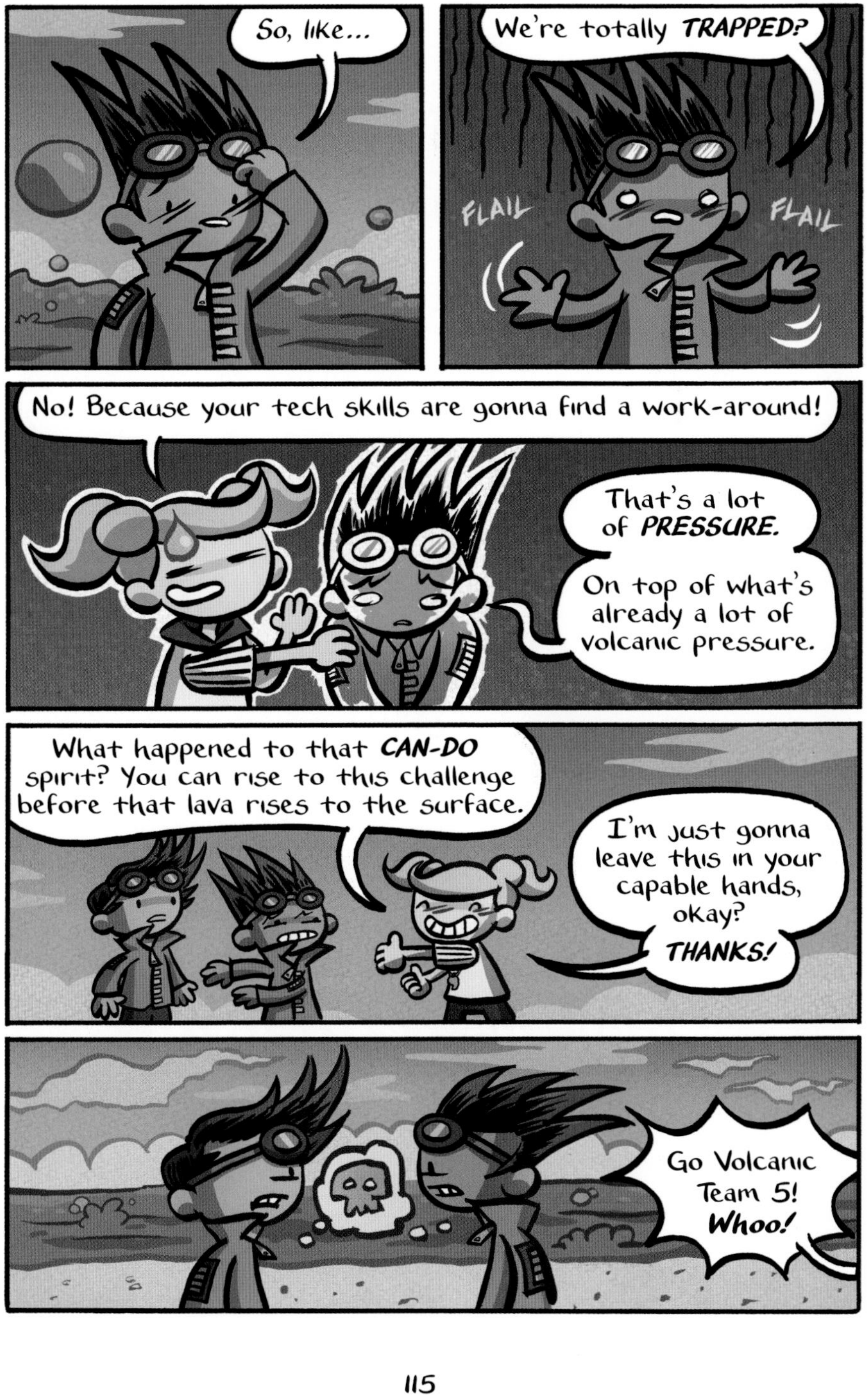
So, like...
We're totally TRAPPED?
FLAIL
FLAIL
No! Because your tech skills are gonna find a work-around!
That's a lot of PRESSURE.
On top of what's already a lot of volcanic pressure.
What happened to that CAN-DO spirit? You can rise to this challenge before that lava rises to the surface.
I'm just gonna leave this in your capable hands, okay?
THANKS!
Go Volcanic Team 5! Whoo!

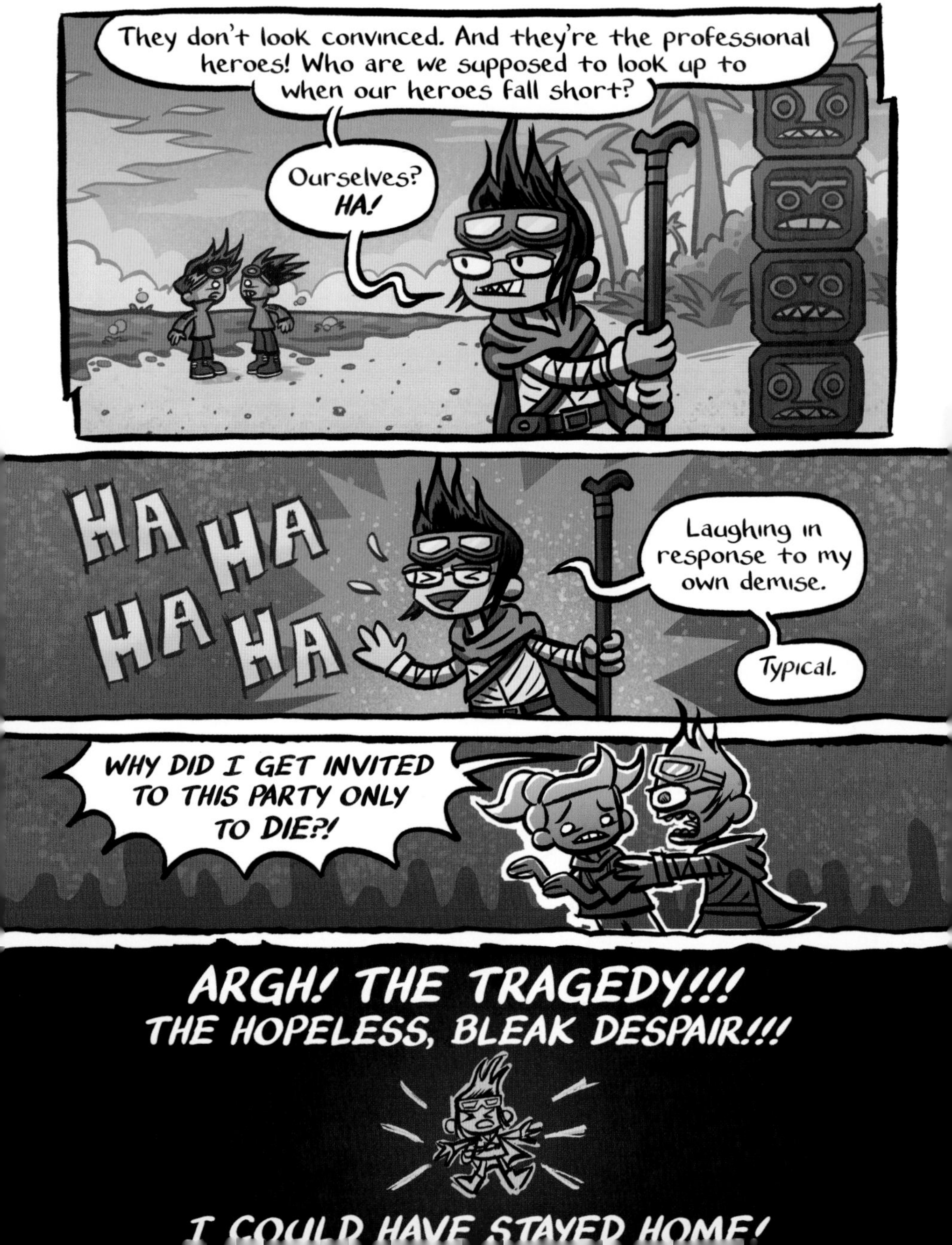
They don't look convinced. And they're the professional heroes! Who are we supposed to look up to when our heroes fall short?
Ourselves? HA!
HA HA HA HA HA
Laughing in response to my own demise.
Typical.
WHY DID I GET INVITED TO THIS PARTY ONLY TO DIE?!
ARGH! THE TRAGEDY!!!
THE HOPELESS, BLEAK DESPAIR!!!
I COULD HAVE STAYED HOME!

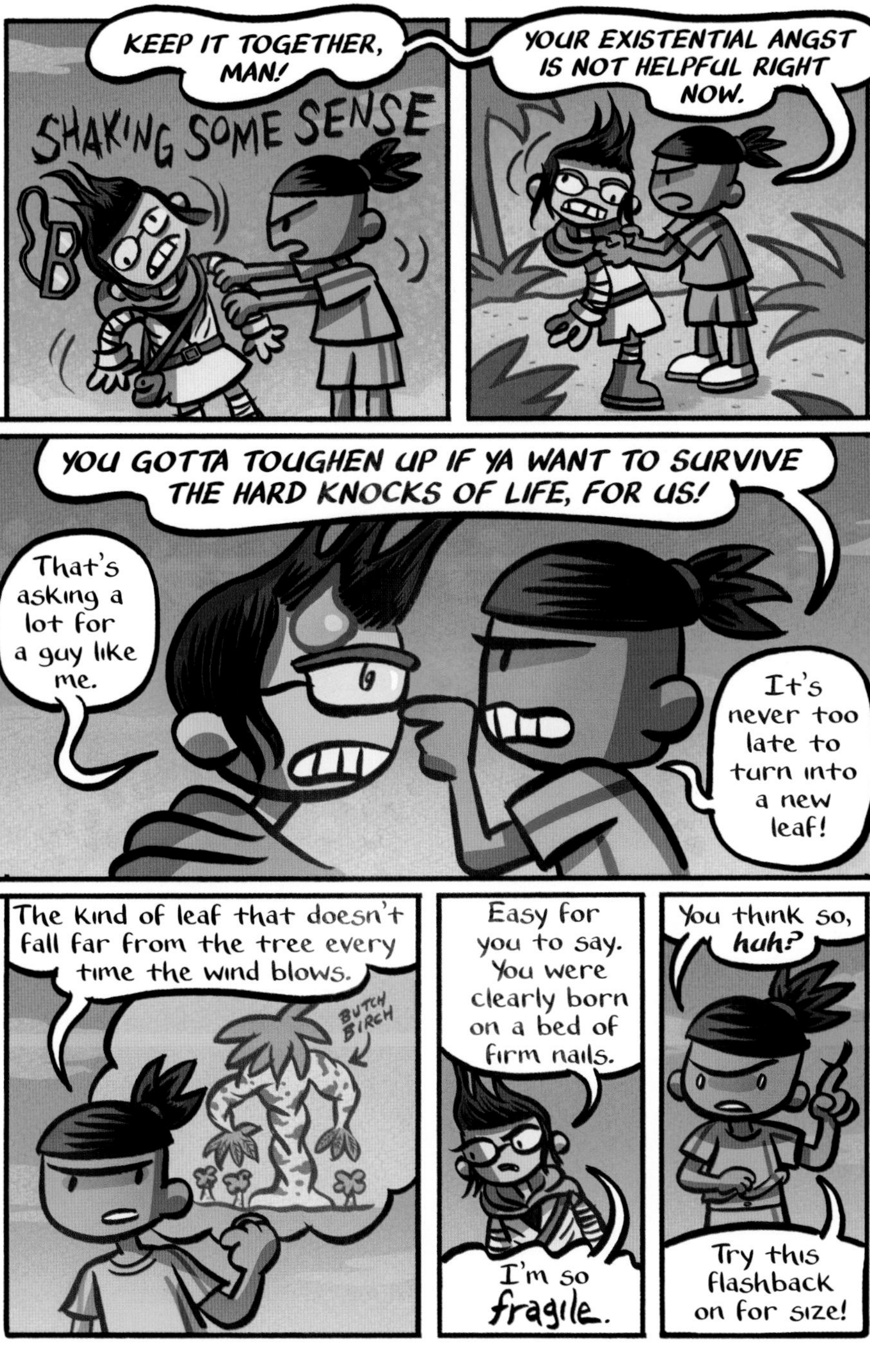
KEEP IT TOGETHER, MAN!
YOUR EXISTENTIAL ANGST IS NOT HELPFUL RIGHT NOW.
SHAKING SOME SENSE
YOU GOTTA TOUGHEN UP IF YA WANT TO SURVIVE THE HARD KNOCKS OF LIFE, FOR US!
That's asking a lot for a guy like me.
It's never too late to turn into a new leaf!
The kind of leaf that doesn't fall far from the tree every time the wind blows.
BUTCH BIRCH
Easy for you to say. You were clearly born on a bed of firm nails.
I'm so fragile.
You think so, huh?
Try this flashback on for size!

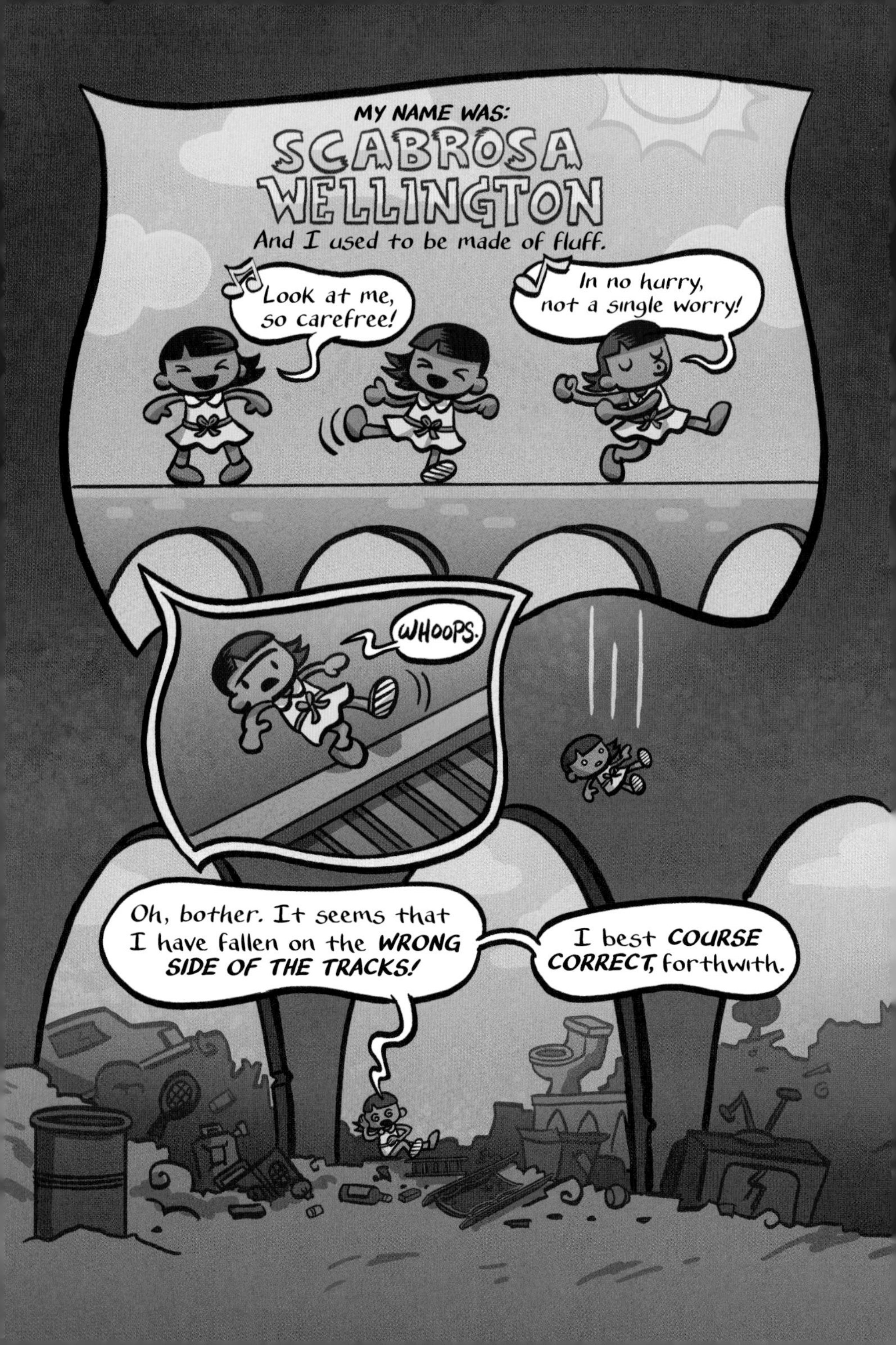
MY NAME WAS:
SCABROSA WELLINGTON
And I used to be made of fluff.
Look at me, so carefree!
In no hurry, not a single worry!
WHOOPS.
Oh, bother. It seems that I have fallen on the WRONG SIDE OF THE TRACKS!
I best COURSE CORRECT, forthwith.

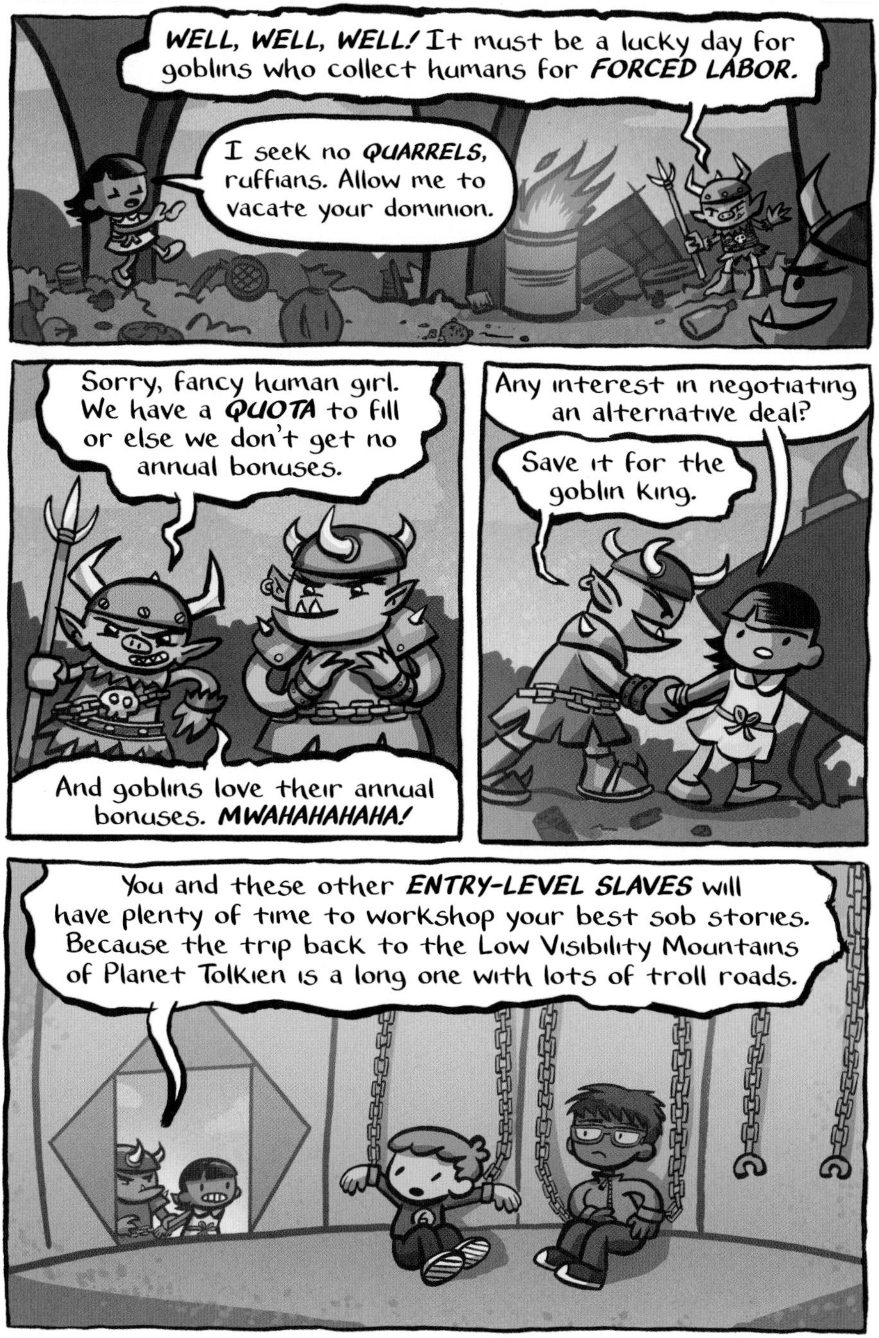
WELL, WELL, WELL! It must be a lucky day for goblins who collect humans for FORCED LABOR.
I seek no QUARRELS, ruffians. Allow me to vacate your dominion.
Sorry, fancy human girl. We have a QUOTA to fill or else we don't get no annual bonuses.
And goblins love their annual bonuses. MWAHAHAHAHA!
Any interest in negotiating an alternative deal?
Save it for the goblin King.
You and these other ENTRY-LEVEL SLAVES will have plenty of time to workshop your best sob stories. Because the trip back to the Low Visibility Mountains of Planet Tolkien is a long one with lots of troll roads.

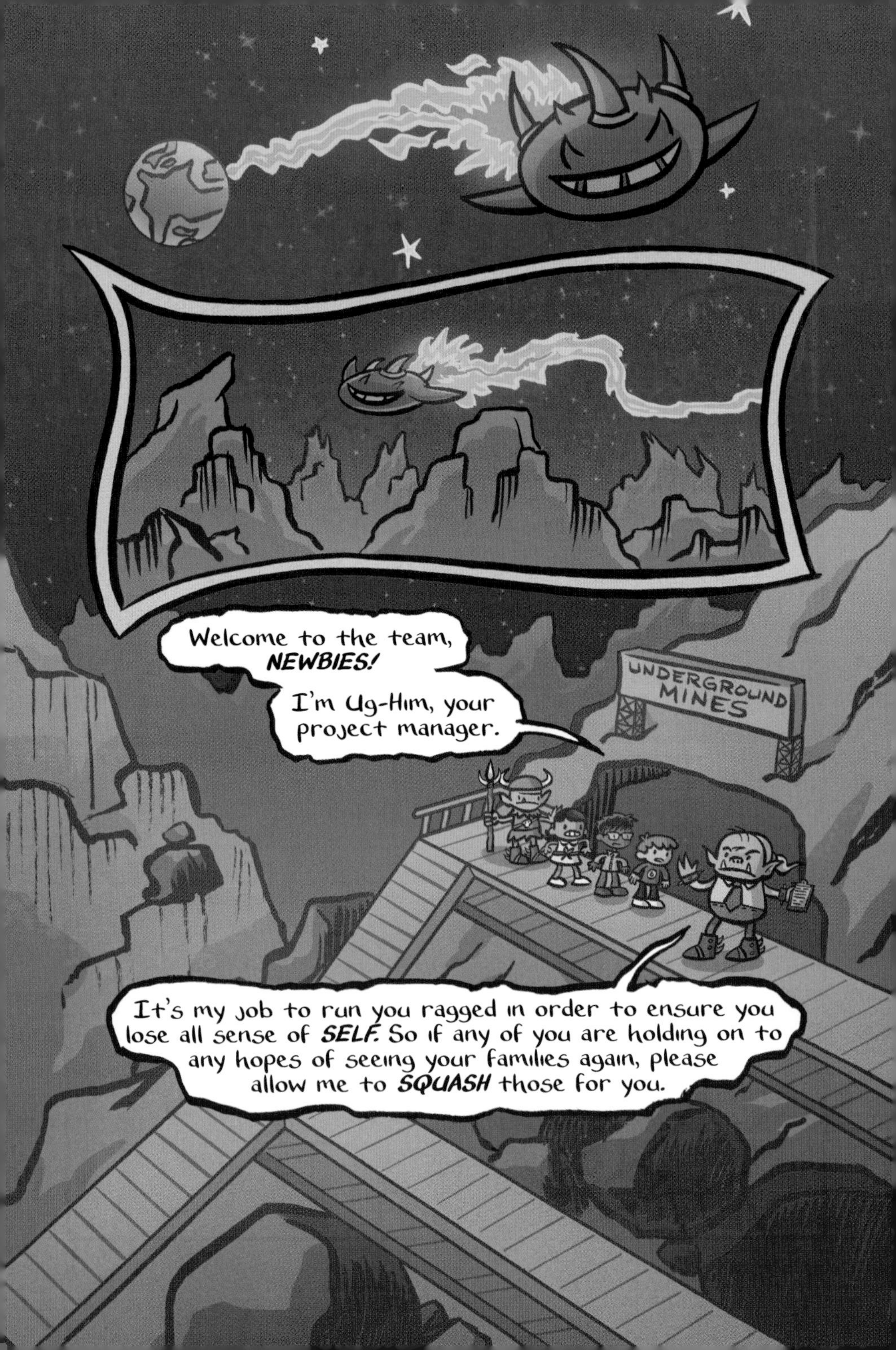
UNDERGROUND MINES
Welcome to the team, NEWBIES!
I'm Ug-Him, your project manager.
It's my job to run you ragged in order to ensure you lose all sense of SELF. So if any of you are holding on to any hopes of seeing your families again, please allow me to SQUASH those for you.

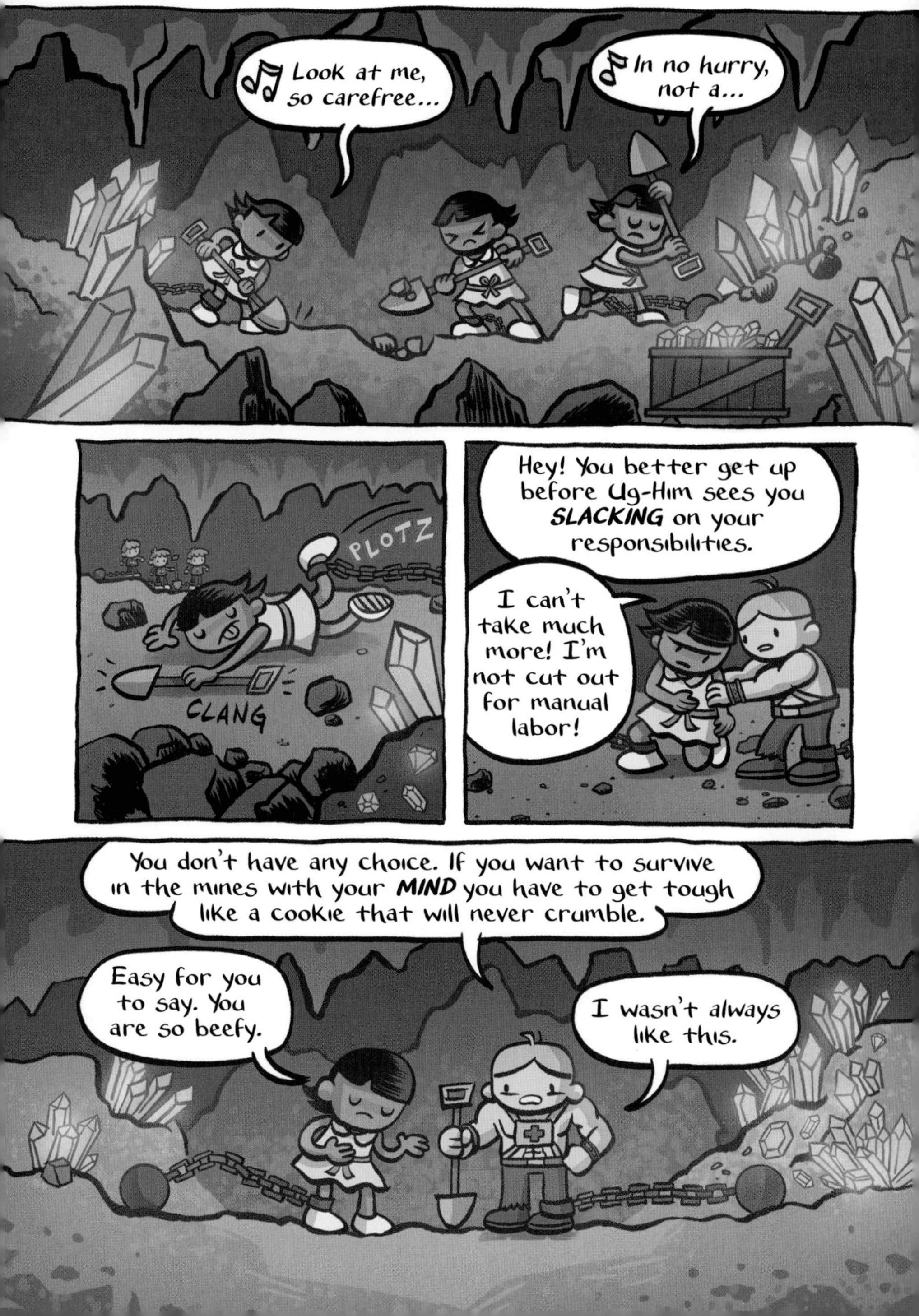
Look at me, so carefree...
In no hurry, not a...
PLOTZ
CLANG
Hey! You better get up before Ug-Him sees you SLACKING on your responsibilities.
I can't take much more! I'm not cut out for manual labor!
You don't have any choice. If you want to survive in the mines with your MIND you have to get tough like a cookie that will never crumble.
Easy for you to say. You are so beefy.
I wasn't always like this.

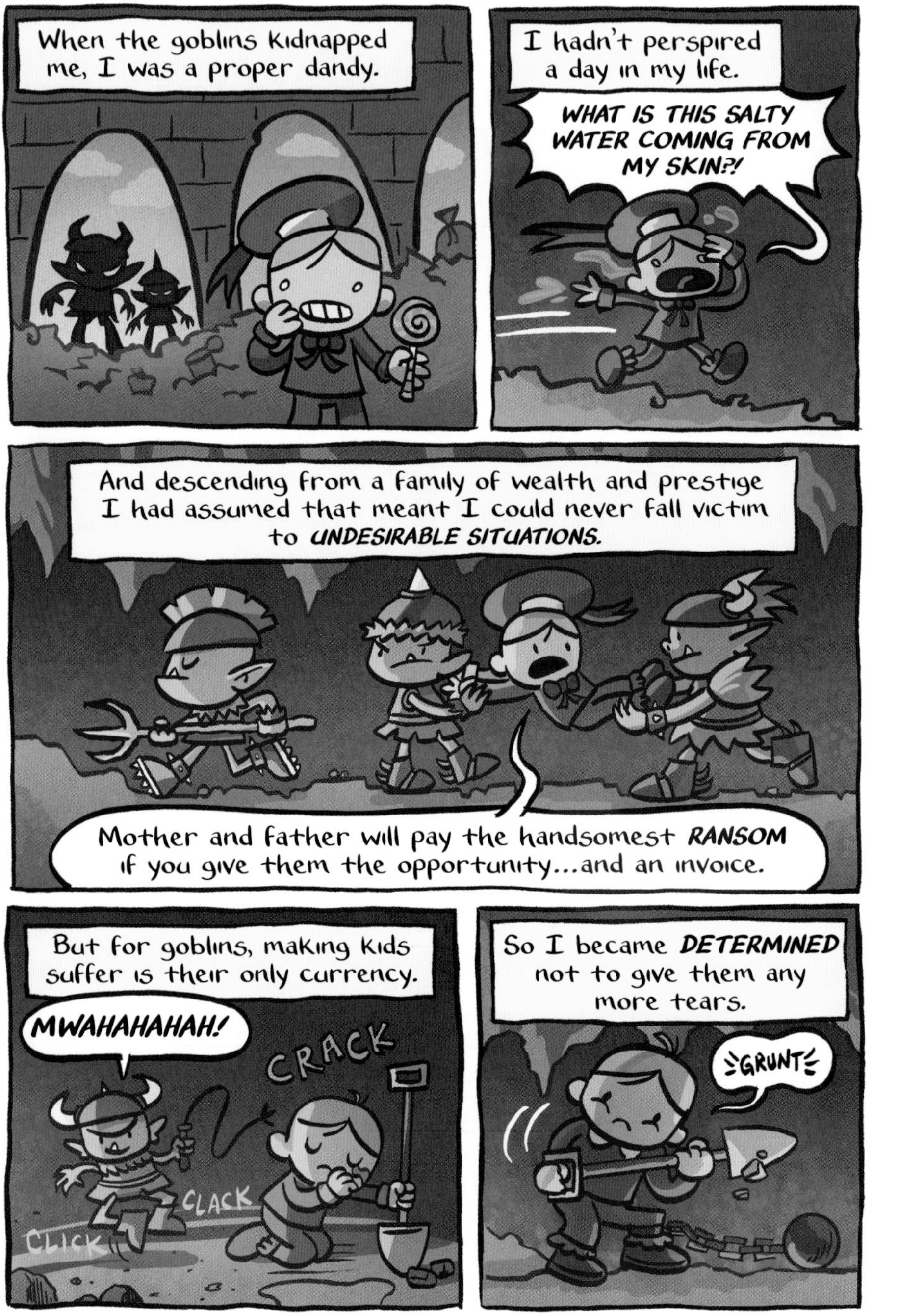
When the goblins kidnapped me, I was a proper dandy.
I hadn't perspired a day in my life.
WHAT IS THIS SALTY WATER COMING FROM MY SKIN?!
And descending from a family of wealth and prestige I had assumed that meant I could never fall victim to UNDESIRABLE SITUATIONS.
Mother and father will pay the handsomest RANSOM if you give them the opportunity...and an invoice.
But for goblins, making kids suffer is their only currency.
MWAHAHAHAH!
CRACK
CLACK
CLICK
So I became DETERMINED not to give them any more tears.
GRUNT

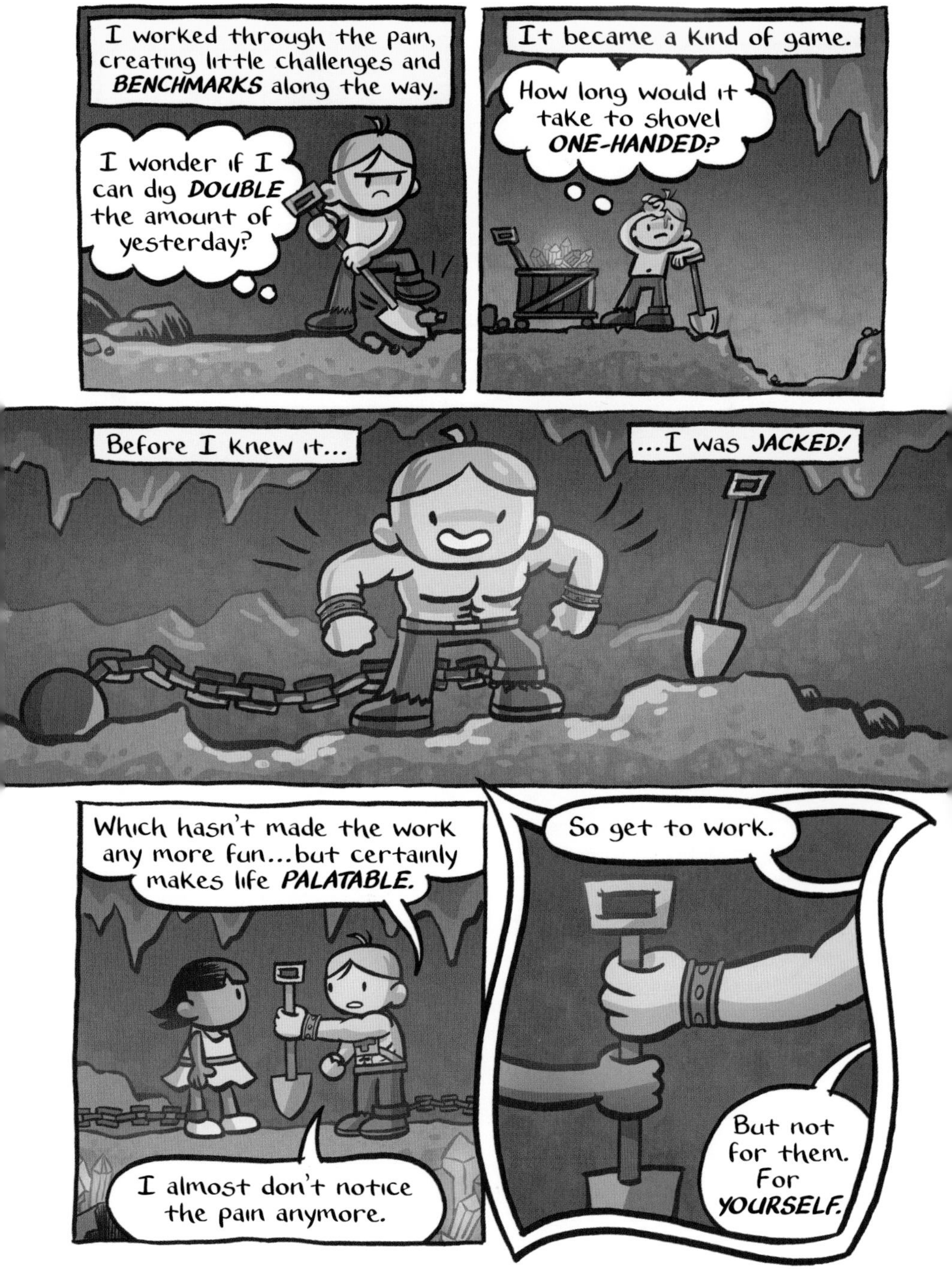
I worked through the pain, creating little challenges and BENCHMARKS along the way.
I wonder if I can dig DOUBLE the amount of yesterday?
It became a kind of game.
How long would it take to shovel ONE-HANDED?
Before I knew it...
...I was JACKED!
Which hasn't made the work any more fun...but certainly makes life PALATABLE.
I almost don't notice the pain anymore.
So get to work.
But not for them. For YOURSELF.

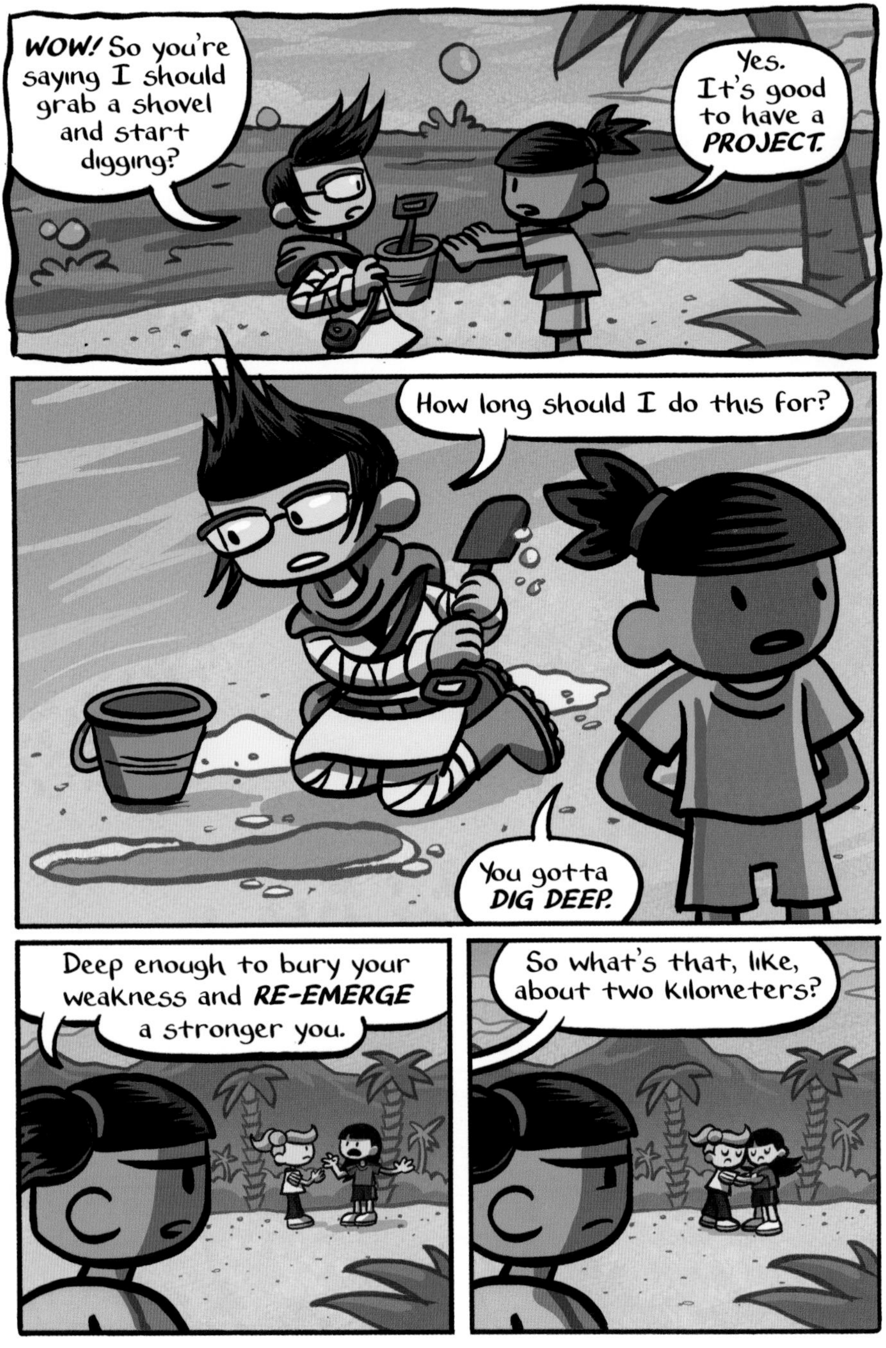
WOW! So you're saying I should grab a shovel and start digging?
Yes. It's good to have a PROJECT.
How long should I do this for?
You gotta DIG DEEP.
Deep enough to bury your weakness and RE-EMERGE a stronger you.
So what's that, like, about two kilometers?

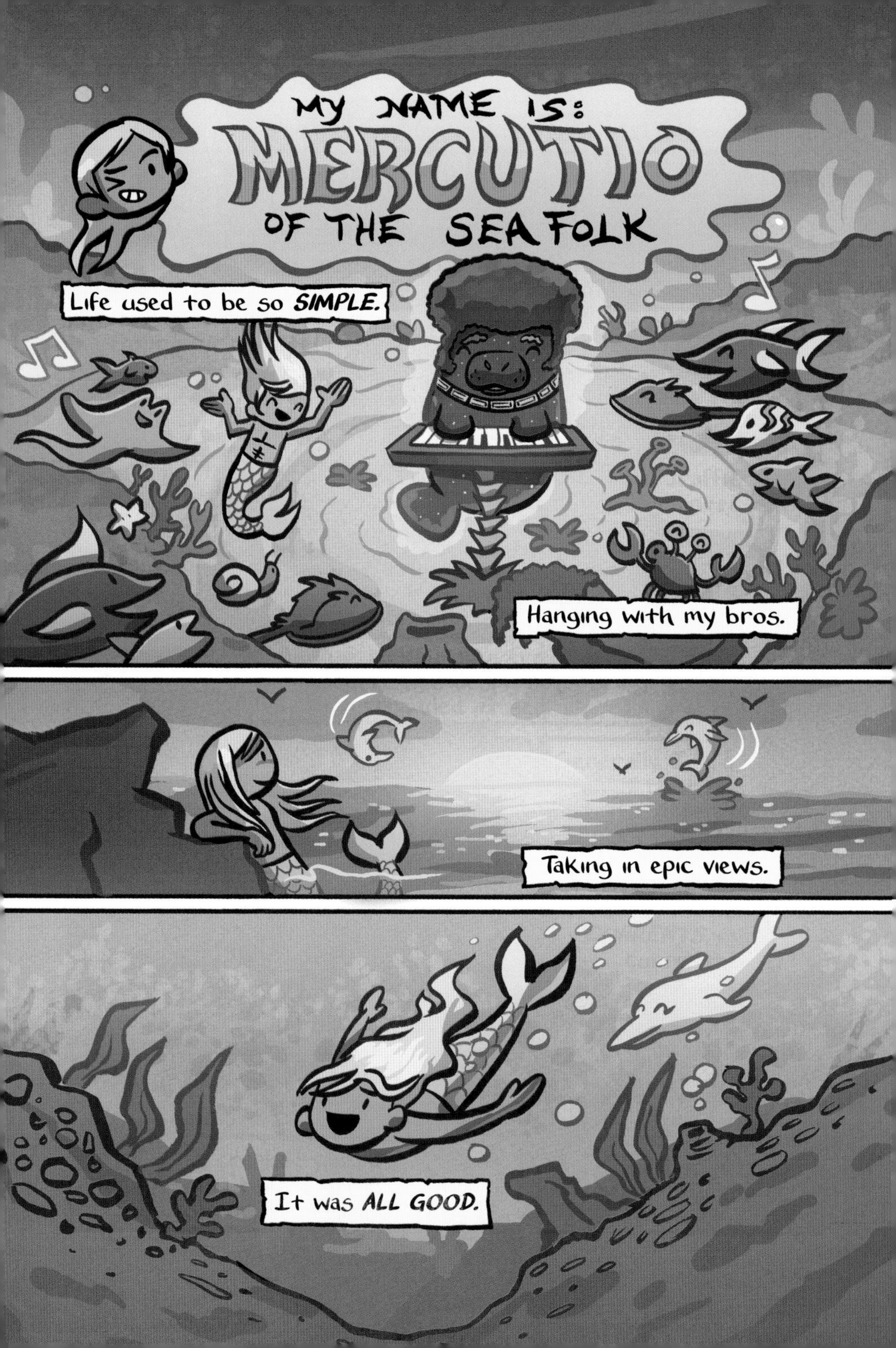
MY NAME IS:
MERCUTIO
OF THE SEA FOLK
Life used to be so SIMPLE.
Hanging with my bros.
Taking in epic views.
It was ALL GOOD.

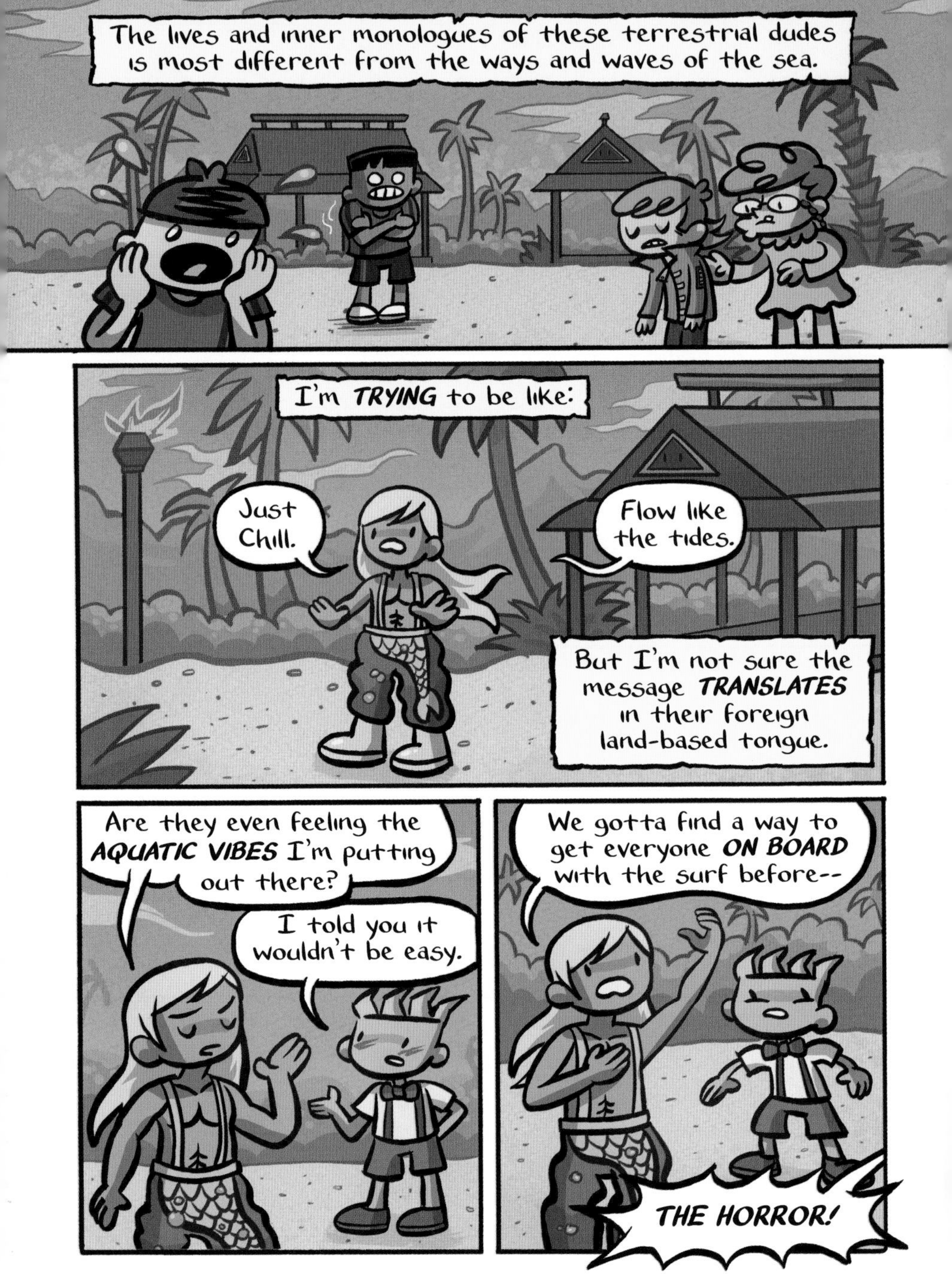
The lives and inner monologues of these terrestrial dudes is most different from the ways and waves of the sea.
I'm TRYING to be like:
Just Chill.
Flow like the tides.
But I'm not sure the message TRANSLATES in their foreign land-based tongue.
Are they even feeling the AQUATIC VIBES I'm putting out there?
I told you it wouldn't be easy.
We gotta find a way to get everyone ON BOARD with the surf before--
THE HORROR!

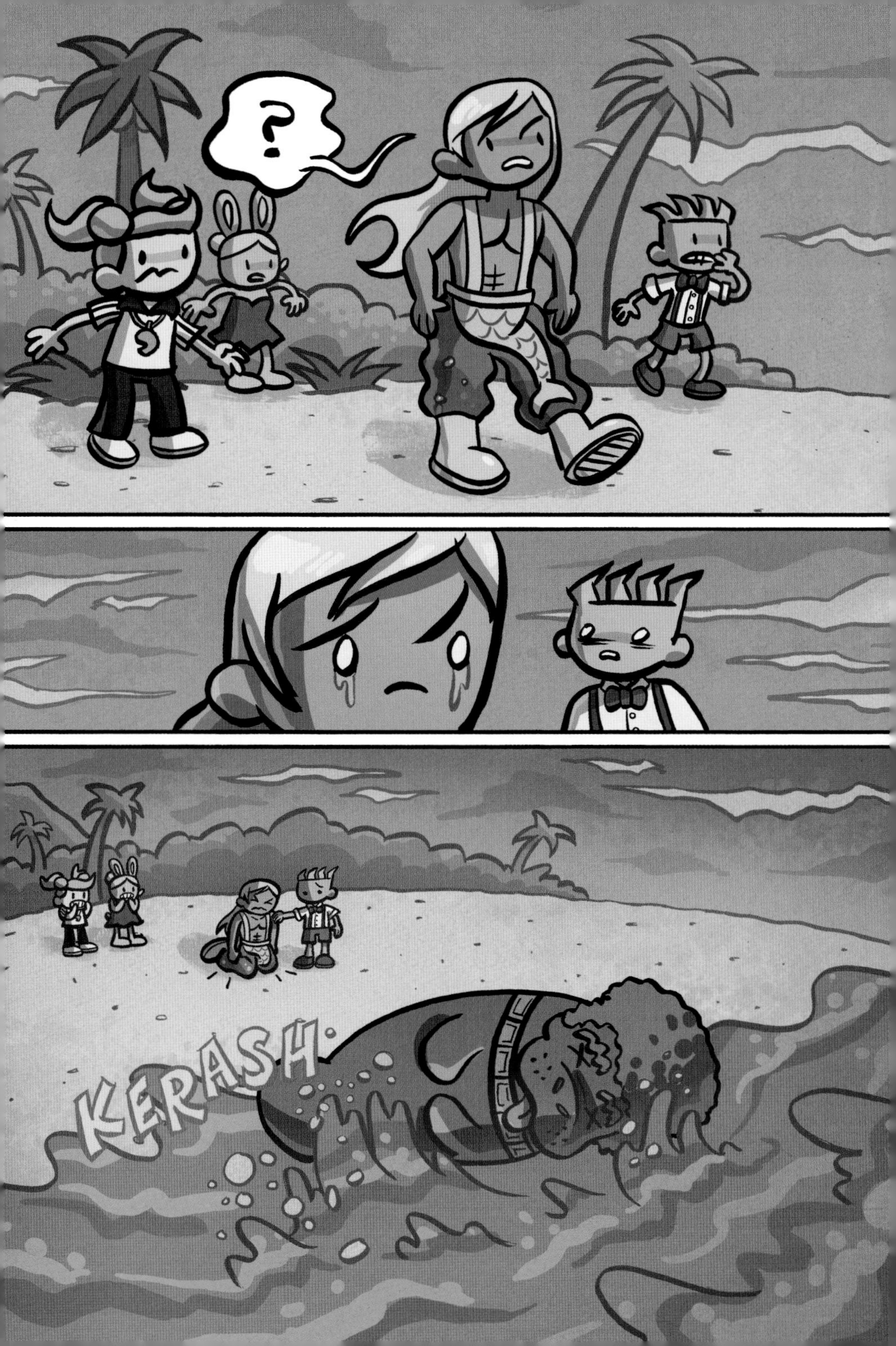
?
KERASH

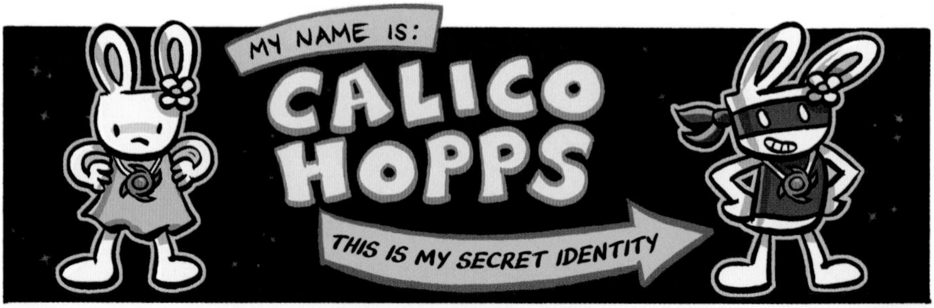
MY NAME IS:
CALICO HOPPS
THIS IS MY SECRET IDENTITY

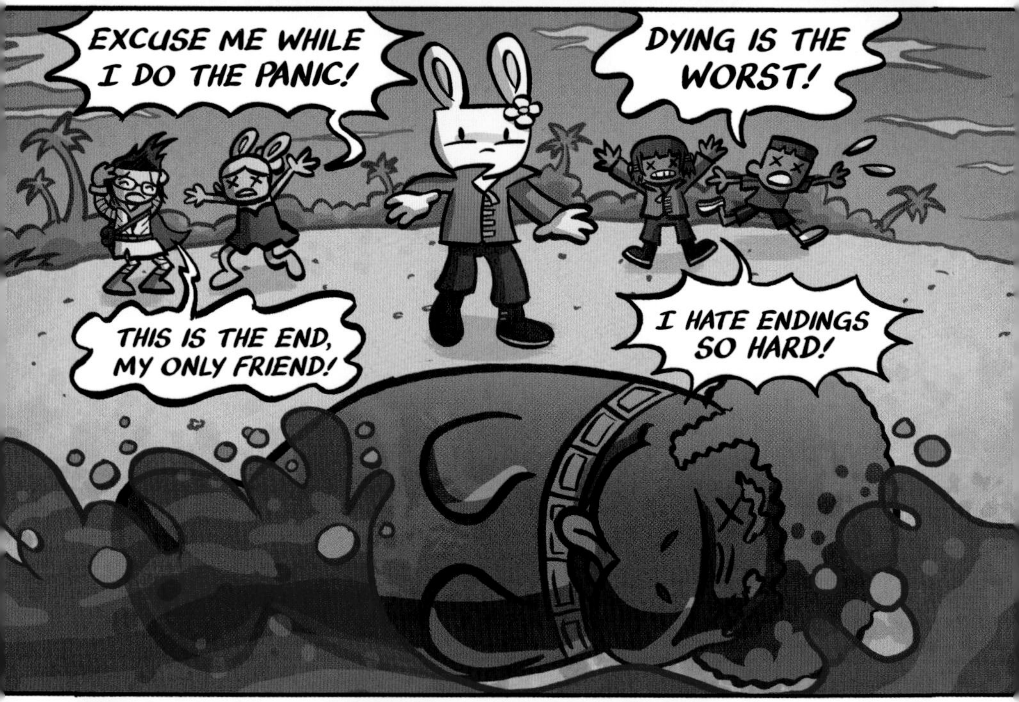
EXCUSE ME WHILE I DO THE PANIC!
DYING IS THE WORST!
THIS IS THE END, MY ONLY FRIEND!
I HATE ENDINGS SO HARD!

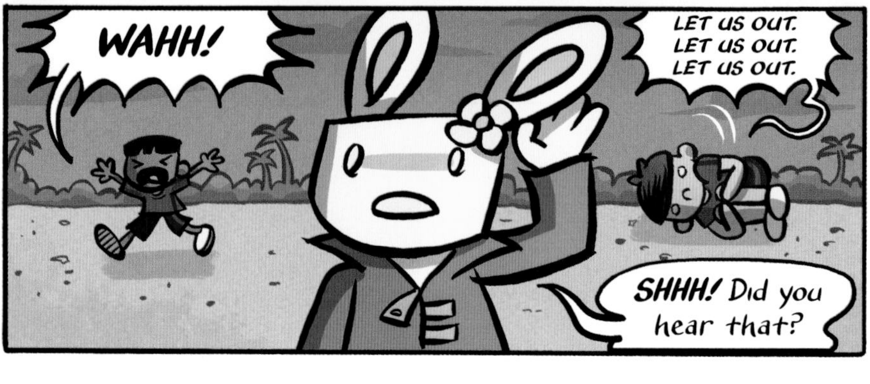
WAHH!
LET US OUT. LET US OUT. LET US OUT.
SHHH! Did you hear that?

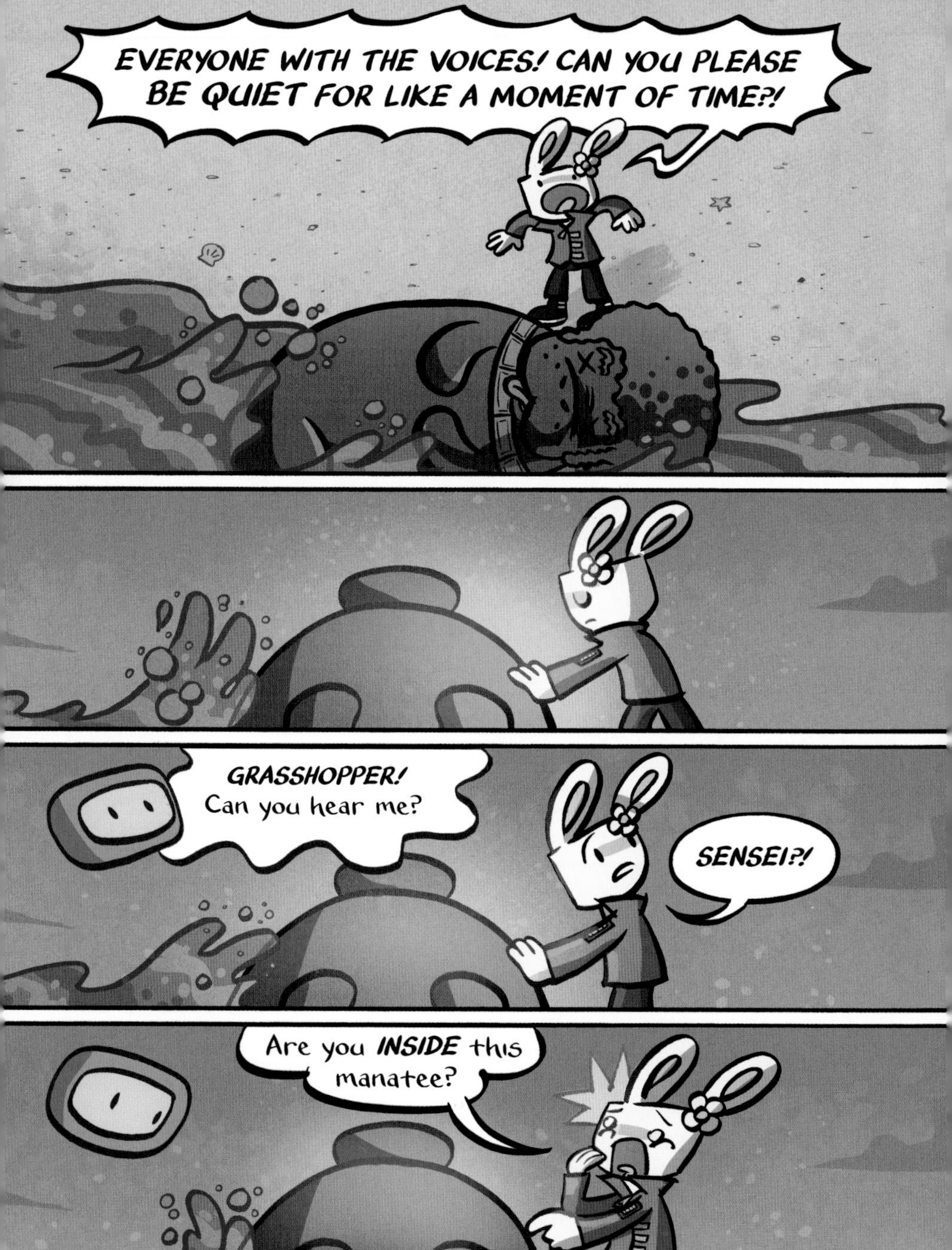
EVERYONE WITH THE VOICES! CAN YOU PLEASE BE QUIET FOR LIKE A MOMENT OF TIME?!
GRASSHOPPER! Can you hear me?
SENSEI?!
Are you INSIDE this manatee?

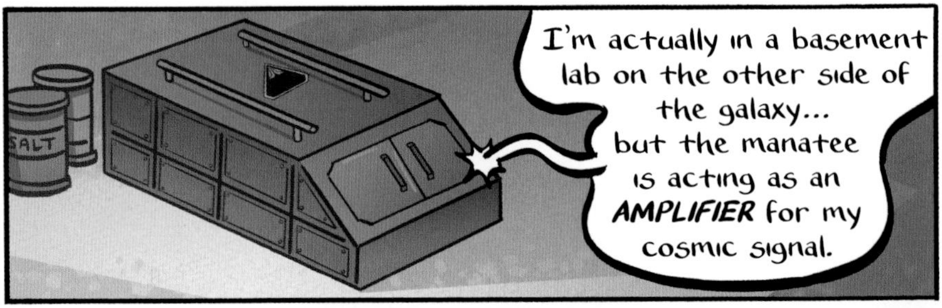
SALT
I'm actually in a basement lab on the other side of the galaxy... but the manatee is acting as an AMPLIFIER for my cosmic signal.

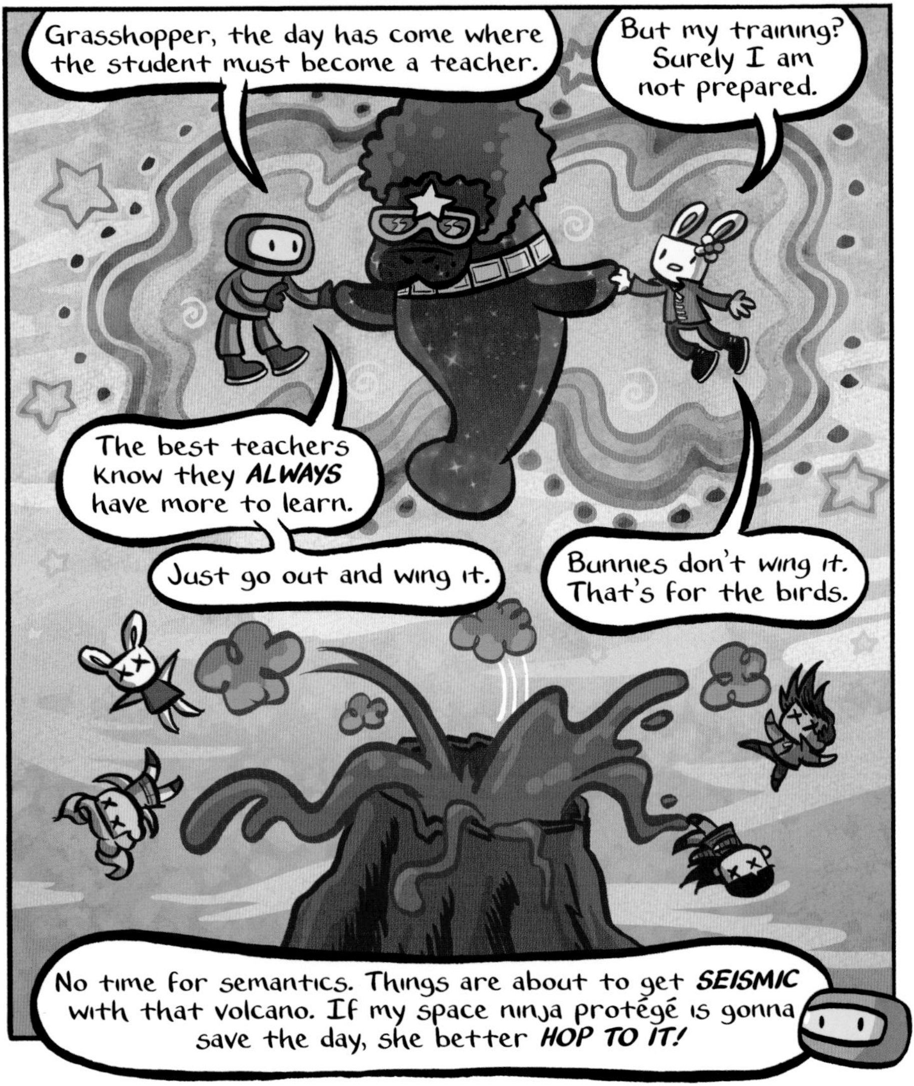
Grasshopper, the day has come where the student must become a teacher.
But my training? Surely I am not prepared.
The best teachers know they ALWAYS have more to learn.
Just go out and wing it.
Bunnies don't wing it. That's for the birds.
No time for semantics. Things are about to get SEISMIC with that volcano. If my space ninja protégé is gonna save the day, she better HOP TO IT!

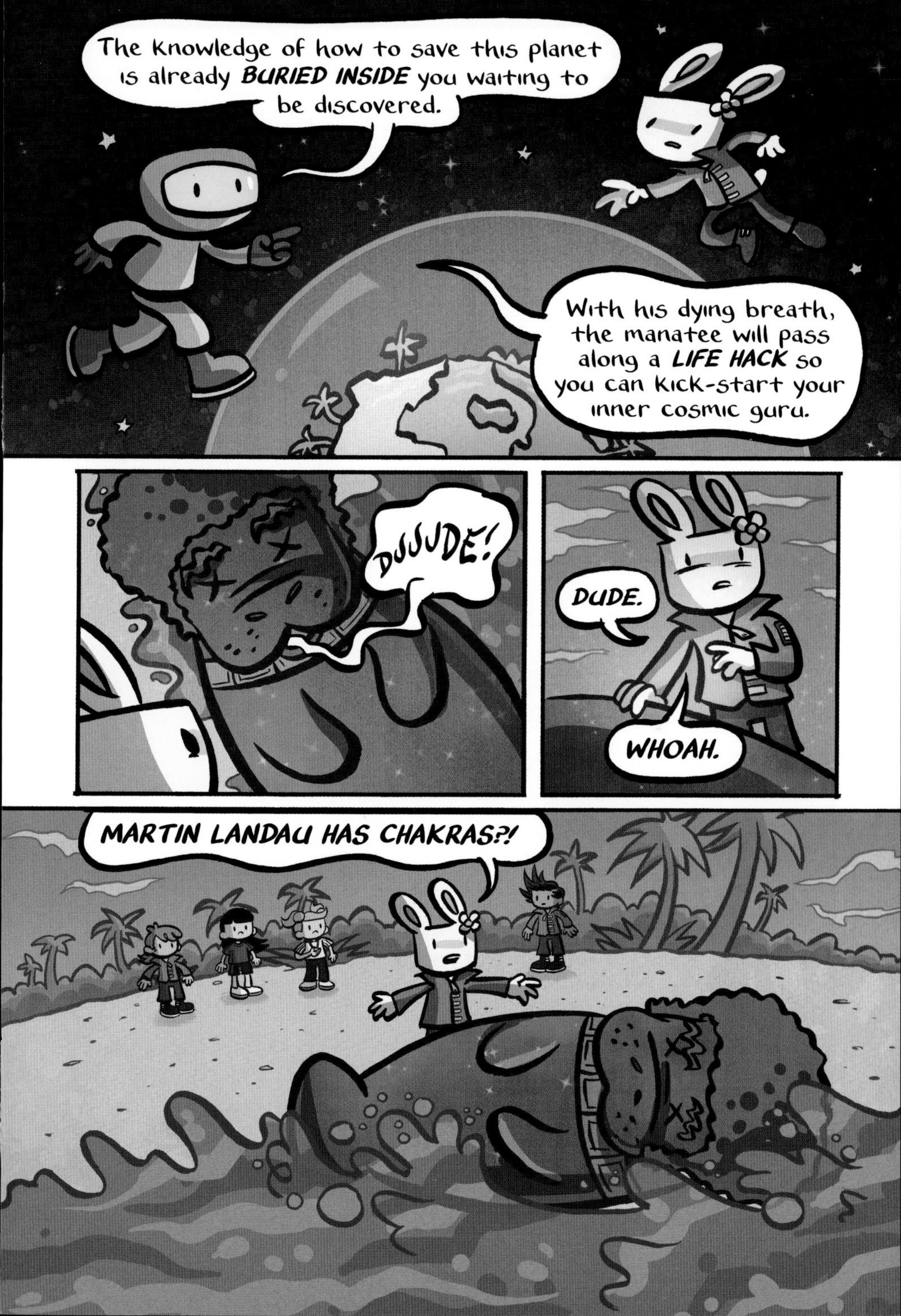
The knowledge of how to save this planet is already BURIED INSIDE you waiting to be discovered.
With his dying breath, the manatee will pass along a LIFE HACK so you can kick-start your inner cosmic guru.
DUUUDE!
DUDE.
WHOAH.
MARTIN LANDAU HAS CHAKRAS?!

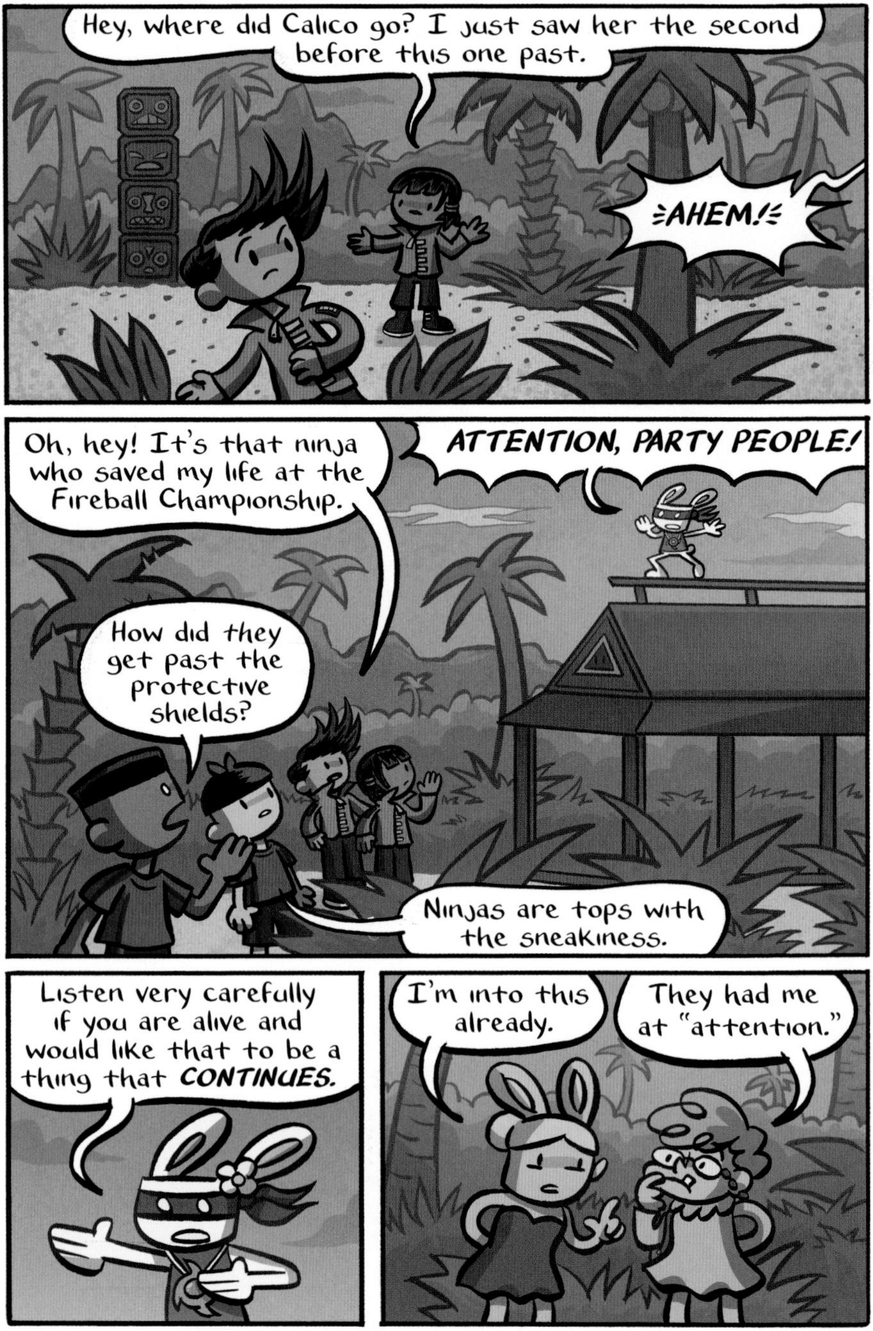
Hey, where did Calico go? I just saw her the second before this one past.
AHEM!
Oh, hey! It's that ninja who saved my life at the Fireball Championship.
ATTENTION, PARTY PEOPLE!
How did they get past the protective shields?
Ninjas are tops with the sneakiness.
Listen very carefully if you are alive and would like that to be a thing that CONTINUES.
I'm into this already.
They had me at "attention."

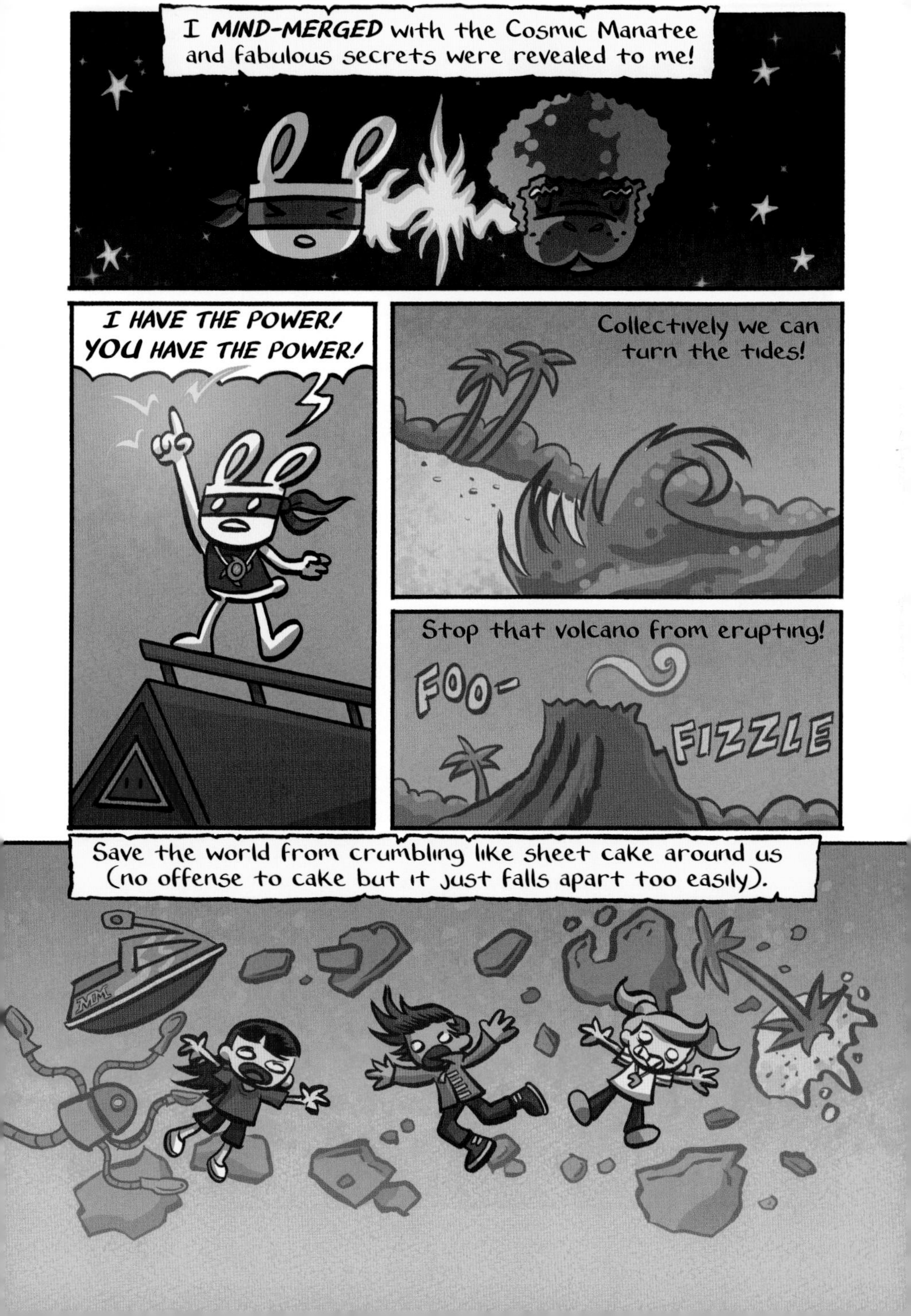
I MIND-MERGED with the Cosmic Manatee and fabulous secrets were revealed to me!
I HAVE THE POWER! YOU HAVE THE POWER!
Collectively we can turn the tides!
Stop that volcano from erupting!
FOO-
FIZZLE
Save the world from crumbling like sheet cake around us (no offense to cake but it just falls apart too easily).
NM

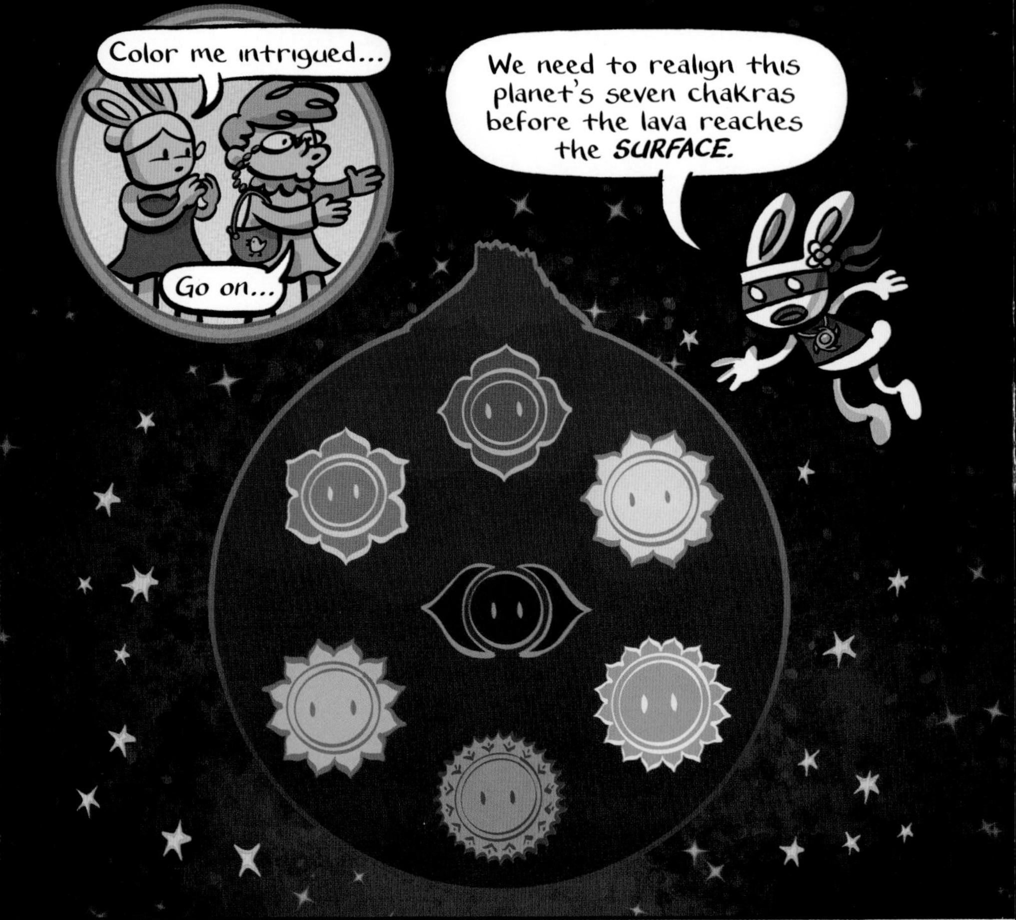
Color me intrigued...
Go on...
We need to realign this planet's seven chakras before the lava reaches the *SURFACE.*

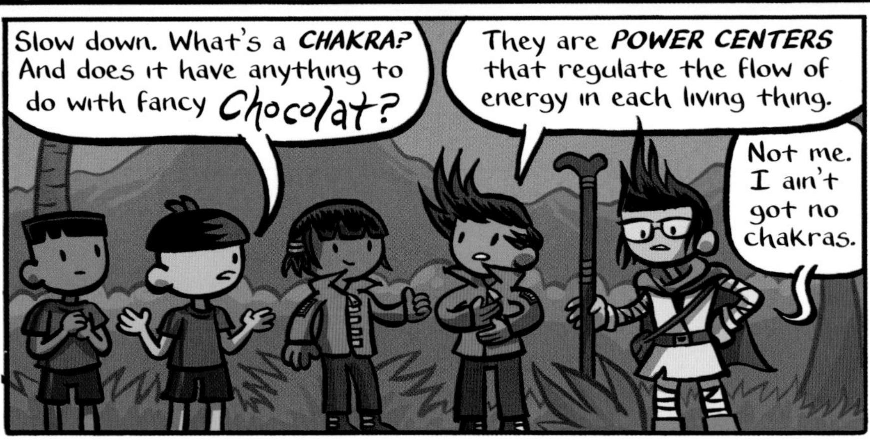
Slow down. What's a *CHAKRA?* And does it have anything to do with fancy Chocolat?
They are *POWER CENTERS* that regulate the flow of energy in each living thing.
Not me. I ain't got no chakras.

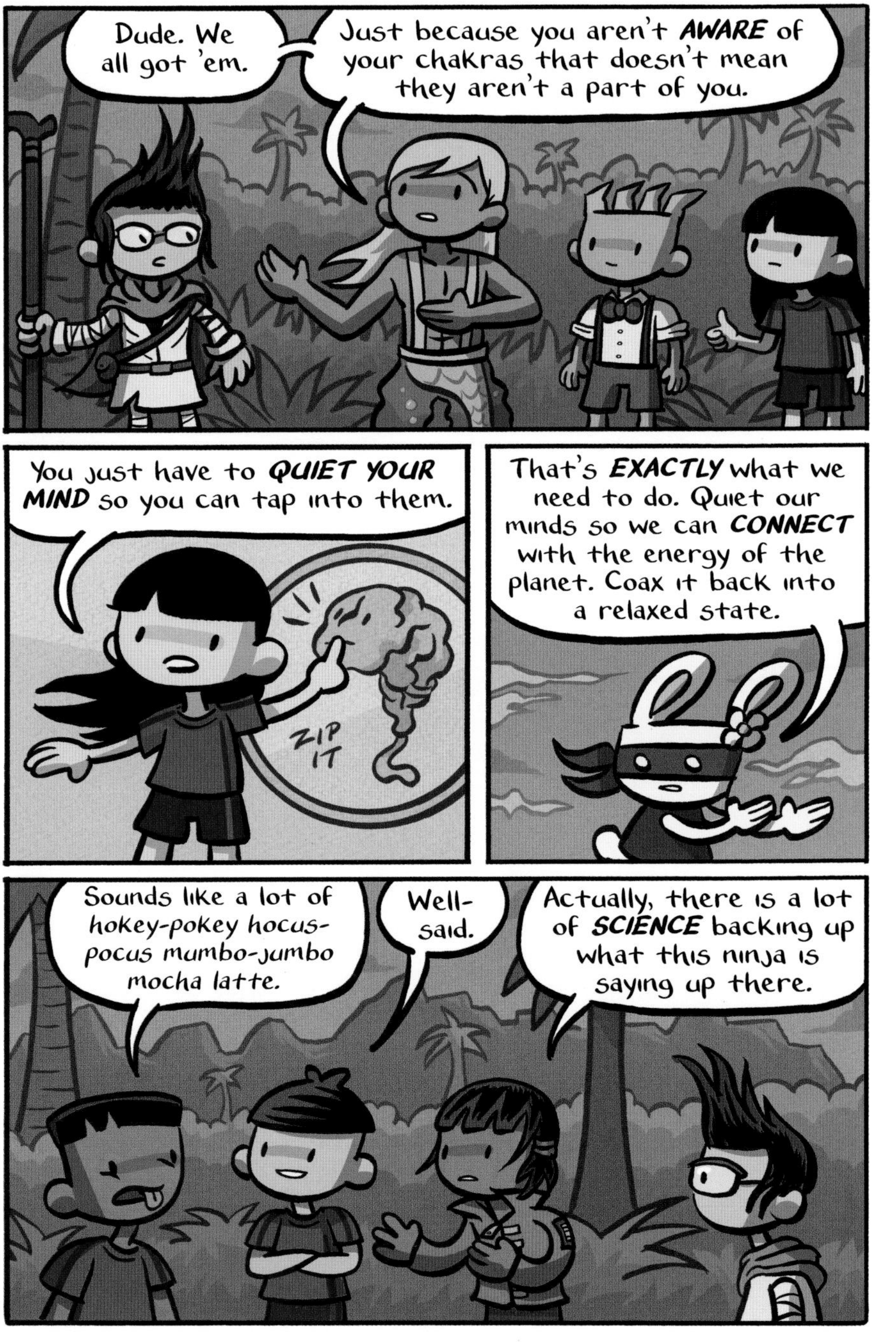
Dude. We all got 'em.
Just because you aren't **AWARE** of your chakras that doesn't mean they aren't a part of you.
You just have to **QUIET YOUR MIND** so you can tap into them.
ZIP IT
That's **EXACTLY** what we need to do. Quiet our minds so we can **CONNECT** with the energy of the planet. Coax it back into a relaxed state.
Sounds like a lot of hokey-pokey hocus-pocus mumbo-jumbo mocha latte.
Well-said.
Actually, there is a lot of **SCIENCE** backing up what this ninja is saying up there.

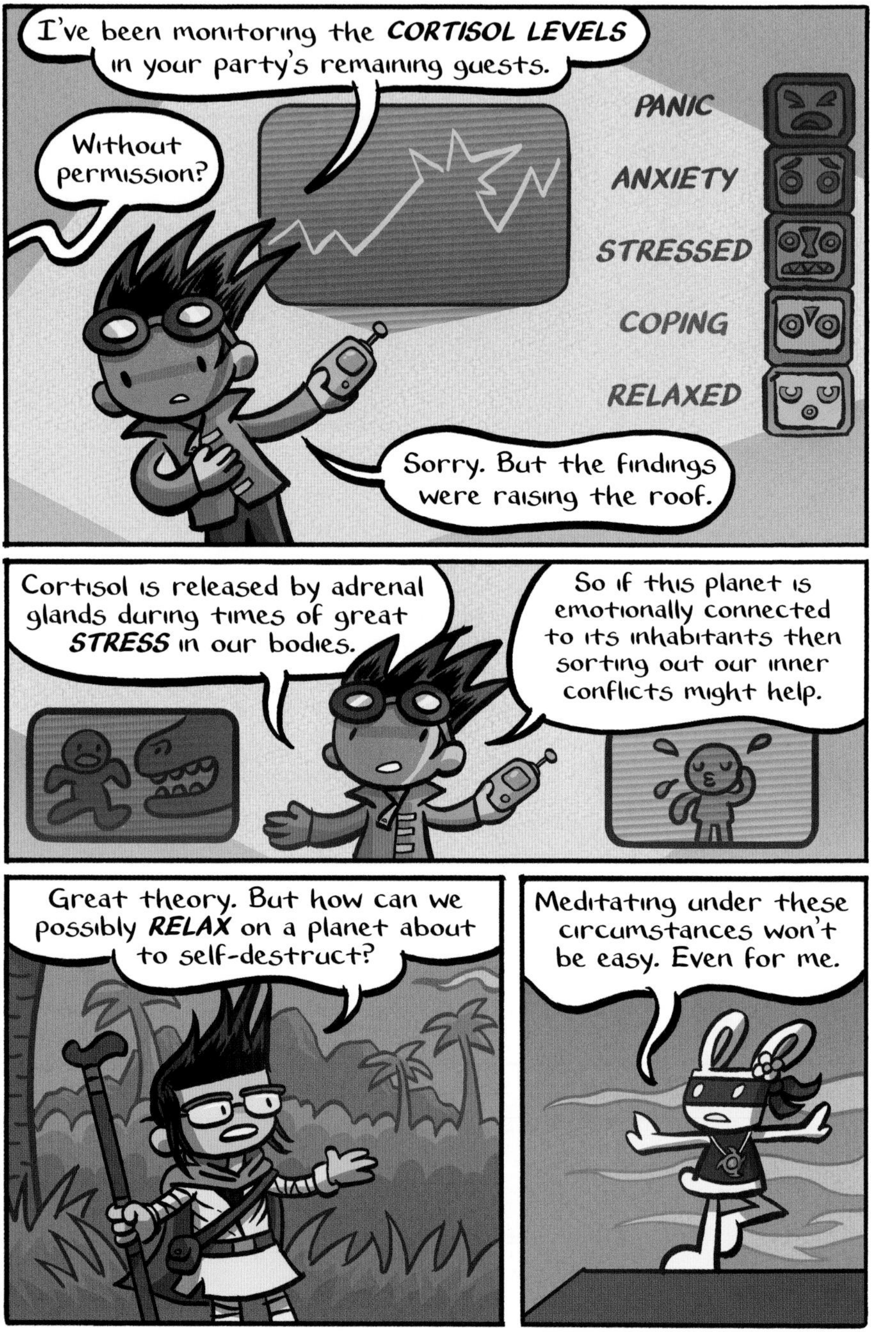

I've been monitoring the CORTISOL LEVELS in your party's remaining guests.
Without permission?
PANIC
ANXIETY
STRESSED
COPING
RELAXED
Sorry. But the findings were raising the roof.
Cortisol is released by adrenal glands during times of great STRESS in our bodies.
So if this planet is emotionally connected to its inhabitants then sorting out our inner conflicts might help.
Great theory. But how can we possibly RELAX on a planet about to self-destruct?
Meditating under these circumstances won't be easy. Even for me.

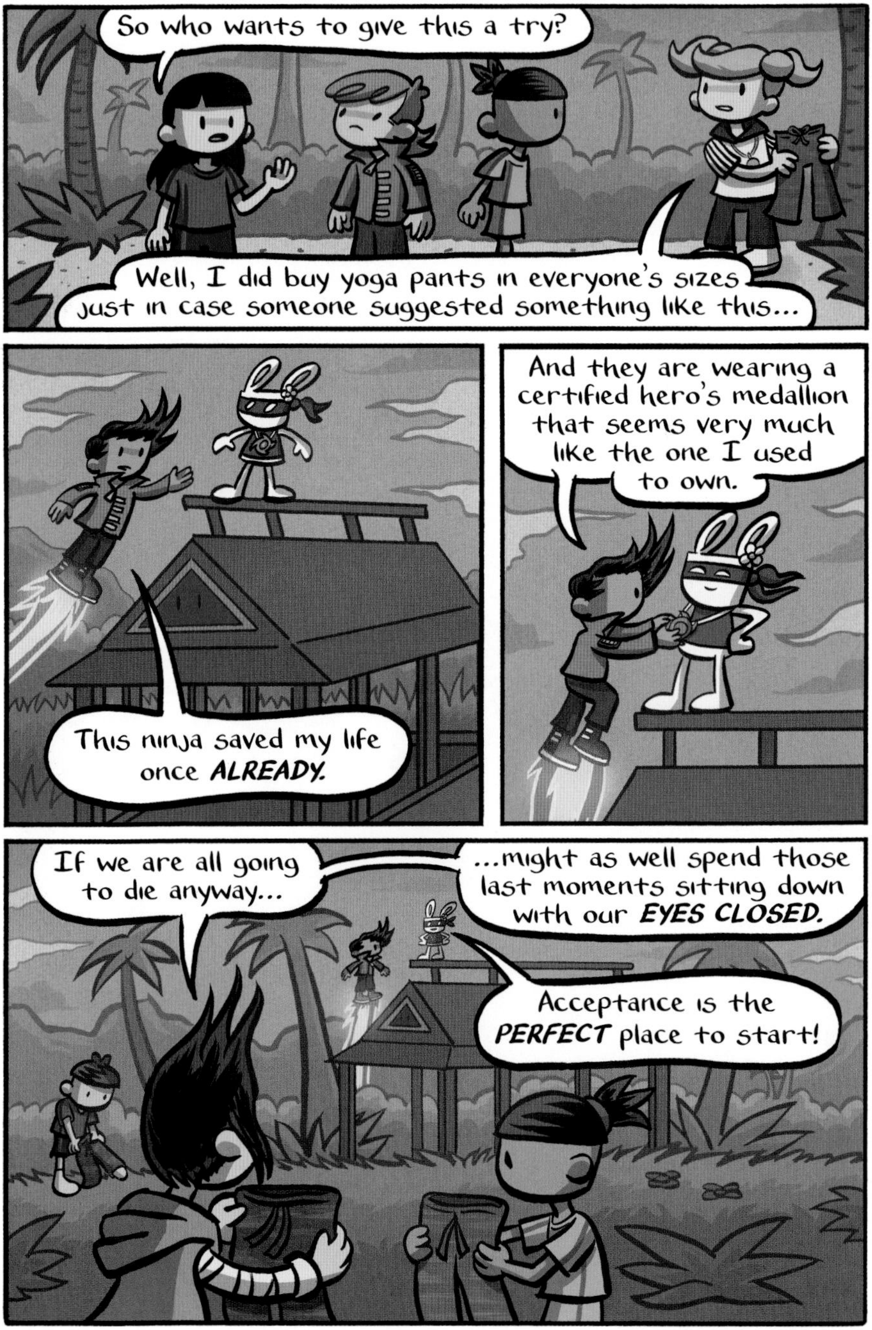
So who wants to give this a try?
Well, I did buy yoga pants in everyone's sizes just in case someone suggested something like this...
This ninja saved my life once ALREADY.
And they are wearing a certified hero's medallion that seems very much like the one I used to own.
If we are all going to die anyway...
...might as well spend those last moments sitting down with our EYES CLOSED.
Acceptance is the PERFECT place to start!

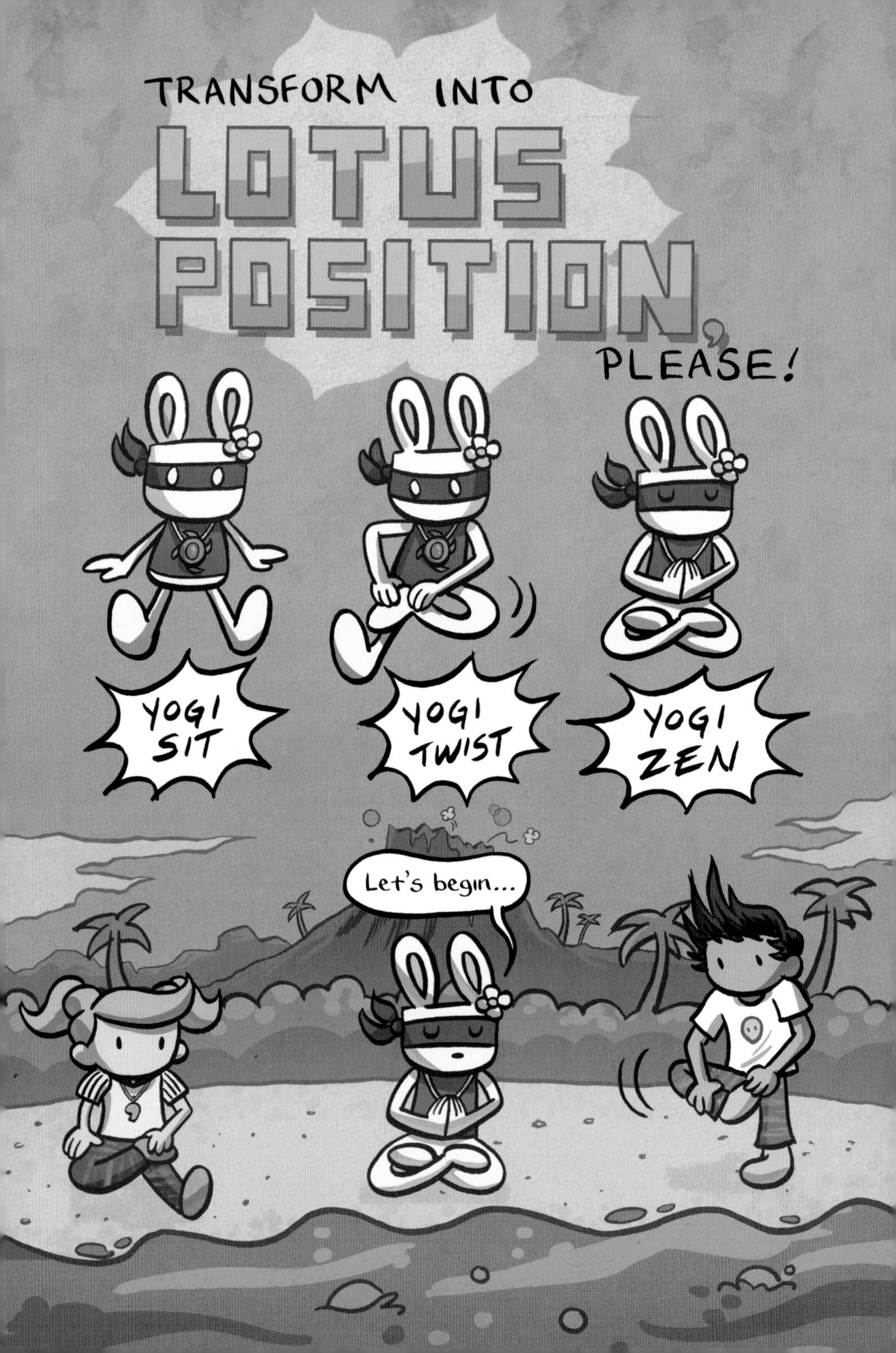
TRANSFORM INTO
LOTUS POSITION,
PLEASE!
YOGI SIT
YOGI TWIST
YOGI ZEN
Let's begin...

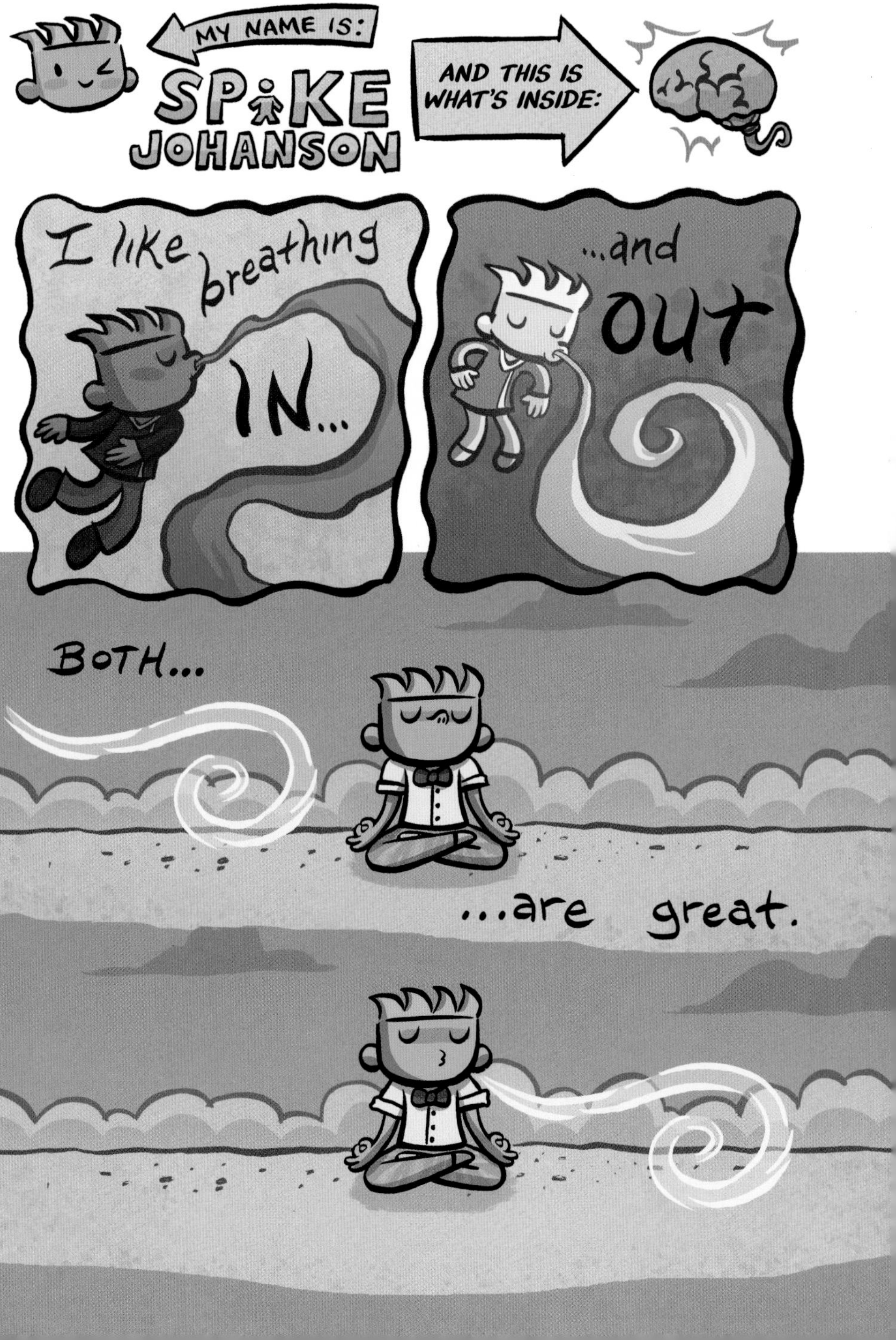
MY NAME IS:
SPIKE JOHANSON
AND THIS IS WHAT'S INSIDE:
I like breathing
IN...
...and
OUT
BOTH...
...are great.

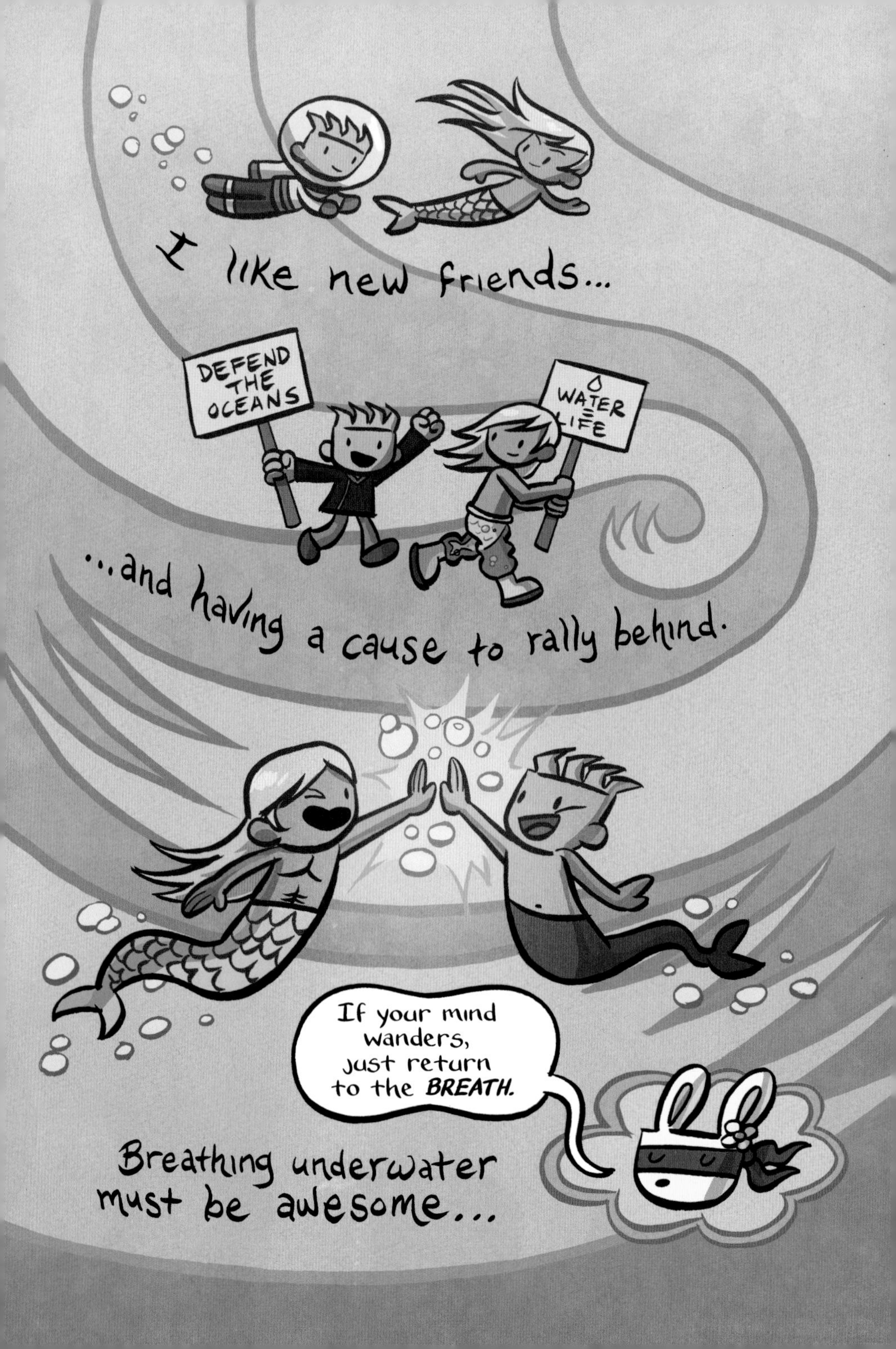
I like new friends...
DEFEND THE OCEANS
WATER = LIFE
...and having a cause to rally behind.
If your mind wanders, just return to the BREATH.
Breathing underwater must be awesome...

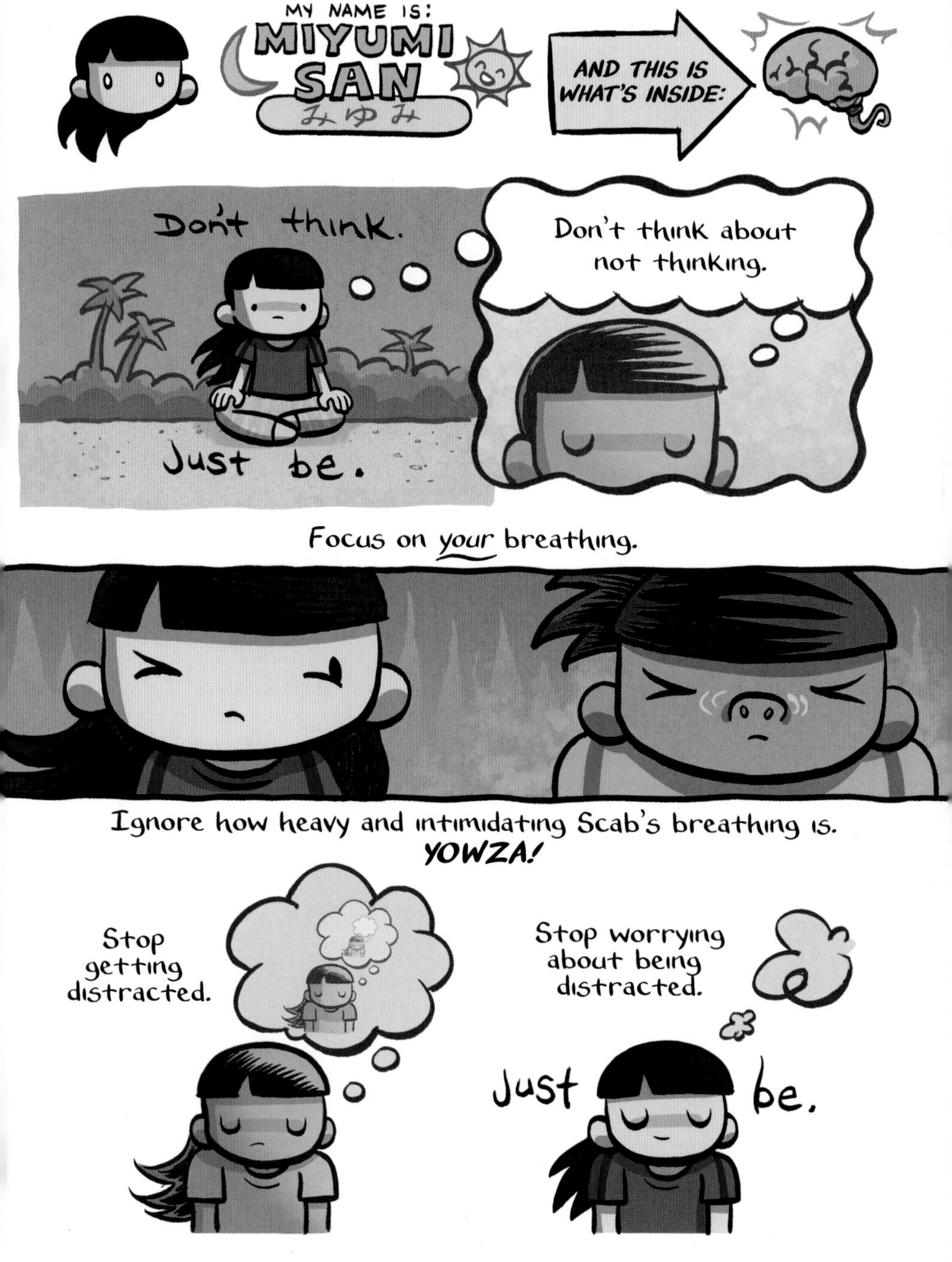
MY NAME IS:
MIYUMI SAN
みゆみ
AND THIS IS WHAT'S INSIDE:
Don't think.
Just be.
Don't think about not thinking.
Focus on your breathing.
Ignore how heavy and intimidating Scab's breathing is.
YOWZA!
Stop getting distracted.
Stop worrying about being distracted.
Just be.

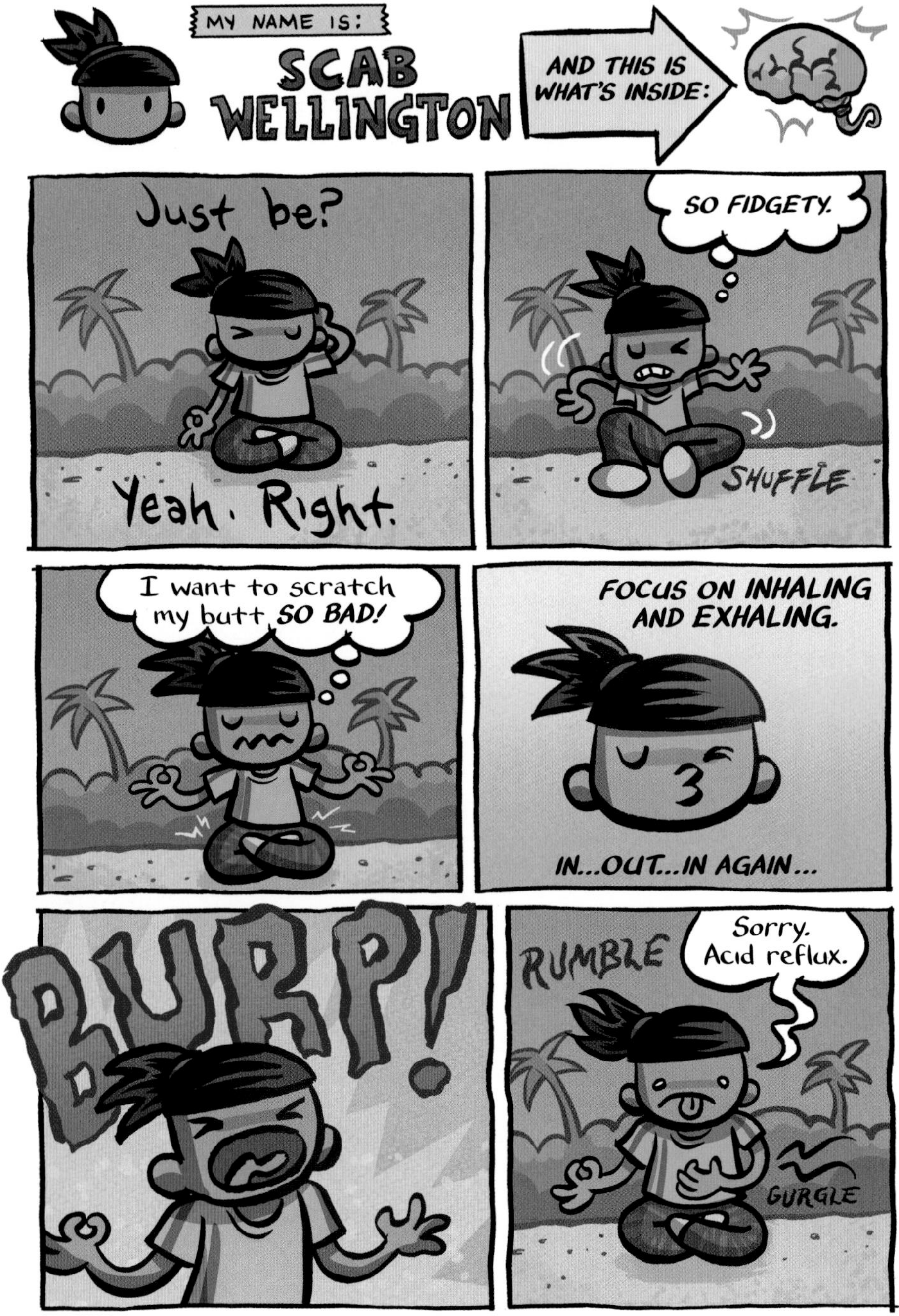
MY NAME IS:
SCAB WELLINGTON
AND THIS IS WHAT'S INSIDE:
Just be?
Yeah. Right.
SO FIDGETY.
SHUFFLE
I want to scratch my butt, SO BAD!
FOCUS ON INHALING AND EXHALING.
IN...OUT...IN AGAIN...
BURP!
RUMBLE
Sorry. Acid reflux.
GURGLE

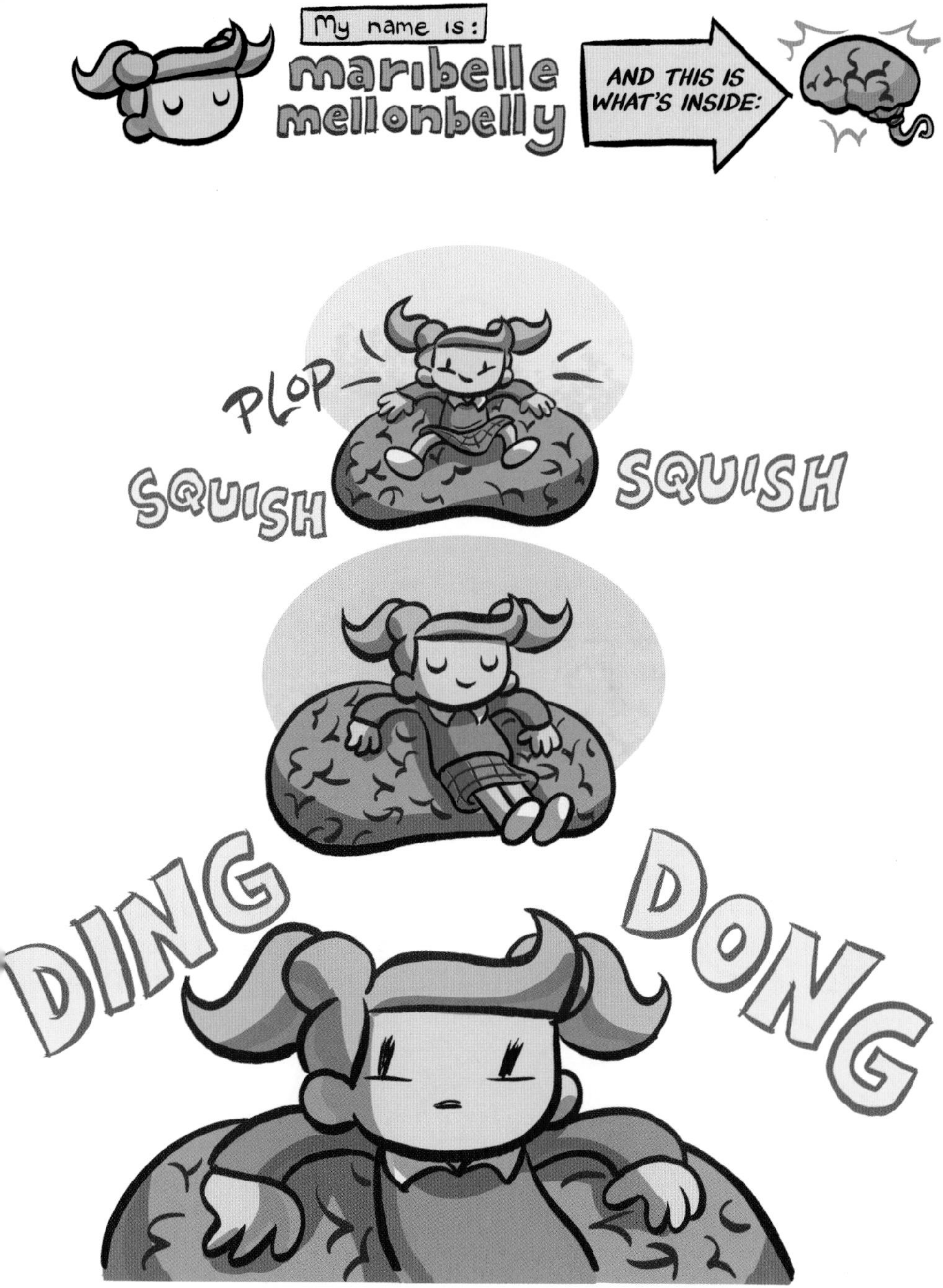
My name is:
maribelle mellonbelly
AND THIS IS WHAT'S INSIDE:
PLOP
SQUISH
SQUISH
DING
DONG

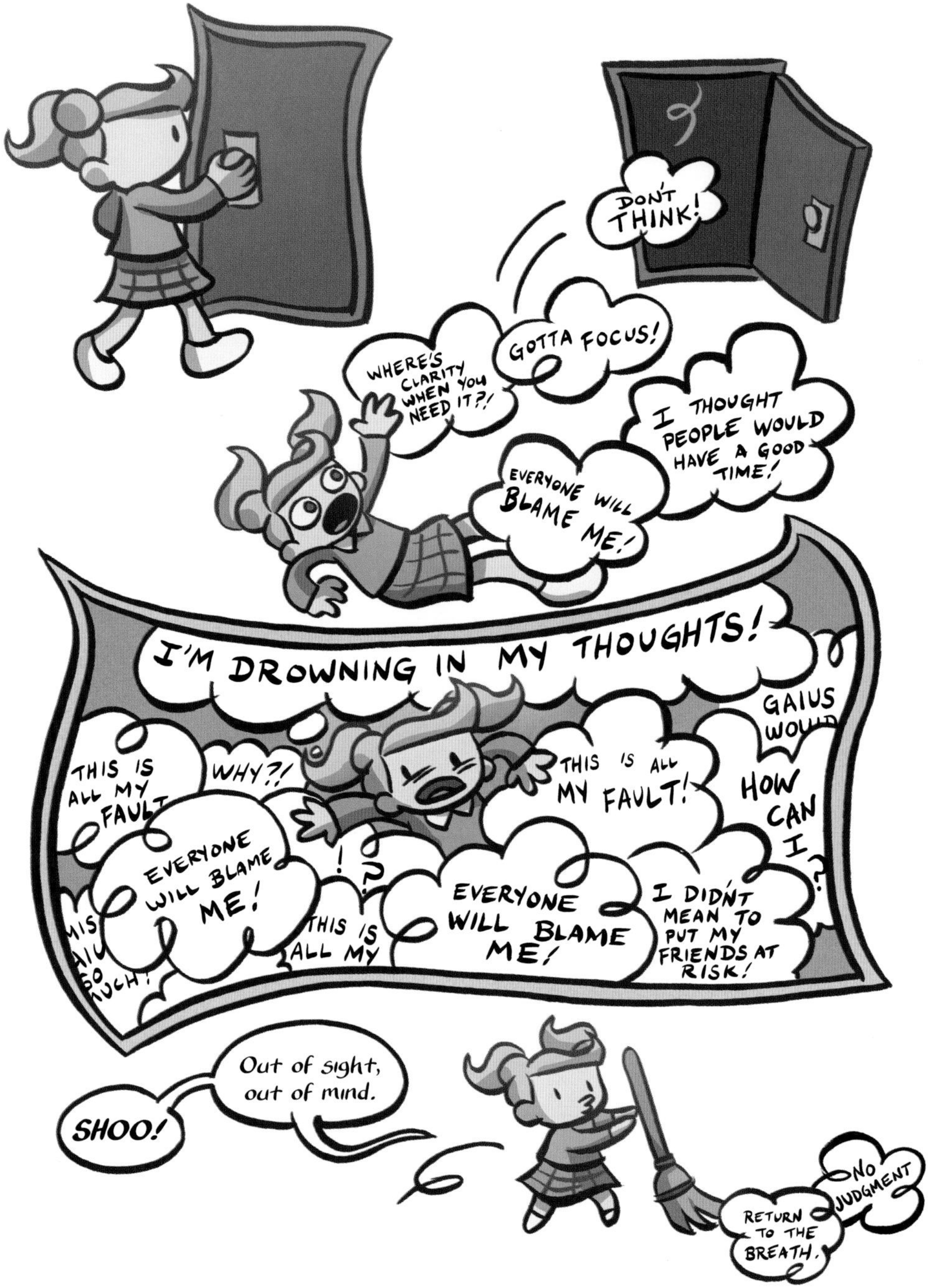
DON'T THINK!
GOTTA FOCUS!
WHERE'S CLARITY WHEN YOU NEED IT?!
I THOUGHT PEOPLE WOULD HAVE A GOOD TIME!
EVERYONE WILL BLAME ME!
I'M DROWNING IN MY THOUGHTS!
THIS IS ALL MY FAULT
WHY?!
THIS IS ALL MY FAULT!
GAIUS WOULD
HOW CAN I ?
EVERYONE WILL BLAME ME!
!?
EVERYONE WILL BLAME ME!
I DIDN'T MEAN TO PUT MY FRIENDS AT RISK!
THIS IS ALL MY
Out of sight, out of mind.
SHOO!
NO JUDGMENT
RETURN TO THE BREATH.

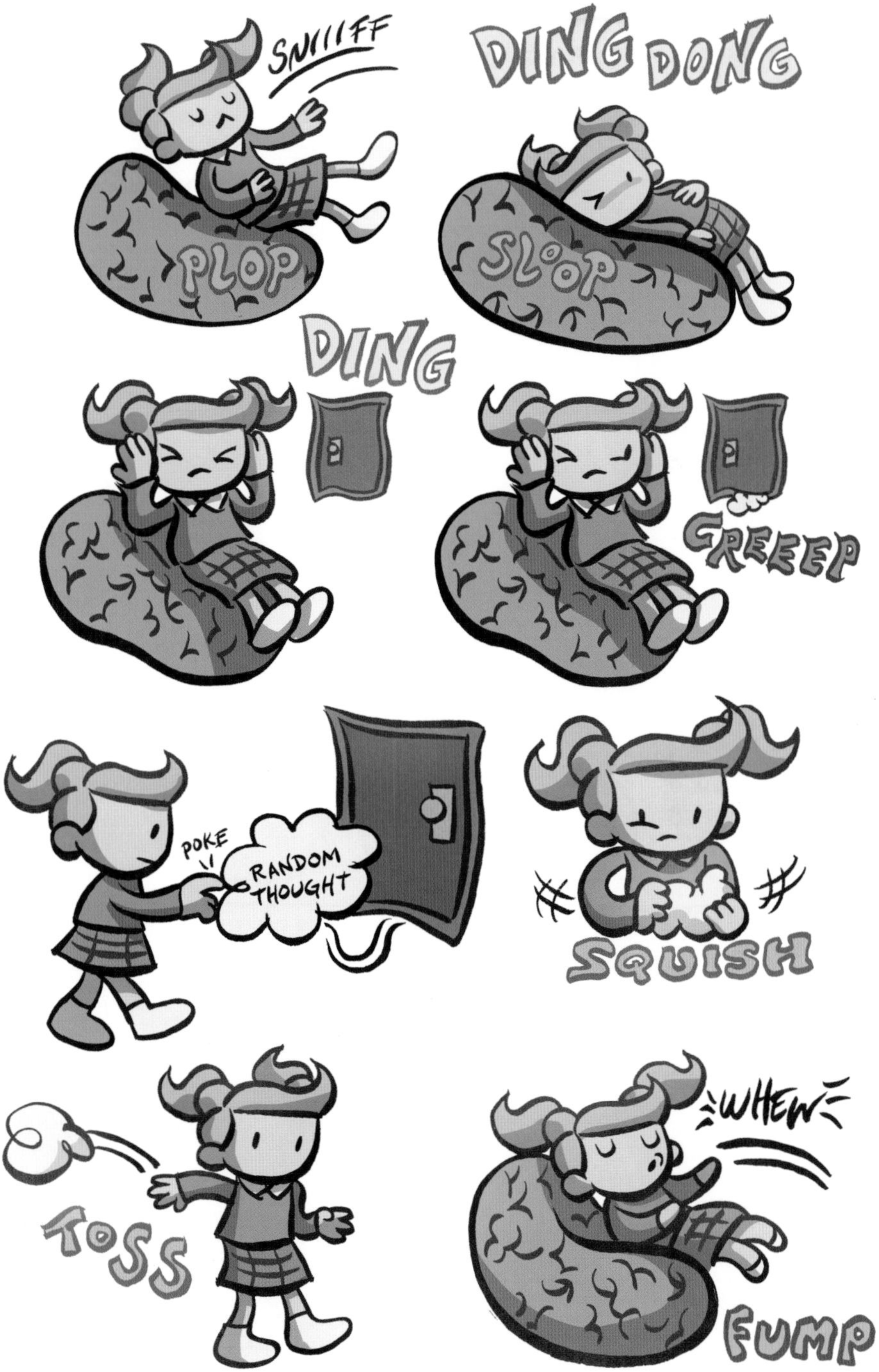
SNIIIFF
PLOP
DING DONG
SLOOP
DING
CREEEP
POKE
RANDOM THOUGHT
SQUISH
TOSS
WHEW
FUMP

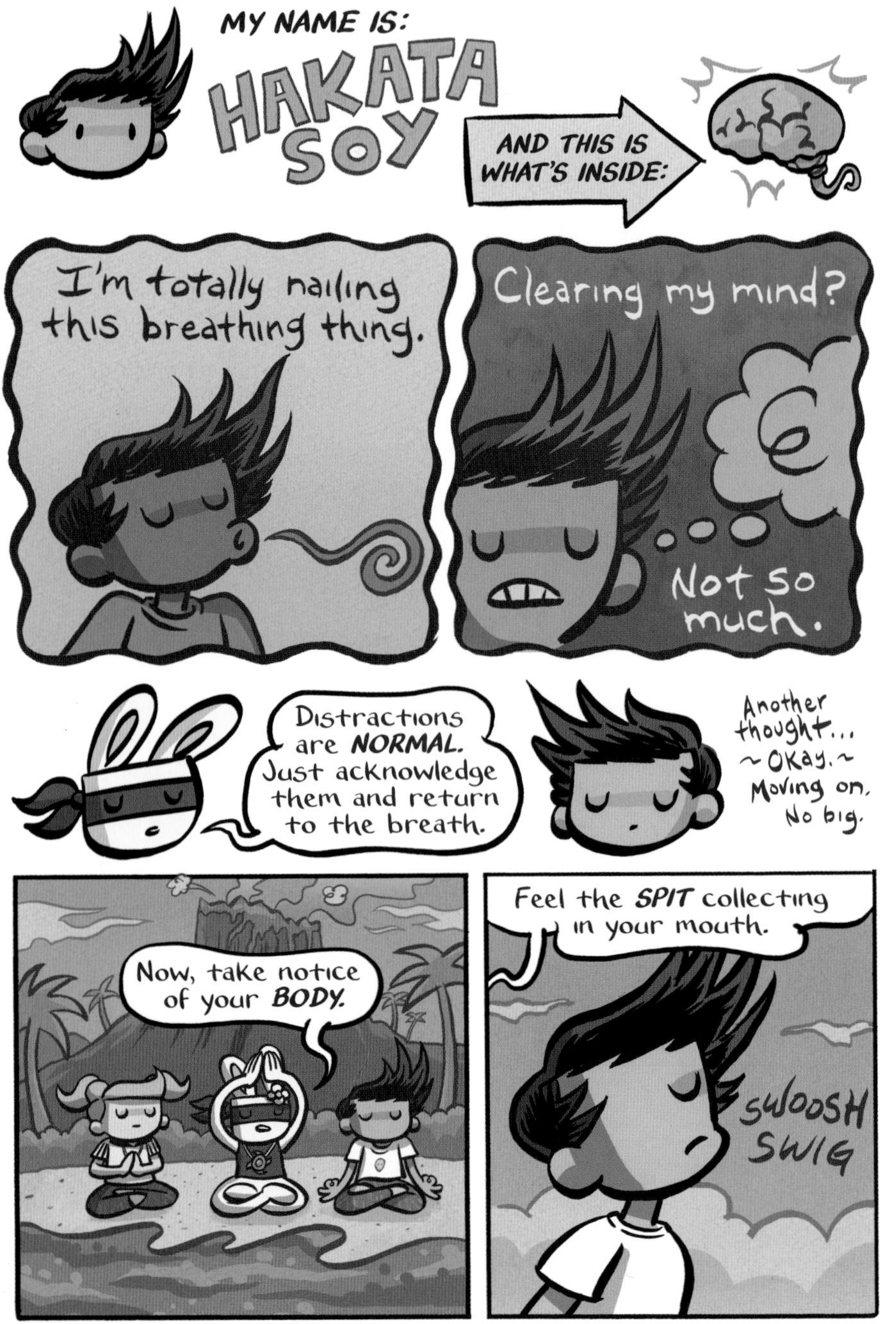
MY NAME IS:
HAKATA SOY
AND THIS IS WHAT'S INSIDE:
I'm totally nailing this breathing thing.
Clearing my mind?
Not so much.
Distractions are NORMAL. Just acknowledge them and return to the breath.
Another thought... ~Okay.~ Moving on. No big.
Now, take notice of your BODY.
Feel the SPIT collecting in your mouth.
SWOOSH
SWIG

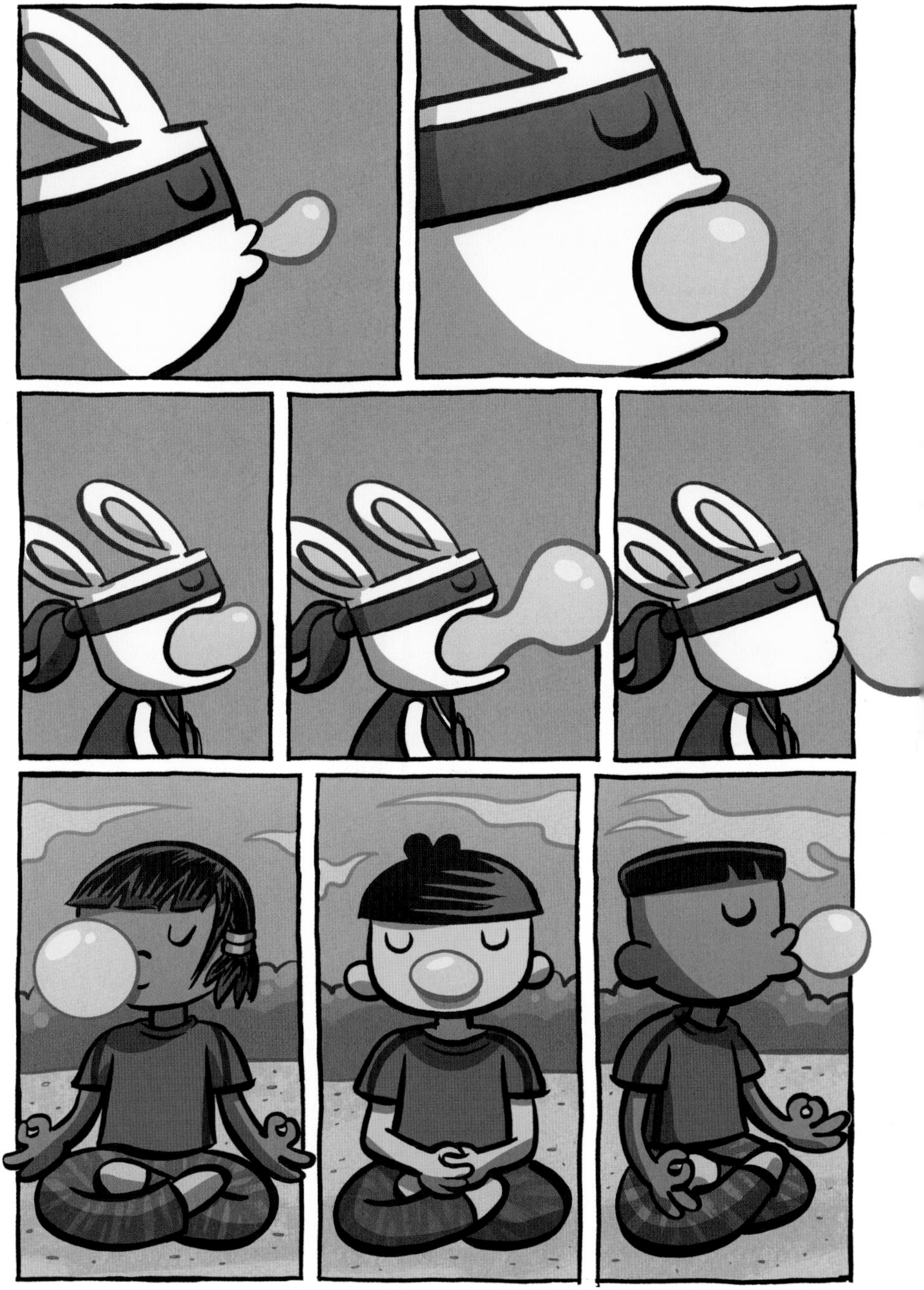

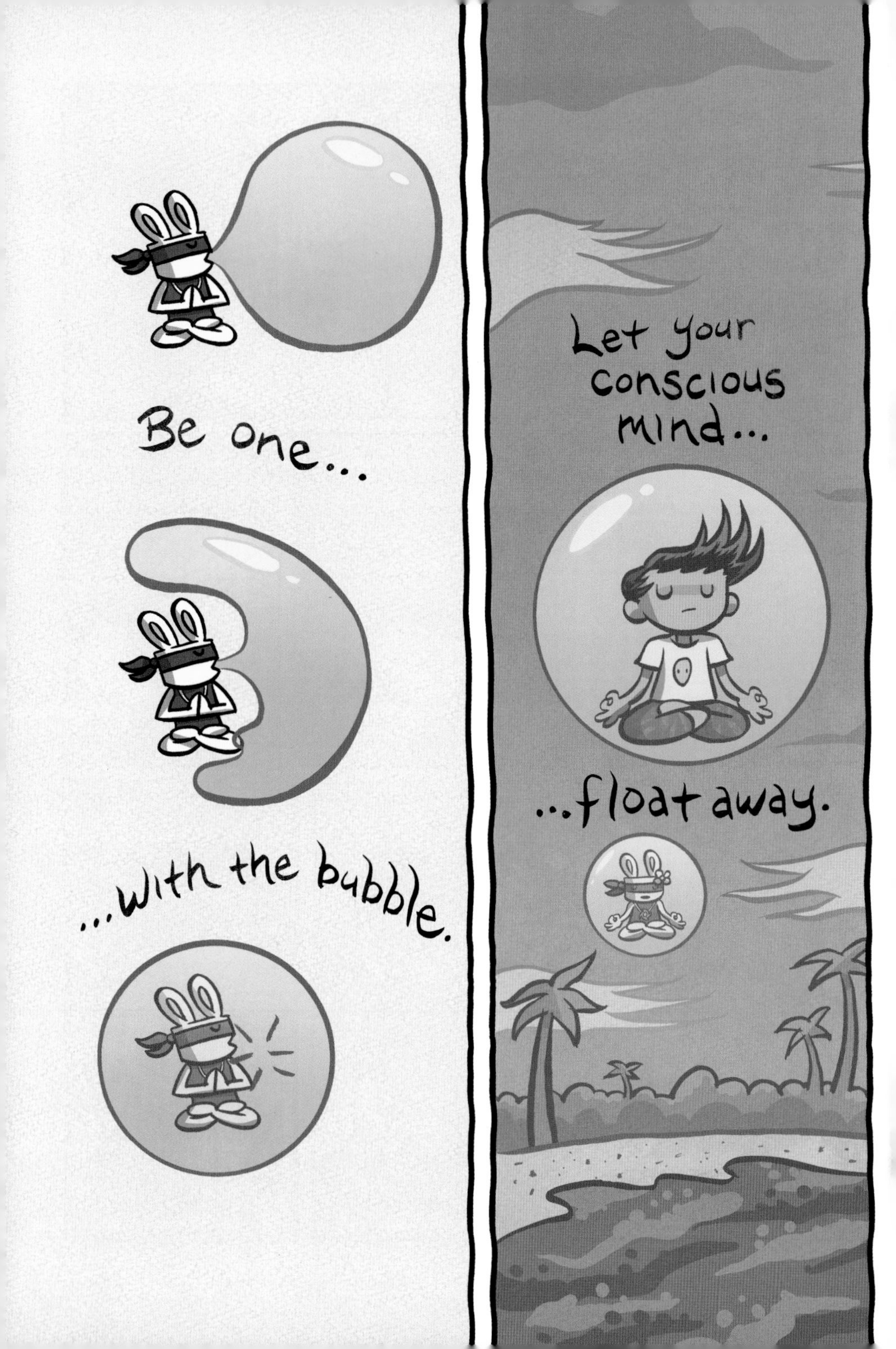
Be one...
...with the bubble.
Let your conscious mind...
...float away.

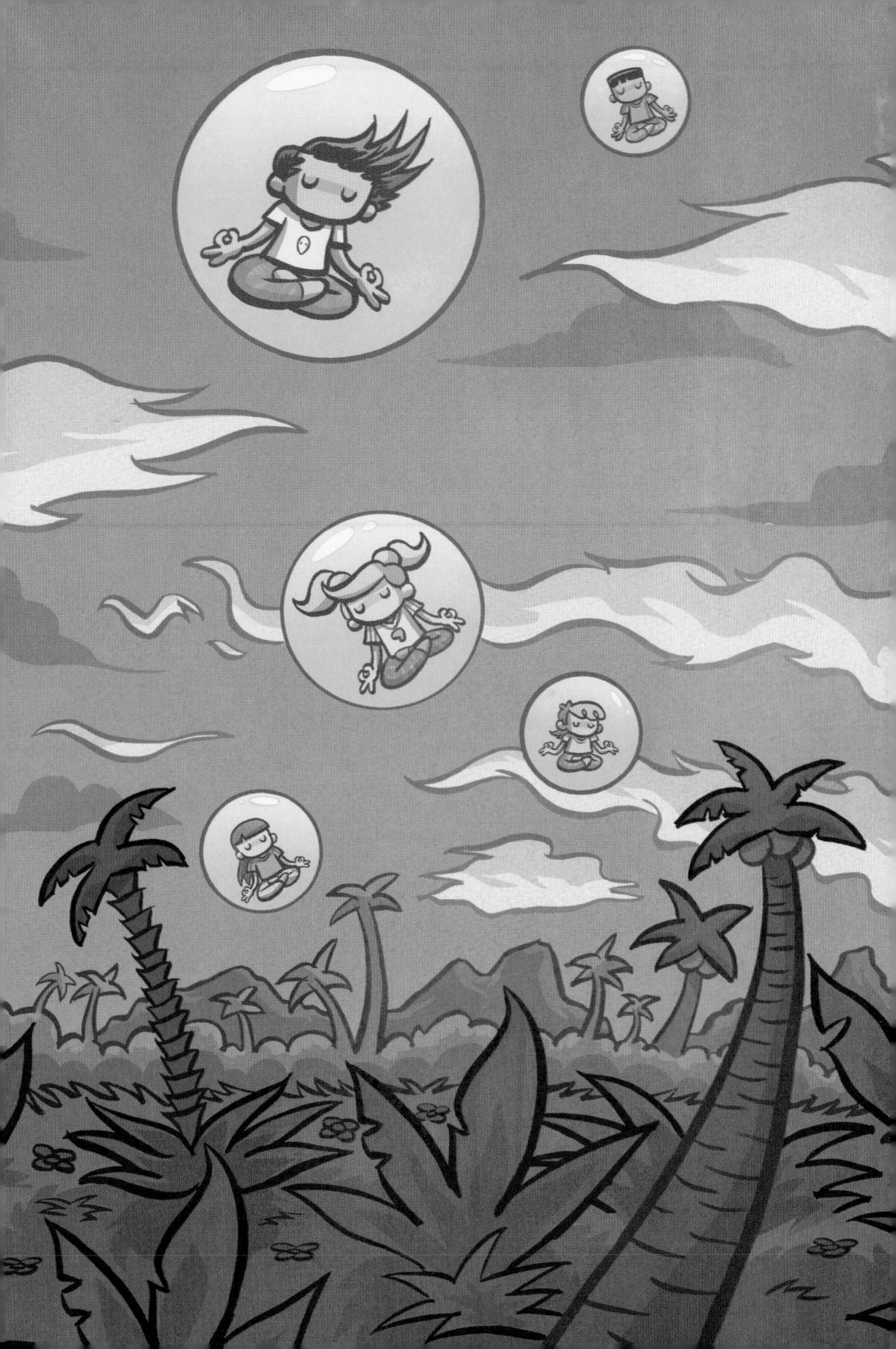

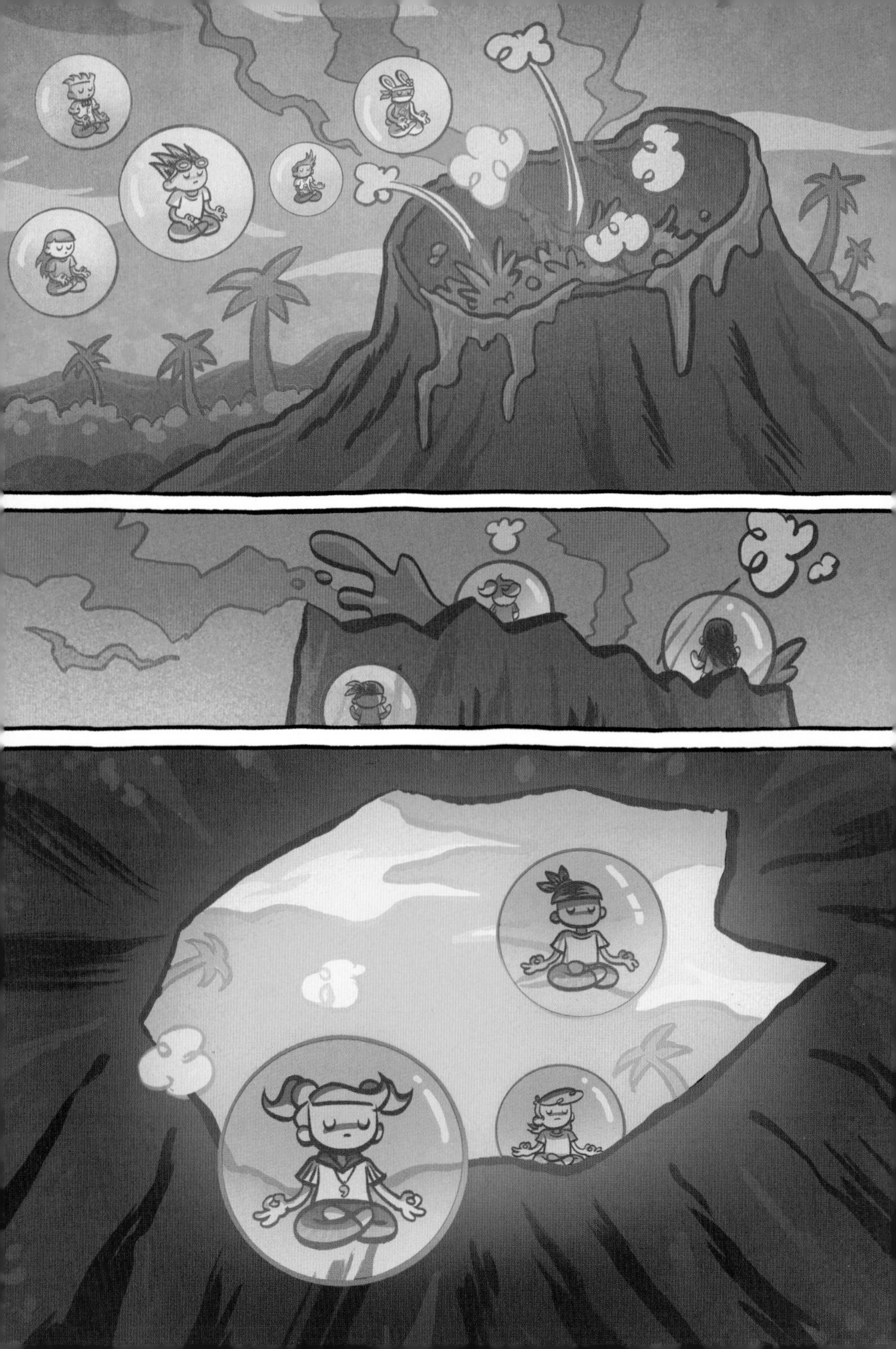

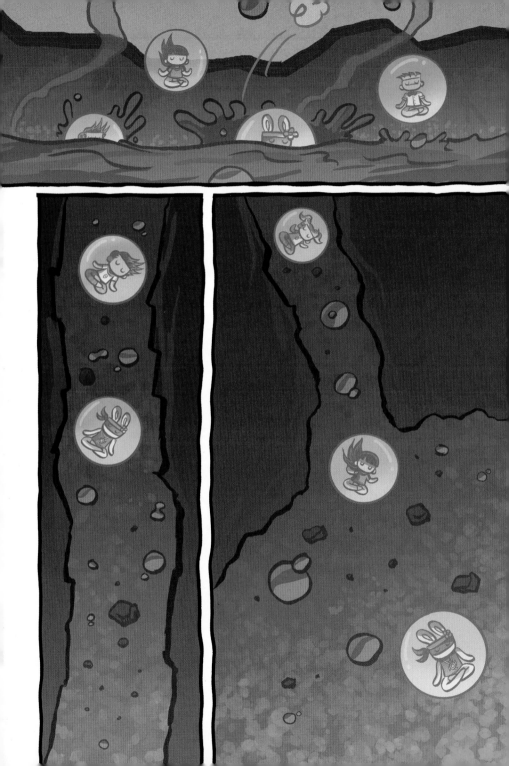

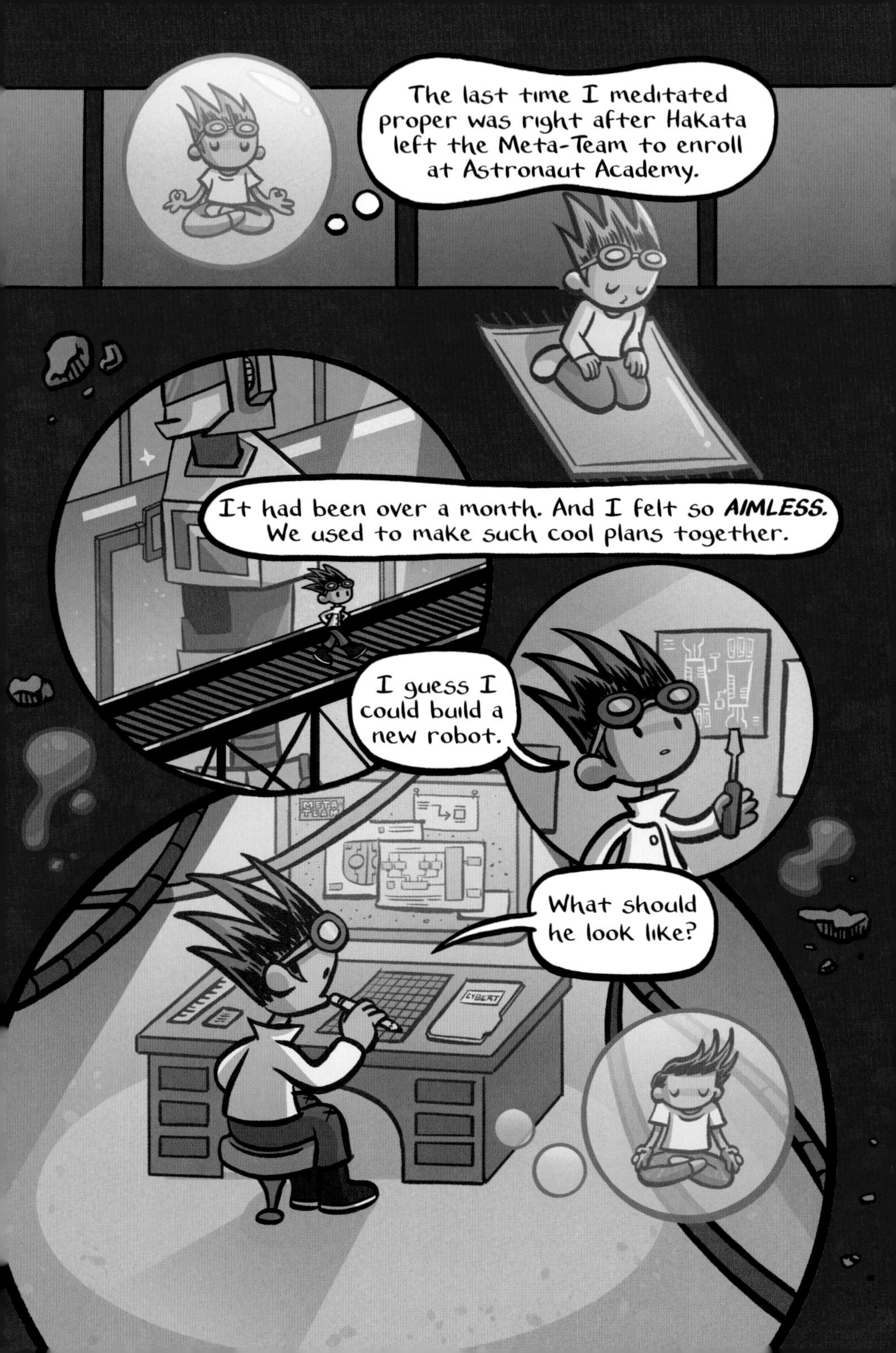
The last time I meditated proper was right after Hakata left the Meta-Team to enroll at Astronaut Academy.
It had been over a month. And I felt so ***AIMLESS.*** We used to make such cool plans together.
I guess I could build a new robot.
META TEAM
What should he look like?
CYBERT

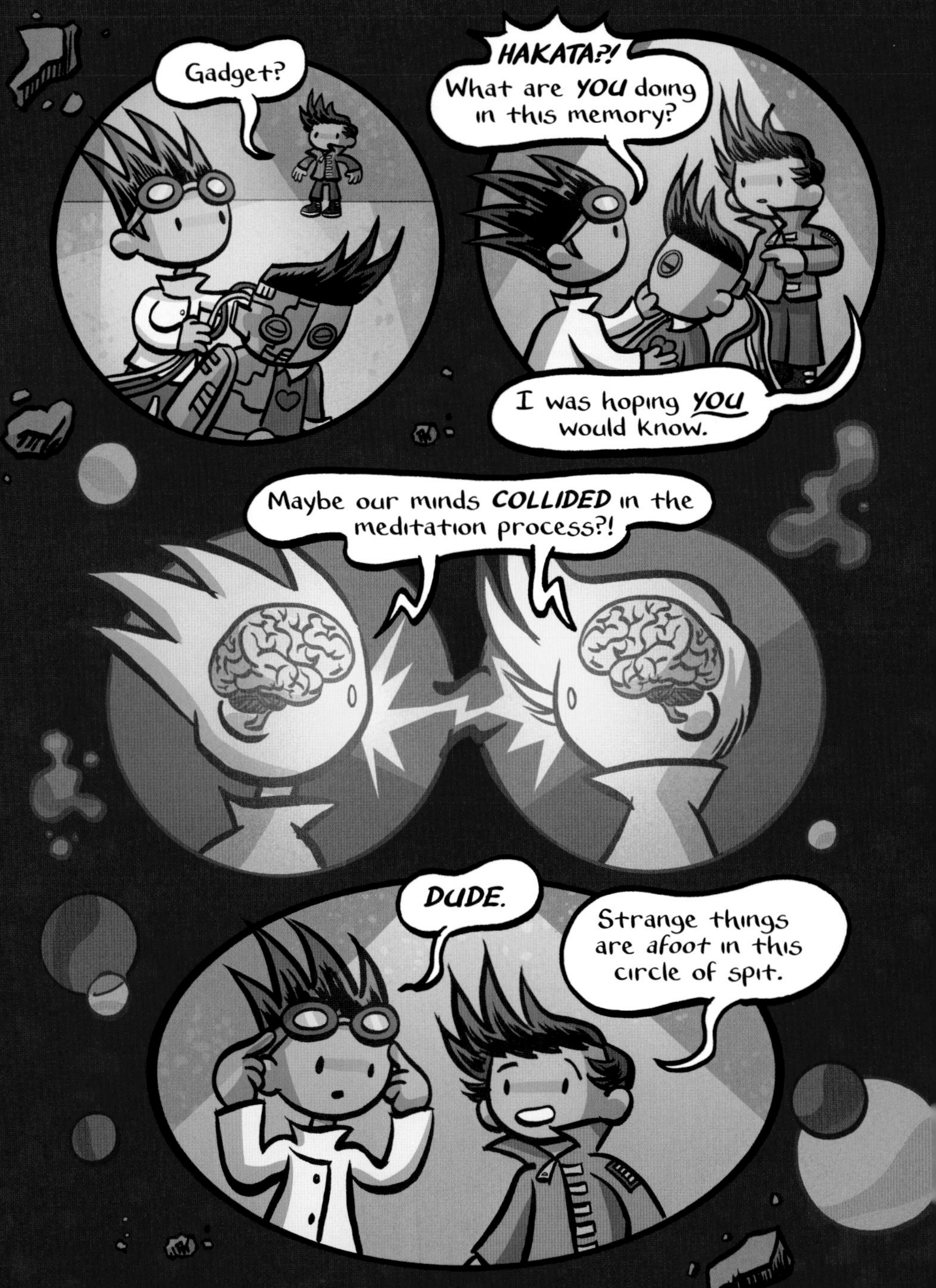

Gadget?
HAKATA?!
What are YOU doing in this memory?
I was hoping YOU would know.
Maybe our minds COLLIDED in the meditation process?!
DUDE.
Strange things are afoot in this circle of spit.

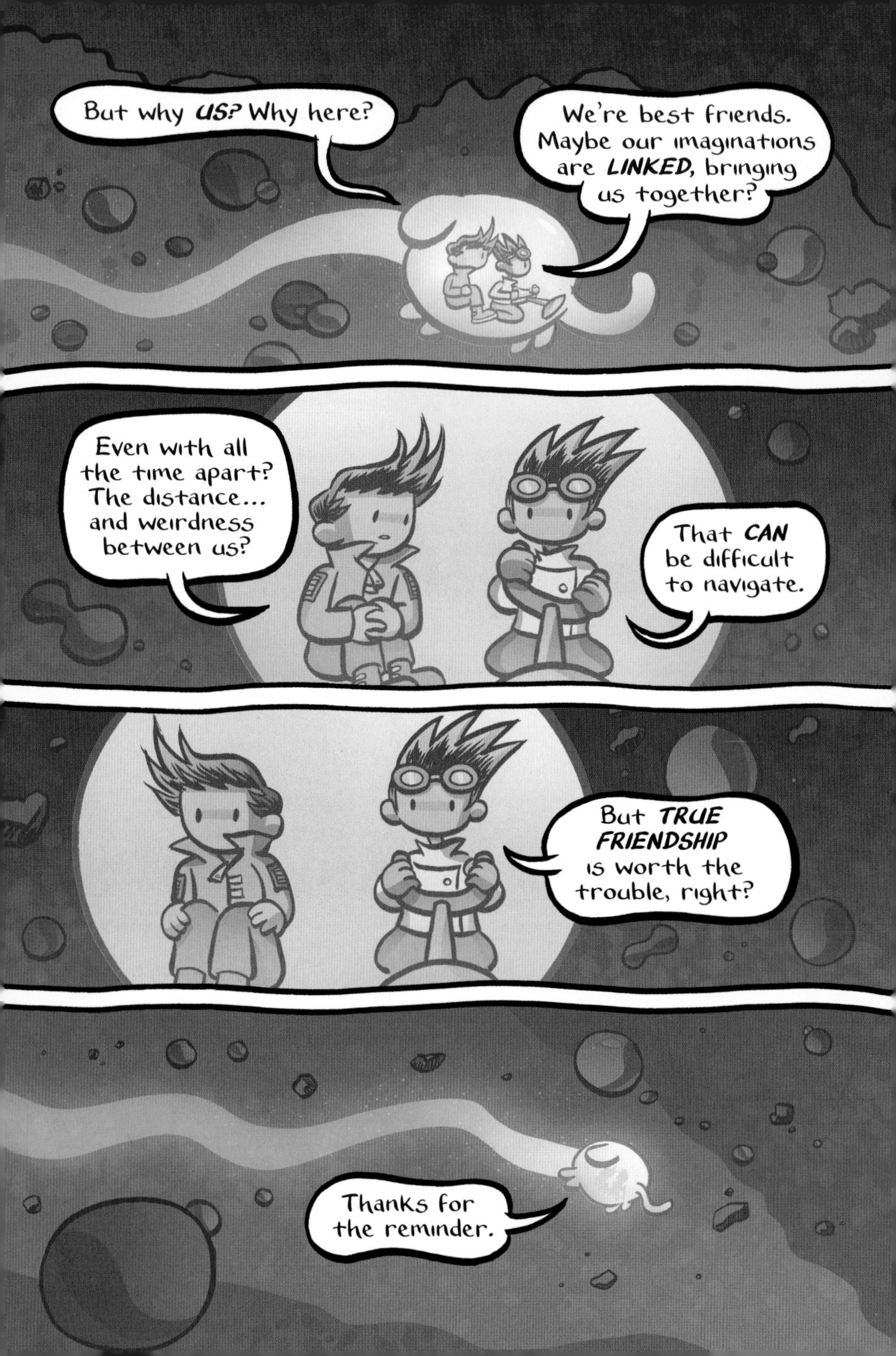
But why US? Why here?
We're best friends. Maybe our imaginations are LINKED, bringing us together?
Even with all the time apart? The distance... and weirdness between us?
That CAN be difficult to navigate.
But TRUE FRIENDSHIP is worth the trouble, right?
Thanks for the reminder.

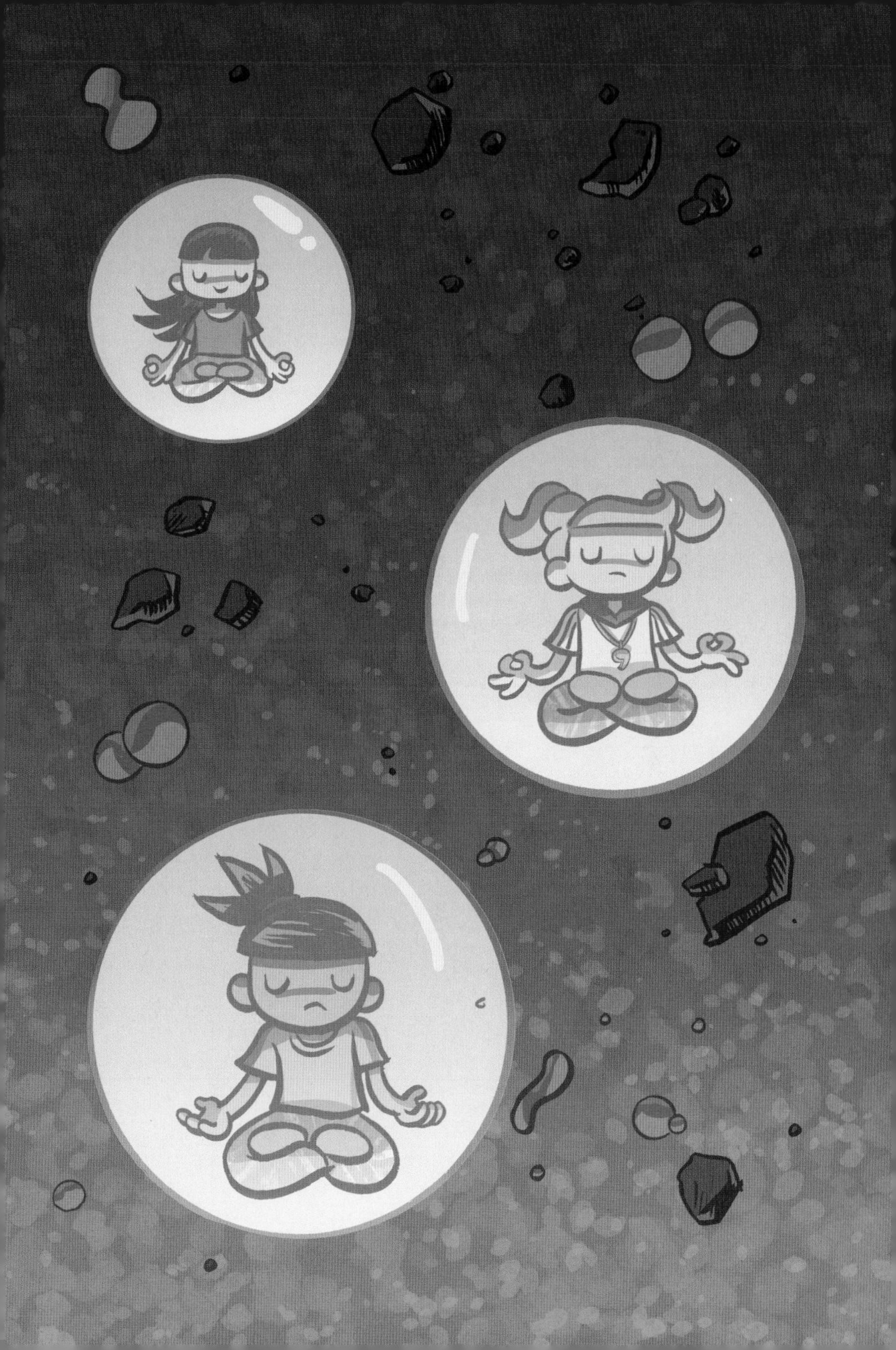

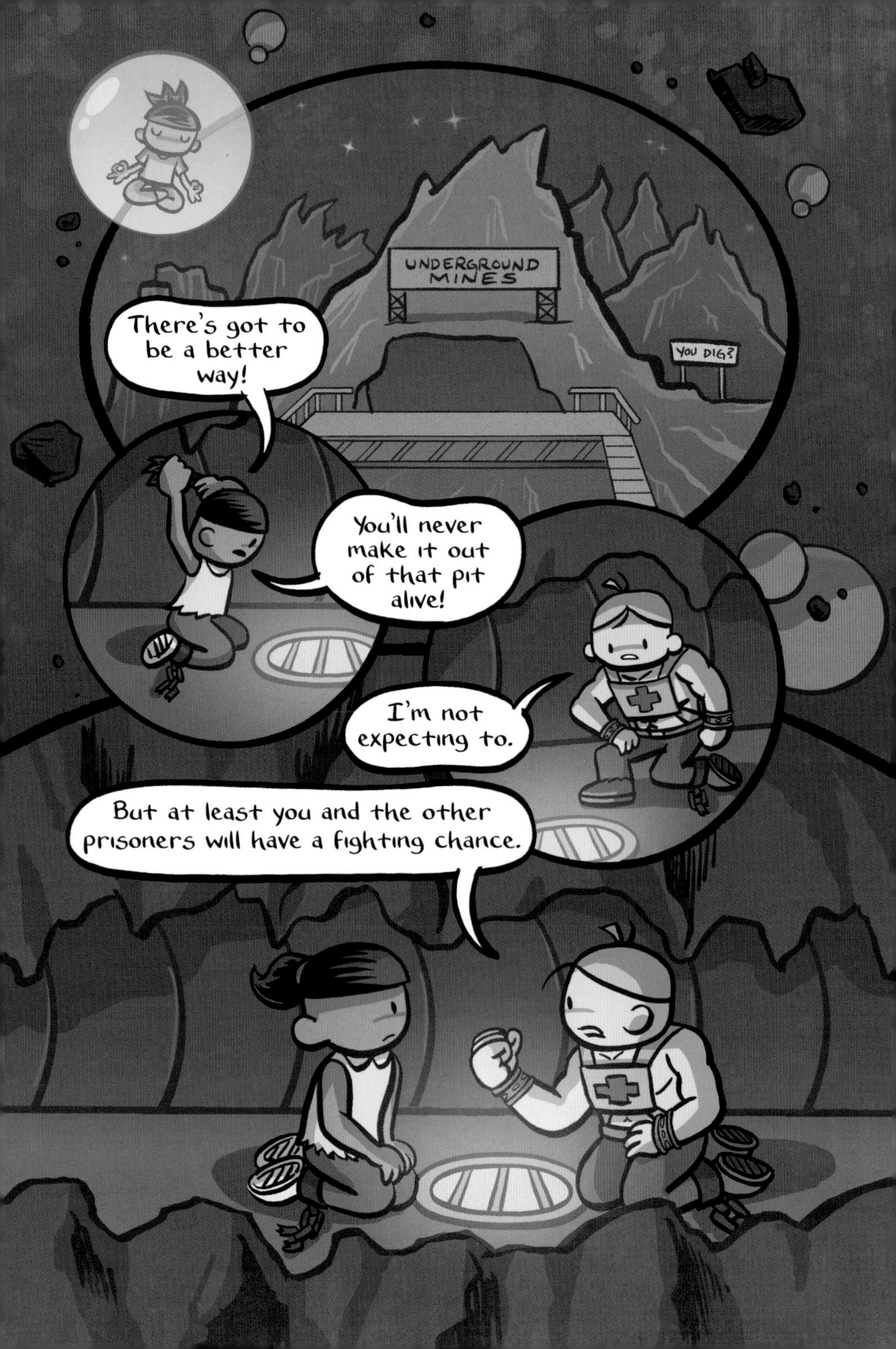
UNDERGROUND MINES
YOU DIG?
There's got to be a better way!
You'll never make it out of that pit alive!
I'm not expecting to.
But at least you and the other prisoners will have a fighting chance.

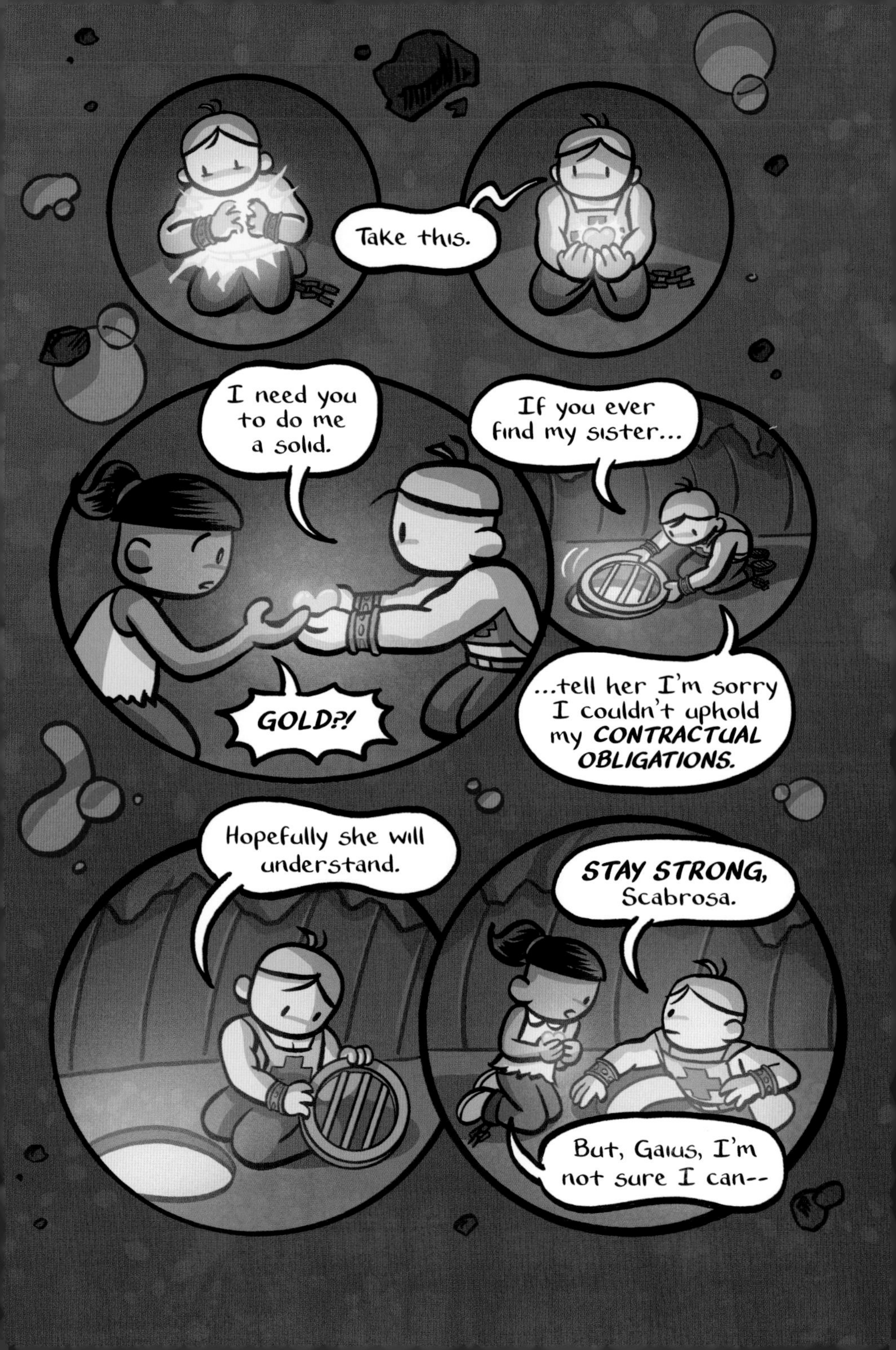
Take this.
I need you to do me a solid.
GOLD?!
If you ever find my sister...
...tell her I'm sorry I couldn't uphold my CONTRACTUAL OBLIGATIONS.
Hopefully she will understand.
STAY STRONG, Scabrosa.
But, Gaius, I'm not sure I can--

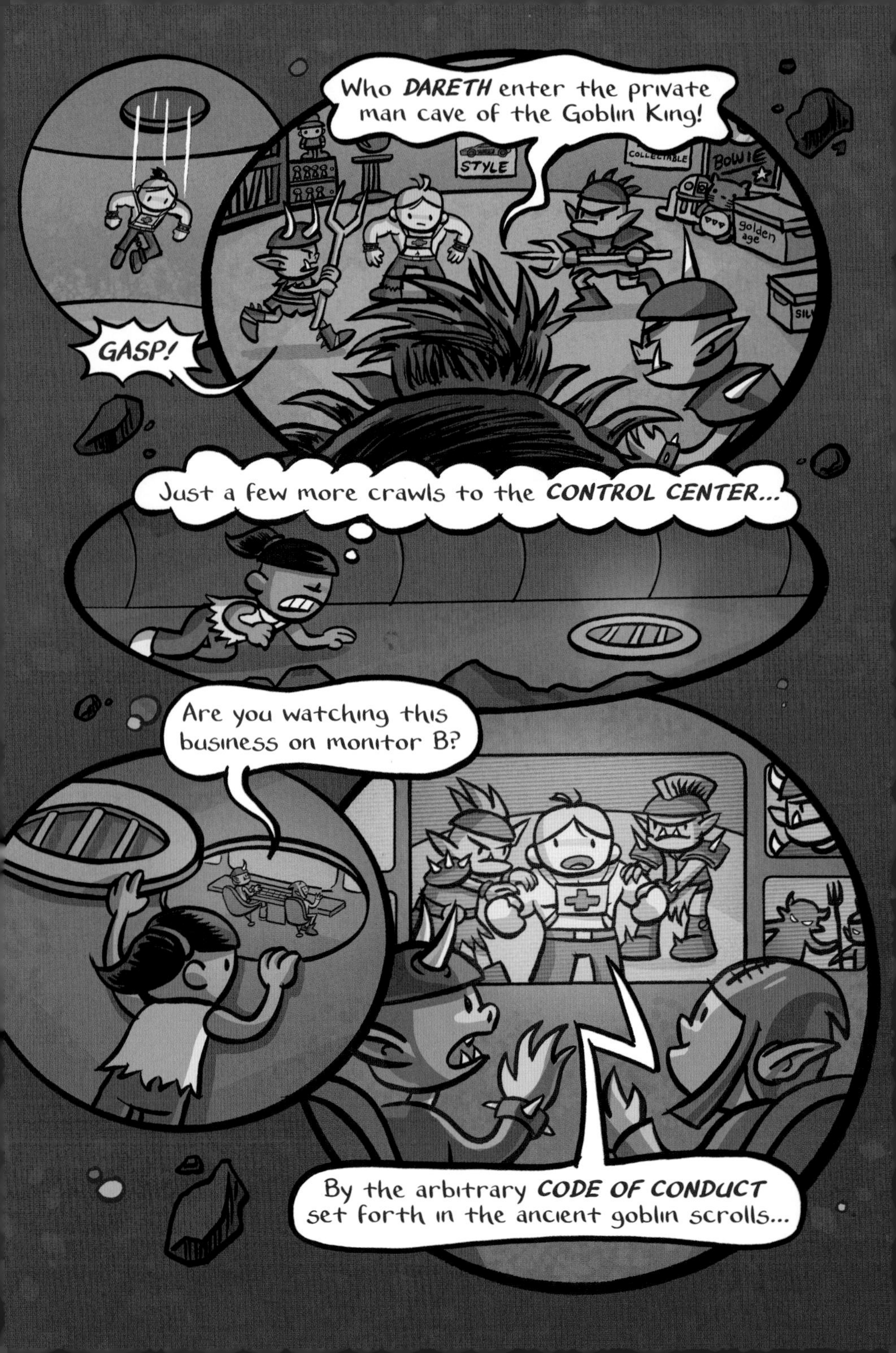

Who DARETH enter the private man cave of the Goblin King!
STYLE
COLLECTABLE
BOWIE
golden age
GASP!
Just a few more crawls to the CONTROL CENTER...
Are you watching this business on monitor B?
By the arbitrary CODE OF CONDUCT set forth in the ancient goblin scrolls...

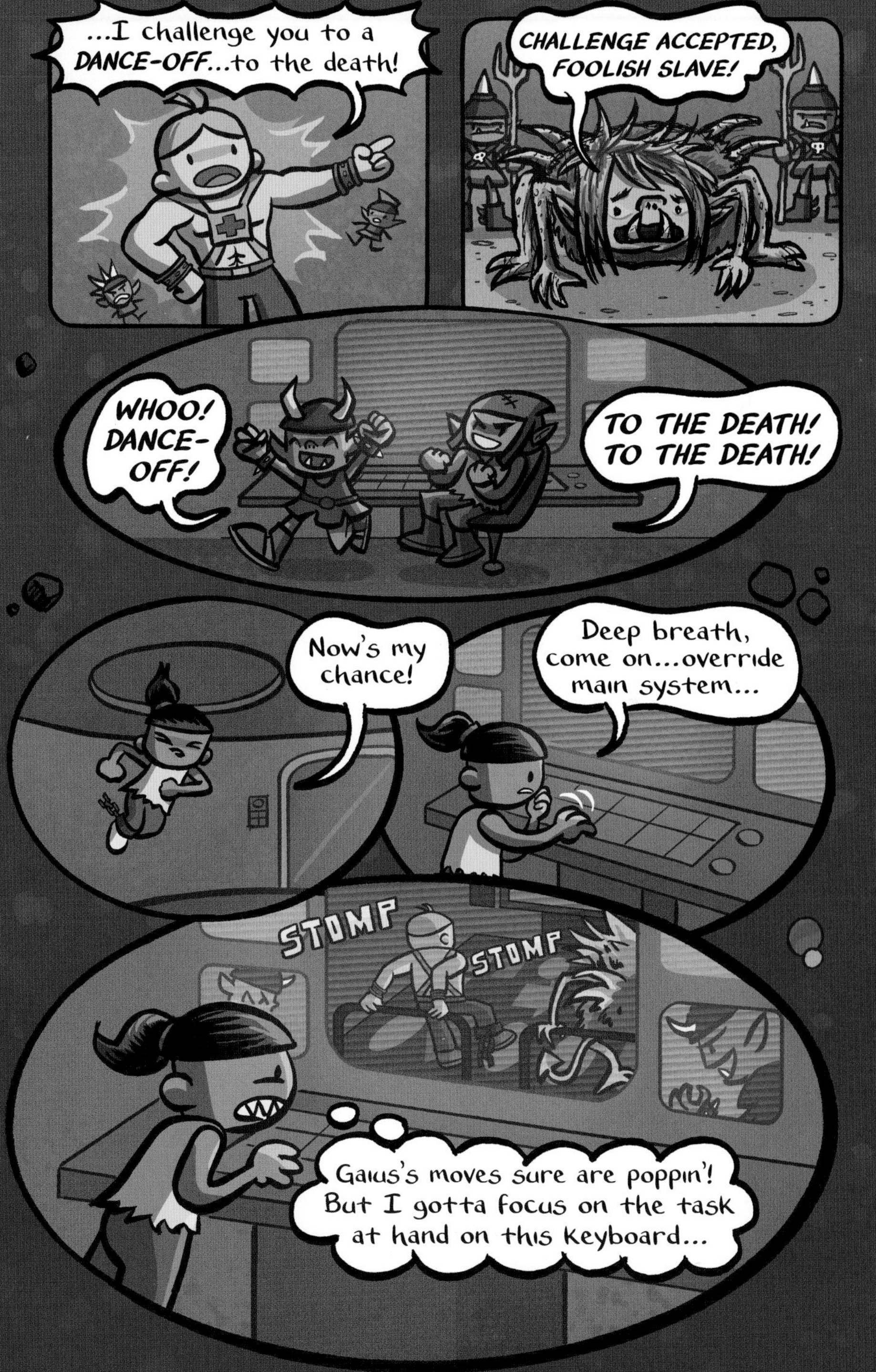
...I challenge you to a DANCE-OFF...to the death!
CHALLENGE ACCEPTED, FOOLISH SLAVE!
WHOO! DANCE-OFF!
TO THE DEATH! TO THE DEATH!
Now's my chance!
Deep breath, come on...override main system...
STOMP
STOMP
Gaius's moves sure are poppin'! But I gotta focus on the task at hand on this keyboard...

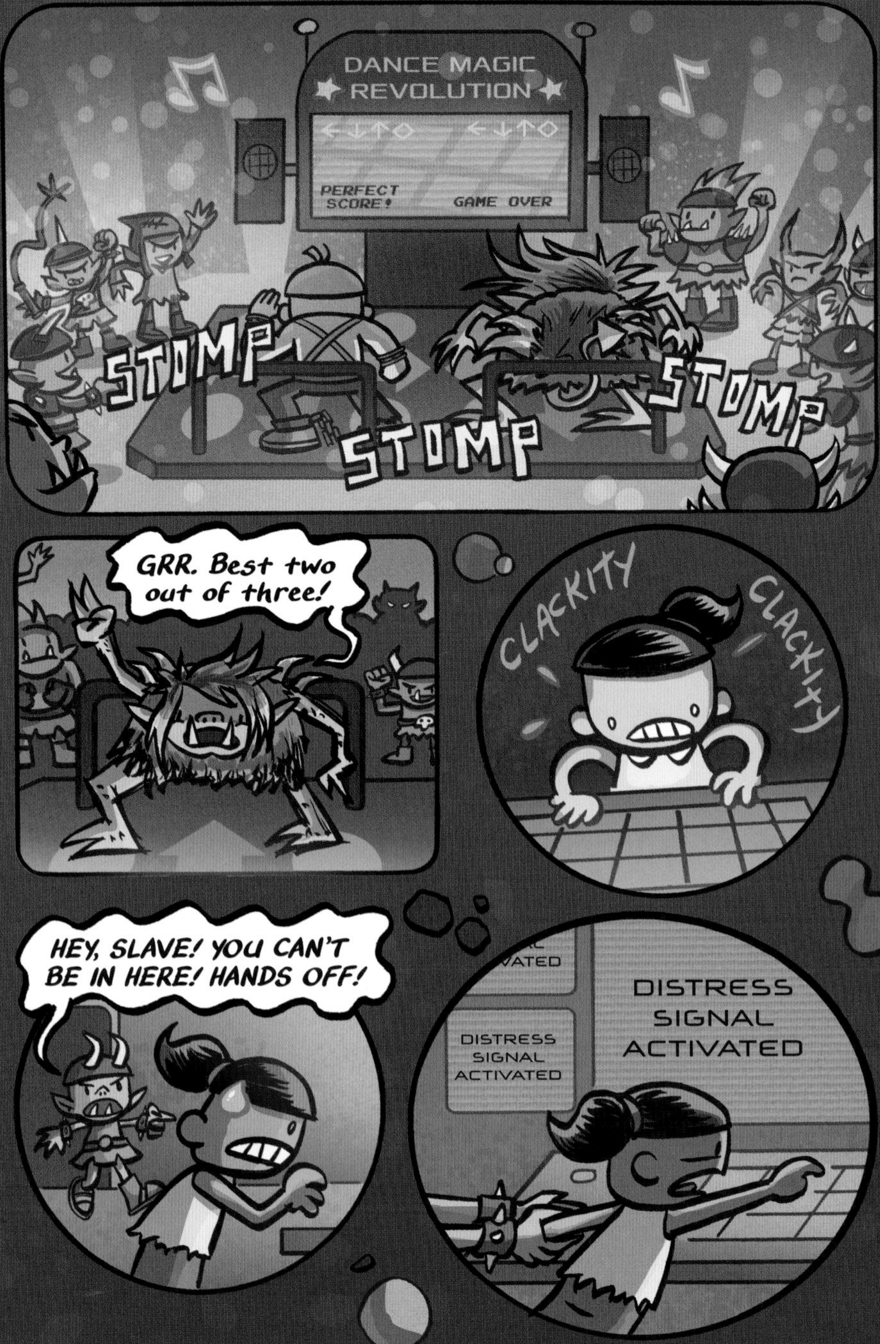

DANCE MAGIC
REVOLUTION
PERFECT SCORE!
GAME OVER
STOMP
STOMP
STOMP
GRR. Best two out of three!
CLACKITY
CLACKITY
HEY, SLAVE! YOU CAN'T BE IN HERE! HANDS OFF!
DISTRESS SIGNAL ACTIVATED
DISTRESS SIGNAL ACTIVATED

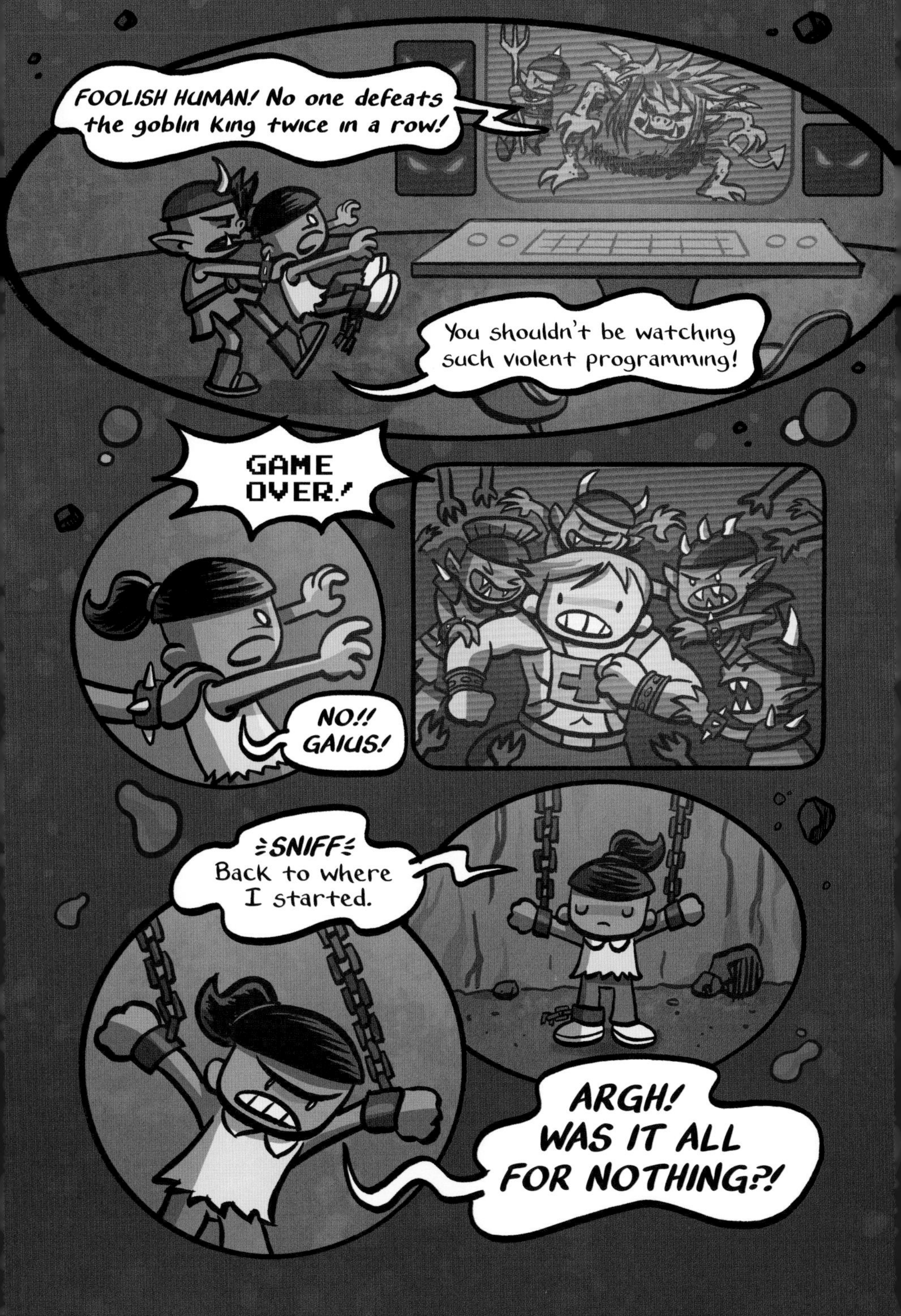
FOOLISH HUMAN! No one defeats the goblin king twice in a row!
You shouldn't be watching such violent programming!
GAME OVER!
NO!! GAIUS!
SNIFF
Back to where I started.
ARGH! WAS IT ALL FOR NOTHING?!

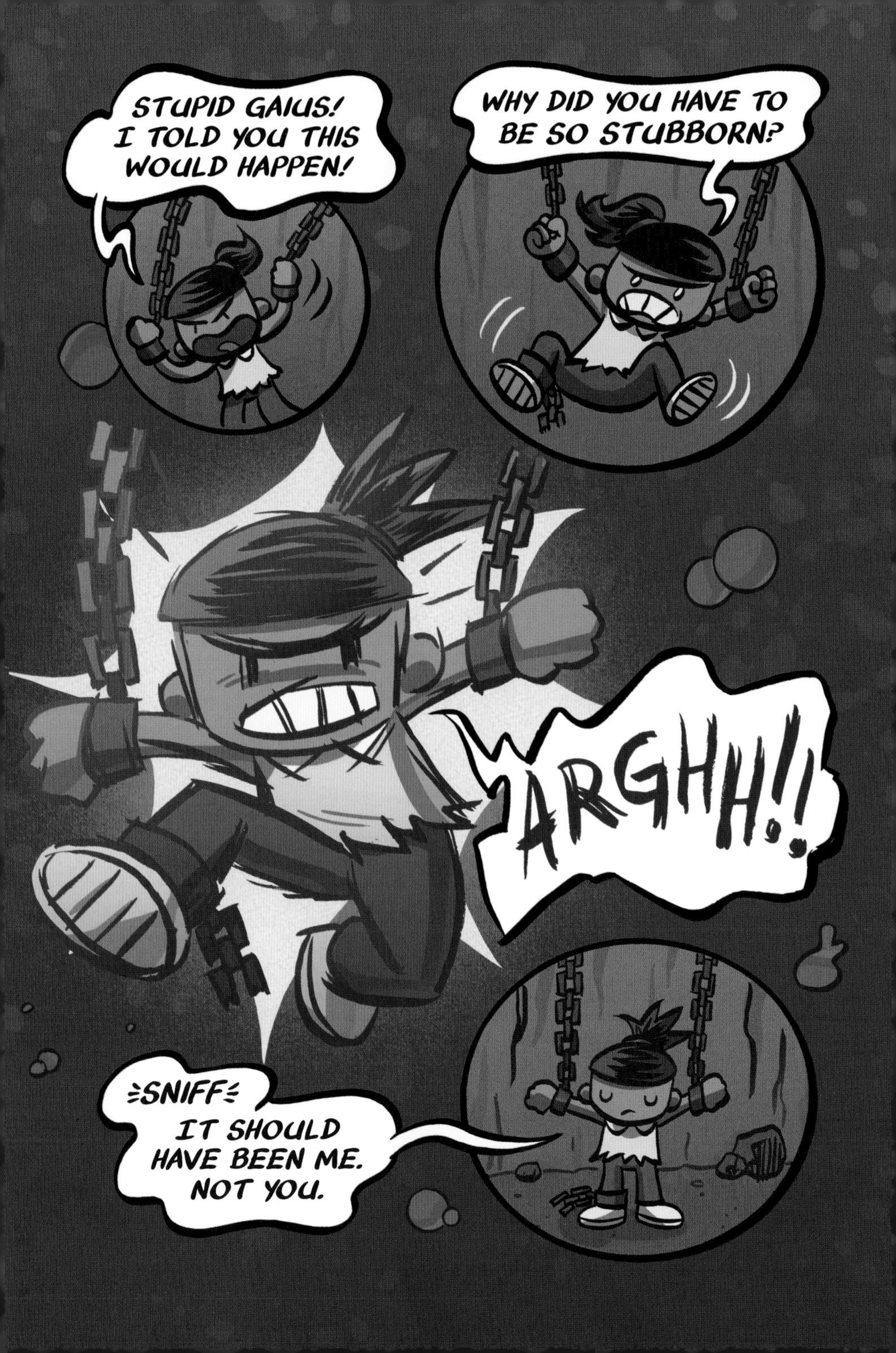
STUPID GAIUS! I TOLD YOU THIS WOULD HAPPEN!
WHY DID YOU HAVE TO BE SO STUBBORN?
ARGHH!!
SNIFF
IT SHOULD HAVE BEEN ME. NOT YOU.

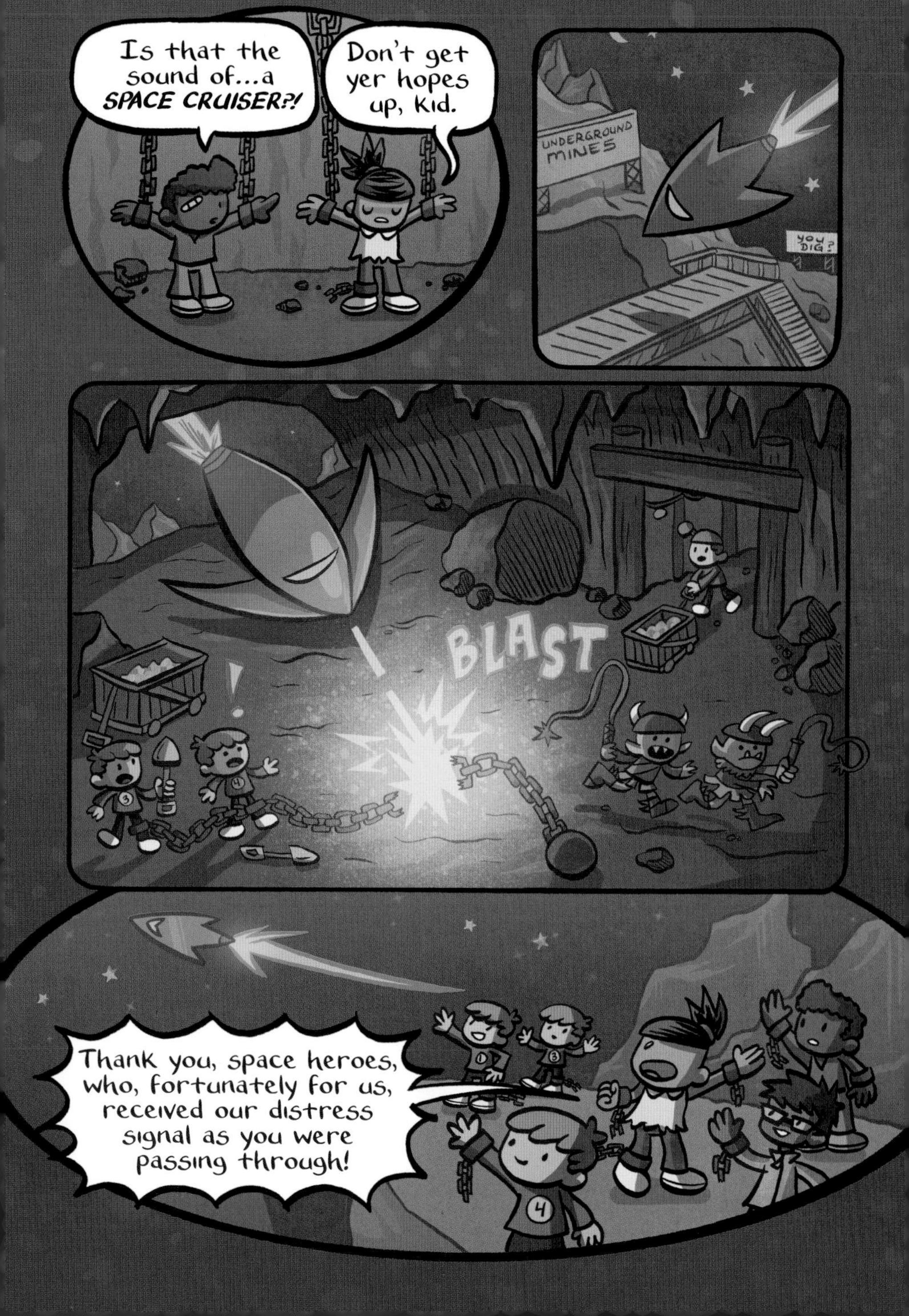
Is that the sound of...a SPACE CRUISER?!
Don't get yer hopes up, kid.
UNDERGROUND MINES
YOU DIG?
BLAST
Thank you, space heroes, who, fortunately for us, received our distress signal as you were passing through!

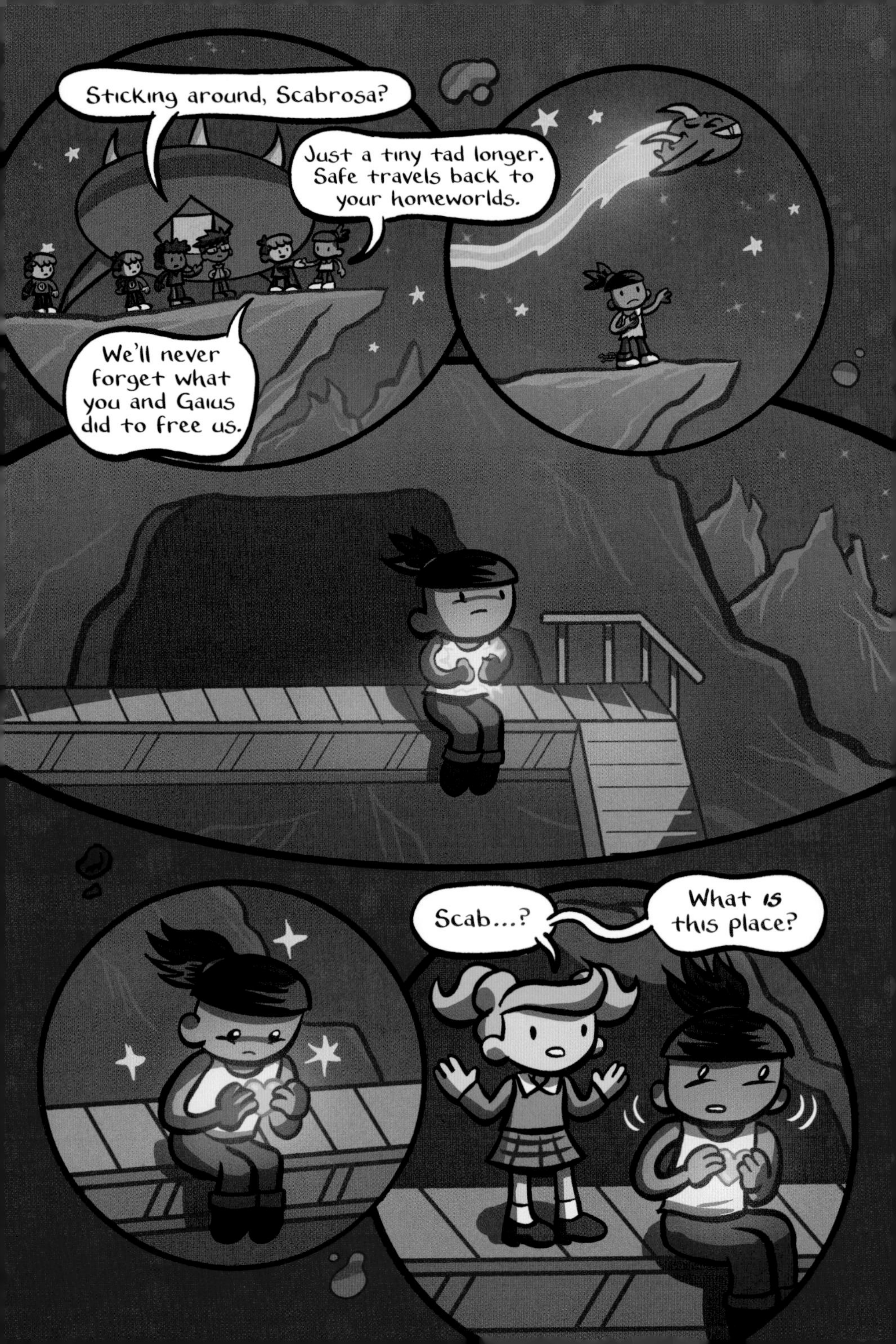
Sticking around, Scabrosa?
Just a tiny tad longer. Safe travels back to your homeworlds.
We'll never forget what you and Gaius did to free us.
Scab...?
What IS this place?

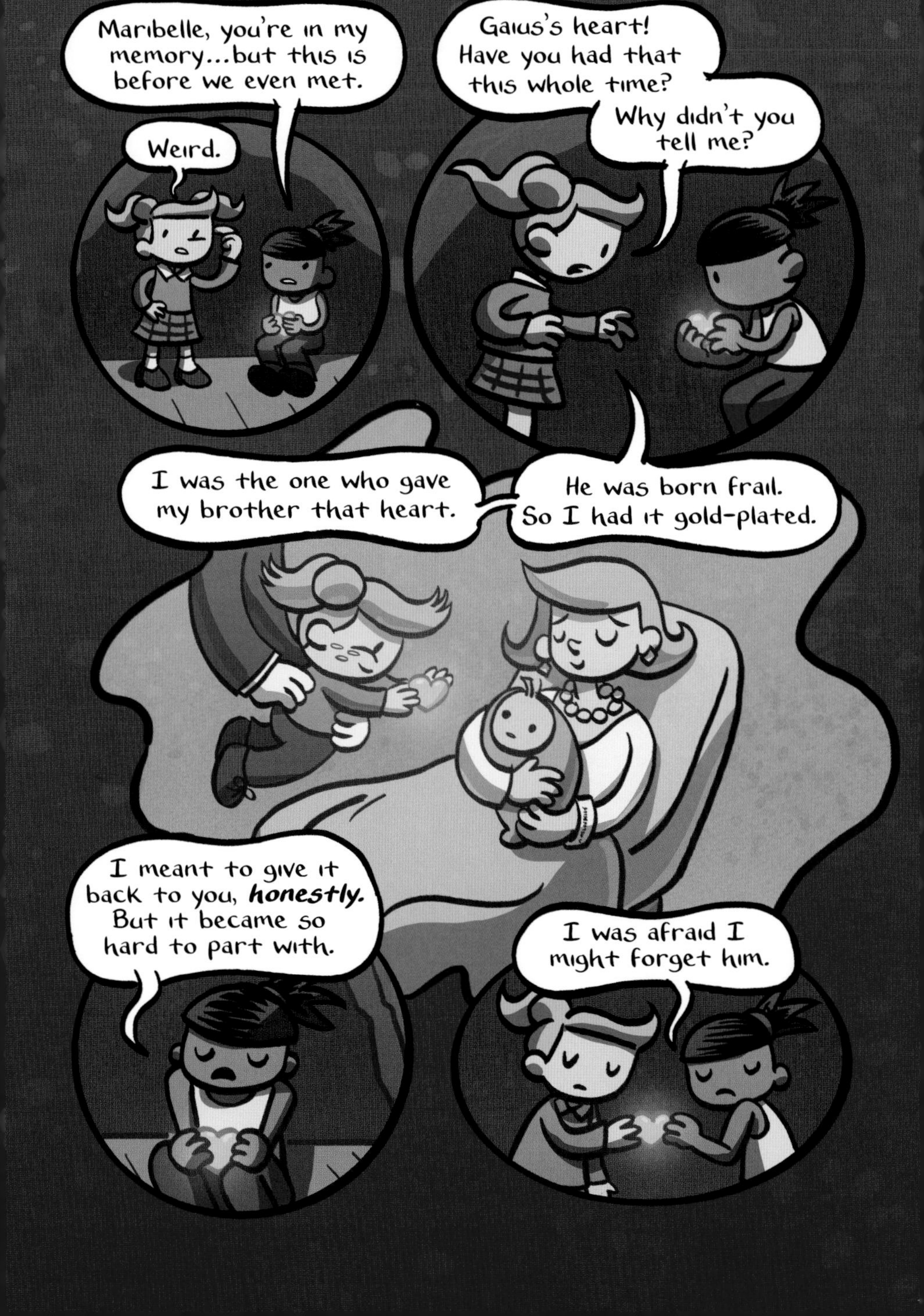
Maribelle, you're in my memory...but this is before we even met.
Weird.
Gaius's heart! Have you had that this whole time?
Why didn't you tell me?
I was the one who gave my brother that heart.
He was born frail. So I had it gold-plated.
I meant to give it back to you, *honestly.* But it became so hard to part with.
I was afraid I might forget him.

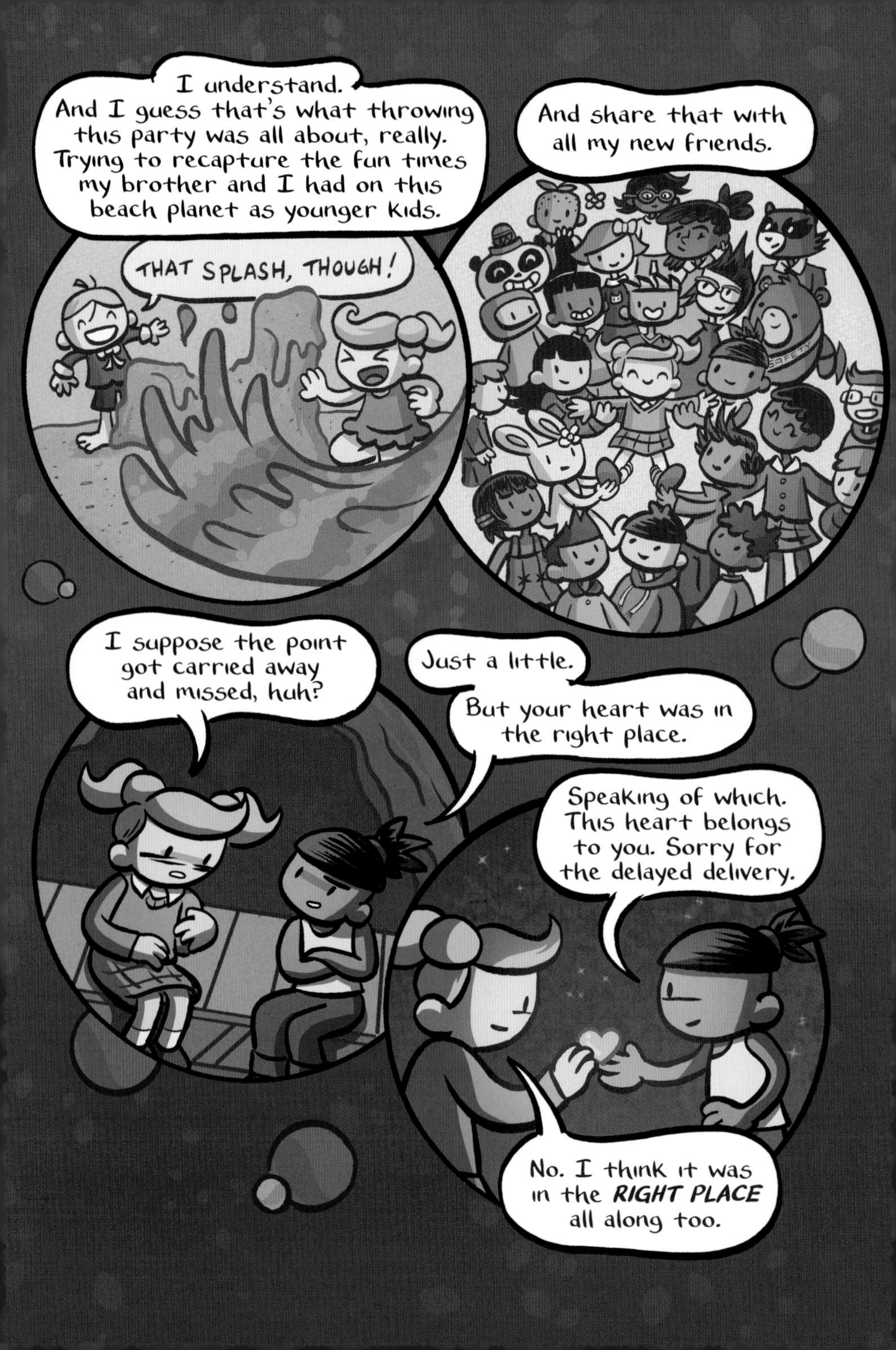
I understand. And I guess that's what throwing this party was all about, really. Trying to recapture the fun times my brother and I had on this beach planet as younger kids.
THAT SPLASH, THOUGH!
And share that with all my new friends.
SAFETY
I suppose the point got carried away and missed, huh?
Just a little.
But your heart was in the right place.
Speaking of which. This heart belongs to you. Sorry for the delayed delivery.
No. I think it was in the *RIGHT PLACE* all along too.

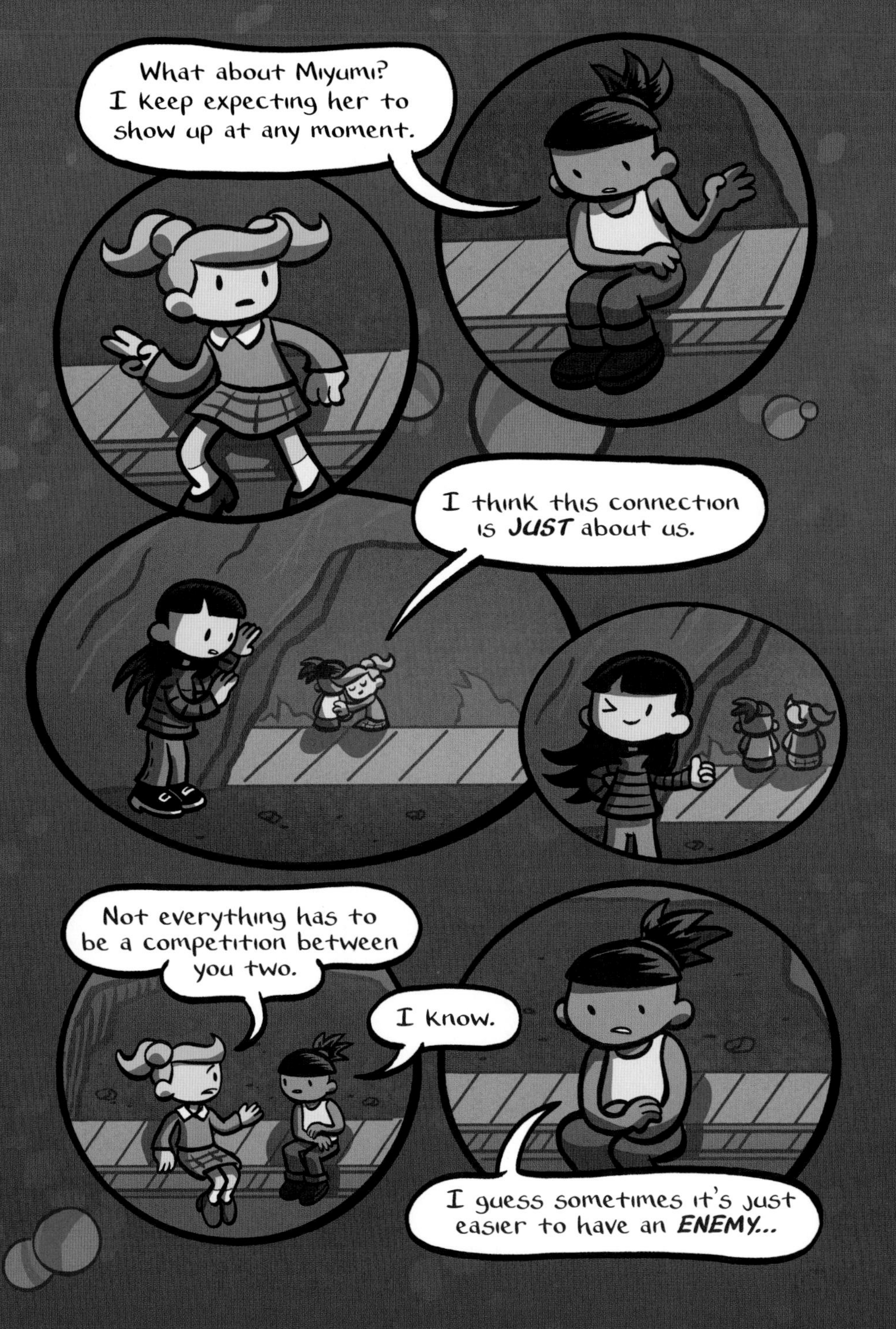
What about Miyumi? I keep expecting her to show up at any moment.
I think this connection is JUST about us.
Not everything has to be a competition between you two.
I know.
I guess sometimes it's just easier to have an ENEMY...

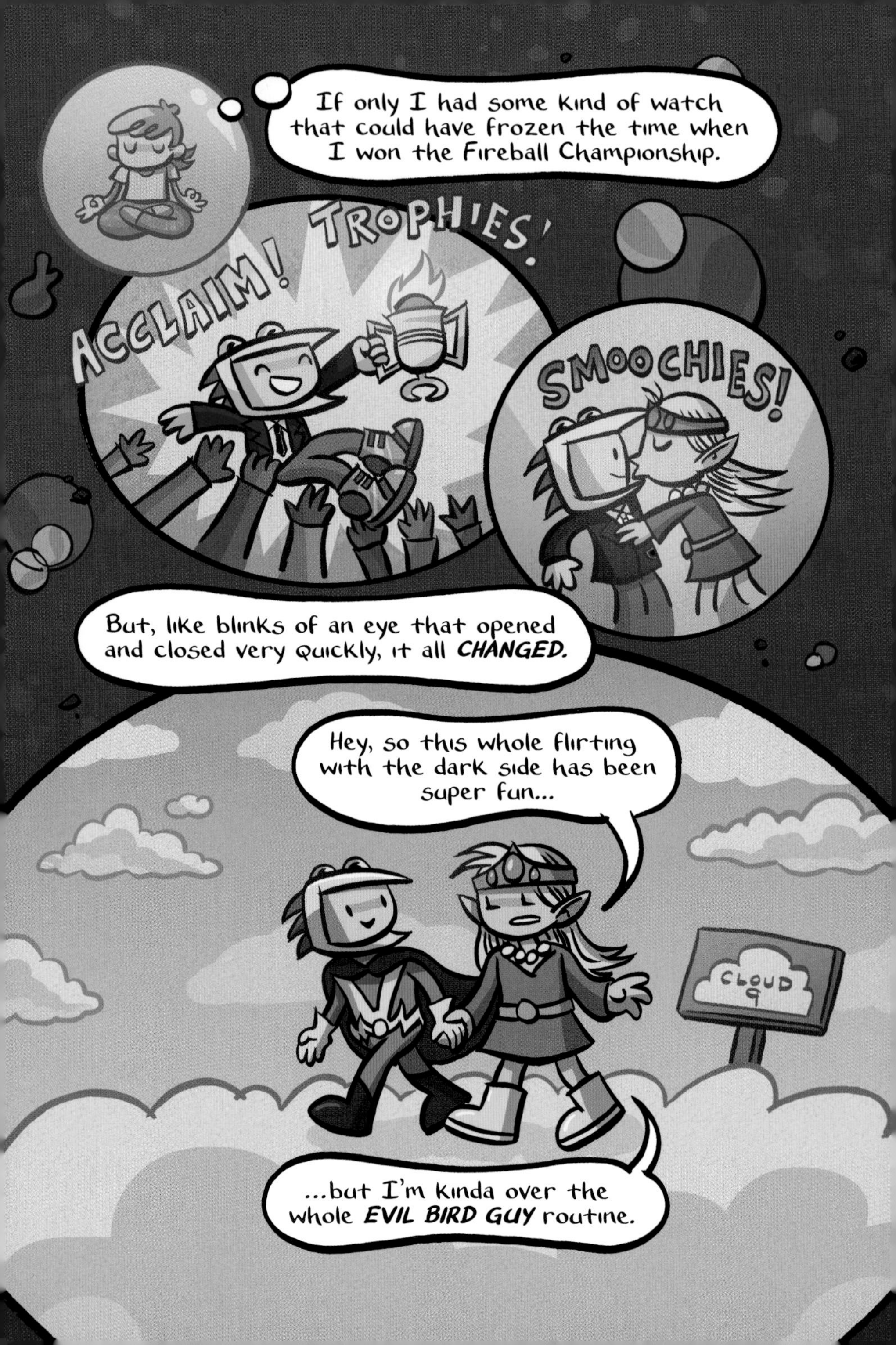
If only I had some kind of watch that could have frozen the time when I won the Fireball Championship.
TROPHIES!
ACCLAIM!
SMOOCHIES!
But, like blinks of an eye that opened and closed very quickly, it all CHANGED.
Hey, so this whole flirting with the dark side has been super fun...
CLOUD 9
...but I'm kinda over the whole EVIL BIRD GUY routine.

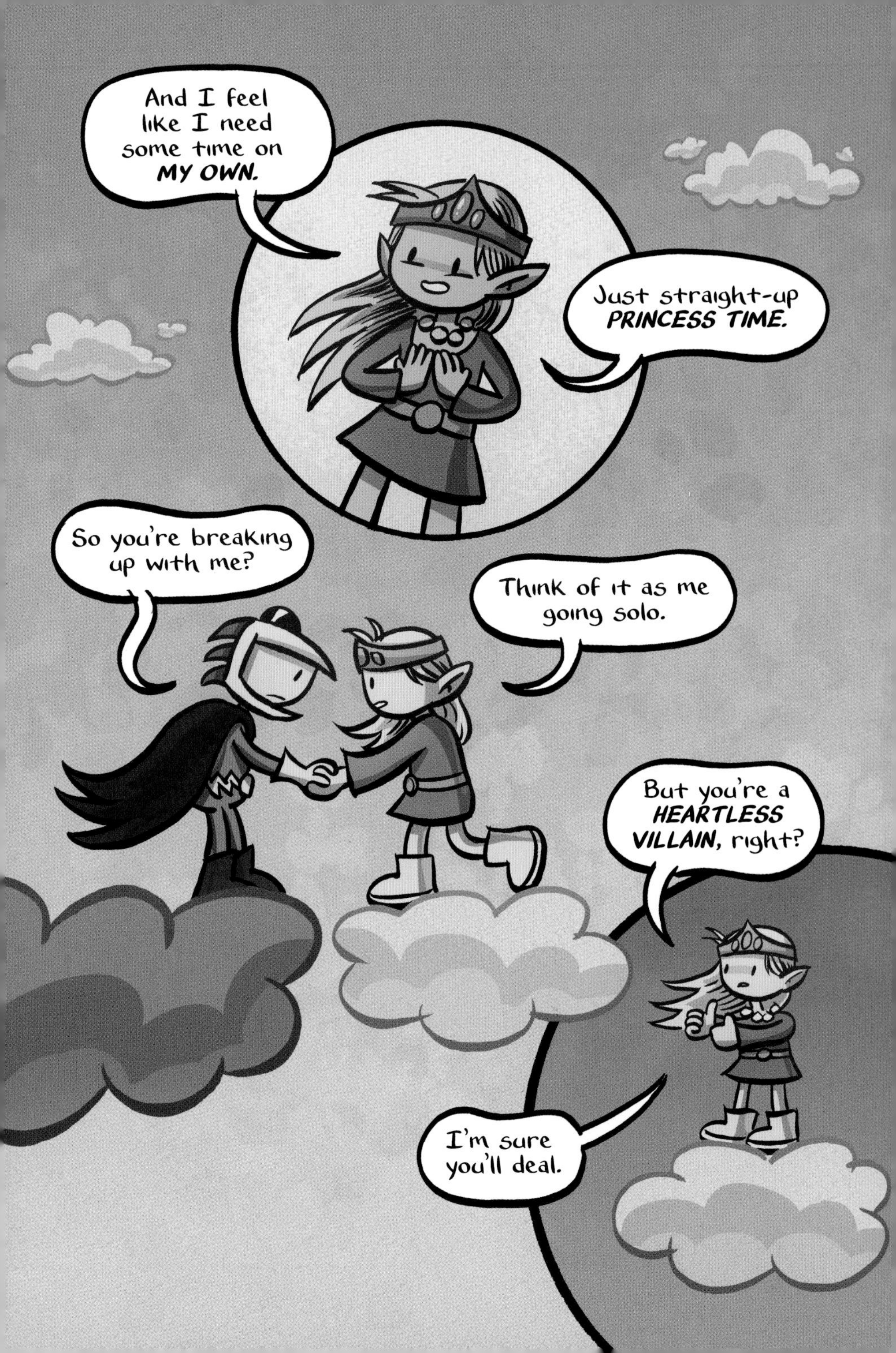
And I feel like I need some time on MY OWN.
Just straight-up PRINCESS TIME.
So you're breaking up with me?
Think of it as me going solo.
But you're a HEARTLESS VILLAIN, right?
I'm sure you'll deal.

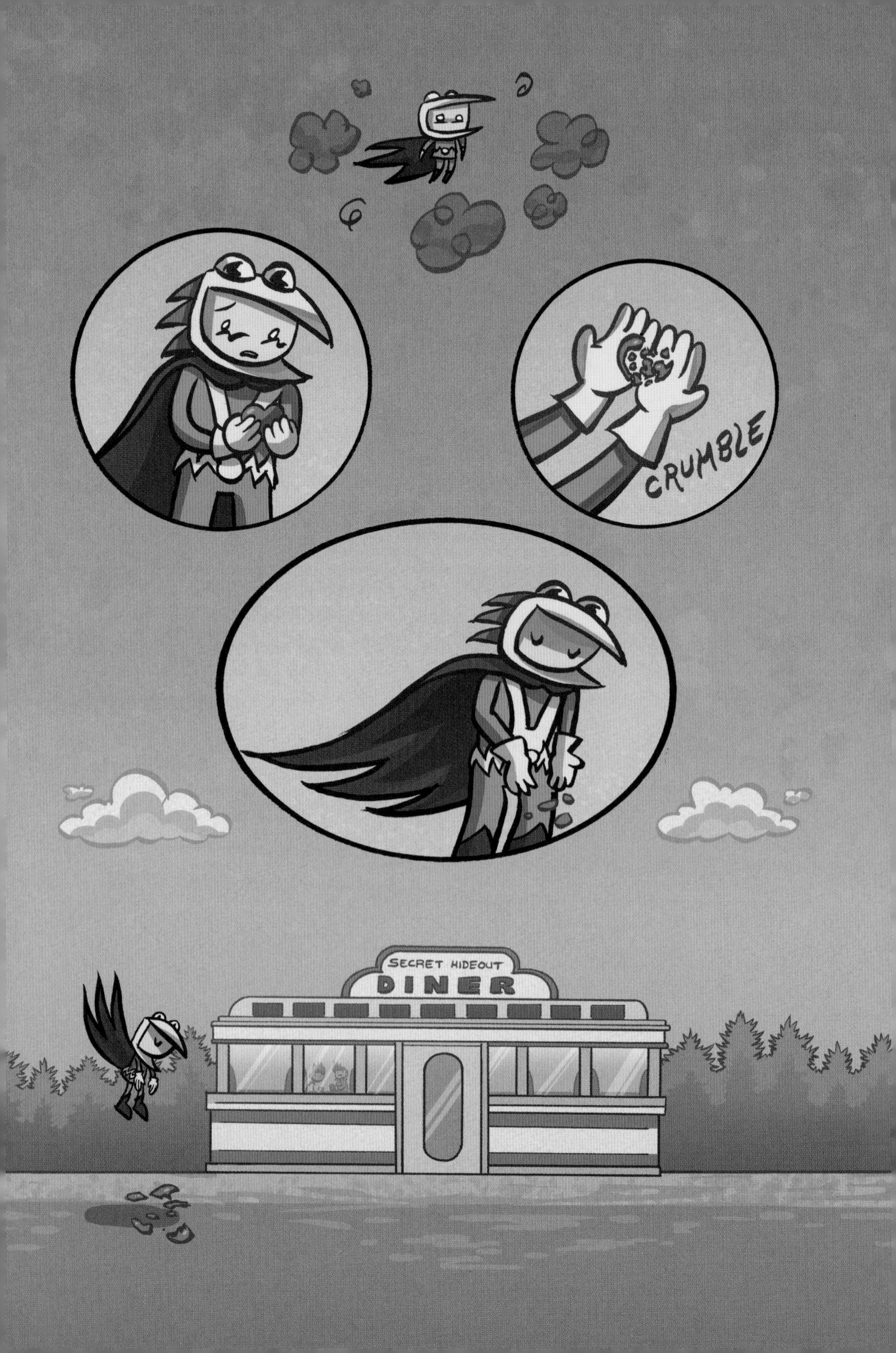
CRUMBLE
SECRET HIDEOUT
DINER

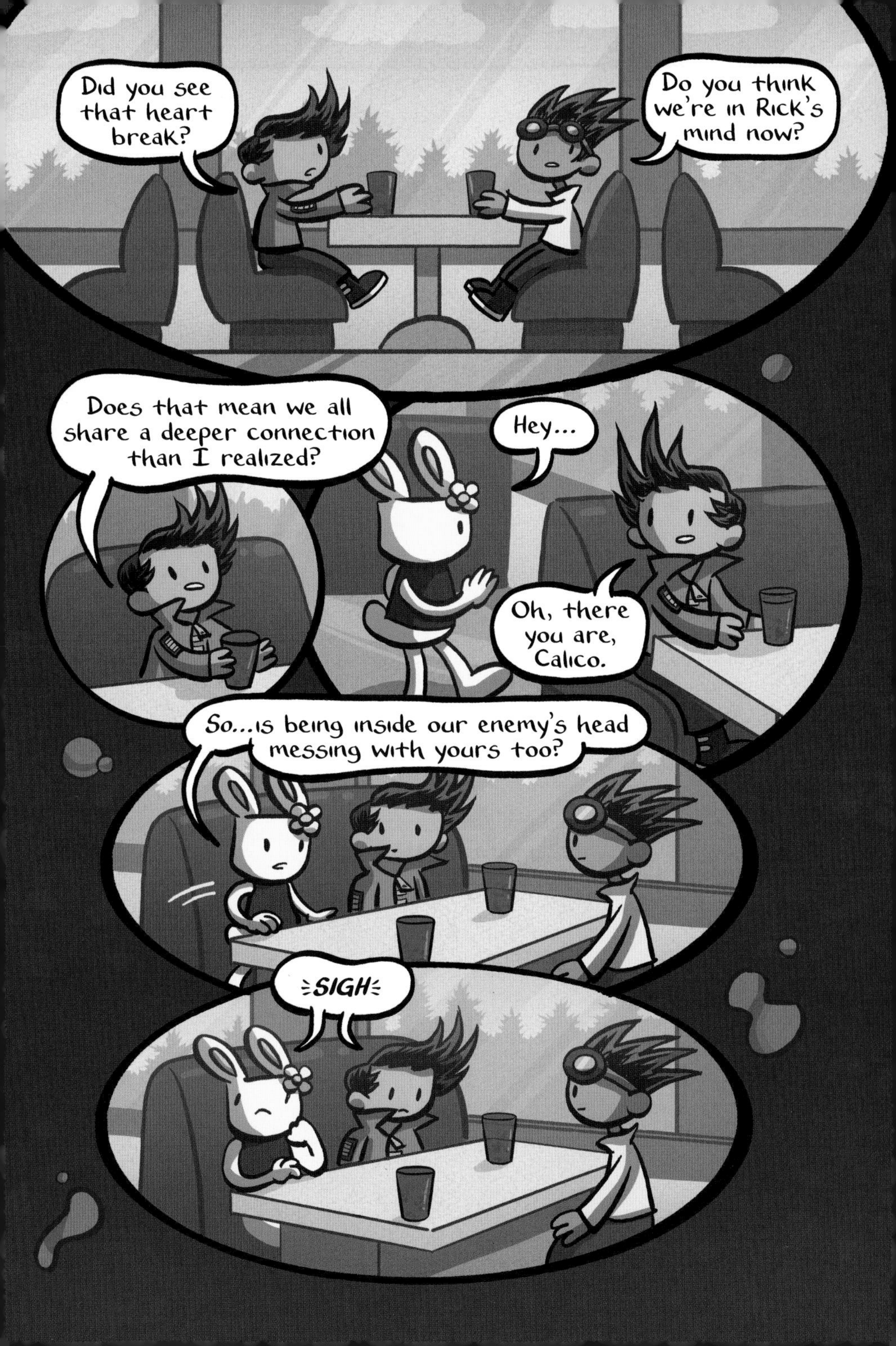
Did you see that heart break?
Do you think we're in Rick's mind now?
Does that mean we all share a deeper connection than I realized?
Hey...
Oh, there you are, Calico.
So...is being inside our enemy's head messing with yours too?
SIGH

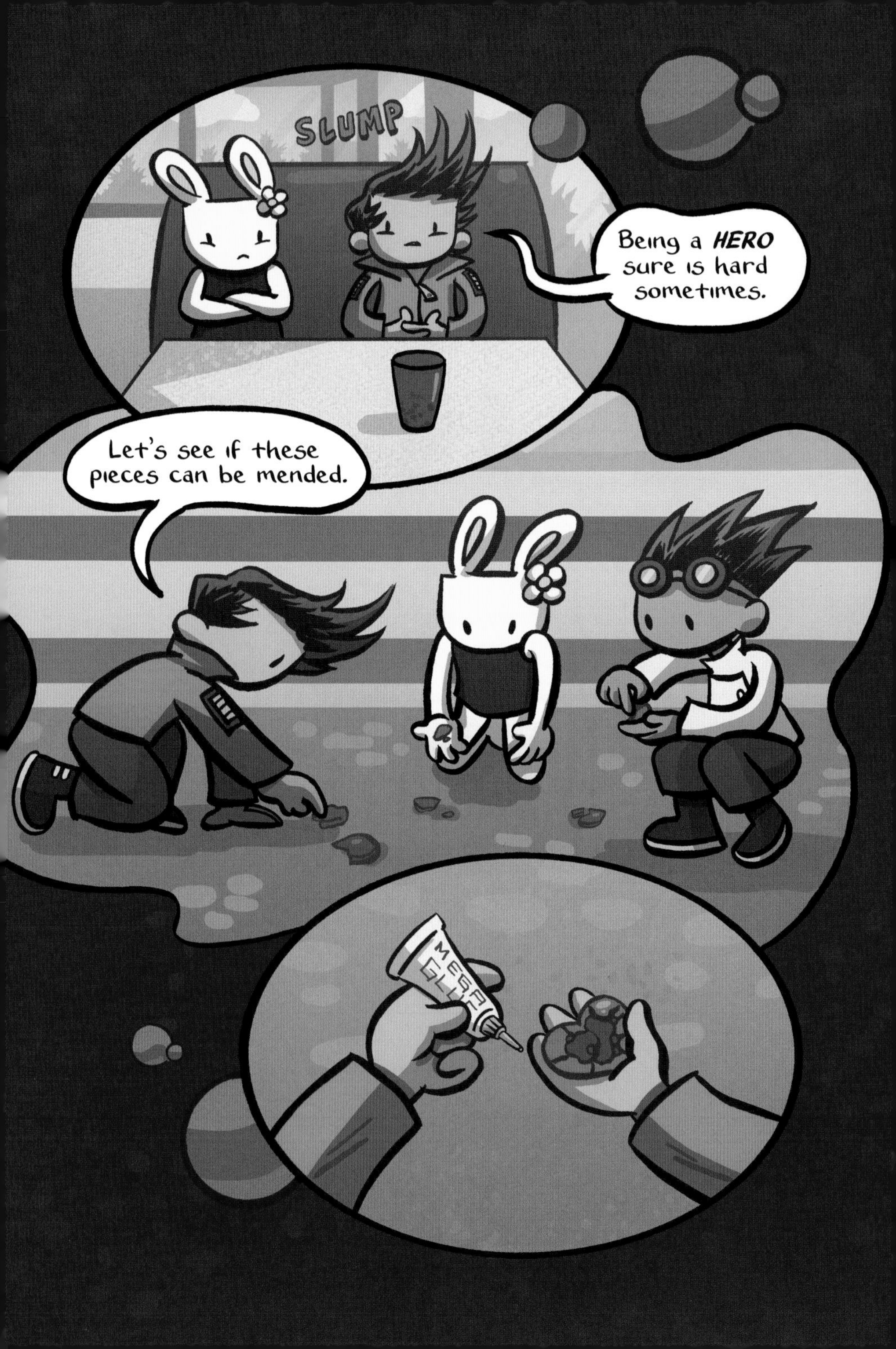
SLUMP
Being a HERO sure is hard sometimes.
Let's see if these pieces can be mended.
MEGA GLUE

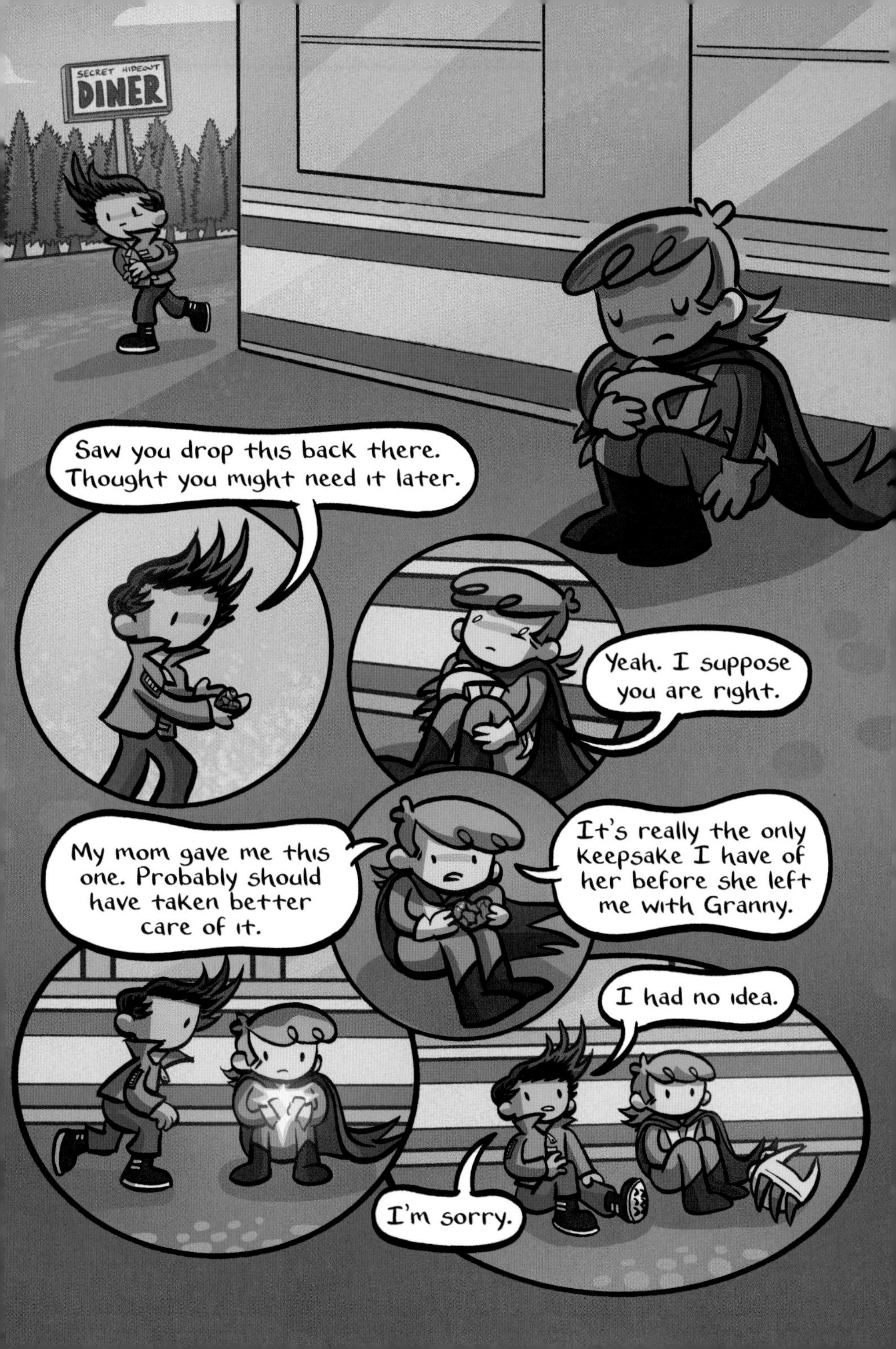
SECRET HIDEOUT DINER
Saw you drop this back there. Thought you might need it later.
Yeah. I suppose you are right.
My mom gave me this one. Probably should have taken better care of it.
It's really the only keepsake I have of her before she left me with Granny.
I had no idea.
I'm sorry.

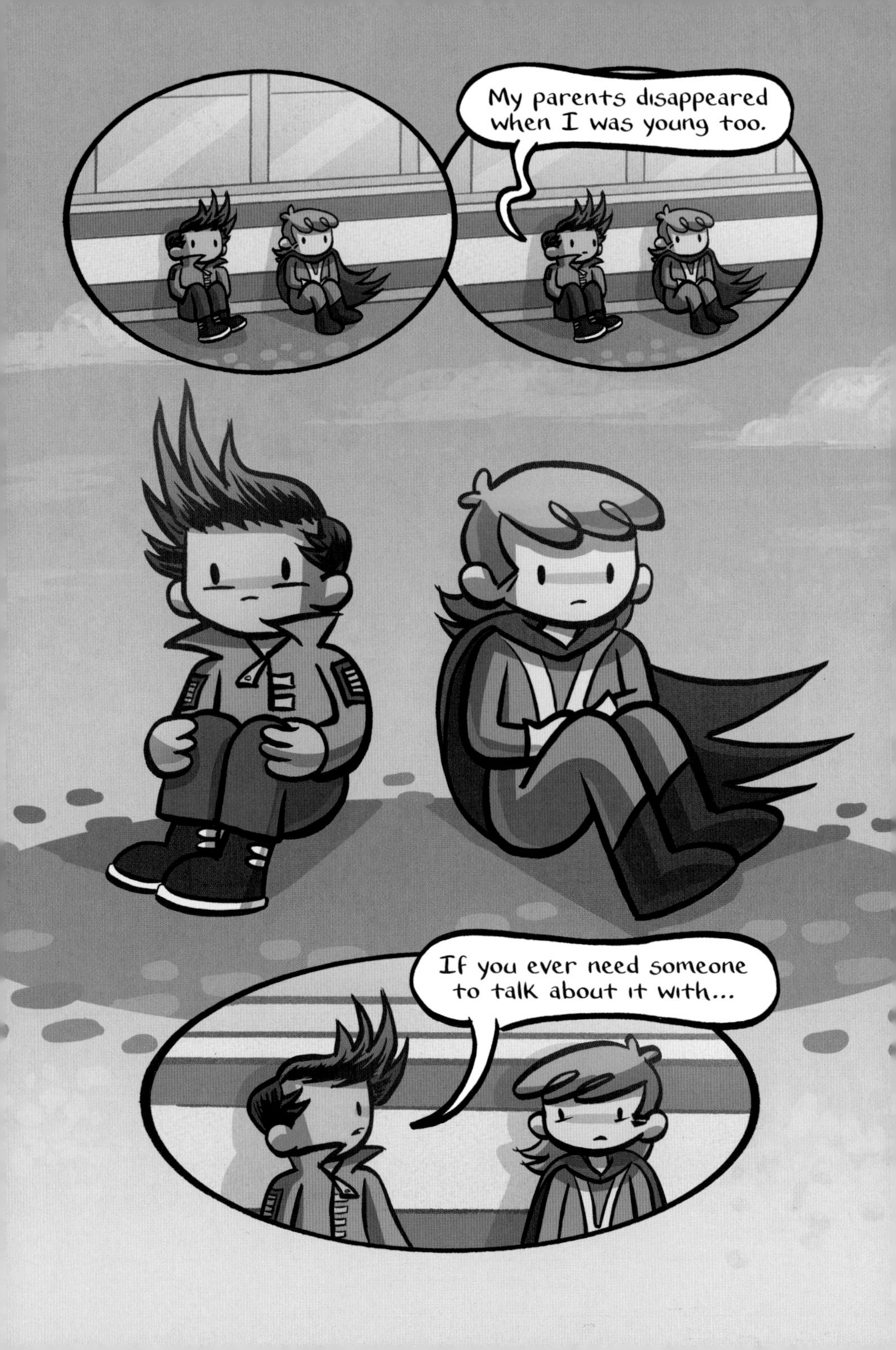
My parents disappeared when I was young too.
If you ever need someone to talk about it with...

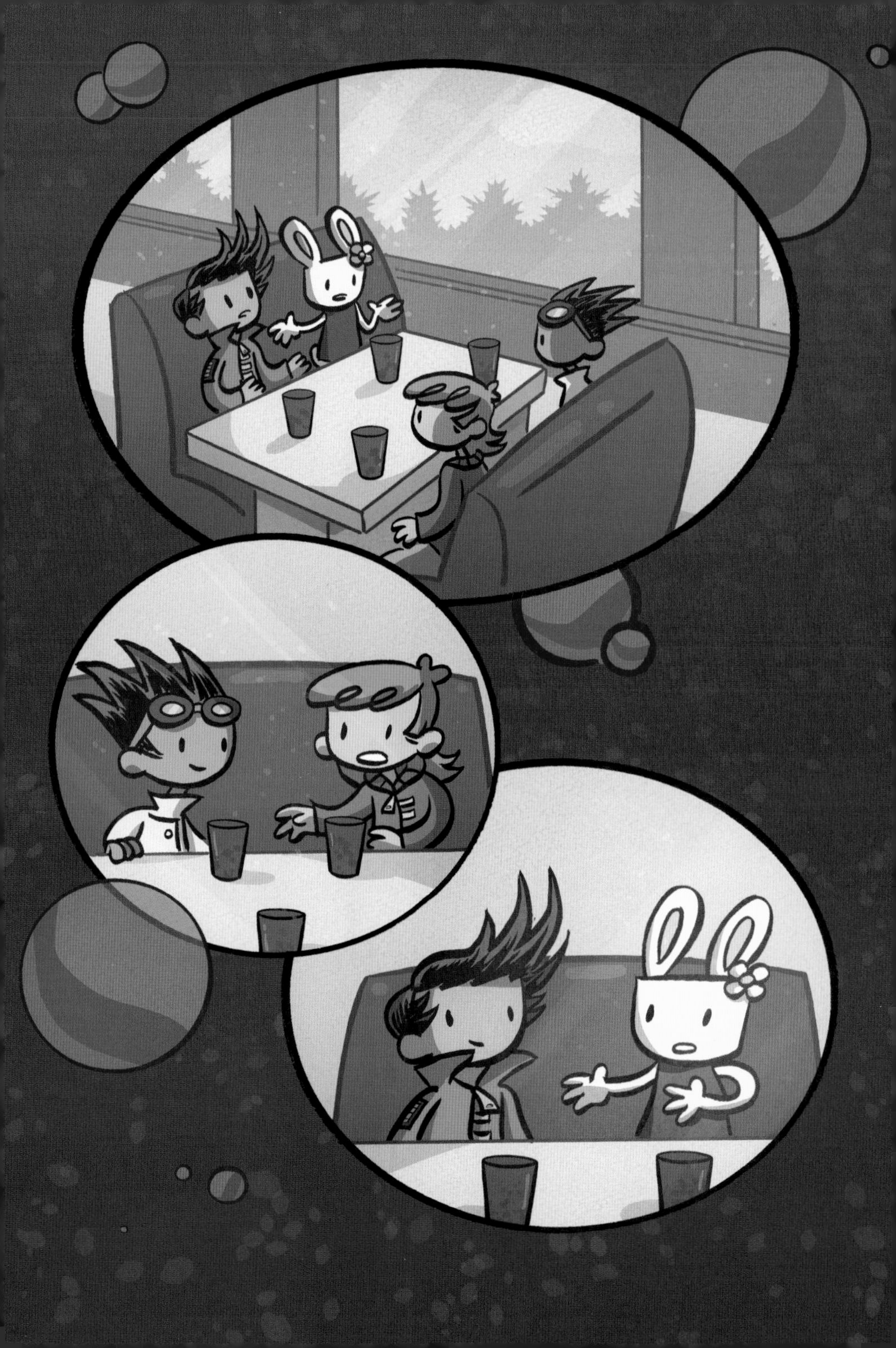

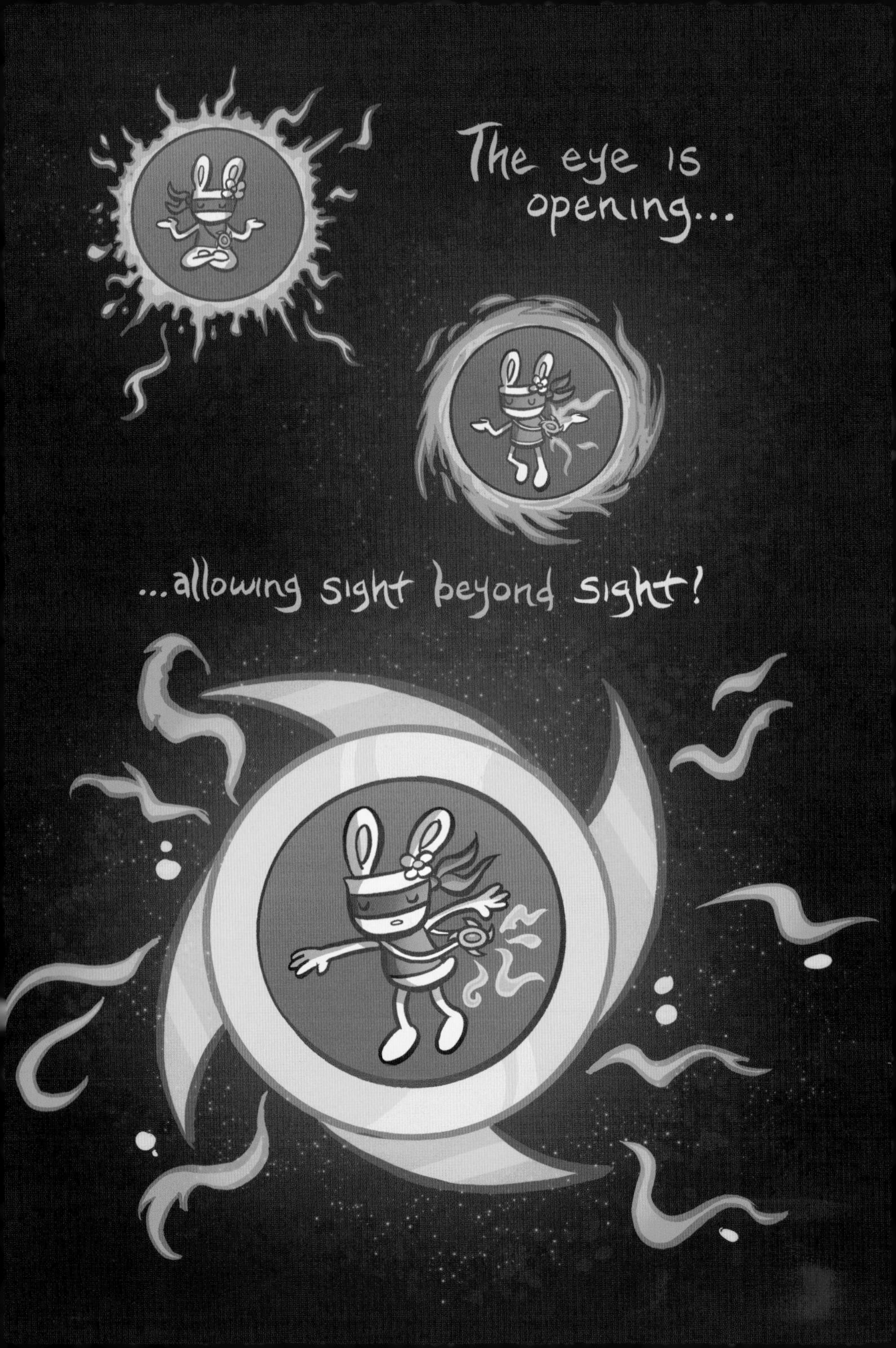
The eye is opening...
...allowing sight beyond sight!

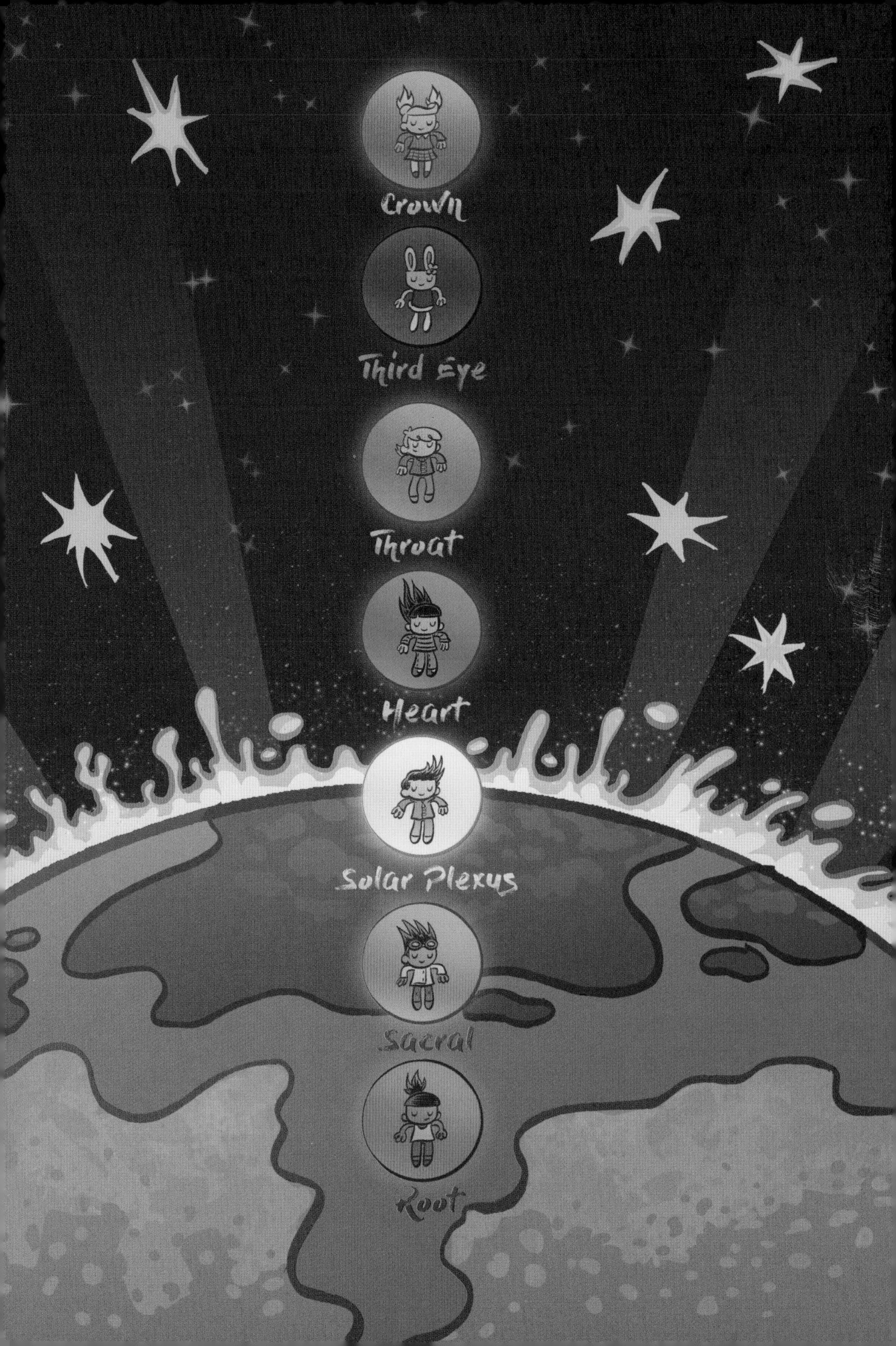
Crown
Third Eye
Throat
Heart
Solar Plexus
Sacral
Root

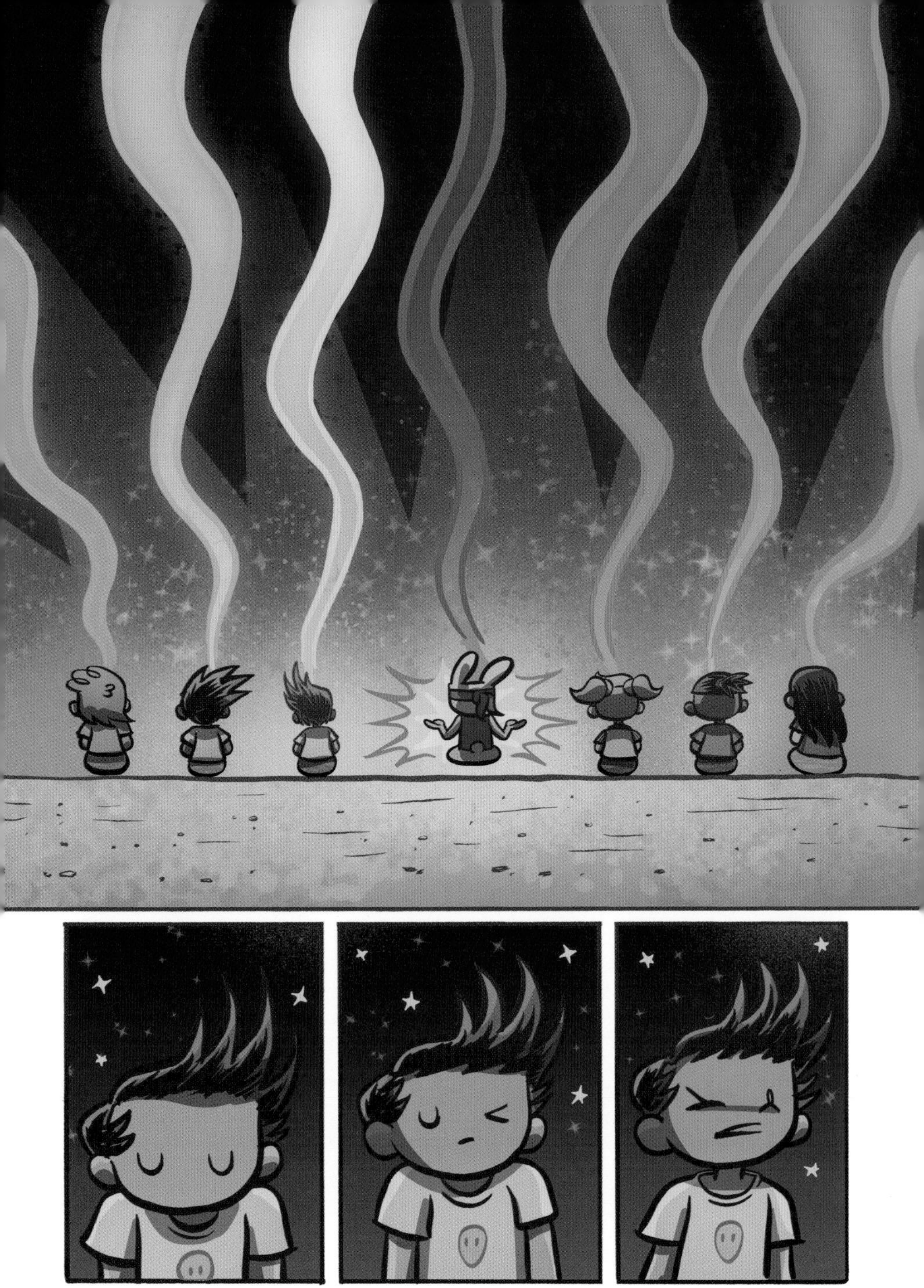

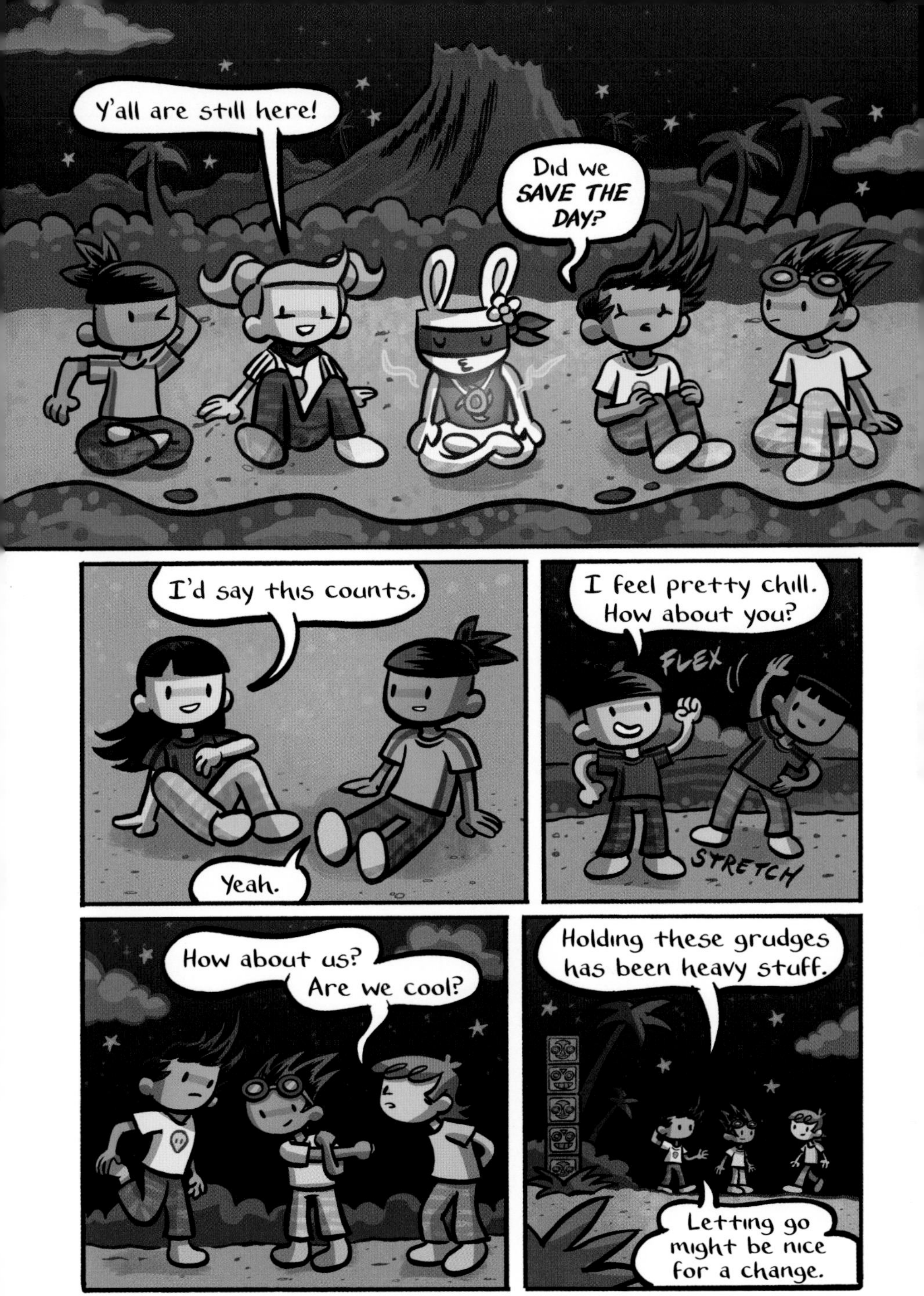
Y'all are still here!
Did we SAVE THE DAY?
I'd say this counts.
Yeah.
I feel pretty chill. How about you?
FLEX
STRETCH
How about us?
Are we cool?
Holding these grudges has been heavy stuff.
Letting go might be nice for a change.

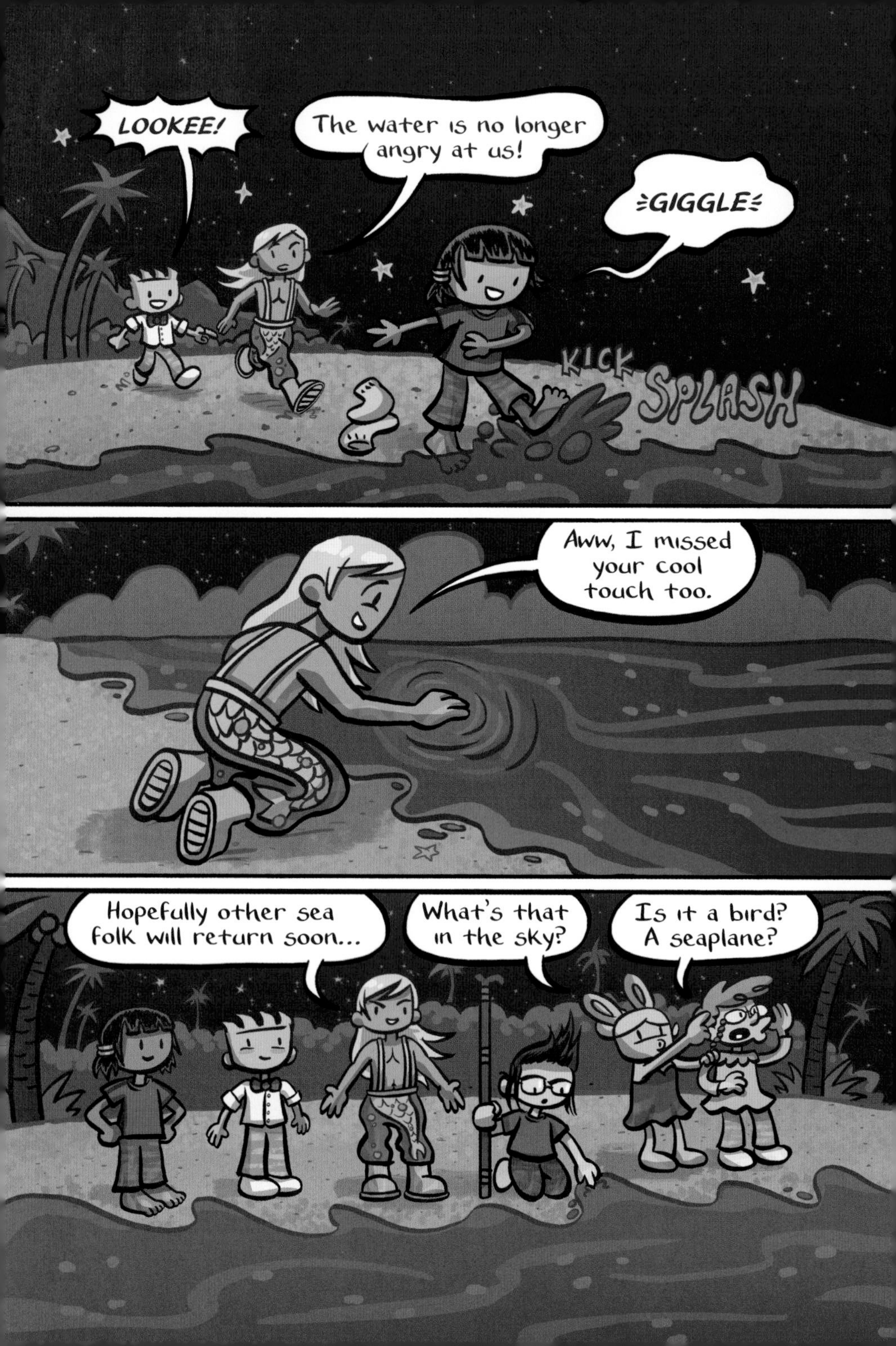
LOOKEE!
The water is no longer angry at us!
GIGGLE
KICK
SPLASH
Aww, I missed your cool touch too.
Hopefully other sea folk will return soon...
What's that in the sky?
Is it a bird? A seaplane?

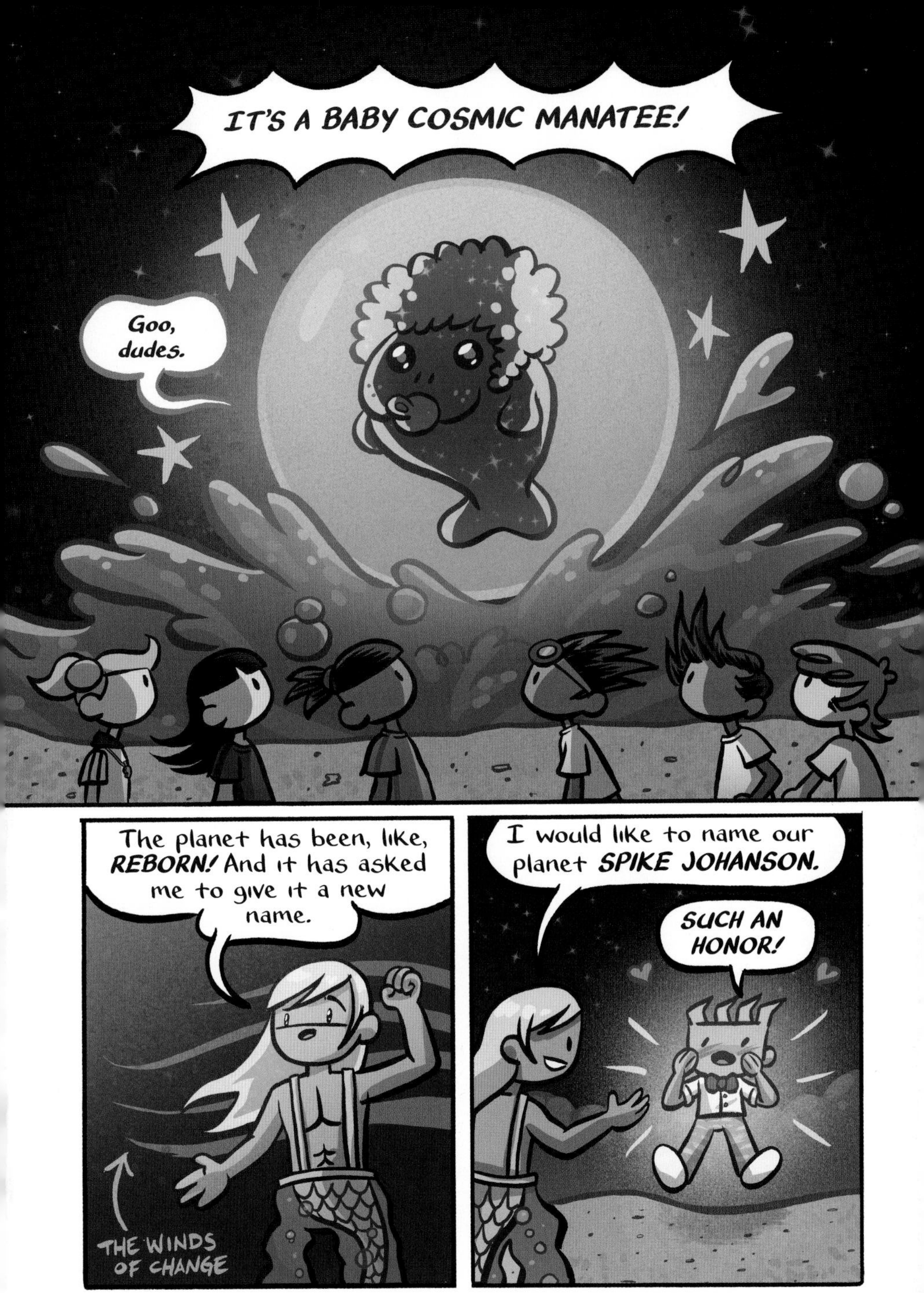
IT'S A BABY COSMIC MANATEE!
Goo, dudes.
The planet has been, like, REBORN! And it has asked me to give it a new name.
THE WINDS OF CHANGE
I would like to name our planet SPIKE JOHANSON.
SUCH AN HONOR!

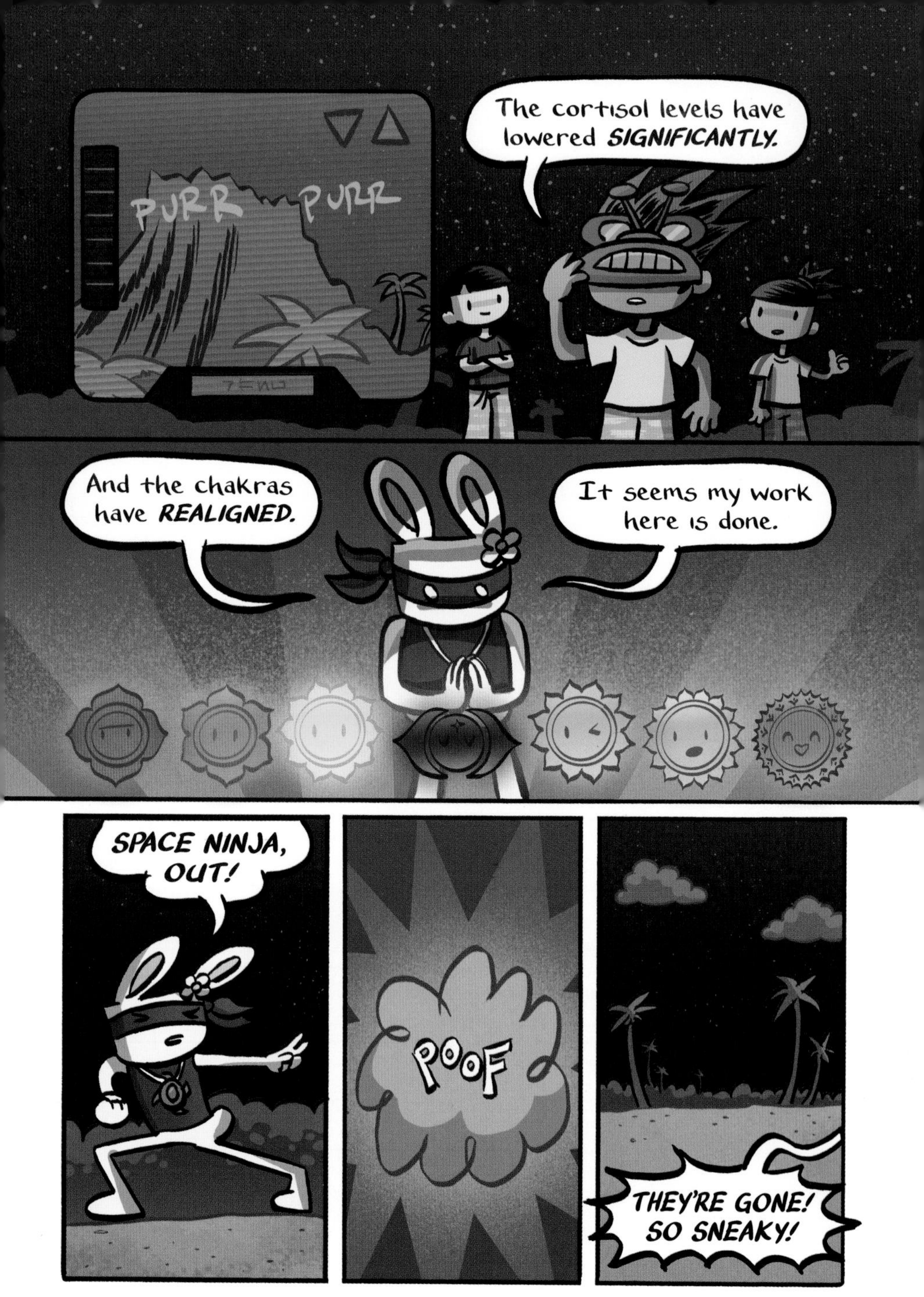
PURR PURR
The cortisol levels have lowered SIGNIFICANTLY.
And the chakras have REALIGNED.
It seems my work here is done.
SPACE NINJA, OUT!
POOF
THEY'RE GONE! SO SNEAKY!

I'm not sure if this was the best party ever, but it was the only one I've ever been to, so who am I to judge?
But I would like to go home now if that's an option.
Thanks for STICKING around as long as you did. Here. Take a goodie bag before you head out.
PARTY FAVOR
Huh.
PARTY FAVOR
Neat.
Guess this is the part of the party that winds itself down?
Yeah.
Actually...

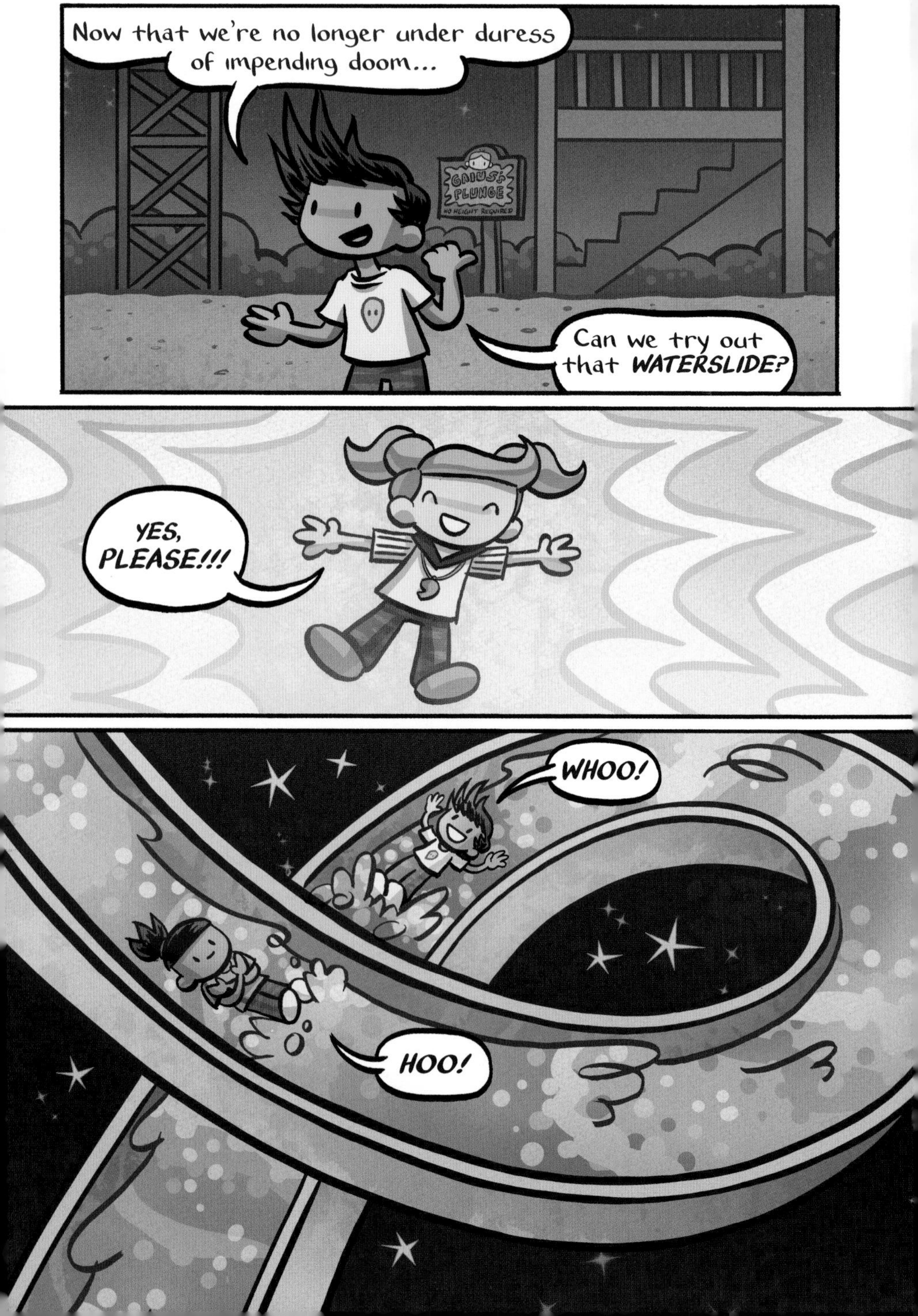

Now that we're no longer under duress of impending doom...
GAIUS'S PLUNGE
NO HEIGHT REQUIRED
Can we try out that WATERSLIDE?
YES, PLEASE!!!
WHOO!
HOO!

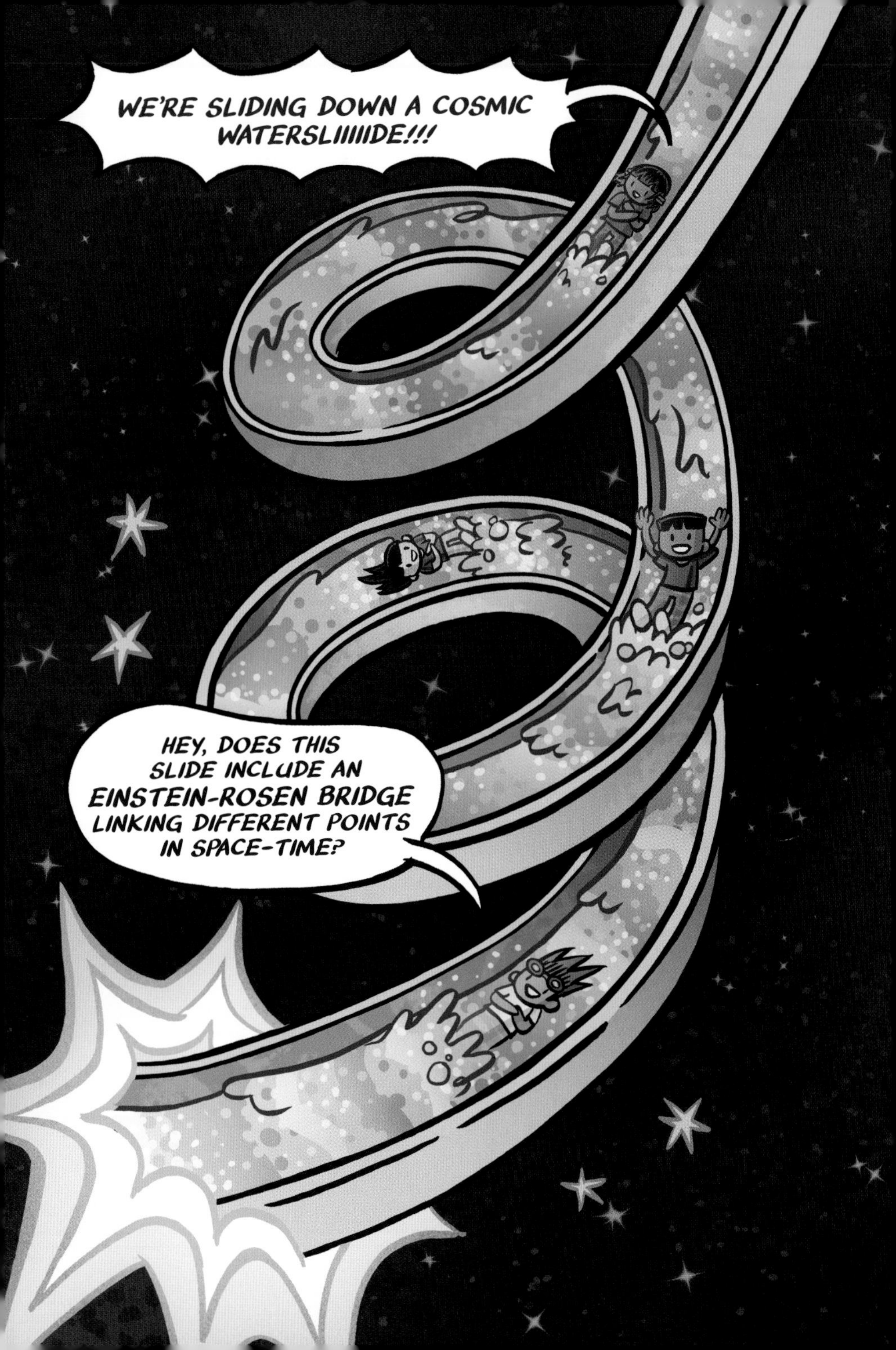
WE'RE SLIDING DOWN A COSMIC WATERSLIIIIIDE!!!
HEY, DOES THIS SLIDE INCLUDE AN EINSTEIN-ROSEN BRIDGE LINKING DIFFERENT POINTS IN SPACE-TIME?

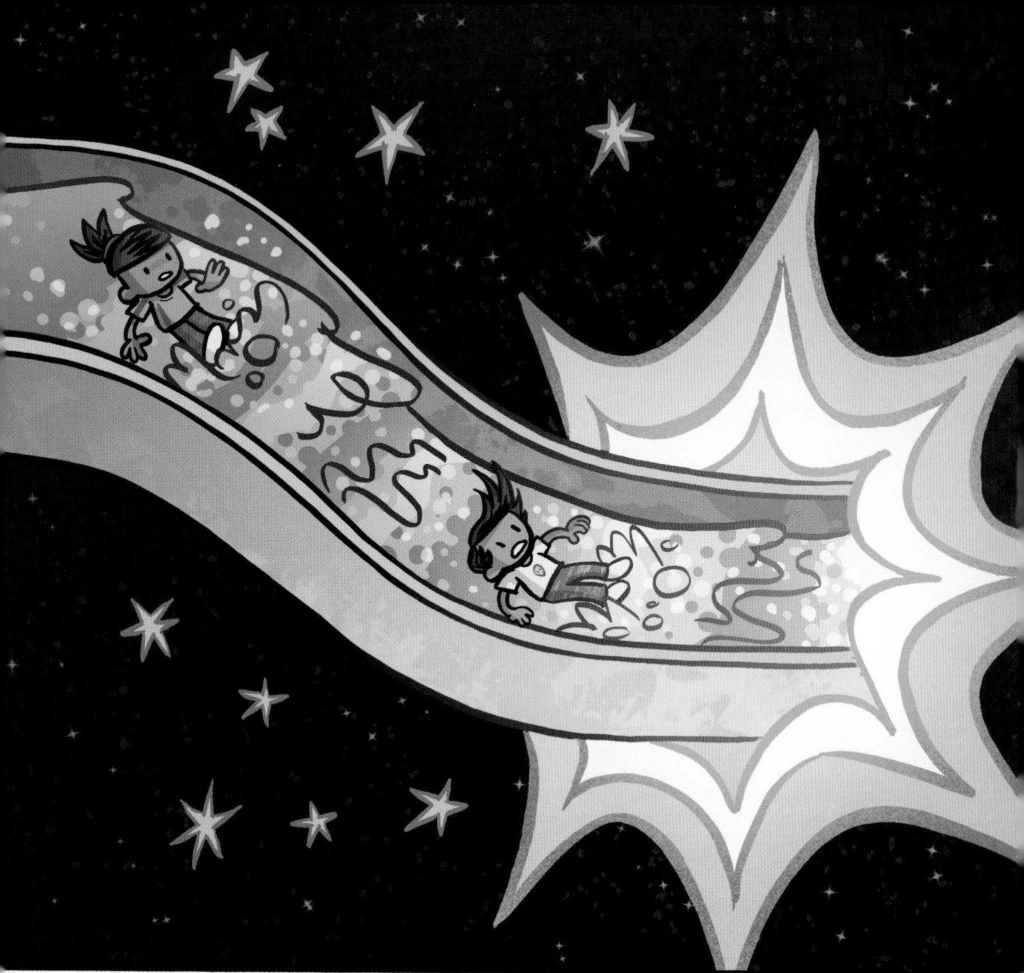

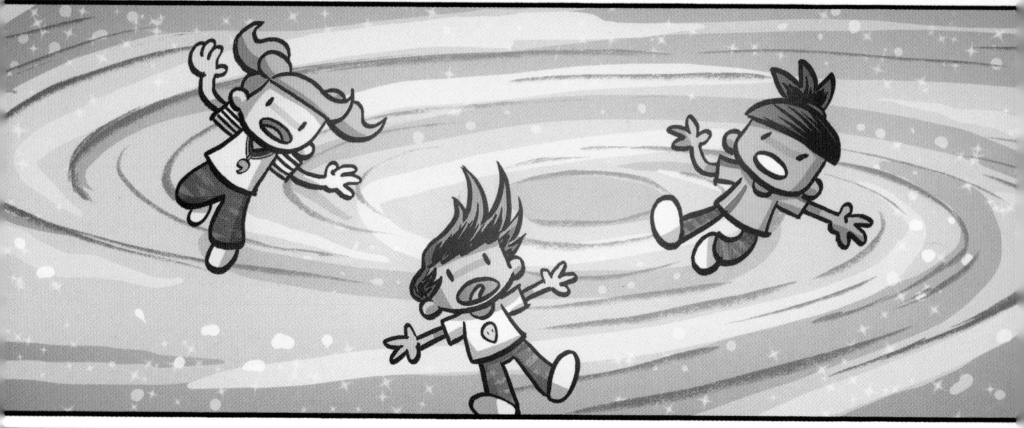

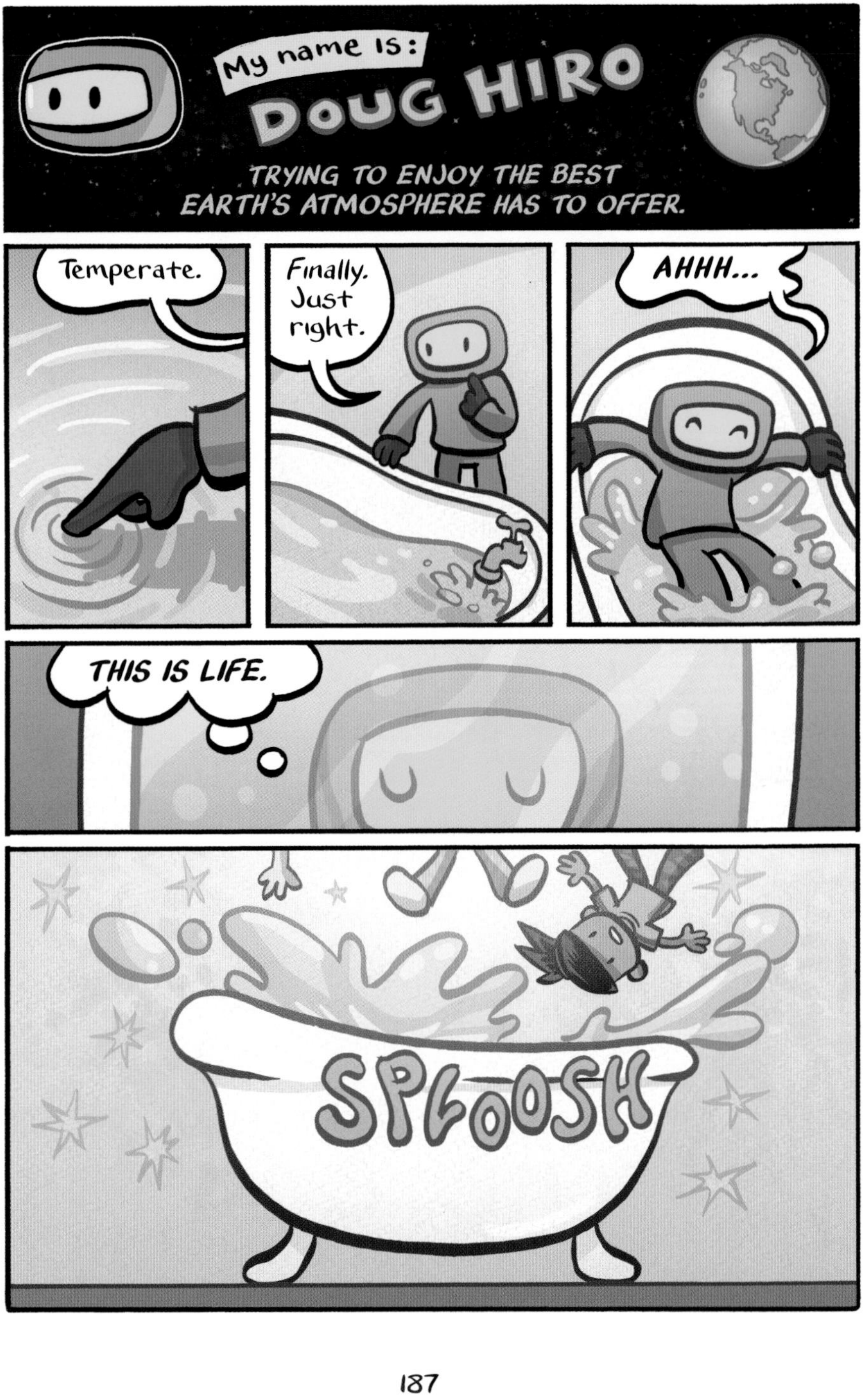
My name is:
DOUG HIRO
TRYING TO ENJOY THE BEST EARTH'S ATMOSPHERE HAS TO OFFER.
Temperate.
Finally. Just right.
AHHH...
THIS IS LIFE.
SPLOOSH

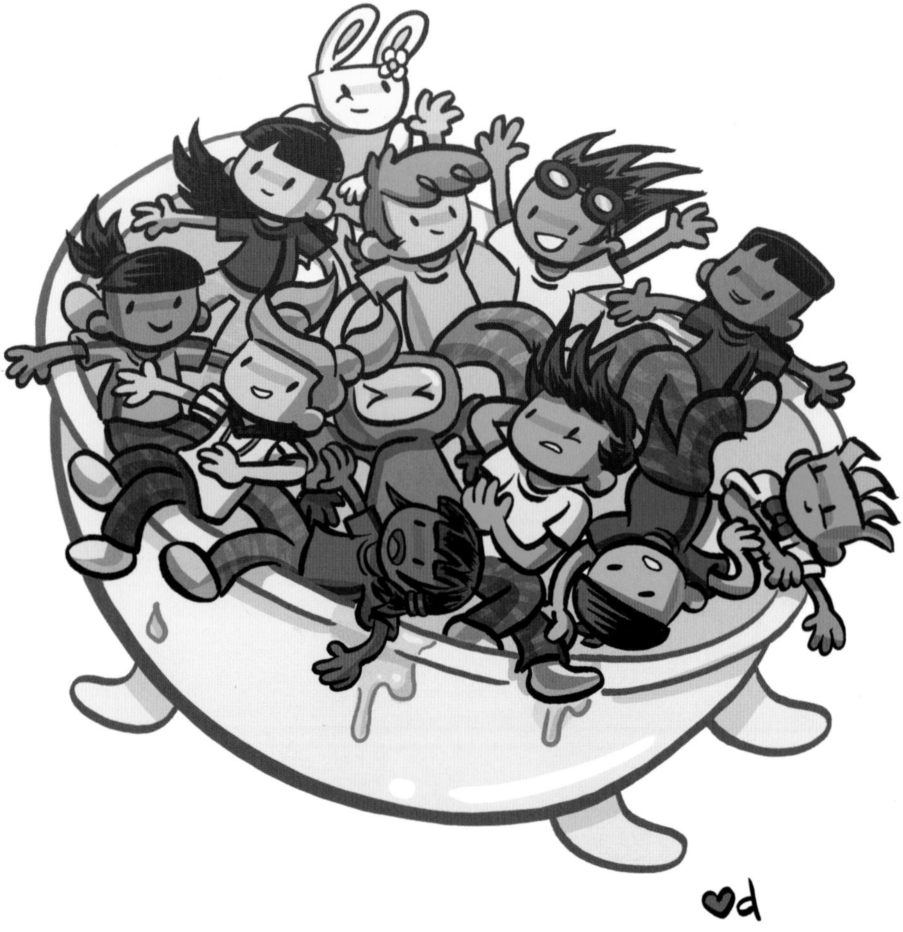

The end